KU-361-231

Praise for *The Thinking Woman's Guide to Real Magic*

If Hermione Granger had been an American who never received an invitation to Hogwarts, this might have been her story."
—*People* magazine

A marvelous plot, clever dialogue, and complex characters. . . . Fun, seductive, and utterly engrossing."
—Deborah Harkness, author of the All Souls trilogy

To read *The Thinking Woman's Guide to Real Magic* is to enter a lush, fantastical dream filled with beauty and strangeness, love and cruelty, playfulness and gravitas."
—Sara Gruen, author of *Water for Elephants* and *At the Water's Edge*

A clever and scrumptious debut fantasy, the kind you happily disappear into for days."
—Kelly Link, author of *Magic for Beginners* and *Get in Trouble*

Emily Croy Barker has written a sophisticated fairy tale that has one foot through the looking glass and the other squarely planted in the real world. . . . An imaginative synthesis of the stories that delighted us as children and the novels that inspired us as adults."
—Ivy Pochoda, author of *The Art of Disappearing* and *Visitation Street*

A wonderfully imaginative world of illusion and real magic that reveals the importance of a curious and open mind, learning, and love."
—Karen Engelmann, author of *The Stockholm Octavo*

Also by Emily Croy Barker

The Thinking Woman's Guide to Real Magic

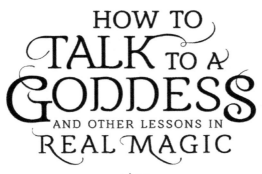

HOW TO TALK TO A GODDESS
AND OTHER LESSONS IN REAL MAGIC

EMILY CROY BARKER

Semrland Books

Copyright © Emily Croy Barker, 2021
All rights reserved. No part of this book may be reproduced, scanned,
or distributed in any printed or electronic form without permission.
Please do not participate in or encourage piracy of copyrighted materials
in violation of the author's rights. Purchase only authorized editions.

ISBN 978-1-7364071-0-3

Published by Semrland Books
P.O. Box 207
Southport, Maine 04576
United States of America
emilycroybarker.com

1 3 5 7 9 10 8 6 4 2

Book design by Iram Allam
Set in Fournier

This is a work of fiction. Names, characters, places, and incidents
either are the product of the author's imagination or are used fictitiously,
and any resemblance to actual persons, living or dead, businesses,
companies, events, or locales is entirely coincidental.

For my mother,
who first taught me the magic of writing

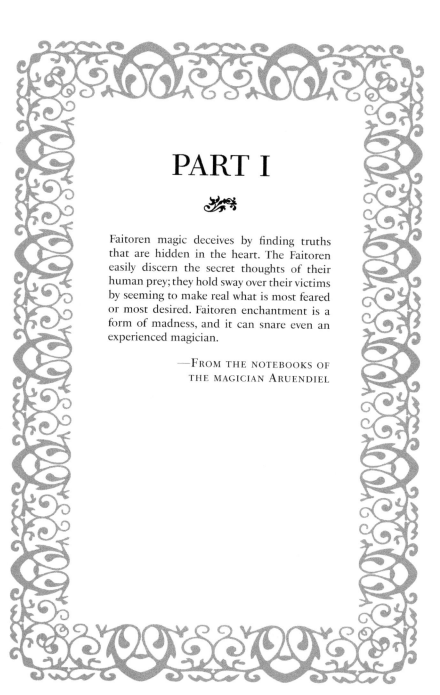

PART I

Faitoren magic deceives by finding truths that are hidden in the heart. The Faitoren easily discern the secret thoughts of their human prey; they hold sway over their victims by seeming to make real what is most feared or most desired. Faitoren enchantment is a form of madness, and it can snare even an experienced magician.

—FROM THE NOTEBOOKS OF
THE MAGICIAN ARUENDIEL

Chapter 1

Letting the heavy doors swing shut behind her, Nora stood on the steps of the neo-Georgian box that housed the English department and let out a deep breath. The campus bell tower had just finished striking: three o'clock on a balmy spring afternoon. The dogwoods in the quad blazed with white glory, but Nora barely noticed them as she walked slowly down the steps.

She discovered that she was still holding the manila folder that Naomi had given her, clutching it so tightly that her fingers had already left smudges on its creamy surface. She opened the folder, just enough for another glimpse of the letter on the department's good stationery, the dean's signature in blue ink at the bottom. *I am pleased to inform you that in recognition of outstanding scholarship—*

The breeze making the dogwood blossoms dance suddenly ruffled the papers in the folder and tugged them free from Nora's grasp. She snapped the folder shut, but a half-dozen sheets were already spinning away from her and fluttering across the grass. "Gods!" Nora swore under her breath, snatching back one of the papers, then running after the others, which seemed ready to take flight with the next gust of wind. One by one she trapped them.

"Thanks," she said to the pink-haired boy who came loping over with a sheet that had blown across his path. The undergraduates now looked even younger, more dewy-faced, than she recalled. Automatically she thought, I need to hurry up and finish my thesis. This was the first time in a year she'd felt that particular stab of anxiety, and it hadn't lost any sharpness. But she had the Blum-Forsythe now. She would go to England and write a brilliant thesis that would make her thesis adviser swoon and regret ever having expressed any doubts about Nora's abilities. Well, actually, Naomi would never swoon about anything, but she might narrow her eyes in appreciation and give a wolfish, approving smile, just as she had ten minutes ago when she told Nora about the fellowship.

All the stuff that had blown out of the folder was probably online, Nora reflected, but it would be nice to keep the original of the dean's letter. It wasn't in the sheaf of papers she had recovered, however. She circled in place to see if she could spot the letter anywhere on the lawn.

Someone held out a piece of paper to her, and she began to say an automatic thank-you. "Nora?" he said.

It took her a second to realize that the man, who had wire-rimmed glasses and a puckish look, was Adam. Her first feeling was annoyance, as though he had deliberately tried to take her by surprise.

"I thought that was you," he said. "I heard you had resurfaced."

Nora took the paper from him. Yes, the dean's letter. She wondered if Adam had read any of it in the ten seconds it had been in his hand, and hoped that he had. "Why are you here? Aren't you still living in Chicago?"

"Oh, I'm just here for the weekend. Ted Drumm's bachelor party." He gave a wry, deprecating grin—Nora knew it well—that hinted at how amusingly banal bachelor parties were. Even if he had come all the way from Chicago to attend this one. "What are *you* doing here?"

"I was just talking to Naomi," Nora said, closing the folder and sliding it into her bag. She studied Adam's neat features, his vigilant brown eyes, the small smirk that lingered in the corner of his mouth, and she could not resist adding, "I got a fellowship for next fall. I'll be in England. Cambridge."

"The Blum-Forsythe? I heard! That's really great."

Of course Adam knew about it already, she thought. Two years since he'd finished his thesis and taken his doctorate, but he still had allies and admirers throughout the English department. He probably knew they were giving her the fellowship before the dean did.

"Congratulations," he was saying, "it'll be huge for you, it's about time you got some recognition." He did sound genuinely excited.

"I wasn't expecting it," Nora said. "I mean, last year, I had a conversation with Naomi, and she was not, um, very encouraging—but anyway they liked the paper I wrote on Dickinson, her strategies of absence—"

"Yeah, I remember, you showed it to me. It's a good paper. That's what saved your fellowship. They wanted to yank it at one point, you know." Adam gave her a shrewd glance. "Did Naomi tell you about that?"

"She said they had to be resourceful—that was her word—and read the rules a certain way, to keep the award for me. Because they couldn't reach me. I wasn't around."

Adam nodded. "That's right, basically. It was a little more complicated. I heard Brett Vance raised hell, saying his candidate should get the fellowship because you were nowhere to be found. But Naomi shut him down. She got Nina Blum, the donor, to read the proposals from all three finalists, and Nina hated Brett's guy, and she loved you."

"Oh. Brett Vance. I see." Any hint of his involvement would be enough to propel Naomi into action. Vance was her archenemy, guarding the fiefdom of Southern literature—once the glory of the department—from the encroachments of the feminists and the critical race theorists. He had a small but devout following of students, who— Naomi had once observed—were all white men with incipient drinking problems and half-finished novels overgrown with kudzu.

"I see. It wasn't necessarily my brilliant paper that landed me this fellowship," Nora said. "It was politics."

"Well, it always is," Adam said. "But you wouldn't have the fellowship without the brilliant paper, either. Anyway, where the hell were you?" he added. There was perhaps a hint of grievance in his tone. "You just disappeared off the face of the earth. It's been, what, a year since that weekend?"

"Not quite," Nora said.

"There were all these wild stories going around—that you were murdered or you got mixed up with a drug gang or joined Antifa." She could feel his eyes lingering on her scarred cheek. "And the sheriff's deputies and then this Asheville detective kept asking when I saw you last and what was I doing between seven and noon on May 11. I thought I was going to have to get a lawyer. They always suspect the ex."

The notion of Adam being a suspect in her disappearance had not occurred to Nora. Once she would have taken a vengeful pleasure in the thought of Adam trapped in an interrogation room, trying to meet a cop's dead-eyed stare. Now the picture only seemed rather funny. "Did you tell them it was more likely I'd murder *you?*"

"They were not kidding around," he said resentfully. "I just told the truth, that everything—our breakup—was very amicable."

"That's the worst thing you could have told them. No wonder they were suspicious."

"I actually wondered if this whole thing was a setup, if you ran off to make me look bad."

Nora gave an incredulous snort. "Adam. Please. Not everything is about you."

"Well, I didn't know what to think. I knew you were kind of—upset."

An amicable breakup, he'd said. Nora shrugged. "Not upset enough to frame you."

"Thanks for that." He smiled. "Anyway, so what did happen to you?"

Nora slung her bag over her shoulder. "Oh, nothing as interesting as being in a drug gang," she said. "I had a stupid accident in the mountains, I broke my leg, some people found me, and then I was kind of stuck for a while." She began to walk along the brick path that crossed the quad. Adam kept pace with her.

"Well, fortunately, enough people saw me drinking mimosas at the brunch that day to give me an alibi." He shook his head, bemused. "An alibi. I actually had to have an alibi."

"Well, anyway," Nora said. "So how are things with you? How's married life?"

"I wouldn't know," Adam said. "I'm not married."

She frowned at him, uncertain as to how to take this revelation. He'd been quite clear about his intentions when he was breaking up with her. "You were planning to get married in the fall. Last fall."

"It didn't happen."

"Oh. Is it going to happen?"

"Not with Celeste, that's for damn sure." He spoke with feeling.

Nora registered a fleeting sense of vindication. "Better luck next time." By now they had crossed the quad and were approaching the old library. Several possible escape routes lay ahead. "Well. I need to get my car."

"It's great to see you. We should talk more," Adam said, with an air of sudden decision. "How about dinner tonight?"

Nora already had an excuse: "I'm having dinner with Maggie. I'm staying with her."

"Oh, how is Maggie?" Without waiting to hear Nora's response, he said: "How about a drink beforehand, then? Five thirty, six?"

Nora tried again. "What about the bachelor party?"

He waved away her objections. "It won't get started until late. What's your cell? Is it the same number?"

As though he remembered the old one. But she gave him her new number, then turned down the walk that led past the old library, toward the parking lot.

The Blum-Forsythe fellowship. She resisted the temptation to pull out the dean's letter again. So—she was not a failure after all. She'd been judged and for once was not found wanting. Perhaps she had finally mastered the knack of impressing the stubborn, guarded, supercilious ranks of the departmental priesthood—even Naomi, who last year had made it clear that Nora wasn't going to cut it much longer in grad school. But Nora was a credit to Naomi now, a trophy from her successful tussle with Brett Vance. A pawn that had turned into a queen.

But still Naomi's pawn. Nora's mood darkened a shade. Still, this was an amazing chance. One thing she'd learned was that after a certain point in grad school, there were only winners, because all the losers had been eliminated. Maybe it was that way in other professions, too, but certainly the cozy inclusiveness of the university was a myth, and for a long time she'd feared that she had already taken her place on the losing side. Now she had a real opportunity to scramble up into the ranks of the winners. She could have her old life back, after this lost year, except better.

Nora looked around the quadrangle as though seeing it for the first time. In the shade of arching oak branches, students hurried past, chattering to each other or staring at their phones. The trim, antiquated facades of the classroom buildings looked down at her with stately patience. Everything in view was civilized and orderly, full of grace and purpose. The air felt luminous with promise. She had a place here after all.

Why, then, was her heart squeezed tight and her breath locked inside her chest?

At ten to six, Adam was already waiting for her—that was new—at the zinc-topped bar of the Italian restaurant near the bookstore. He had always liked the place because of its wine list; Nora because of the name, Petrarch. In fact, the selection of wines by the glass was rather limited, but by the time Nora got there, Adam had already persuaded the bartender to pour him a glass of Gavi from the bottle-only menu.

By the time she finished her drink, Nora had heard more about Adam's complicated relationship with Celeste and its demise than she really cared to. But Adam was smart enough not to make a play for her sympathy, not overtly. Instead, he treated the whole episode as an absurdist comedy of manners. Despite her intention to remain cool, collected, and fundamentally unsympathetic, Nora found herself snickering, not sure whether she was laughing at him or with him.

"—so obviously I was upset to find my fiancée boinking another man, and not even the man she claimed to be boinking—"

Who said "boinking," anyway? Adam had always been overfond of Briticisms—an occupational hazard of the study of English literature—but Nora wondered how often even the Brits said "boinking." Well, she would find out soon enough. She was thinking of the Blum-Forsythe with a touch of complacency, mixed with anxiety—moving to England for a year, so much to do—when she became aware that Adam had stopped speaking.

"Well, it doesn't always work out," she said, a tiny hidden dagger in her smile. "Does it."

"Thank God, it's so much better this way. But listen—" Adam leaned toward her. "I want to hear more about what's been going on with you."

He gestured to the bartender to refill Nora's empty wineglass, although she was shaking her head no, no more for me.

"I want to hear about how you got married," he said.

"I didn't get—"

"What about the ring? That's a wedding ring."

So he'd noticed, although she'd been careful to let her left hand dangle behind the barstool where she thought he couldn't see it.

"Oh, the ring. It's not exactly what it seems." That was certainly true. "And it won't come off." Also true.

Adam arched his eyebrows in theatrical disbelief, as though daring her to try to evade telling him all. Nora sighed and nodded to the bartender, hovering with the bottle.

"Yes, I did get involved with someone," she said, keeping her eyes on the wine flowing into her glass. She took a sip. "It wasn't a legal marriage. And then it was over." She shrugged her shoulders lightly.

"That's not good enough, Nora. I told you all the sordid details of my misadventure."

As though I wanted to hear them, Nora thought. She began the same story that she had told Naomi, her family, and everyone else. Getting lost in the woods, breaking her leg. A long recovery in an isolated household, off the grid.

"They were basically Sixties refugees," Nora told him. "Maybe ex-Weathermen or something, although they never said anything about that." The ring? A memento of the dreamy man who turned out to be an abusive liar. There was a subtext there—*see what you let me in for when you dumped me, Adam!*—but she tried not to overdo it. Finally, her return to civilization.

Adam nodded as he listened, but something hard and attentive in his eyes made Nora know that he didn't believe a word of what she was saying. She felt a sharp, unexpected thrill: he still knew her inside and out. It was strangely flattering.

"You were a prisoner, is that what you're saying?"

"No, nothing like that." She had to be careful here, or he'd want to know why the police or the FBI weren't investigating. In fact, Nora had been surprised and slightly chagrined at how quickly the police had closed her missing persons case once she was no longer missing. "I wasn't locked up. It was just so isolated."

"Sure, but these are the mountains of North Carolina we're talking about, not the Himalayas. You couldn't have been that far from civilization."

"It was far enough." She took another sip of wine. "In winter it was hard to get around."

"OK, then spring comes, and this creep lets you go?"

"There was another man who helped me." Nora made her tone casual, but there was a new gleam of interest in Adam's eye.

"Oh, who was that?"

This was a mistake, talking to Adam at all, trying to keep him at bay with half-truths. The wine wasn't helping. She was homing closer and closer to the full truth the longer they went on, because part of her wanted to tell it. When you'd had a chance at love and magic and turned it down, it was hard to stop confessing, like the Ancient Mariner after he shot the albatross.

"He was just one of the other men in this little colony. Like I said, he helped me out."

Adam wasn't willing to let it go. "What was his name?"

"Ar—" She stopped herself. How could she explain the name, so uncommon, so obviously foreign, without raising any more questions?

"What did you say?"

"Aaron," Nora said, pleased by her own resourcefulness. "His name was Aaron." She waved her hand in a vague gesture of unconcern and managed to knock her wineglass off the bar.

"Oh, shit." She grabbed for it uselessly and braced for the sound of smashing glass.

With a sort of unhurried assurance, the wineglass rose through the air, intact, and alighted gracefully on top of the bar.

"Fuck, did you see that?" Adam asked.

He looked down at the glossy black tiles of the floor, plainly expecting to see shards of glass there, and not seeing them. "What happened?"

Nora laid her hand gently on the base of the wineglass, as though to anchor it to the bar. "See what?" she asked.

Chapter 2

"That's good," Ramona said, when Nora told her about the wineglass, back in New Jersey, as they were walking home from the public library. It was the first chance she'd had after her visit to school to speak to her sister alone; at the house, their father or their sister Leigh or Nora's stepmother always seemed to be in the room, too. Ramona was the only person in this world who knew, sort of, how Nora had spent the past year.

Now she seemed more interested in what Nora considered a side issue. "Why were you with Adam? I thought you guys broke up."

"We did. It was just a friendly drink."

"But he was a jerk to you, wasn't he? Why were you having a drink with him when you could have changed him into an ant and stepped on him?"

"I don't hate him that much," Nora said.

"Then don't step on him." Ramona was nothing if not practical. "Or—I know—give him a dog's head. An ugly dog. Or poison his drink, turn it into something really gross."

Nora snorted. "One of those Australian chardonnays he hates."

"I was thinking of warm spit."

"The chardonnay would be worse."

"Whatever." Ramona shrugged. "You could make warts grow all over his body, or turn him into a fat old lady, or make it so flies come out of his mouth every time he talks."

"That's disgusting," Nora said, chortling. She had a quick mental picture of Adam lecturing to a classroom full of undergraduates, trying to ignore the cloud of flies buzzing around his head. "I wouldn't be that obvious," she said. "I'd—oh, I'd make his face break out." Was there a spell for ensuring that he'd never get tenure? "Or I'd make him just a little bit shorter." Adam was already sensitive about his height.

"Make him a lot shorter! Two feet tall. And everything he eats will taste like old sneakers."

Mentally Nora ran through some of the curses she had read. Many of them had to do with weakening an enemy in battle or harming his livestock, or they involved various intimate matters that she thought—she hoped—her eleven-year-old sister would not understand. "He'll be stricken with fear at, um, faculty meetings, his books will get bad reviews, and he'll fall in love with a fish."

"A fish?"

"It's actually a fairly harsh curse," Nora said. "Depending on the kind of fish. People have gone crazy or drowned. I'd be nice—I'd make it a goldfish, and Adam could just keep it in a bowl."

"Make it a shark."

"A jellyfish."

"That's not a real fish. An electric eel."

"Doesn't matter. An octopus."

"OK, an octopus," Ramona agreed. "'Give me your arm, darling. And your other arm. And your other arm—'" With a melting gaze, she tenderly reeled in the multiple limbs of Adam's imagined paramour.

Nora lost her composure and had to lean against a maple tree to recover. Then she wondered if anyone had heard them, their shrieking, their unguarded talk of spells. She glanced around. The street was quiet, nothing moving except an SUV pulling out of a driveway a few houses down.

"Well?" Ramona asked, suddenly strict. "Can you do it?"

Nora grimaced. "No."

"Can't or won't?"

"I can't."

One of the first, most elementary spells she'd ever learned was for levitating objects. Now Nora thought of all the things she'd tried—and failed—to levitate since that evening at Petrarch with Adam: an earring, a cotton swab, a pretzel, a crumpled-up tissue, her toothbrush, a penny, a dime, a five-dollar bill, a spoon, a Styrofoam peanut, an actual peanut, a packet of sugar, her phone, a pencil stub, a bookmark, a bottle cap, the driver's license she needed to renew, several pebbles, too many fallen leaves to count, a Subaru station wagon—that was just for the hell of it—and a subscription card to the *New Yorker*.

Practice, she kept telling herself. It will come back. I just need to practice.

Now, as they passed under a cherry tree, she tried to levitate a pink petal from the sidewalk. It danced into the air, and she felt her heart race. But when a corps de ballet of other petals rose, too, Nora reluctantly concluded that it was the wind, not magic, that had lifted them up.

"I'm still stuck. I can't work any magic," she told her sister. "Except for the wineglass, that one time."

"Why?"

"I don't know. Maybe it's just harder to do magic in this world."

Ramona pondered this for a while, looking down at the pavement. "Arundill could do magic here. He could make animals talk."

"Aruendiel," Nora corrected, privately savoring the name. It had almost escaped when she was talking to Adam last week. She wondered how much longer she could keep it locked away. Such a relief to talk to her sister about magic, but Ramona was only a little girl. There were other things she couldn't begin to explain. "I never learned that spell. I was still a beginner when I left."

Ramona rolled her eyes. "Why didn't you study harder? Is that why you can't do magic now?"

"Are *you* really going to lecture me about studying harder?" Nora asked. She reminded Ramona about the wineglass; it wasn't as though she could do no magic whatsoever.

"But you didn't plan to make the glass float," Ramona said. "It was a reflex or something. The magic's not as good if you can't control it."

That was just what Aruendiel would say—she needed to work on her control. She wished she could hear him say it. "I know," she said.

The discouragement in her voice must have been obvious, because Ramona gave her a worried look and changed tactics. "You just have to keep trying," she said, punching the air with a small fist. "Don't give up."

"All right."

"It's all mental. You have to believe in yourself."

Nora felt fairly sure that Ramona was repeating life lessons from her soccer coach. She sighed. "It's not exactly like that. True magic isn't really about you. It's about making a connection with the world. It comes from understanding the things around you, their inner life, and drawing on their power. Does that make any sense?"

"I guess."

"It's hard to explain. Aruendiel used to tell me that you can't understand real magic until you've done it, which I thought was massively unfair, but it's true."

Ramona was quiet for a minute. "When you first got back, you said you didn't want to do magic anymore."

"Well, I was wrong." The rescued wineglass had filled her with more, and more lasting, elation than any wine ever could. "I miss it. I really miss it."

"I thought maybe you could teach me some magic," Ramona said, sounding unusually shy.

"I wish I could," Nora said. Disturbed by how sad she sounded, even to herself, she tried to be more cheerful: "What, you want to make flies come out of Leigh's mouth when she talks?"

Ramona wasn't buying it. "But I bet you won't even have time to try to do magic. You're going back to North Carolina this summer, and then you're going to England."

Nora's spirits sank even lower, and she suddenly understood that for the past few days, almost since her conversation with Naomi, she had been trying not to think about school or her fellowship or the entire enticing future that it had just opened for her.

"I suppose I will be pretty busy," she said.

Perhaps, Nora thought, she didn't understand the secret life of matter here. Or perhaps the reverse. Aruendiel had speculated that her ability to work magic had been awakened because she was a foreigner in a strange world where everything was new to her. Now, on her home turf, her senses were probably dulled, stupefied; her magical abilities had been quelled. She had become an ordinary person again. What was that word that Ramona had once used? *Muggle.* Even without having read the Harry Potter books, Nora thought it sounded unfairly pejorative.

It was also possible, she thought with a sense of heaviness, that she could not levitate a cherry blossom petal or a pretzel or a piece of paper with magic because there was no such thing as magic, just as there might not be any such person as Aruendiel or any world other than the one she inhabited at present.

Nora contemplated this idea, not for the first time. Accepting it, she could see, would make resuming her old life easier. There would be no more unease over telling her family and friends only part of the truth. And she could tell herself—what? A head injury, or maybe she really did spend the past year stoned out of her mind. It would be easier to forget Aruendiel if she had only hallucinated his existence, had mistaken a dream for reality.

No, it wouldn't. Disbelieving in Aruendiel would only make her regret his absence more, she felt keenly. And anyway she could not unwind her certainty of his existence. She knew him too well for that, no matter how much he'd tried to hide himself from her. She had memorized him—his searching gray eyes, his secret, lonely kindness— the way she learned poems she loved, although that was not enough and would never be.

The kiss she had never given Aruendiel weighed down her heart more than ever with a kind of exquisite, impatient grief. He was real, he existed somewhere—bent over his books in the tower study, or wandering in the shadows of snowy pines, or turning his watchful, battered face toward the light of a dying fire. Whether she liked it or not, some deep part of herself remained with him, awake and alive in a way that she could remember but never quite recover. For a tantalizing, dangerous moment, Nora let herself crave everything she had lost.

The magic existed, too, even if she could no longer find it. She had turned her back, she was marching away, she was doing the responsible thing, and someday in the unknown future she might even resign herself to the fact that she'd made a terrible, idiotic mistake and would never see him again—but at least she was not fool enough to think that she could erase his existence entirely.

After a week in New Jersey, Nora drove south in a rented car to her mother's house in Richmond. Her mother and stepfather had salvaged the stuff from her apartment when she went missing; now it was all in cardboard boxes in her mom's garage.

The day she arrived, she opened a couple of cartons and experienced some surprise at how random and unfamiliar the contents seemed, even the books. It felt like the kind of voyeuristic browsing that you did at a yard sale, marveling at how anyone could have bought those shoes or those dishes in the first place.

"You're not really planning to go back to school, are you?" her mother asked the next morning. They were having breakfast in the sunroom, a term that Nora always considered somewhat misleading, because sunlight flooded through enormous windows into almost every single room in the house, including some of the walk-in closets. It was mid-April, and the air-conditioning was already going full blast.

Nora said that she was, yes.

"You can do so much better for yourself! It's just a waste of your time."

Nora put down the piece of toast she had been eating, secretly uncertain which side of the argument she preferred to be on. "What would be a better use of my time?" she asked mildly. She mentioned the fellowship again.

"That's so wonderful, Nora. I'm so proud of you. But being an academic—it's not what you're called to do. I see that now."

In spite of herself, Nora was intrigued. Her mother sounded so certain. "All right. What am I called to do?"

"You'll find the right path"—her mother looked serious and hopeful at the same time—"if you let God show you."

She should have seen that one coming. "Fine," Nora said, "but I wish he would hurry up."

"You don't need to scoff, Nora. God really does have plans for you."

"But I can't wait for God. I have to figure something out soon. How old am I? Thirty?" The question was not entirely a joke. Time didn't seem to sync up exactly between Aruendiel's world and her own. "I have to get moving."

"Then don't waste any more time. Life goes so quickly. It really does." There was a catch in her mother's voice, so slight that almost anyone else would have missed it, but Nora knew what she was thinking. The date had just rolled around again, the anniversary of the accident. The night when the police came to the door, and Nora was roused out of bed by her parents so they could all go down to the hospital, and nothing was ever the same again.

"I know, Mom," Nora said, as gently as she could, although part of her wanted to scream.

"Your brother had so little time, it still hurts. He was so gifted. He could have done anything, really. And then at the end," her mother said, some steel coming into her voice, "we took away the time he had left."

Nora stared at her mother's thin hands, wrapped around a coffee cup, and noticed how dark and ropy the veins had become. "He was gone, Mom." They had been having this conversation for seventeen years. It would never be finished. "We waited weeks, and he was already gone, the doctors all said so. We could have waited forever and nothing would have cha—"

"I would have waited forever. It's not your fault, Nora," her mother added quickly. "You were so young. And your father was so—"

"I wasn't a little kid! I knew what we were doing. It was the best thing for EJ."

"We'll never know, will we?" Her mother's eyes blazed a fierce blue. "Well, I praise God that you are here, and well."

A moment of silent guilt for all those months of absence. Nora frowned apologetically at her mother. "I'm sorry. I really am. For, well— for all the anxiety I caused—"

"Well, don't you ever do that again!" Her mother pressed her lips together, visibly holding herself in check. In a slightly different tone, she went on, "I want you to be happy, Nora! I do. I would feel so much better if you could be doing the work God has for you, no matter what, no matter where. When you do find the right path, you follow it. Don't waste a minute." Nora sighed, and her mother shook her head vigorously. "And no, I don't mean that job at Scott's office, either."

It was an entry-level marketing position. Scott, Nora's stepfather, had already mentioned it twice.

"He's just trying to be helpful, but it's not for you. You should be helping people," her mother went on. "You have a good heart, and you're so smart. Medical school, even."

"Oh, Mom." Would studying magic be an acceptable substitute for medical school? But it was too late, she was back in her own world, she had missed her chance.

"It's just a thought. But I'm serious, Nora. Don't underestimate yourself. And you don't want to start a family too late, either." If EJ were still alive, Nora wondered, would Mom be so obsessed with planning my life? "Of course you need to find the right man," her mother finished reflectively.

I might have, and then I lost him. "Oh, now you're asking the impossible," Nora said lightly, but her mother frowned over the brim of her coffee cup.

"You're not still brooding about Adam, are you?" she asked.

"Absolutely not."

"We heard he'd gotten engaged to someone else. He never even got in touch with us to say he was sorry you'd disappeared." Her mother's mouth tightened with disapproval. "Anyway, I was just going to say, he wasn't right for you. He didn't respect you enough."

"You're certainly right about that," Nora said. "Getting engaged to someone else—not very respectful."

She spread more jam on her toast and then bit into it. She knew without looking up that her mother was staring at the wretched ring again.

"That gadget I ordered over the internet didn't help?" her mother asked.

Nora shook her head, swallowed. "It didn't work."

"It's amazing. I can't believe that thing won't come off."

"I know, it's bizarre. Believe me, I've tried to get it off." Some of the most powerful magicians in the world—although not this world—had tried. Actually, Aruendiel had managed to get it off briefly, but Nora began turning to stone, so the ring went back on her finger. Would that curse work in this world? Nora wondered, not for the first time.

Her mother took another sip of coffee. "Mmm. Maybe you really don't want the ring off your finger."

There was a tiny grain of truth in the idea. The ring was a small, stubborn reminder of another world, another life, that was now out of reach forever. And Faitoren magic exploited your inner wishes, it was tricky that way. Although Aruendiel had said the spell wasn't a conventional Faitoren enchantment. Nora twisted the ring on her finger, considering. "I don't think it's that kind of magic."

"What did you say, Nora?" Her mother's eyes were wide, her mouth was an almost perfect O. She should have looked faintly ridiculous, but she didn't. She had used the exact same words and the exact same tone the first time she heard Nora use the word *fuck*.

Nora looked back at her, horrified. Her mother, she suddenly realized, was one of the few people who might actually believe something close to the truth of where she had spent the past year. In her mother's church—the one she'd joined after EJ died—there were no metaphors, only what its members considered to be unvarnished facts. Her mother might easily grasp that Nora had been ensnared and misled by ungodly powers. Anyone who wielded those powers, including Nora herself, could be considered an official emissary of hell.

"Did you say 'magic'?" her mother asked.

"Yes," Nora said in as neutral a tone as she could summon. "Something I just—well, those people I stayed with, they believed in some strange stuff. Um, superstitions."

"They weren't Christians."

Definitely not. "They were good people, but no."

"While you were away, I saw you in a dream." Her mother's voice sounded rich with emotion. "You were staring at a candle. Transfixed. I could tell you were trying to commune with the fire—you were worshipping it. It wasn't normal."

Nora looked worriedly at her mother. "That was a dream," she said quickly. "I don't worship fire." Just practicing some basic fire magic, that was all she'd been doing. "I don't worship anything."

"Oh, I'm afraid for you, sweetie. What have you been doing?"

Nora took a deep breath. "Don't worry, Mom. I haven't been worshipping Satan." A mistake to mention the Evil One by name; her mother's expression was pained. "Or false idols or anything. You know, I'm just not a believer, period."

Her mother looked even more distressed. "Don't close your heart to God. It's the worst thing you can do."

"I haven't closed it, I'm just agnostic."

This was another discussion they'd had before. Actually, Nora was relieved to be treading familiar ground. Defending her own godlessness was safer than trying to explain what she had meant by Faitoren magic. (She was still unnerved at how easily the word *magic* had slipped out. As though she wanted her mother to know everything, absolutely everything.)

The funny thing, Nora thought as she argued with her mother, is that I have secretly joined the White Queen's party, I am used to believing six impossible things before breakfast. I have met demons, if not the Devil. I have seen the dead come back to life. There is much, much more in heaven and earth than Horatio and his philosophy ever dreamed of.

And yet, she thought, I still can't call myself religious. Why not? For a moment she envied her mother's certainty, her trust in a mostly benevolent if judgmental power.

Aruendiel had a different kind of certainty about the divine. The gods existed. He didn't like or trust most of them, but he acknowledged their existence the same way he accepted the reality of, say, furniture or horses or magic itself. She recalled how matter-of-factly he had mentioned a job he'd done for a merchant not so long ago, something about removing a sea-god's curse from a shipping fleet.

Nora thought it would be impolitic to mention this to her mother, who was now talking—delicately, as though it pained her to mention it—about some of the horrors awaiting those who rejected God's infinite, demanding love.

"I meant to ask, how are Kimmy and Nate?" she asked abruptly. Scott's grandchildren had been visiting the week before.

Her mother hesitated, visibly reluctant to change the subject, but she reached for her phone. "Well, I have to show you the cutest picture." A small figure in red rain boots, a grinning fuzzy dog. "That was the day we all went to the park," her mother said, disappointment and regret erased from her voice. Nora bent over the screen, feeling relieved, a tiny bit jealous.

Adam called one night while Nora was still at her mother's.

He was back in Chicago. He was not getting along with his department head. He was having trouble getting a paper on Virginia Woolf published. He had a slight cold. He said he wanted to see how Nora was doing.

"Oh, I'm fine," she said, thinking that she would never have heard from him if he hadn't been having a bad day. She was not sure what to say to him, so she began to talk about her new car.

It was not, strictly speaking, a new car, but her mother's four-year-old Volvo. Her mom had been ready to trade it in for a new one, but she and Nora's stepfather had decided that Nora should have the car instead. Last year, after packing up her things in North Carolina, they had tried to drive her old car back to Richmond and ended up selling it for scrap. "I couldn't start it, Scott couldn't start it," her mother said. "It would have cost more than the car was worth to fix the electrical."

"There was a trick to it," Nora said, wondering whether she had unknowingly developed a capacity for magic after years of coaxing her ancient Saturn to life. Magic required a certain empathy with the elements, Aruendiel said.

Adam listened to Nora's account of the new car with more enthusiasm than she would have expected. She had started to tell him about the courses she was going to teach in summer school, when he suddenly uttered an indeterminate syllable, then swore.

"What's wrong?" she asked.

"Another mouse. It just ran out of the closet." She heard a thump; he must have thrown something. "The exterminator was just here last week. Shit. I'm going to move."

"Yikes. I had mice in my old apartment," Nora said. "I found a mouse in the kitchen one morning, stuck on a glue trap."

"Dead, I hope."

"No, still alive." It came back to her now. She had taken the animal outside and freed it by pouring olive oil over the mouse to dissolve the glue.

Nora started to tell Adam the story, then remembered that morning more clearly. It was only a few days after he'd dumped her. Abruptly the misery, the naked loneliness of that day came back to her. (No wonder the Faitoren had found her such a willing victim.) She felt a surge of new resentment toward Adam—and at herself for even taking his call, for letting him seek even the faintest trace of sympathy for his ridiculous grievances. She told Adam something was boiling over on the stove, and she hung up.

The mouse in the trap. She hadn't thought about it for a year at least. That was the day she went to the mountains with Maggie for the wedding, the day before she wandered into a different world.

There were mice in Aruendiel's house, too, but somehow, she had never minded them so much. They did not seem as out of place in the odd corners of a drafty, dilapidated castle as on the pink-and-gold vinyl tile in the kitchen of her old apartment. Aruendiel ate mice sometimes, when he was an owl. Nora had been reading up on owls lately, when she should have been working on her thesis. She thought about how an owl's wings were fringed with soft feathers so that it could fly silently through the darkness; she imagined those feathers brushing the skin of her hand, her cheek.

None of the nature books mentioned anything about magicians who turned themselves into owls, or the transformation spells you'd need to know to do that. But then, most people would not consider that a significant omission.

Chapter 3

Adam called again, a week or so later. This time, Nora was back at school, in her new sublet, getting ready to teach a summer class and going through her notes on Donne's Holy Sonnets, a more stressful process than she had expected. Many of the poems seemed newly obscure—her old readings strained, overcomplex, or simply trite. Other poems, unread for a year, had bloomed into new life that she found a little startling; one of the two thesis chapters that she'd completed would have to be rewritten, Nora realized with dismay. She found herself grateful for Adam's interruption.

She could tell at once that he was in a more upbeat mood this time, no need for commiseration. He was coming to town next weekend. Could they get together?

"Why are you coming?" Nora asked suspiciously. "You were just here."

"Oh, my parents are moving out of their house. To Cardinal Hill." It was the retirement community favored by former academics. Adam's parents were retired history professors. "I'll be coming down every few weeks this summer to help them move."

Nora considered this. "Well, why don't you call me when you get in?" she asked finally. If she made plans with Adam now, she thought, he would only find a way to break them once a better offer came along. And she was willing to bet that he wouldn't call her when he arrived anyway.

He did call. He insisted on taking her to dinner. "We didn't have enough of a chance to talk last time," he said. What does that mean? Nora wondered. Certainly, conversation had stalled after the floating wineglass incident. Nora had been too elated to talk much, and Adam had seemed baffled, slightly annoyed.

She was feeling hopeful about magic again because yesterday her new watch—she had left the old one in the other world—had fallen off the top of the dresser while she was on the other side of the room.

The watch had been lying close to the edge, admittedly, but not that close. She'd been running late, thinking, "Where is my watch?" and then she heard the small metallic thunk on the hardwood floor. (Control, you must improve your control, she could hear Aruendiel saying.) The crystal was cracked now. Would she be able to mend it herself, with magic, or would she have to take it back to the jeweler?

"Still married, I see," Adam said, glancing at Nora's left hand when they met at the Mexican place next to the food co-op. Nora had chosen the restaurant because it was crowded and noisy and not particularly romantic, and because she was still craving chili peppers after a year in a world without them.

Nora laughed brightly. She was now attempting to camouflage the gold ring with a couple of other rings stacked on top of it, as though she really, really liked rings or was making a fashion statement of some sort.

Thankfully, Adam said nothing more about the ring. He complimented her new haircut. Nora asked about his work, and he began to discuss departmental politics with a sort of amused resignation that suggested he was well above the fray and only paid attention to the machinations of his colleagues because they made such good spectacle. She did not believe in this posture for a second. His stories were funny, though. He asked about her thesis and had a couple of good suggestions about dealing with Naomi. They talked about mutual friends. He wanted to know more about her fellowship, and she talked about her plans with determined cheerfulness, although the idea of spending a year in Cambridge doing research on John Donne was now giving her the serious willies.

The restaurant's margaritas were stronger than Nora remembered. Still, it was shaping up to be a perfectly pleasant, rather tame evening. Then Adam said, licking a speck of sour cream from his lip: "Tell me more about this fellow Aaron."

"Aaron?" Damn. He meant Aruendiel. She took refuge in a swallow of margarita. "Well, what can I tell you?" she said, trying to sound brisk and casual.

Adam smiled. "What does he look like?"

Adam knew something. She had barely mentioned Aruendiel—Aaron—last time, but she must have given herself away somehow.

"What does he look like?" Nora repeated, as if Adam's question were pure irrelevance. "Well, he's tall. Long dark hair." Here was an opening to swat down Adam's suspicions. "He walks with a limp because of an accident years ago. It also left his face terribly scarred." She swept a hand vaguely across half of her own face.

"Oh." Adam nodded, his eyes tracing Nora's scars. "How old is he?"

Another opening. "Oh, much older. I'm not sure. A hundred and eighty." She laughed as though she were making a joke.

Adam laughed, too. "But his hair's dark. Maybe he dyes it?"

Nora hesitated, then said: "He looks younger than his age."

"How much younger?"

Nora shrugged and took another sip of margarita. She had just seen Aruendiel in her mind's eye—his black eyebrows lifting, his gray eyes meeting hers with a steady light—and now she had to look away from Adam for a moment.

"He helped you get away from the guy who was not so nice to you, right? Evidently he's not completely decrepit."

"Oh, no." Nora shook her head. Adam had been a reporter before going to grad school. He must have been better at dragging facts out of unwilling sources than she'd thought.

"Are you going to see him again, do you think?"

"I can't." There was too much hopelessness in her tone. She tried to recover. "I mean, I don't even really know how to get back there." With mock severity, she added: "You know, I didn't expect the Spanish Inquisition."

"Nobody expects the Spanish Inquisition," Adam shot back. "Our chief weapon is surprise, surprise and fear—"

Good, he would have to go through the whole routine now. Adam recited the lines with a tinge of irony, as though he were mocking the men—they were usually men—who believe there is a Monty Python quotation appropriate for almost every situation in life, but the truth was, he was one of them. It was one of the few chinks in the armor of his intellectual snobbery.

He surprised her, though, by breaking off before he got to the nice red uniforms.

"Sorry," he said. "I don't mean to be a jerk. Tell me if I'm being annoying." He grinned at her. "It might be none of my business, but I'm interested in what happened to you. And maybe I'm wrong, but I'm getting the sense that you cared about this man, Aaron. So I'm just wondering what he was like. Am I out of line?"

"It wasn't a relationship," Nora said warningly. Was Adam jealous? Or just prepared to be entertained by whatever unusual amatory adventures Nora had embarked on after he himself had cast her off?

"No, but you liked him." Adam paused; she did not contradict him. "Did he like you?"

Nora remembered Aruendiel's face at the end, pale and strained, the way his eyes glittered too brightly in the moonlight. She was going to tell Adam no, or that she didn't know, but then she thought, why don't I just tell him the truth?

"Yes," she said, startling herself with the conviction in her tone. "He did."

"No wonder," Adam said, with a faint smile. She could sense him trying to decide what to ask next. "What sort of person was he? What did he do?"

Nora in turn took a moment to consider her response. Why bother to lie? "He's a magician," she said matter-of-factly.

Adam thought she meant the kind with a top hat and a rabbit. "He had a magic act?" he asked. She could have retreated, waffled, come up with some kind of fib, but the delighted incredulity in Adam's tone goaded her, and the truth tasted too good in her mouth.

"No, he works magic. Real magic." She sat up straight in her chair and smiled at Adam. "Not wizardry—nothing to do with demons or spirits. Just natural magic, real magic."

"Oh," Adam said, not showing much reaction, which meant that he was trying to figure out what the hell Nora meant—was she nuts, was she speaking figuratively, was there a joke there he had missed? The waitress came back to their table and asked if they wanted dessert.

"I'll have another margarita," Nora said.

After a moment, Adam agreed: "Another round." Nora was amused by his hesitation: did he think she was already drunk? She was not as drunk as she wanted to be.

When the waitress left, Adam said to Nora, a little too carefully: "So—magic. You were saying?"

"Maybe I'd better begin at the beginning," Nora said. "I glossed over some things before. The day I got lost on the mountain, I found this old graveyard—"

She told him about the spell on the tombstone and how it had opened a door to another world. How she had fallen in with the lovely, deceitful Faitoren and been seduced by their beauty, their careless pleasure-making, their apparent kindness—but mostly by the spells they put on her. "They're what we would call fairies. But not Tinkerbell-sized," Nora explained. "Normal height."

Adam nodded, as though what she said was perfectly reasonable; the strain showed only a little around his mouth.

She told him about Ilissa, the Faitoren queen. "Her magic is essentially that she gives you what you want. It's an illusion, but it's very powerful. And me, I wanted to be pretty and popular—and rich—and I wanted to meet someone new, since you'd dumped me." (Adam had the grace to flinch faintly here.) "And I got all those things. I ended up marrying this man who seemed absolutely perfect. Raclin." She pronounced the name with distaste. Adam followed her lead and frowned.

"That's where the ring came from." She held up her hand. "Only, Raclin wasn't as perfect as he seemed to be. Nothing was."

The new margarita had arrived while she was talking. She pulled at the straw and went on: how she discovered that Raclin turned into a sort of dragon during the day—"a small one," she specified. Nora touched the scars on her cheek. "It wasn't a bear that clawed me. It was Raclin. And Aruendiel—his name is Aruendiel, not Aaron—helped me escape." She explained that he had tutored her in magic, when it turned out she had the ability for it.

She still left out quite a bit. There was no reason to talk about monster babies or ice demons or the less savory details of Aruendiel's past.

Adam listened, leaning on one elbow, his mouth now hidden by a curled hand. His eyes darted over and around Nora as if in search of some confirmation for her story. Only as she finished did he speak:

"And the reason your ring won't come off is because of mag—" He gestured as though he preferred that she say the word.

"A magical spell, yes," Nora said. "That's right."

"Has anyone else traveled to this other world?" Adam inquired.

"Yes, the Faitoren came from this world. That's why we have legends of fairies. There's another magician from the other world here now, I believe. A friend of Aruendiel's—I don't know him. Mitch—" She stumbled over the name, the tequila slowing her tongue. "Micher Samle."

"What's the name of this other world?"

Nora spread out her hands. "What do we call our world? We call it the world. They do the same."

"And do they speak English there?" Adam smiled, too broadly.

"Of course not. I learned how to speak Ors—the language they speak in Aruendiel's country—when I was there."

Adam laughed. "You always were good at languages, Nora."

"Thank you," she said, pleased that he had remembered.

"And you say you were able to come back because a door opened up, just like that, between this world and that one?"

"It happens sometimes. Not often."

The restaurant was quieter now, only a few other tables occupied. How long had they been talking? Nora took another draw at her straw and discovered that her glass was empty. Adam looked around the room, too, and then back at her with an odd smile. "And you were studying magic there. What kind of spells?" After she had rattled off a few—levitation, mending pots, light-casting—he asked genially: "And can you do magic here?"

"Well," she said, "remember when I knocked the wineglass over, that night at Petrarch, and it floated back up to the bar?"

Adam hunched his shoulders. "I didn't really see what happened."

Nora felt deflated. "But you were right there," she said. "You said, 'Fuck, what happened?'"

"I'm sorry, I just don't remember."

Nora shook her head. She didn't really care whether Adam believed her story about the other world or not. She was content simply to have told it and to be free from having to lie again. But she felt disappointed in Adam for conveniently forgetting what he could not explain, when it was something he had seen with his own eyes. She had expected a little more intellectual integrity from him.

Adam, meanwhile, was studying her again. "That's quite a story," he said. "You should write it down."

He didn't believe her. "You think so?"

"It's amazing stuff." He gave a rueful laugh. "So many wonderful narrative elements. So much resonance. An anti-Cinderella story that's also reminiscent of Cupid and Psyche. This Jane Eyre situation with your friend—Aruendiel? And he's kind of a Jungian archetype, the Magician."

Nora laughed, too. "Not bad. You could look at it that way," she allowed. "I didn't, since I was busy living it. Although certainly I agree, one lesson is that fairy godmothers are not all they're cracked up to be."

"Thank you for sharing this with me, Nora. All I can say is—" Adam paused, then threw up his hands and emitted a long sigh, like the air hissing out of a balloon. She was startled to see what looked like real concern in his face. "I don't know what you went through, what kind of trauma you experienced out there, but I—I want you to know that I have nothing but admiration for the way you've survived. It's amazing to me."

Taken aback, Nora shifted slightly in her chair. "Thanks."

"And the way you're dealing with it now—" Adam paused. "Again, I admire you. You've been through *hell*, and you've found a resourceful way to process it. Fictionalizing a bad experience is healthy, my shrink used to say. Better than so many other ways of dealing with it."

"Mmm." Nora thought of those short stories Adam used to write, where not much happened. "I see. You think this is all a fantasy—a metaphor—to cover up a terrible reality. I guess that makes sense." She grinned at him. "Yeah, we all have our own ways of handling the truth when it's hard to understand."

"I can tell how bad it was, just from your story." Adam looked intensely uncomfortable. "This place wasn't good for women, was it? A keep-'em-barefoot-and-pregnant kind of culture?"

Nora gave him a sharp look, surprised that this particular insight would strike him, and wondered how much he might have guessed about some of the parts of her story that she had chosen to keep to herself. But then Adam took some pride in his ability as a feminist critic; it had been useful more than once in forging intradepartmental alliances.

"Yes, basically. Women aren't educated, no legal rights, they're like livestock, basically. What made it bearable was learning magic." Why Aruendiel would have chosen to teach her in the first place—to spend hours each day correcting her mistakes, drilling her on the most basic of spells—Nora was still not entirely sure. There were very few female magicians. The only one whom Nora had ever met had also been taught by Aruendiel.

Adam apologized. This development was so unexpected that at first Nora could not take in what he was saying, but as she listened, she gathered that he was sorry for whatever he had done that had driven Nora to get lost in the mountains; he hoped that he hadn't contributed much to the trauma that underlay her fantastic story. He spoke haltingly, his eyes troubled behind the glitter of his eyeglass frames. Nora thought about telling him how attractive sincerity looked on him, he should try it more often.

Then she felt ashamed. For a moment, she had the urge to reach out and squeeze his hand.

He finished up in a more self-justifying vein, talking about how they'd grown apart after he'd moved to Chicago. He'd thought she was secretly ready to move on as well.

"That wasn't true," she said. "It really wasn't."

"I know. And I'm sorry." He looked at Nora as though expecting something. She nodded gently, which seemed to satisfy him. "I'm glad we talked about this," he said.

"Me too," Nora said.

She was still luxuriating in the warm sense of freedom that came from being able to finally, finally talk about the other world. She hadn't expected that Adam would be the one to open that particular door, and she felt oddly grateful to him for doing it.

But she lived in this world now. The other world—and magic, and Aruendiel himself—might as well be a fantasy for all the good it would do her.

The waitress slipped the check onto the table. Adam grabbed it, and Nora let him. She was starting to feel poor again, grad-student poor, after weeks of reveling in the incredible luxuries of electric light and hot showers and owning more than two changes of clothes. The fellowship stipend was generous, but it didn't start until September.

Outside, Nora said that she'd walk home, it was only a few blocks, it was not that late.

Adam said that he'd walk with her. It was almost eleven, he said in a serious tone, as though he were concerned for her safety. He added: "I'd like to see where you live."

He can't possibly be that interested in my sublet, Nora thought as they turned down a street of tidy brick houses. What exactly is he getting at? It was a luscious spring night, full of fresh green leaves, promising summer. She was picking up odd signals—Adam's hand brushing her elbow, a sideways glance infused with a confident energy that she recognized from the past. Could he possibly want to spend the night? Surely not. She felt unaccountably distracted. He was confusingly real—annoyingly obtuse about some things and yet kinder and more perceptive about others—not like she had been remembering him for the past year.

She was casting about for a suitably neutral subject of conversation when someone came up behind them, slightly out of breath.

"Miss, I'm sorry to bother you." She couldn't place the voice, but it sounded familiar.

In the streetlight's orange glow, she recognized the hardscrabble beard and the red plaid shirt: Farmer Dahmer, the homeless man who hung around the campus. She experienced a twinge of unease that he was so close, standing right next to her and Adam, then felt guilty about her distaste. He's weird but harmless, she reminded herself.

"It hasn't closed up," Farmer Dahmer said earnestly. "Not completely. You want to be careful with that."

"Don't worry." Nora shook her head politely. "It's fine." Now she remembered how she had bumped into Farmer Dahmer once before and how he had babbled about peanut butter. And something about a reward. She had noted then, as now, that he carried himself with remarkable dignity. But perhaps you needed more dignity when every-one thought you were crazy.

The collision with Farmer Dahmer had happened the same morning she'd freed the mouse, Nora thought. Funny. Hadn't there been peanut butter in the trap?

Adam rounded on him. "Sorry, we don't have any change."

"I'm not asking for money. I'm just warning the lady." To Nora, he said: "You could fall through again, if you don't watch out. Or someone else could."

"Thanks for the advice." Adam took Nora's arm and pulled her firmly away.

They walked on. "Farmer Dahmer's not dangerous," she said. "I used to see him sometimes in the library, writing notes to himself."

"I used to smell him sometimes in the library."

"I never noticed before—he has some kind of accent, doesn't he?" Like a Scottish burr, but more guttural, almost Russian sounding.

As they passed under a streetlight, Adam gave her a look that indicated Farmer Dahmer's origins were of no concern to him. "So, this magician of yours—" he began.

"What about him?"

"Did you and he ever, well—make magic together?" Adam asked. Nora frowned. "Sorry," he said. "I didn't mean to make fun."

"That's all right. He never—well, no, we just didn't."

"No? Why the hell not?" The outrage in his voice was rather cheering. "He didn't appreciate a beautiful, intelligent woman like you?"

"It was complicated," Nora said, giving the answer that should have ended the matter. But once again the chance to talk more about that lost, secret year was too enticing.

"*He* was complicated," she said. "I think, um, he did care for me, but he didn't act on whatever feelings he—he had." She laughed, with some bitterness. "He tried to get me to marry someone else at the end, a younger man he thought would be more suitable." Thinking about that interview in Lord Luklren's library, when Aruendiel had all but ordered her to marry Perin, still made her wince inwardly with rage—at Perin, for his tactless, blockheaded good intentions; at Aruendiel, for his blindness and his pride; at herself, for a failure she could not even begin to name.

"Another beau? You were racking them up," Adam said. "Why was the other man more suitable?"

Perin was the obvious better choice: honest, stalwart, shrewd, innocent. Nora wondered, in an abstract way, why she hadn't preferred him.

"He was more respectable. Safer, perhaps. Aruendiel had done things—well, he murdered his wife when she was unfaithful. A long time ago," Nora added hastily, as if it would reassure Adam to know that Aruendiel had not been violent recently. "He knew he'd done a terrible thing. He felt guilt over that, and for being alive."

Nora was trying to decide whether to go on and explain that Aruendiel had died and then been returned to life by a couple of other magicians, against his own wishes—another reason for the darkness that edged all his humors—when Adam broke in, wanting to know how Aruendiel had killed his wife.

"He stabbed her," Nora said.

She felt the sudden weight of Adam's arm on her shoulders. He pulled her close in an embrace that felt correctly fraternal but nevertheless— she had an inkling—could still develop into a more passionate clinch. "Jesus, Nora," Adam said into her ear.

"It wasn't that bad," she said, trying to get her balance.

"I hate to think of you surrounded by people like that."

"He was good to me, I told you. And look, I survived."

"I'm so glad you did," Adam said. His arms tightened around her.

Adam's body was an adamant, familiar presence. He was still working out, she guessed from the feel of his shoulders. He was exactly three-and-a-half inches taller than she was. Nora knew the precise angle to tilt her head to meet his lips. Against her thigh—hello, hello—she could feel his cock wedged into his jeans, the way she had so many times before.

I can't believe this, she thought, Adam's turned on by the fact that I was in love with a murderer. Men are so weird. She felt his breath warm against her neck, shorter breaths now. This is all wrong, she thought wildly. But this is now. Adam's here. She sighed.

"I missed you," he said.

On some level—Nora realized, pressed against him—she had wanted him to say those words for a very long time. Adam was no magician, certainly not, but there are some incantations that never lack power. *I missed you.* Under the circumstances, she could extract all kinds of delicious meanings from those words: I was wrong. I love you. Let's go back to the way it was. She saw that, in sharing confidences, she and Adam had begun to rebuild their old alliance, and tonight or not much later she would likely follow him into bed again. Why not? He was tangible, close—not a ghost in her memory, like Aruendiel.

His lips touched her cheek. He always liked to come in from the side, finding the corner of her mouth and then working around to the front. She ran her hands over his shoulders and down the compact muscles of his back, her palms slipping over the thin cotton of his shirt.

Her old life back, but better. Was that what she really wanted?

Be careful what you wish for, Nora thought with rising panic. She wished, absurdly, that Farmer Dahmer would happen along to interrupt them again. Then a couple of different thoughts came together in her mind, like a chord.

You want to be careful with that, Farmer Dahmer had said. Careful of what? You could fall through again, he'd said. And she knew where she'd heard that accent before.

Nora jerked free. "Oh, my God," she said. Adam looked at her with surprise and some annoyance. "I have to go back. I just remembered—" She gestured vaguely, trying to think. "I forgot something. Back at the restaurant. Um, my bracelet."

Turning, she broke into a half run, heading back the way they had come.

There was no sign of Nora's lost bracelet at the restaurant, which was not much of a surprise to her. Nevertheless, while Adam waited next to the cashier's desk, she searched diligently under the table where they had sat and in the restroom.

Adam said that he didn't remember her wearing a bracelet that evening, but Nora said she was sure she'd put it on—she'd had some trouble getting the clasp to fasten. He looked aggrieved. "Well, no wonder you lost it."

There was no sign of Farmer Dahmer, either, on the streets near the restaurant. His absence Nora found much more disappointing. All the way back to her apartment, she was on edge, swiveling her head to look down side streets, until Adam asked whether she expected to run into someone else wearing her bracelet.

"It's not especially valuable, is it?" he asked.

"Sentimental value, that's all."

"Did the magician give it to you?" He sounded as though he were trying to be funny.

"Of course not," Nora said. "My grandmother."

Adam did not attempt to embrace her again. The low hum of erotic attraction that she had detected before had dissipated. But when they reached her apartment, and Nora pulled out her keys, she could feel his eyes on her, as though he were taking the measure of her readiness, her desire.

She told Adam that it had been very good to see him, and she would love to offer him a drink, but that the apartment was a mess and she had to get up early the next morning.

Did a flash of relief cross his face? He said that he had to get up early, too; his parents were expecting him. "Something about dismantling a sideboard." He smiled to show how ridiculous the task was.

"Well, have fun," Nora said, feeling relieved, also wistful, and she smiled back more warmly than she would have a minute before. On an impulse, she added: "Thanks for listening."

"Anytime." Adam looked at her for a moment, and she thought she saw both concern and wary bafflement in his face, as though he were trying to figure out just how crazy Nora might be, and exactly how he felt about her. He swiped her cheek with an ambiguous kiss. "I'll talk to you soon," he said.

Closing the door behind her, Nora briefly considered waiting a few minutes for Adam to disappear and then going out again to scour the neighborhood for Farmer Dahmer. Reluctantly she abandoned the plan: it was almost midnight, and she had no idea where to look. He could be a mile away by now or bedded down in whatever alley or abandoned building he called home.

Nora woke early the next morning, Saturday. It was cooler than the day before; there was dew on her landlord's lawn when she left the apartment just after seven. She had dressed a little more carefully than she normally did on Saturdays: her lovely clunky handmade boots that had gotten so many compliments; a denim skirt; her new blouse in the cool vintage print; the bead bracelet that she'd described so carefully to Adam last night, the one that had been in her jewelry box the whole time, right where she knew it was. She wanted to make a good impression. She also had a faint, squeamish feeling that her feet should be well protected.

Farmer Dahmer was not near either of the coffee shops she passed; nor was he on the main drag or any of the side streets in the business district near campus. A man was sleeping on the bench in front of the post office, but it wasn't Farmer Dahmer. She tried to think about all the times she had seen him in the past. An eccentric street person was ubiquitous until you actually wanted to find him. She decided to try the campus. Scanning for the red shirt, she looked for him in the main quad, then the two side quads, then circled back past the student union.

She started asking people if they'd seen Farmer Dahmer, and most of them looked at her as though she also might be cracked. Then a girl playing the recorder under a tree scratched her pierced nose thoughtfully and said she believed she'd seen him not too long ago, going into the main library.

Right, Nora thought, I should have known. What was I telling Adam last night?

She found him on the eighth floor of the library's east tower— in the sociology stacks, of all places. Through a gap in the shelved books, she glimpsed the red shirt, and then she heard him muttering to himself. He was sitting at one of the tables in an open space near the bathrooms, hunched over a fan of papers, just as she had seen him on other occasions. Many different kinds of paper, she saw as she approached: graph paper, sheets torn from a spiral notebook, standard-issue white copy paper, the backs of colored handbills from campus bulletin boards. All were covered with closely spaced lines of tiny handwriting that went up and down the page like a thicket of saplings.

Quietly Nora took up a position at the side of the table, to Farmer Dahmer's right, and craned her head to look more closely at what he had written on the sheet of paper nearest her. His handwriting was even more difficult to read than Aruendiel's. Some notes about the weather. A word that she recognized, after a moment, as a phonetic rendering of *air conditioner*. It was the rough draft of a cooling spell.

Farmer Dahmer finally noticed Nora. The mumbling stopped. He looked up at her with an air of being both affronted and apprehensive.

Nora glanced around quickly to make sure there was no one else within earshot. Only one of the nearby carrels was occupied, and the student inside was bent over his phone, his thumbs busy.

"Excuse me," Nora said to Farmer Dahmer in Ors, "but you had something to tell me, and I wanted to make sure I understood. That's why I came to see you here.

"My name is Nora. I think I have the honor of addressing the magician Micher Samle, is that right?"

Chapter 4

Nora took a sip from the glass of Fanta and glanced around again, taking in her surroundings. She hadn't been sure what to expect when Farmer Dahmer—Micher Samle—invited her back to his house. Not this clean, bland space in one of the newer apartment complexes near campus.

"Aruendiel said that you used to live in a cave," she said.

"I'm not as young as I used to be," he said.

Nora had been giving him news from the other world, telling him about her months there. He sat upright on the couch beside her, rocking slightly, showing very little reaction except that he blinked more rapidly whenever she first mentioned a name that was familiar to him: Aruendiel, Hirizjahkinis, Dorneng, Ilissa, Nansis Abora. She fought off the faint worry that she was boring him. He might simply be uncomfortable. Micher Samle did not strike her as someone who had many visitors. He was sipping his Fanta from an empty peanut butter jar because he had courteously allotted his one drinking glass to Nora.

"Dorneng never had any sense about women," was the only comment he made, after Nora recounted how his former apprentice had joined forces with Ilissa.

After she had finished, there was a silence. Micher Samle finally broke it. "And you remember nothing about the other wishes?" he said reproachfully.

"That's the only one I remember making—that my life were different. It certainly came true. The other two, I have no idea.

"You could have told me that you had granted me three wishes," she added. "Then I might have remembered them."

"I thought it was very clear."

"Well, how would I know that you were the mouse that I saved? Not that I would have believed it. Or believed in three wishes, either.

Still, it would have been nice to have some warning. Do you know how dangerous that is, granting someone wishes without telling them? Especially in this world, where people don't expect it?" She didn't want to be too hard on him, but he had to understand the risks here.

"Probably you used the other two wishes on trivial things—wished for something good to eat, for example," Micher Samle said, as though he had not been paying attention to her. Behind the dry scrub of his beard, he looked disappointed.

"Sorry," Nora said. "But again, if I had known—"

"Now, if you'd wished to live forever, or to be rich, that might have been more interesting." He shook his head solemnly. "Well, I'm afraid my wish spell isn't what it should be. You asked for a different life, and it simply sent you to my own world. No inspiration there. Millions of other possibilities. The spell failed to consider them."

"Oh, it could have been a lot worse," Nora said hastily. "At least the spell didn't change my life by giving me a heroin habit or a degenerative disease or making me enroll in business school. Overall, I think things worked out all right."

Without answering, Micher Samle stared at the peanut butter jar that he held in his lap, scraping absently at the label with a dirty fingernail. Nora sipped her own drink again, inhaling the scent of orange soda as an antidote to Micher Samle's unwashed staleness. The fug that clung to him was all the more noticeable in this pristine apartment. But then he came from a world where most people rarely bathed or changed their clothes. Had she smelled that bad when she came back? Micher Samle used to live in a cave, she reminded herself.

She changed the subject: "This other thing, what you warned me about. You're saying that when I came back from your home world, the door didn't close properly?"

With difficulty, Micher Samle pulled himself away from what was evidently a more interesting line of thought. "That's right."

"And it's stuck to me, more or less." He nodded mechanically, so she went on: "So there's a rip in the universe that's basically been following me around ever since I got back."

"Yes, yes. It's not extremely large."

"And it leads back to your world?"

"No, that's not quite right. It leads out of this world."

"And where does it go?"

"Well, it might lead to my world," he allowed. "It's hard to say. The two worlds could have drifted apart, you understand, since you passed from that one to this one."

"And if it doesn't lead to your world?"

"It would go to the place between worlds."

"What is that?"

"No place. In fact," Micher Samle corrected himself, "I should not even call it a place. There is nothing there."

Nora remembered that moment of crossing the void, of feeling completely alone except for her panic. "And so what do I do about this gap, this hole? Can you close it?"

"Oh, no, I don't think so. If the fissure has been accompanying you all this time, then I think clearly it is under your influence. It is yours to resolve. Yes, that would be best." He gave a succession of rapid nods, closing his eyes as he did so.

"But how do I close it? Especially since"—she dropped her voice slightly—"I can't really do magic in this world."

He pursed his lips. "That should not matter. The fissure will respond to you. You will see." The explanation for closing the gap was long and technical. Micher Samle swayed back and forth as he outlined what had to be done, and his voice dropped to a mumble again. Unlike Aruendiel, who always grew more animated on the subject of magic, Micher Samle seemed to withdraw into himself when speaking of it.

Nevertheless, Nora got a general idea of what was required. It was her pot-mending spell writ large, only here what she had to anneal was the stuff of the world, the rich fabric of ordinary reality. "All right," she said finally. "I think I understand."

"Good, very good." Micher Samle took a long swig of Fanta, as though he needed the refreshment badly.

"But just to be clear," Nora said, her voice rising nervously, "you say it's also *possible* that someone could go through the door and reach your world?" She flashed Micher Samle a smile that attempted to look casual, but this was the question she had been burning to ask ever since recognizing him the night before: was there a way back?

"Possible, yes."

"Can you tell for sure?"

Micher Samle seemed surprised by the request, but he stood up and began to walk around the room, circling the couch, his eyes searching out a few places in the empty air that only he seemed to know about. Finally he stopped and squinted at Nora.

"The connection still exists."

"Really. All right." She nodded, taking in the information, trying to think carefully.

She could go back. It was possible. The stories that she'd told Ramona and Adam and herself would be real again. She would see the sky of another world overhead, its sun and moon and weather, not so unlike their equivalents here but different all the same. Because she, Nora, would be different there. She would be a magician again, knowing the life of the world around her in a way that she could not here, even though it was home. And she could pick up the thread of the conversation that her heart had been having with Aruendiel's and find out where it led.

And where would it lead? She thought she knew, but there was only one way to be sure. Only one. Nora felt her pulse race so fast that she knew her mind was already made up. "I want to go through," she said. "Back to your world."

"You want to go back?" Micher Samle was dubious, a little flustered. "I should say, it's not a strong connection. Not at all. It would be much safer, much, much safer, to close up the fissure, not try to pass through it."

"But I could pass through it?"

"Probably." He chewed his lip. "Once, maybe. I don't know if you could come back the same way."

There was always a catch. Nora paused, and then—as Micher Samle's brow wrinkled further—she decided she could not afford to let him see any signs of indecision. And he might be wrong.

"Well, I want to try. You'll help me, right?" She smiled as winningly as she could. "Just help me through, and then I'll stop bothering you."

Micher Samle blinked rapidly, and at first she thought he was going to say no. But evidently the prospect of having her disappear and being left to his own thoughts was too enticing. "Yes, all right," he said.

They had only a few preparations to make. Micher Samle showed her exactly where the hole began. Once she felt the gap, it was impossible to mistake: the air itself seemed flimsy and rough, as though space were unraveling under her fingertips. Then she remembered the rope that Aruendiel had given her last time. At her urging, Micher Samle transformed a candy bar wrapper into a length of nylon cord.

While he was doing that, Nora rummaged in her bag for her phone, recalling something that her sister Leigh had said once. There was a text from Adam, sent an hour ago. She glanced distractedly at the first few words on the small, bright screen—"Hey Nora would you like to meet"—and then deleted the message without reading more.

She texted her youngest sister instead, choosing her words carefully: "Ramona, there's a door. I think I can go back. You know where."

Almost instantly, her phone quivered. Saturday-morning soccer practice must be over. "You mean THERE?" Another electronic shudder. "2 see Aroondeel???"

"Yes."

A line of smiling faces and hearts. "How long will u b gone?"

Now her fingers were trembling slightly as she typed: "I don!r knoe." The autocorrect kicked in.

"Can I come with u?"

"No," Nora texted back immediately. "It's risky," she added. "I don't know if/when I can get back here." Then: "Maybe I won't go."

"Go!!!!! Now!"

Nora laughed aloud. Micher Samle glanced up, looking worried again. "It's all right," she said.

"I cant believe u would even think that," Ramona texted furiously. "Just go y would u want to stay in this boring world. Besides u will b magician and—"

"But I will miss you so much." Nora hit send.

"—u will find magic to come back and also bring me to other world. Promise ok?? I cant wait 2 go." Then: "R u going?? GO."

After a moment, Nora wrote, "OK. I love you. Tell Dad and my mom I'll be OK."

Once you find the right path, her mother had said, follow it. Even if this probably wasn't exactly what she'd meant.

"I love u 2!" Ramona wrote back at once, and Nora changed her mind about leaving again, until the next text: "Do lots of magic! U r coolest sister ever." Nora laughed again, her breath catching in her throat. The white words in their fat blue bubbles onscreen blurred slightly as she read them over again.

"Love love love. I will find way back, promise."

"GO!"

"Miss?" Micher Samle asked.

She shivered. "I'm ready."

It occurred to Nora, as she was tying the cord around her waist, that Micher Samle might be blamed for her disappearance. Witnesses would come forward to say that she had been asking about Farmer Dahmer shortly before she vanished. She must have been seen walking across campus with him, perhaps even going into his apartment. But when she mentioned this, with some trepidation, to Micher Samle, he shook his head and gave a shy smile.

"No one will remember anything."

"And you? You don't want to go back?" Nora asked. The company of an experienced magician would not be a bad thing in a journey from world to world.

"Oh, no," Micher Samle said. "Why would I want to do that?"

"Well, it's your home." Awkwardly, she added: "You must feel a little out of place here." She felt it would be impolite to point out that he was generally considered a vagrant and a madman. Did he know about the Farmer Dahmer nickname?

"Oh, no, I'm very comfortable here. This world has excellent libraries, better than in my world."

"You don't miss your friends in the other world—other magicians?"

"Well, you have given me recent news of some of my friends, which is all that I really desire. You will give them a good account of me, I hope?"

"Oh, yes. I'm sure they'll be very interested."

"Good. I suppose that I will return someday," he said. "But there are things in this world that I would miss." His eyes went to the flat-screen TV opposite the couch.

Nora turned to look at it, too. Should she take some books, so she'd have something to read this time? No, she decided swiftly, with a glance at Micher Samle, there was no time for a lightning trip to the campus bookstore. If she was going to do this, she had to do it now, before the hole to Aruendiel's world closed or she lost her nerve or Micher Samle decided that he'd had enough interruptions for one day.

"I'm ready," she announced.

"All right." Micher Samle rocked back and forth. "You know what to do, then?"

Move with purpose, Aruendiel had scolded the last time. She could still hear the raw emotion in his voice, more than one might have expected even from a magician with a short temper instructing a hesitant pupil in a piece of strong, risky magic. She wanted to hear his voice again, for real, saying anything at all. "Yes. I have to go forward with strong intent," Nora said. "Concentrate on my destination."

It would not be hard. She had had enough of dithering and uncertainty.

"Yes, yes, you must move fast, decisively. Strange the connection has lasted this long. It's not very trustworthy. I don't know if—" Micher Samle chewed his lip. "Well, you will probably be all right. But," he added, "you don't want to be stuck in the middle of nothing. Very unpleasant."

Nora frowned. "You'll pull me back if I can't get through, right?"

"Oh, yes, yes," Micher Samle said, with a faint air of surprise, as though he had forgotten about the rope.

"Actually—let's just tie the rope to something solid." Nora took the other end from him, glanced around for something to fasten it to, and finally settled on the kitchen doorknob. She wrapped the rope around the handle three times and knotted it as tightly as she could, then walked back to the middle of the room. She picked up her bag from the couch and slung it over her shoulder.

Fingers outstretched, she felt for the edge of the hole in the air. "Here goes," she said. And went.

Micher Samle was right, there was nothing on the other side of the hole. Perhaps not even Nora herself. She could not see her hands in front of her. There was no sensation in them, either. Nothing to tell her that she even had hands.

She could have been traveling a thousand miles an hour, or she could have been motionless—she could not tell for sure. It was not dark, exactly. Darkness—shadows, midnight, the great vacuum of outer space—is the absence of light. Here was neither light nor its opposite.

How long had she been here? Her mind's inner clock seemed to be leaking time. It was hard to keep her thoughts in order. But surely she should have been in the other world by now. The place where she wanted to be.

She wasn't, though. She was here. She was nowhere.

Something had gone terribly wrong, Nora thought without much interest.

Chapter 5

Aruendiel left Luklren's castle as soon as he could, which was not as soon as he wanted to.

Even after the peace treaty was finally signed—the Faitoren took an unconscionable time to approve it, quarreling among themselves and demanding various ridiculous amendments—there was still the last ceremonial banquet to get through. The other negotiators on the king's side agreed that Aruendiel should share the first cup of peace with the Faitoren, since he'd been known as their most implacable enemy for so many years. Otherwise, they hinted, the Faitoren would not consider the treaty truly binding.

It chafed him to have to be so solicitous toward a treacherous, criminal, conquered race—not even human. At the banquet, he went through the ritual mechanically, passing the bowl back and forth with a Faitoren—Vulpin, the one who now styled himself their leader. Aruendiel only wished that the meaningless display would be soon. The wine seemed to have no effect on him, except to make him feel duller than usual. The sound of the bowl smashing on the floor, the end of the toast, caught him by surprise.

Aruendiel returned to his seat and watched the other toasts. The hall grew noisier with talk and laughter. Some of the younger knights had started dancing at the far end of the room, their arms flailing as they whirled. It was a country bull-dance. The Faitoren guests looked on, amused. Then a few Faitoren got up and joined the dance, too. Monstrous, half-human figures—yet they moved with quick, uncanny grace. There was something satiric in the studiously precise way they emulated the human dancers, copying the drunken sway of their bodies, stamping with exaggerated force.

"Never thought I'd be entertaining that rabble under my roof." It was Luklren, their host, bawling through the din into Aruendiel's ear. "And I'll tell you—after tonight, never again."

Aruendiel nodded curtly. He was in full agreement, but there was no need to state the obvious. Besides, he doubted that the Faitoren had any great desire to socialize with Luklren any more than they were required to.

"Hideous, aren't they?" Luklren continued. "I can hardly stand to look at them. That one with the mouth—ugh. And they say they want to look this way. Why? That's what I want to know. It's not natural."

"Natural for them," Aruendiel corrected him. "And in any case, the new treaty prohibits them from using their old glamours."

Luklren went on, unheeding: "How could you want to look like that?" He pointed at a Faitoren whose eyes swiveled restlessly on fleshy stalks. "I liked it better when they took the trouble to look human. You remember that girl we picked up last year, up Sheepfold Hill?"

"She was no Faitoren. I told you then."

"Wasn't she? That little beauty with the tits?" Luklren looked puzzled, then took another swig of wine. Aruendiel turned away. The stupid doll's countenance hiding Nora's own sweet, clever face—if anything, the memory of her Faitoren enchantment made him angrier now than it had before.

He suddenly wished that at this very instant he could look into her clear brown eyes, so steady and bright with understanding. Then he pushed that thought away.

This defeat of the Faitoren was a flawed, rotten victory, Aruendiel thought. There was no reason to celebrate when Ilissa and Raclin, his real enemies, were still at large. When his old friend Hirizjahkinis was dead—or as good as dead, even if Nansis Abora was right—and even faithful, stubborn Mrs. Toristel, who had spent all her life in his service, was gone.

But at least he had resolved the question of Nora. That was perhaps the one fortunate result from this whole fiasco, Aruendiel reminded himself. He had handled the matter honorably, restored her to her family and friends, and put her safely beyond Ilissa's reach. He had nothing to reproach himself with. All very satisfactory.

She was beyond the boy Perin Pirekenies's reach, too. That thought gave him pleasure, although not as much as it had previously. If Nora had decided to stay to marry Pirekenies, she would be here now in this banquet hall, near at hand. She would be watching intently the toasts and the dancing and all things that were new to her, the way she always did. And sitting at Pirekenies's side, wearing the red betrothal veil. She might spare an occasional smile for the old, crippled magician who had taught her. Then she would turn back to Pirekenies, their heads close as she spoke to him.

Foolishness, Aruendiel rebuked himself. It was hard enough to see her go into the other world without trying to imagine what her future would have been in this one. Then he realized someone had touched his shoulder to get his attention, and that it was the boy Pirekenies.

"What do you want?" Aruendiel asked roughly. He was pleased to see that the younger man moved back a half step.

"To inquire after Lady Nora," Pirekenies said. "She said she would try to return to her world. Has she—?"

"Yes. She has gone back to her people."

Pirekenies looked steadily at Aruendiel. "How do I know you are telling the truth?"

"What?"

"All I have is your word that she traveled into another world"— Pirekenies frowned, as though it disturbed him to repeat such nonsense—"and did not meet some other, worse fate."

Wonderful, the boy's stark foolishness. Aruendiel stood up, his hand on his sword hilt, and glowered down at Pirekenies. "What, you suspect I murdered her?"

"I'd simply like an assurance of her safety."

"You think I would have harmed Nora?" He added, more menacingly: "You doubt the word of a peer and a magician?"

"I don't mean to insult you," Pirekenies said. Evidently he was not a complete idiot. "I only want your reassurance that she is well."

"She is well," Aruendiel said. "She reached her parents' house in safety. I can attest to this."

In fact, Aruendiel had done the observation spell that very afternoon, finally succeeding, after several tries, in finding his way to Nora's father's home in the other world. There he had moved around the house like a restless ghost, looking for Nora. She was not in the house, but he overheard her being discussed by her father and a woman who was no doubt her stepmother. They spoke too quickly for him to make out all the English words. He gathered, though, that Nora was buying food at the market, that she would cook the dinner that night. (Just as she had done in his own household, he thought.) They were concerned about her—he could hear it in their voices—but from what they said, as far as he could tell, there was nothing wrong with her health or spirits.

He had waited, hoping to see Nora when she came home, but his candle had gone out and the spell had ended before she appeared.

"If you doubt me," Aruendiel said to Pirekenies in a more measured tone, "you can speak to the magician Nansis Abora, who also saw her travel back to her own world."

"Another magician," Pirekenies said, with a distrustful smile.

"Yes, and an honest man. If that is not enough for you," Aruendiel added reasonably, "my sword can continue this argument with yours."

Pirekenies stood stock-still for a moment, as though considering Aruendiel's offer, then smiled again. "It's not necessary. I'll accept your reassurances. Thank you." He bowed, then went back to his seat at the other long table.

Aruendiel did not resume his own seat. Instead, he made his way through the crowd, out of the hall. The insult from the boy Pirekenies had roused his blood, but then his anger had lost its savor. Now he felt only a great weariness. There was nothing to keep him in this place any longer. Going to the stables, he shook a dozing groom awake and retrieved his horse and saddle.

The night was blessedly cold and silent as he rode away.

There had been a thaw in the Uland, so that all the snow had melted, and then the weather had turned cold again. Stripped of winter's white blanket, the village, the fields around the castle, even the deep woods beyond the river had a tired, dirty look, still unprepared for the slightest shoot of green.

The castle, however, was very clean. Aruendiel could not remember the last time it was so tidy or smelled so strongly of beeswax and rosemary.

That was Lolona's doing. She and two of her daughters had apparently spent the days after her mother's death sweeping, scrubbing, buffing the castle's living quarters to a high polish in a way that Mrs. Toristel had not had the energy to do for decades, even with Nora's help.

They had already burned Mrs. Toristel's body, in the Pelagnian way. It was what she would have wanted, Lolo said; Pelagnia was her mother's birthplace, after all, and she'd always considered it home, even after so many years in the Uland. Aruendiel visited the large, blackened patch where the pyre had been and smeared a dark line of ash down his face. Mrs. Toristel would have been pleased by the remembrance. Still, Aruendiel felt unexpected regret that she had not been buried properly, like an Ulwoman, her curled body shrouded in wool and set to rest in earth—or better, the castle vault. His ancestors were also hers, although she'd never known that. It would be more fitting for a daughter of his line to rest with them instead of being roasted like a piece of meat.

Aruendiel also braided a white ribbon into his hair, as was correct. It caused some comment among the villagers, who thought it was odd that he would wear mourning for a servant. The ribbon was for Hirizjahkinis, too, although they could not be expected to know that.

He was startled, though, when one of the village girls stopped him on the road one morning to ask if he was wearing the white ribbon for Nora.

"Of course not! What idiocy!" he snapped.

The girl shrank back, looking terrified, although she was a strapping young woman, almost as tall as he was. Morinen, that was her name, he recalled. She had been friendly with Nora.

In a gentler tone, he told her the same thing he had told Pirekenies, that Nora had returned to her people. Unlike Pirekenies, Morinen did not doubt him.

"Ah, that is good," she said with obvious relief. "I was afraid—we heard she'd been taken away by the lady that killed Mrs. Toristel."

"She is safe now," Aruendiel said.

"Well, I will miss her. She was a funny one, but I liked her. I could always tell her anything, it felt like."

"Yes," Aruendiel agreed, frowning slightly.

"She would listen so carefully, and then say something that I never thought of before. I liked to listen to her."

He'd noticed the same acuity in Nora, so many times. This girl Morinen was not as foolish as he'd thought. He nodded. "Mistress Nora was ever perceptive, with a rare gift of discernment. Conversing with her was a singular—happiness."

"Oh, yes! I used to laugh at her sometimes, her odd notions. But I don't think she ever minded, she was so kind and good-hearted."

"Yes. She was." He corrected himself: "She is."

"And I wanted her to come to my wedding!" The girl beamed, obviously very proud. "She would have liked to hear that I'm getting married, especially since she introduced me to my fiancé."

Aruendiel now noticed the red scarf covering the girl's hair and perceived that congratulations were in order, so he gave her good wishes for a warm hearth and a full cradle. Morinen's husband-to-be, he discovered, was his own manor tenant, Peusienith. A very good match for a girl from one of the largest and poorest families in the village. Nora had apparently made the introduction during the last Null Days.

"He doesn't mind that I'm so big," Morinen added. "He likes it! I wish I could tell Nora."

"She would be happy to hear your news," Aruendiel agreed. His own spirits felt lighter, to hear Morinen rattle on.

"But it's good that she's back with her people," Morinen said. "She talked about her world a lot, how different it was. I didn't understand everything she said, but it must have suited her. Well, now maybe she'll be able to marry, too! It'll be easier for her to find a husband there, where her family is, won't it?"

"No doubt," Aruendiel said, his mouth twisting. He tried, without complete success, to keep the ice out of his voice, not wishing to frighten the child again. "Good day to you, Mistress Morinen."

Nora's wax tablets, her stylus, and the books she had last consulted still lay on the table in his library. He could not bring himself to put them away. She had made notes both in Ors—some observations he had given her on water magic—and in her own language. It was immediately obvious how much more assured her flowing, horizontal English scrawl was, next to her clumsier Ors script. Aruendiel thought he should take some comfort in that. It was a sign that she was back in the place where she belonged.

There were very few other traces of Nora in the castle, perhaps because of Lolona's formidable housecleaning—perhaps because whatever Nora had made with her own hands had been foodstuff, consumed and forgotten—perhaps because she'd had few possessions of her own. Aruendiel had gone through her room himself. Her clothes were still folded in the wooden chest—the rough blue breeches and thin, shapeless shirt that had come from the other world (did women really wear such garments there?); some linens; a woolen dress that he recognized as one of the two that had been made from the cloth he had bought in Semr. It was the dark red dress, the one he liked better on her—it looked so warm against her lightly tanned skin. Nora was all different shades of brown, like a wren. On the floor by the bed was the bracelet that she wore sometimes. She'd said once that the bracelet was a clock that would not work anymore because some part of it was dead. Aruendiel had not known exactly what she meant but had not wanted to reveal his ignorance by asking further questions.

Also in the room was the book that Nora had been translating for him. An uneventful story, hardly worth the paper—girls seeking husbands—but once you started following the narrative, it was surprisingly engrossing. Nora had gotten halfway through, and then he had stopped her. Why, he was not sure now. He had looked forward each day to reading what she had translated.

Aruendiel flipped through the book. The black lines of print were alien, inscrutable. He had never learned to read English when he was in Nora's world so long ago, and now there was no Nora to tell him what the words meant.

Nora's belongings were here. Where was she? The possessions of the dead are a puzzle that can never be solved again. But she wasn't dead, Aruendiel reminded himself irritably. He was as bad as that village girl. Yet it was better to think of her as dead.

Not long after, he did the observation spell for the last time. He knew the way now. And this time, prowling unseen through Nora's father's house, he saw Nora herself. She was lying on a divan, reading, the book propped up against her knees. Her sister—the child he'd met before—lay on the same divan, facing Nora, also reading.

He watched them, transfixed, from an arm's length away. Nora turned a page, then another page. Her eyes moved easily, contentedly through the maze of sentences. (But had she not seemed just as happy and absorbed when she sat reading in his own library?) Her hair was unbraided, flowing over her shoulders. She was wearing the same kind of long, coarse breeches that he had just seen in her clothes chest. Apparently women did wear clothes like that in her world. She was still lovely in her strange dress. After a while, her sister spoke to her, and Nora responded, squeezing the girl's foot affectionately. What were they saying? The English words slipped past him too fast for comprehension, but he listened hard anyway, relishing the sound of her voice.

Then he noticed that the child seemed to be staring directly at him. Once before, she had seen him when he cast the observation spell. Could she see him now? In some confusion, he blew out the candle that governed the spell. He had no wish for Nora to know that he was secretly observing her. Spying on her, in fact. Well, he was finished with spying. He had established beyond any doubt that Nora had survived the passage to her world, that she was happy, that she was at home in all senses of the word.

That was all to the good, so why did he feel more restive and bereft than ever? Yes, it would be better to think of Nora as dead, removed to some peaceful, inaccessible heaven.

Aruendiel found himself grateful that Lolona had stayed in the castle after her mother's death. Not so much for the castle's unaccustomed cleanliness or even for the meals she cooked for him—Lolo was a better cook than her mother, although not as good as Nora—as for the sound of her voice and her footsteps moving through the house during the day. On a few evenings he even went across the rear courtyard to the Toristels' small dwelling, to sit at their fireside for an hour, drinking a tankard of Lolona's excellent ale. If Lolo was surprised to see him there, she didn't show it. She was a loud, cheerful talker with news from Barsy and her brewery to share, as well as strong views on the state of local agriculture—the farmers were not growing enough hops to suit her, and the price was getting too high—and on many of the villagers, although her observations were never malicious enough to qualify as gossip. Rather, it was more that she felt an honest regret that many other people around her were not industrious or intelligent or disciplined enough to take advantage of the opportunities that life offered them.

Mr. Toristel sat close to the fire, saying little. He had aged in the weeks since his wife's death. There was a watery look in his old eyes, and a noticeable hunch in his spine. Looking at him, Aruendiel felt twinges of both sympathy and fear, but he only allowed himself to think, I will have to hire a new groom soon.

From time to time, one of Lolo's daughters would get up to adjust her grandfather's shawl or to pour him more ale. The two girls were fourteen and sixteen. Lolo had no compunction about dissecting their marriage prospects in front of them, while they giggled or rolled their eyes. Aruendiel had little to contribute to this kind of discussion, but it was more absorbing than he would have expected. It reminded him of Nora's book. And then, he reflected uneasily, the girls were his descendants, even if he was losing count of how many generations they were removed from him.

Nora had urged him to tell Mrs. Toristel the truth, that he was her ancestor. She'd been fiercely insistent; it would make Mrs. Toristel so happy, she'd said. Now it was too late. What about telling Lolo? Aruendiel considered the idea. So much time had passed, perhaps he could avoid the troublesome question of exactly where everyone fit on the family tree.

In practice, though, he could not bring himself to say anything of the sort to Lolona. All he could manage, one evening, was an awkward remark to the effect that he had always viewed Mrs. Toristel as a sort of daughter.

Lolo gave him a curious, half-amused look. "Did you, now?"

"Yes," Aruendiel said, wondering if he should say more, then thinking better of it. "She came to work for me when she was just a child."

"Oh, and Ma always said how handsome you used to be back then."

Lolo gave a spurt of laughter. "Like a king, she said. And your great estate—she loved to talk about those times. I used to feel jealous that I'd never gotten to see how things were in the old days."

Aruendiel smiled thinly and changed the subject. He did not mind Lolona's allusion to his broken face. She had been bracingly matter-of-fact about his appearance since the age of four, when she boldly asked him why he was so ugly. He liked less the thought of Mrs. Toristel dwelling fondly on his lost good looks. Some misguided fancy from her girlhood, nothing he'd ever cared to encourage.

Then, several weeks after his return, Lolona informed him that she would be returning to Barsy and taking Mr. Toristel with her. "He can't live by himself," she told Aruendiel severely, as though he were pressuring her to leave the old man behind.

"Of course not," Aruendiel agreed. "He should be with you. But you do not want to stay on in your mother's place?" he added hopefully. "You are quite welcome to take her position at the castle."

Lolona thanked him profusely. It was obvious, though, that she had no wish to be his housekeeper, even for the honor of following in her mother's footsteps. No doubt Lolo could make a far better living brewing beer in Barsy, he thought.

With Lolo and her family gone, the castle sank deeper into silent torpor. For the first time in years Aruendiel found little joy in his books. Finishing a chapter, he could not always remember what its subject had been. Sometimes, after woolgathering, he would pick up his brush to complete a sentence and discover that the ink in the pot had already dried.

Nora's tablets were still collecting dust on the library table. A few lines written on wax, that was all she had left behind. Why had he been so stingy and not given her parchment to write on, real notebooks? And yet it hadn't seemed to matter to her. She'd been as enthusiastic a student as he could have wished for. He could still picture the light in her face when she tried a new spell. The magic she conjured was fresh, sweet, impatient. She would have been a great magician—he would have made sure of it. As good as Hirizjahkinis. Better.

Lolona had engaged a woman from the village to cook and clean for him. He refused to allow her to bring his meals up to him in the tower, so she left food for him in the great hall. He ate it when he remembered to. Or, as the night stretched on, he changed shape and flew out the tower window to hunt in the forest. It was easier to be an owl than a man, in some ways—his emotions sharper and simpler; his thoughts focused on flying and killing. But transformation was a temporary respite, and even then he kept finding his concentration was somehow askew. Too many times he dove, then rose back into the night with empty claws.

He was sitting over his books one afternoon when his reverie was disturbed by someone calling outside.

A woman with bat's wings and indigo skin was flapping through the air, circling the tower. She grinned at him, pointing at something white that she held in her sharp, pointed teeth.

A mail demon—he had not seen one for years. Cautiously Aruendiel opened the window and took the letter from the carrier, trying to keep his hands away from her teeth. The letter was from that great fool, the wizard Hirgus Ext. He might have guessed it. Who else would send a missive by such a showy and archaic messenger? He read:

To Lord Aruendiel of the Uland, magician, greetings from the learned and puissant wizard Hirgus Ext of the Court of Fragrant Jasmine, Mirne Klep. (Gods, could Ext be more pretentious or effete? Court of Fragrant Jasmine, indeed.) *Sir, notwithstanding our differences in the past, I address you with honest goodwill, extending the hand of fellowship in the hope that you and I may find common cause against a most repulsive enemy* (Interesting. Did he mean Ilissa?) *and come to the aid of a mutual friend. I trust that you will not scorn this application when you comprehend the nature of my proposition.* (Why not get to the point, then?)

Both I and my beloved spouse were grieved to hear the dark news from the north—to wit, that the lovely and most noble Lady Hirizjahkinis, who had been our houseguest until recently, was the victim of an attack by a foul fiend, her own trusted servant the Kavareen. I am sure that her comrades on the battlefield were not more shocked or distressed than we are.

Yet I dare to remind you that all hope is not lost. It is known that some demons can be induced to regurgitate their prey, under sufficient duress. Therefore I would like to propose that you and I, skilled and learned magic workers both, combine our formidable powers to trace the monster that has devoured our friend, and force it to give back its prize. In broaching this endeavor, I appeal to your affection for Lady Hirizjahkinis as well as your sense of honor and justice. I am confident that our shared efforts will meet with success and release our friend from her horrific captivity.

Aruendiel's initial impulse was to laugh, the first time he had found anything amusing in days. Ext was so obviously afraid to go after the Kavareen by himself, and yet so determined to rank himself on the same level as Aruendiel. Refolding the letter, Aruendiel waved the mail demon away—no response.

But Aruendiel could not dismiss the letter out of hand. "Our friend," Ext had written. Simple words stronger than all the florid pomposities littering his message. Ext was ridiculous in his presumption, a fool, but he had proposed a brave and honorable mission, and Aruendiel felt piqued that he himself had done nothing to free Hirizjahkinis.

That was assuming that Hirizjahkinis could be freed. Nansis Abora, who liked to ponder odd magical problems, was fairly sure that she survived inside the Kavareen, along with everything else the Kavareen had ever swallowed. But then the Kavareen was not an ordinary demon; it was the ghost of a demon. Anyone or anything in its belly might well have undergone some transformation impossible to predict by the usual demonic physics.

Aruendiel considered this new project for a day or so, feeling oddly sluggish and indecisive. Then he concluded that he could not, on principle, ignore a chance to rescue his old friend Hirizjahkinis. In the back of his mind, he reflected that Kavareen might be useful to himself, too, without spelling out, even in his own mind, what its uses might be.

He had only a few matters to settle before leaving. He made himself give planting directions to the peasants—they expected it, it reassured them—and he renewed the protection spells on the castle and the valley. Idly he wondered how long the magical barriers would last without him. From a niche in one of the castle's ruined towers, he retrieved a few silver dishes engraved with the crest of his mother's family. Mrs. Toristel had disapproved when he sold the family silver. She thought he didn't know she'd held back those dishes and hidden them there, but there is no concealing anything from a magician in his own house. He had the silver sent to Lolona in Barsy. What Lolo would make of the gift, the legacy, Aruendiel did not know, but as he told Nora's watchful shade in his own mind, it was the best he could do. Her own clothes, still in the chest in her room—he meant to tell the new housekeeper to give them to someone in the village, but it kept slipping his mind. They were still there when he rode away very early one morning.

Aruendiel had no intention of accepting Ext's offer, so he did not turn his horse's head toward Mirne Klep. In fact, he had very little idea of where to look for the Kavareen. But he knew of a scroll in Hajgog, in the library of the Old Temple, that described the monster, its habits, and the rituals the priests had once used to control it. When the priests had set the Kavareen after her, Hirizjahkinis had consulted the scroll—in the guise of one of the temple's sacred cats—and some of what she learned had been useful when she finally subdued the demon and made it her slave. So she'd said, anyway. Hajgog was as good a place to start as any. He would make his way to the southwestern coast—avoiding that reeking anthill, Semr, and its court—and take ship for the southern continent.

As he rode, passing through the rocky Uland and then into the richer lands beyond, his spirits changed slightly. They did not lift, exactly, but he found it refreshing to have a sense of purpose again. A long, difficult journey, the prospect of challenging a wickedly powerful adversary—these things quickened the blood. And the possibility that he would not defeat the Kavareen after all—that was also sweet in its own way.

The route he had chosen took him south through Pelagnia. With no conscious intent, he rode through country that he had passed through long ago. The market town of Kilmsy was very little changed from the old days, except that the inn he remembered was long gone. They still told stories in the town about how a mysterious green fire had burned it to the ground, and how every building erected on the same spot had also burned, until the site was finally abandoned.

He passed within two *karistises* of Forel, but only to glance at the manor farm where his daughter Blackberry had once lived. The farmhouse had been enlarged; the place looked more prosperous than he remembered. He had ridden into the dooryard so many times to see Blackberry and her children. But they knew him only as a distant kinsman, some relation of Blackberry's dead mother. Those visits, always joyful but faintly unsatisfying. He had a sudden stab of regret for those past lies, for having made Blackberry an orphan.

He had no desire to see the officially recognized remnant of his family, his grandniece and her brood, although Pusieuv would no doubt be delighted—if surprised—to see him ride through her castle gates. Another opportunity to harangue him about how her daughters needed Lusul, his wife's estate, for their dowries. And if he told her that he'd been ready to give Lusul to Nora for her dowry? Aruendiel smiled crookedly to himself: Pusieuv's outrage would be gratifying, although it would not outweigh the deadly tedium of a visit.

But Nora had refused his offer of Lusul, looking sickened, as though he'd insulted her with such a magnificent gift. Did she not understand that he was trying to protect her? Even if Pirekenies were mad enough to marry her without a dowry, that would hardly protect her from the scorn of his family. And Pirekenies himself might eventually lose respect for a poor wife.

Gingerly he recalled that last day with Nora, the strained conversation in Luklren's library. It baffled him still, that rage of hers, when he suggested that she marry Pirekenies. What did she expect? She had to marry someone, it seemed, and there was no more eligible candidate than the boy. He was well-born, amiable, young—truly young, not an old man pickled in magic. And she was fond of Pirekenies. You could tell when you saw them together. Yet she was furious when Aruendiel did everything he could to convince her of the benefits of the match.

At the time, he'd almost welcomed her anger. It eased the task of saying goodbye to her, a little.

Why, Aruendiel thought suddenly, had he bothered to listen to the boy and his absurd scruples about protecting Nora's good name? If Nora wanted to live under Aruendiel's roof, study magic with him, and destroy her reputation in the process, why was it any concern of Pirekenies or anyone else? The world was officious toward unprotected women, probably because it was also so cruel to them.

And if she had stayed—? To lose himself again in conversation with her, to walk with her in the forested hills around the castle, to relish her quick wit in magic—he would have been content, almost. I could tell her anything, the village girl had said; there was so much more he wanted to say to Nora. And if one day he took her into his arms, kissed her pretty mouth? Would she have smiled back at him? Looked at him with sweetness and desire? Pure foolishness to even dream such a picture, but it made his pulse quicken.

What had he lost when Nora went away? Not only her, but some part of himself, fresh and fond and hopeful, that she had awakened, that he missed now.

He was still puzzling over these things as he came to Taslonr's Mountain. It had also changed. A village had grown up at the foot of the hill, as though the place had lost its malign reputation. It had been generations now since the Lady of the Mountain had disappeared. Did the inhabitants even remember Olenan, how their great-great-grandparents had sought her out to beg for favors, how they'd tried to appease her?

Most of the hill was stripped of trees now, turned to grazing land. Aruendiel tied up his horse and walked slowly uphill, his boots squelching in the thawing mud. There was no trace of Olenan's presence. He had not expected any, after all this time. At the top he gazed blankly at the view—rolling brown fields, dappled here and there with unmelted snow, with the foggy humps of mountains in the east and north.

How had Olenan done it, he wondered. More than one hundred years, and he had never come across any trace of her. As the years passed, he understood better the bitterness of passing time, how even without growing old you could lose everything that mattered to you. It had become obvious to him what she had done.

The deed was hard for a good magician. Your magic almost had a will of its own; it was nearly impossible not to save yourself, not to work a spell in the last extremity. You could take poison, but your body would reject it; you could plunge a dagger toward your heart, only to have the blade turn to water when it touched your breast.

Years before, when the pain from his injuries was unceasing, Aruendiel had stepped off the northern battlement, the one built on the cliff. He'd died in a fall once before, he reckoned—why not again? Instead, he found himself floating among the treetops on owl's wings. He had changed shape in an instant, without conscious thought. He tried again, unsuccessfully. The fall that had killed him in that long-ago battle, he decided regretfully, had been a fluke.

If any magician had the fortitude, the magical control, for a deliberate death, it was Olenan. Aruendiel doubted that she would have done violence to herself. She would have chosen a more passive method. Perhaps turned herself into a deer—Olenan liked to do that sometimes—and then let herself be hunted to death.

Or, he thought with repulsion, it could have been something like what that treacherous calf of a magician Dorneng did to me. She could have walled herself up, away from all sources of magic, and let herself wither, dwindle, and die.

There was always the Kavareen, Aruendiel reminded himself as he descended the hillside. The trick would be to have it maul and kill you without swallowing you, but that could be managed. A quick death, an honorable one. He reclaimed his horse and rode westward, wondering the whole time how—with all his power and magic, with intelligence and honor and good intentions—he could have made so many idiotic mistakes in his long life, and found so many ways of ruining his own happiness. But looking ahead, he was resolved and darkly expectant.

Chapter 6

Nora floated silently in blurred gray dreams, in bland, formless peace.

Emptiness frayed and dissolved her thoughts, dispersing their dust across infinite expanses of quietude.

Occasionally some fragments of her lost self drifted close enough together for a spark of mutual recognition, a momentary flare of consciousness. And then she thought confusedly: is this all? Is this how it ends?

Words came to her out of oblivion, unexpectedly solid and familiar. *I am re-begot...* She clung to them, waiting. There was more. . . . *Of absence, darkness, death. Things which are not.* She repeated the line, even as the void encroached again and the words began to lose meaning for her. Other words curled closer. *For I am every dead thing...*

How did the poem go? That's right, it was a poem. Poems had existed, once, somewhere. *For I am every dead thing, in whom love wrought new alchemy.* Love? It had a comforting sound, but the meaning felt elusive. She tried to picture it and could not.

Another word approached, demanded her attention. A name. Nora thought, Aruendiel?

Aruendiel. She could picture him, when she could see nothing else. Details, trivialities, as though she could not encompass him in a single glance. But she could piece him together even from fragments: his dark head bent over a manuscript; how he splayed his long, square-jointed fingers on the table as he talked; the wiry black hairs on the back of his wrist; the way he'd held tight to her shoulder as she helped him out of the dungeon; the warm light in those cool eyes when he watched her in the ruddy glow of an improvised Christmas tree.

And then she knew with a pure conviction exactly what he was doing right now.

He was on horseback, riding along a dirt track. She could not see him, but she could sense the chuff of the horse's breath, its weight on the road, the creak of the saddle as Aruendiel changed position slightly, the breeze touching his face and ruffling the hem of his cloak—testimony from a multitude of witnesses that he was alive and moving through the world.

Aruendiel rode on through the material universe, distant, inaccessible, and Nora, hidden in nonexistence, traced his path. When he stopped to water the horse, she knew it, from the way the water filled the horse's mouth; she knew by how Aruendiel's shadow cooled the ground that it was a sunny day.

These fragments were not enough.

Again Nora felt the void scattering her thoughts, lulling her into forgetfulness, eating away with soft persistence at the boundaries of her soul. The great emptiness would make her its own forever.

Elsewhere, very far away, a pebble skipped into the air because Aruendiel's horse had stuck it with an iron shoe. Nora followed its brief trajectory with despair. These tantalizing clues, these dropped hints from the real world—they would not save her from annihilation.

Aruendiel had the distracting and unwelcome sensation of being watched, even after he had cast a series of spells to reveal the invisible and to frustrate the vision of unwanted onlookers. A half-starved wolf wandered out of the underbrush, looking dazed, but it was only an ordinary animal, not a werewolf or a disguised and hostile magician.

As his horse drank thirstily from a stream at the side of the road, Aruendiel wondered whether someone was using an observation spell on him. Could Nansis have been fool enough to share the rediscovered Blueskin spell with another magician? Remounting, Aruendiel passed a quarter of an hour working out a counterhex in his head, and then tried it out, but the uneasy feeling that he was not alone remained. Perhaps, he thought with a sense of cool anticipation, the wait for his next battle would not be as long as he had expected.

Suddenly there came to mind an old tale—people used to tell it when he was younger, did they still?—about the young man who went to look for Death. Aruendiel had heard different versions. Sometimes the young man was seeking out Death to beg a reprieve for his sick father; sometimes he wanted to challenge Death to a duel; sometimes he was simply a curious fool. Whatever his motive, he arrived at Death's domain and made his way to Death's magnificent ivory palace—built of the teeth of all the humans and animals who had ever lived and died—only to find the halls deserted. Eventually the young man gave up his search and returned home, and his family, who had given him up for lost, rejoiced and threw a feast to celebrate.

In the middle of the festivities the young man, having drunk his fill, went out to relieve himself in the yard. But his family had dug a new latrine in his absence, and in the darkness, befuddled, he fell into the hole and drowned.

All of the stories went into some detail about the vile soup in which the young man perished. The point of the tale was that the young man was punished for his presumption. To pay a call on Death—one still heard that expression sometimes—was to be naive or arrogant or both.

The fact remained, Aruendiel thought grimly, that the young man succeeded in his quest.

He was riding through a belt of dry, low hills, lightly forested. By now he was only about a day's ride from the coast, and the new spring was further advanced here than where he had come from. A few of the trees were misted with sprays of green. The sun shining through naked branches was so strong that Aruendiel unfastened the front of his cloak and began to think of removing it altogether.

Squinting up into the light, Aruendiel became aware of an anomaly that he had not noticed before, something that might explain his intuition that all was not right. He stopped his horse and dismounted. There was a sort of dullness in the air; he probed it tentatively with a finger. Yes, the place felt rough and thin. Not an outright breach in the wall of the world, but a weakness.

Strange to find this, just a few weeks after he had dispatched Nora through a gap that led to her world. Was there to be a glut of these things?

He tested the spot again. His fingers could press deep, but he could find no edge. Micher Samle believed that such thin, bruised places in the world's skin were purely transient, and that they turned into holes, gateways into other worlds, only in those rare cases when they happened to align with a worn spot in another world's hide.

There was little chance that this oddity connected to another world. Within a short time—hours or days—it would likely disappear.

Detachedly, he told himself: there is nothing on the other side of this crack in the wall of the world. Nothing. He could not use this opening as a doorway to some mad, misguided quest across worlds to recover a woman who had never been his in the first place. If he did go through it, the emptiness on the other side would no doubt kill him. Tear him to pieces, quickly or slowly. It is not easy to kill a magician, but this would be one way to do it.

No, Aruendiel thought. No, I will not do this. But he could not quite bring himself to get back on Applenose and ride away.

For a moment he stood there, tight-lipped, considering. Then he began to work a spell. It was a variation of magic designed to rip a mountain to pieces. Kemis the Stout was the first on record to use it, and the mountain he destroyed in pursuit of the Larger Goblin of Hnos has been a gravel plain ever since. To this Aruendiel added a utilitarian door-unlocking spell and, for good measure, a spell to let large objects pass through small openings.

An experiment, he told himself, to see if he could blast a hole in the world.

The air groaned, a wild noise that echoed in the trees and earth around him. Applenose whinnied, but Aruendiel ignored the horse. He was watching his outstretched hand shudder as though seized by palsy.

Then something gave way. A broken edge beneath his fingers. He lost sensation in his hand and forearm, and they disappeared from view, gone to a place where his eye could not follow them.

He felt a strained sense of triumph. It could be done. Whatever he was doing. He looked at the trembling horse and thought: at least I should unsaddle Applenose and make sure the poor beast can fend for himself, before I finish this.

He began to withdraw his hand from the hole. There was more resistance than he expected. It felt, in fact, as though his fingers had been caught in something. With an effort, and some apprehension, he jerked his hand back.

Here was the explanation, of a sort: another hand grasping tight to his own. Smaller, lightly tanned. A woman's hand.

Instinctively, he tugged on the hand, harder, and he repeated the spell for letting objects pass through openings smaller than they were.

An arm emerged from the air, a swirl of brown hair. Nora blinking up at him. Impossible. Another heave, and she came sideways through the gap, staggering against him.

Aruendiel stared down at her, not daring to let go of her hand, which was ice-cold. She looked wan, clammy. Her hair was shorter, falling to her chin like a boy's. But it was certainly Nora. There was a leather bag slung over her other shoulder and a rope tied around her waist, leading back into the place she had come out of.

Dropping Applenose's reins, Aruendiel reeled in the rope, length after length coiling to the ground, until the end came into view, tied to some metal implement, bolted to a broken shard of wood, that he did not immediately recognize. He turned it over in his hand.

"It's Micher Samle's doorknob," Nora croaked.

Chapter 7

After she had thrown up behind a tree and taken some shaky steps on her numb legs, Nora began to feel better. Her lungs and heart and muscles and joints still worked, apparently. She had the correct number of arms and legs and fingers. She sat down on a rock to feel her toes through the leather of her boot, and they all seemed to be accounted for.

"It is a shock to the system, having a body again," she observed to Aruendiel, who was draping his cloak over her shoulders. He seemed so grave that she smiled to let him know that she had made a joke.

She kept smiling at him as he squatted beside her. Aruendiel was almost exactly as she remembered, perhaps thinner and grimmer than usual. She recognized the tunic he was wearing, black that was fading to a shadowy greenish tinge. There was a streak of white in his dark hair— no, that was a white ribbon, loosely braided with a lock of his hair.

"I thought I would never see you again," she said. "Or anything, for that matter."

Nora was almost whispering; Aruendiel could hardly hear her. She spread her hand on the stone that she sat upon as though reassuring herself of its solidity. "I can't even tell you what it was like. It was so empty, that place. It erased me," she said.

Her words filled him with a sense of oppression. "How long were you there?" he asked.

"I don't know. Hours, days? How did you know to look for me?"

"I noticed something odd in the air. Open your mouth," Aruendiel said, his brow furrowing. He looked into her nose and into her ear, the usual quick tests for enchantments, but she thought there was something hesitant, almost perfunctory about his movements, as though he were not quite sure what he was looking for.

"Here," he said when he had finished. "You should drink something." He conjured up a wooden cup and thrust it into her hand. "Some wine—no, that will be too strong." The red liquid in the cup turned clear. "Drink some water."

Not until she began to drink did Nora realize how thirsty she was. She emptied the cup gratefully. As Aruendiel began to refill it, she said: "Actually, I would like something stronger, too. Please." He obliged. The wine sent a faint glow down her throat and through her newly material body. "Thank you," she said with a sigh.

Aruendiel found it reassuring to watch Nora drink, to watch the muscles in her upper neck contract smoothly, to hear her clear her throat slightly as a small, hidden bubble of air fought its way back to her lips. She was actually here. He was not dreaming. She handed the cup back to him, and her fingers brushed his. They were warmer—that corpselike chill was gone. The wine must be doing some good. He decided to summon a southern breeze for good measure.

Doing the magic had the advantage of steadying his nerves further. Not as much as he would have liked. "You have met my friend Micher Samle?" he asked, choosing at random one of the dozen questions that had occurred to him.

"Yes!" Nora said, her face lighting up. Her voice had regained more force. "And it turns out that I knew him all along. Or it might be more accurate to say that I knew of him. He's this rather strange man who hangs around the university—most people think he's a little mad." She decided she should not mention the Farmer Dahmer nickname, too hard to explain. "But he was the one who sent me to your world the first time, more or less."

She told him how she had met Micher Samle in the street and deduced from his accent and other clues who he must be. "You once told me that Micher Samle liked to transform into a mouse. And then I remembered that mouse in my kitchen, the day before I came to this world the first time. I set him free, and he apparently gave me three wishes, although he wasn't considerate enough to explain what he was doing. And one of my wishes was for my life to be different, and, well, it worked."

Nora looked at Aruendiel a little shyly as she said this. He had not smiled once during the entire time they had been talking. She had expected—well, she was not sure what she had expected, but certainly some signs of enthusiasm, relief, affection. Now she uneasily remembered that last day at Luklren's castle: how they'd argued, how distant Aruendiel had been on the sleigh ride, how he had practically bundled her through the hole to her own world as she was still trying to find the words to say goodbye. Not to mention that he had also tried to marry her off to another man.

Back in her own world, everything had seemed so clear. From a distance, she could look back and pick out the traces of his love as easily as finding stars in the sky. Now she wondered if, in discovering how much she needed him, she had simply assumed that his need for her was just as powerful. Quite possibly her reappearance had plunged Aruendiel into deep gloom—the return of a troublesome burden.

But she had seen Aruendiel's face when she stepped back into the world. And she had felt how tightly, urgently he gripped her hand. Those things could not be entirely discounted.

"Where are we?" Nora said aloud, looking closely at her surroundings for the first time. The scrubby slope where they sat was broken with long, bluish rocks like the backs of whales. A few massive oaks reared up out of the low brush, too far apart to count as forest. A gold haze burned in the undergrowth here and there, the first blooms of spring. "Do I know this place? It doesn't look familiar."

"We are—" There was unexpected pleasure in being able to hear Nora say *where are we*, because it meant that he and she were in the same place. "We are some four dozen *karistises* west of Pelagnia's borders, about two days' ride from the coast. About a week's ride from the Uland," he added, as Nora worked out their position on her still-vague mental map of this world.

"That's to the south," she said with a trace of uncertainty. "I thought Lord Luklren's castle was northeast of the Uland."

He perceived that she thought he was still making his way home from the Faitoren campaign. "I have already been home to the Uland," he said. "This is a new journey that I have undertaken."

"Where are you going?"

It took him a half second to recollect his destination. "To Hajgog, on the southern continent." He fought down a slight feeling of furtiveness. "I want to consult a scroll in the temple library. A book dealing with the Kavareen."

"The Kavareen! You're going to rescue Hirizjahkinis!"

"I intend to try."

"I'm so glad!" Nora said. "That is wonderful news. I thought you might do something like that—and I'm going with you."

She knew that Aruendiel would say no automatically, but as he shook his head, he was not frowning as deeply as he might have been. He began to say all the things she expected about how dangerous it would be. Nora pointed out that the last time Aruendiel had left her behind in supposed safety, she had been kidnapped and almost murdered—although she'd gotten out of that tangle handily enough, hadn't she?

"And if you're going to say it's improper for me to travel with you," Nora added, thinking that she might as well head off any possible objection, "that's not a consideration. Not at all. You know as well as I do that I don't really have any reputation to speak of, and even if I did, I'd ruin it in a second to save Hirizjahkinis. I don't know what it must be like for her inside the Kavareen, but if it's anything like that hideous nowhere I just got out of, we can't leave her there. We can't."

"No, we cannot," he agreed somberly.

He rose and looked around. In all this time, he had given no thought to the horse. Happily, it was grazing near the stream at the foot of the hill. He went over to the animal with careful steps, clucking under his breath, and managed to catch the reins even as Applenose tried to sidle away. Nora watched him from a distance, thinking that perhaps—unbelievably—she had convinced him to let her accompany him on this new quest. She would have to learn to ride better. And learn more magic. She touched the stone she sat on again, then smoothed her hand across her thigh. Everything still felt real.

The horse securely tied up, Aruendiel climbed back up the slope with long strides. "Nora," he said, "how is it that you have come back here?"

"Micher Samle thought I could come back through the same hole—probably—so I decided to try."

"Micher Samle was mistaken."

"Yes, I realized that. Very quickly." Nora looked down, brushing a strand of hair out of her eyes.

Aruendiel could not make up his mind about her hair being chopped off like that. No grown woman cut her hair; it made Nora look absurdly young and coltish, and yet no one would ever mistake her for a child. And the outlandishly short foreign skirt she wore— far shorter even than the skirts women wore in his youth. Was everything in Nora's world so abbreviated? He kept seeing other fine differences the more he looked at her. During her absence Nora seemed to have been newly purified, remade out of more pristine, select materials. Her skin and hair fairly shimmered, they were so clean, as though she had bathed every day for a month. Even her fingernails had taken on a high gleam, subtly pink, like tiny shells. So this was her chosen appearance, Nora as she went about her life in her own world. The transformation was fascinating, distracting; it showed how far she had gone away from him. And yet here she was, back again. By her own will, she said.

There was a change in her gaze, he thought. Her brown eyes looked into his with the same directness he remembered, but he saw a new shadow in them, the trace of suffering. Perhaps it was the lingering chill of the emptiness between worlds.

"It was miserably careless, very poor practice, of Micher Samle to let you go through the gate," Aruendiel said. "I never knew him to be so slipshod in the past."

"He told me it was risky. I insisted."

"Then you should have known better. Traveling between worlds is dangerous magic in the best of circumstances."

"It was what I wanted."

"Nora, why—"

A panicked whinny from the horse cut across Aruendiel's words. Both he and Nora turned. Applenose was rearing, yanking at his tether. The horse whinnied again.

A snake was Aruendiel's first thought. This southern country was full of them. Then he saw that a clump of grass near the horse's front hooves was unusually pale in color, almost papery. As he watched, the clump seemed to ripple, like a reflection in water, and then it disappeared. What was left had no shape or color—or, at least, his gaze could not hold on to it.

"It's the same hole, isn't it?" Nora said with a sharp intake of breath. "It ate that patch of grass. It almost ate Applenose."

"I think," said Aruendiel, "that it's time to close this door, and to lock it."

He started down the slope. Nora kept pace with him. He turned to tell her to keep back, to stay a safe distance away, but she shook her head impatiently.

"Let me try," she said. "Micher Samle told me how." What must be done was clearer now than it had been in Micher Samle's living room. The door was a ragged wound in the smooth, bright flesh of the world, and all she had to do to heal it was pull the edges together.

She thought there was a gleam of satisfaction in Aruendiel's hard glance. "Together, then. Which spell do you prefer?"

"I think Horn Marn's mending spell will work," she said promptly. "The second variation."

"What about the Ytrevik binding spell?" he asked, raising an eyebrow.

Another spell she'd learned for mending pots. She shook her head. "That would work, but the Marn is simpler and stronger. Honestly, I don't think it has to be that complicated. This hole is unnatural—it wants to close, you can tell."

"Very well," said Aruendiel briskly, and they began to work the spell, Nora counting off the steps under her breath. She pulled magic from the stream at the bottom of the hill and from a wood fire in someone's hut nearby, and she felt Aruendiel calling magic out of trees and stones. The air sang.

Together they pulled shut the door that led out of the world and held it closed. Then she knew that the gap had disappeared and that this world—unblemished again, finite, self-absorbed—had forgotten it already. With both exhilaration and unease Nora thought: there is no way back now. Micher Samle's apartment, Ramona, Adam, the bed where she had woken up this morning, a million other familiar things—they were gone, they might as well not exist. But I don't know that I'll never see them again, she thought. The only way I'll find out is by going forward.

"That was fine work," Aruendiel said.

"Thank you." She was exhausted, and yet she felt as though she had never been truly awake until this moment. This was why she had come back to this world, to be able to know the hidden life of mute things like fire and water, and to weave alliances with them. Now she could see how you could live to be a hundred and eighty—a thousand years old—by doing magic. Aruendiel looked brighter, less strained. It helped that he had smiled for a moment.

A few drops of rain splattered down, then a few more. The branches of the trees nearby rustled and swayed in a sudden swift breeze.

"You're still having that problem with the rain, I see," Aruendiel said.

"I don't know why. I tried to be neat." She sighed.

"You need to work on your control," he said, as he always did, then added: "Otherwise, when you get to weather magic, you will be raising hurricanes and blizzards."

The rain was developing into an actual shower. Nora raised her face resignedly to the heavens and let the raindrops touch her face like confetti, and she couldn't help being secretly proud of them, no matter what it said about her lack of control. After a minute, Aruendiel swung his arm in the air over her head and his, as though tracing the brim of an invisible umbrella. The water arced over the circle his hand described, sluicing down on all sides, but leaving them standing dry in a shining tent made of rain.

"When will we get to weather magic?" she asked.

"Soon. There is more to learn about fire first."

"Will you show me how to do what you just did?"

"Of course." Aruendiel looked at her intently. "Nora, why did you come back?"

A simple question, with another question hidden inside. "I couldn't stay there," Nora said.

He looked serious, and anger stirred in his voice as he asked: "Did your people cast you out?" She must have told them too much about the Faitoren abduction for the family honor to bear, he thought.

"Oh, no, nothing like that!" Nora shook her head. "My family was great. They were happy to see me. They didn't blame me for being away for so long—not too much, anyway—and it was all fine. And the university was ready to take me back, and I found out that I'd even won a prize, an honor that I didn't expect. It was mostly because of a paper I'd written," she added, wondering if Aruendiel might be impressed, "on the poet Emily Dickinson.

"And it even seemed"—Nora looked unwaveringly at Aruendiel as she said this; he might as well know everything—"that I could have taken up again with the man that I used to care about."

One of the black eyebrows twitched, then steadied again.

"I couldn't do it," she said.

"Why not?" Aruendiel asked curtly. "When all things were set to prosper?"

"Because these things that I'd worked so hard for in the past—I didn't want them so much anymore. What I mean is, I could see that they had value, and I was grateful for them in some sense, but they felt as though they didn't have much to do with me."

"You did not want to resume your old life?"

"It wasn't my life anymore! I'm different, more than I thought. I've had experiences that I couldn't even tell people there about." Nora was quiet for a breath. "Ramona, my sister, she was the only one who had any idea. And she's just a little girl. I did tell someone—Adam, the man I just mentioned—and he didn't believe a word of it. He thought I made it all up because I'd been hurt, abused, so badly I couldn't face the truth."

She smiled ruefully, looking down. Aruendiel felt an obscure disappointment at losing sight of her clear, brown gaze. "I saw you and your sister once," he said, the confession escaping him abruptly. "I did the observation spell."

He was gratified as her eyes met his again, brightening, wondering. "You did? I wish I'd known!"

"It was to see that you had arrived safely in your own world," he explained.

"What were we doing?"

"You were reading, both of you."

"Oh, yes." Nora smiled wistfully. "I did quite a bit of reading."

"You looked well. Happy, I thought."

She didn't answer for a long moment. Then she said: "I'd thought that going home would be like waking up after a long dream. Even before you open your eyes, even before you're completely conscious, you know that the dream is gone and you're back in real life. If it was a nightmare, you're relieved that it's over. If it was a very good dream, you're regretful. Either way, you always know instinctively that you're back where you're supposed to be.

"But it wasn't like that at all, Aruendiel. I got back to my own world, and whenever I thought about this world, both places still seemed exactly equal to me. Neither of them was more real than the other. But at the same time, I'd made a choice, and it seemed to me that I had to live up to it. To forget about other realities, other lives I could have had.

"Except that I couldn't. I didn't want to. I couldn't bear to live like that, pretending to everyone else and even to myself that I'd never walked on the soil of another world, or worked magic, or known you."

"You were not there for so long, were you?" Aruendiel asked. "A few weeks have passed here."

"A little more than a month there," she admitted.

"Perhaps if more time had passed, you would have begun to think of this world and everything in it as a dream." Speaking the words did not seem to give him any pleasure; he did it like a necessary task.

"I kept thinking that would happen, and it didn't." Nora paused, wondering how to summon the nerve to say the words she wanted to speak, until something in his face beckoned her on. "Aruendiel, I missed you too much to let you slip away like a dream. I came back to see you again."

His gray eyes searched hers, and it seemed odd that she could ever have thought that they were cold and unreadable.

"I didn't know it would be so hard to leave you," she said. "I couldn't even say goodbye. When I looked at you just before I went through that gate, for the last time, I thought my heart would break."

Aruendiel was silent for a moment. "And mine," he said.

He bent toward her hesitantly, like a tree pushed by the wind. Nora reached up, her fingers spread as though to brush away the raindrops that still hung like a constellation in his hair, but instead she found her hand cupping the back of his neck, and all at once his arms encircled her, his hands sliding confidently over the curve of her waist as though he already knew every inch of her by heart. She stepped closer, pushing herself tight against him, as he leaned down to sink a deep, ravenous kiss on her open mouth.

So, Nora thought dazedly, was it always this simple? All this time? Aruendiel smelled of horse, wet wool, woodsmoke, and underneath it all there was a slight, tantalizing astringency that she could not quite identify, although she felt willing to spend as much time as necessary to figure it out, to track the scent through his clothes and all over his long body. He was not as rickety as he looked, once she had him in her grasp. She could launch herself against him, and he met her easily. Her lips ran over his face, questioning, affirming. At first, out of pride it seemed, he wanted to keep his head turned slightly, presenting her with his unblemished side, but she was adamant and thorough. The scarred skin on his cheek and jaw was warm and only a little uneven under her kisses, like the tooled binding of a book that one has held in one's hands for a long time.

After a while, Aruendiel, stooping, murmured in her ear: "Perhaps we would be more comfortable—"

"Yes? Yes."

Plucking his cloak from the ground—at some point it had slid off Nora's shoulders—he shook it out and spread it on the air at knee level. The folds of cloth billowed and then settled, a tolerable approximation of a bed, resting on nothing. Nora laughed as he pulled her down.

A resolute, pleasantly heated struggle ensued, as each of them tried to figure out how to remove the other's clothes. Something about Nora's bra seemed to amuse Aruendiel—more brevity, so unlike the long, modest shifts that other women wore under their dresses—and by a sort of instinct he discovered on his own how to unfasten it. Nora had to show him how the zipper on her skirt worked. Her hands discovered where to loosen the lacings of his tunic, and then he obligingly peeled it off.

As they went on, pressing past each boundary, Nora found that Aruendiel made love the way he did many other things, with seriousness, urgency, and a clear sense of where he wanted to go, but that he was willing to countenance that there were many different routes to that destination, all happy and all worth pursuing. She mapped his body—there were more scars on his back and chest, but she had no time to count—and he took her to himself with rampant joy.

Once, Aruendiel paused and looked at her through tangled black hair. "Nora?" he said. "Are you—this is pleasing to you?" She said that yes, it was, and a small bubble of sound that might have been either laughter or a sigh escaped his throat. "It has been a long time," he said, so softly she could hardly hear him.

Afterward she was a little sore in the hips and thighs, from folding herself so vigorously against him, and chilled in all the places where her naked skin did not touch his. She was glad of the discomfort. This was real, this was no airbrushed Faitoren ecstasy.

Nora and Aruendiel pulled their clothes back on slowly, reluctantly, like tired swimmers who despite the lateness of the hour do not wish to leave the water. It was growing dark. Aruendiel tended to the horse, moving stiffly, as though his back ached slightly. When he returned, Nora had gathered wood and conjured a fire. They ate bread and cheese and dried apples from Aruendiel's pack. Nora found some chocolate in her bag and broke it in two, giving half to Aruendiel. She had to tell him what it was, the English name; he had never had chocolate before. Its musky bittersweetness surprised him.

Years before, when Aruendiel had found it an agreeable game to seduce other men's wives, he'd imposed a strict rule on himself: never to linger long after the first tryst. It was a mistake to leave too soon—women hated that—but it was equally unwise to dawdle with a woman for hours as though he had nothing better to do. Loitering encouraged sentimentality and mistaken presumptions. It was more useful for the woman to understand that she would never quite have as much of him as she wanted. But he could hardly leave Nora alone in the middle of the countryside, nor did he have even the slightest wish to do so.

At his asking, she began to tell him more about what she had been doing in her world. He listened as carefully as he could, puzzling privately over some of the unfamiliar customs she alluded to. But when he did ask a question, she seemed to relish answering it. Aruendiel found himself moved at hearing how she had tried to work magic over and over again, in secret and without success. If she had found magic in her own world, he wondered, would she have returned to his? He watched her in the firelight as she wove the stories, her eyes shining, her mouth smiling at him, and he marveled that she was here, and that he was.

Chapter 8

The morning sunlight felt hot and grainy in Nora's eyes. She blinked uncomfortably, turning her head to elude its unrelenting brightness, until full consciousness returned and she knew that she could not hide from the light any longer.

She had managed to get some sleep. Not much, but a few hours, maybe. The first part of the night, she'd been disturbed more than once by Aruendiel shifting position or by the grunts and mumbles he emitted in his sleep. And when he'd awakened in the middle of the night and reached for her again, there was no sleeping then. It was a miracle that she'd managed to get any rest at all. Her head buzzed with morning static.

Nora sat up slowly and pushed her snarled hair out of her eyes. It already felt lank and oily. She would have to get used to life without shampoo again. It had been easier when she had hair long enough to braid. She groped for her scattered clothes, wrinkled and grubby, and began to pull them on. What a wretched idea to sleep in her clothes, when they all came off during the night anyway. She was going to look like hell today, even worse tomorrow.

She glanced around for Aruendiel and spotted him at the top of the hill, a hundred yards away. He was doing something with the horse. Fine—she hoped he stayed busy there for a while, so that she'd have some time to collect herself.

No such luck. Aruendiel was heading back, leading Applenose. Something in the angle of his head and the set of his shoulders indicated a sense of general well-being, no matter that his night had been almost as sleepless as hers. She reached for her bag and rummaged through it resentfully, looking for her brush and comb. She only had enough time to give her hair a few rapid strokes before he reached her. Aruendiel took in her disheveled appearance with a raised eyebrow and a glance that seemed faintly mocking. Then he leaned down and gave her a quick buss, touching his lips to hers with a sort of possessive nonchalance that was delightful or irritating, Nora could not decide which.

"You slept late, Nora."

"I hardly slept at all."

He laughed proudly at that, pulled her to her feet, and kissed her again, longer this time. Nora leaned her head against his chest and felt perfectly happy for a moment. Then her brief sunny mood dimmed once more. She would have been hard put to say why.

Aruendiel did not notice the fluctuation in her spirits. "I took the liberty of preparing some breakfast," he said. "Perhaps you would have preferred to do it yourself, excellent cook that you are, but I did not wish to wake you."

As though she had risked her life traveling back to this world in order to make him breakfast. "Thanks," Nora said, biting her tongue. "I can smell it."

The breakfast was grilled rabbit. Aruendiel must have killed it that morning. While flying around in an owl's body, no doubt. She felt a spasm of distaste for the heaviness of meat first thing in the morning when what she really felt like was some raspberry low-fat yogurt and coffee; for the way Aruendiel had made these transformations of his into a routine that he tried to keep secret but would not abandon, like a drug habit; for herself, who had slept with a man who could go directly from making love to changing himself into a cruel and stinking bird of prey in order to hunt down small, helpless animals. Almost like Raclin. But Raclin couldn't help it, it was his nature, while Aruendiel could choose. It seemed almost an insult to her that he couldn't stay with her in human form for an entire night.

She forced down some of the rabbit. As she ate, Aruendiel laid out his plans for their travel that day and the next. Her heart sank as she listened. It would take several days' journey before they reached any sizable town. She thought, I gave up a lot to come back here, but I expected to have at least a bed and a roof over my head every night. Aruendiel added, as if to allay her misgivings, that doubtless they would find lodgings with peasants along the way. "We could have pressed on last night—there is a hamlet further down the stream—but the hour was late, and I judged you were fatigued enough. And I had no desire for any other company."

"Oh me neither," Nora said, rousing herself. "Last night was wonderful."

As they set out, Nora jolted along on Applenose's back, trying to feel at ease. Horses were higher than they looked, she discovered again. Aruendiel led the horse, and she watched him narrowly from her unaccustomed height. His limp seemed more noticeable from this angle; his head wagged unattractively as he moved.

Back in my own world, she thought with sudden longing, I could be driving my mom's Volvo, smooth asphalt unreeling in front of me, the AC on, Puccini on the speakers, or Ella, Joni, Alicia Keys, anyone. Or, she amended—testing herself—I might be having another dinner with Adam. Picturing Adam himself left her mostly unmoved, but the idea of being in the civilized precincts of a restaurant was nevertheless appealing. They'd talk more about the Blum-Forsythe. Aruendiel might not understand its significance, but Adam did. He'd have advice for her, how best to use the fellowship to advance her career; no one was better at navigating the treacherous waters of a university English department than Adam. She'd never been good at following his counsel in the past, but things were different now; she could play the game at an entirely new level.

Except, of course, that she couldn't. She'd said goodbye to the Blum-Forsythe and school and career and all that. Gone, gone, discarded in an instant.

Nora felt slightly sick. Her entire life thrown away for a freakish passion, one wild night. She could hardly believe she'd been so stupid. And now what?

From time to time Aruendiel turned to address a comment to her, usually some remark about the country they were passing through. His usual cooler, more sardonic manner had reasserted itself. Nora was pleased by this, because it suited her mood that he not be too amiable, but she was also irritated. The tenderness he'd shown last night—that secret smile, the way he'd said her name—all of it had served its purpose and been packed away, she thought bitterly. He'd taken what he wanted; now there was no more need for soft words. Her own replies were short and as civil as she could manage and did not invite further discussion.

When they stopped at midday to eat a little bread and cheese, Aruendiel asked, "You are in poor spirits, Nora?"

"My head hurts," she said. "The sun is very bright." After lunch, she lay down for a few minutes in the shade of a bramble bush, eyes closed, so that she would not have to talk to him.

Surprisingly, she felt a little calmer. If she had some time alone, a few hours, a day, she thought, perhaps she could regain her equanimity. But solitude was impossible. For now, there was no escape.

Once they resumed their journey, Aruendiel said little. Nora kept her eyes on the landscape rather than look at him, but there was not much to distract the eye. They passed through scrubby forest and pastures where goats were devouring the new green growth. Occasionally there was a cluster of beehive-shaped huts almost too small to be called a village. In the fields, distant figures—so thin it was hard to tell whether they were men or women—scratched languidly at the dirt with wooden hoes.

"In my great-grandfather's time, these lands were called the breadbasket of three kingdoms," Aruendiel observed, breaking a long silence. "Now the people here can barely feed themselves."

Despite herself, Nora was curious. "What happened?"

"The soil is worn out," he said. "And the curse that Fergon Smas put on the land in the Salt War did not help."

She might have known there would be a curse. Aruendiel was no doubt dying to tell her about it, the way he always loved to go on and on about magic, but she was disinclined to give him the satisfaction of being asked. She kept her mouth shut and felt that she had scored a minor victory when he said nothing more on the subject.

It was not so easy to distract Aruendiel from magic, however. Half an hour later, as they approached a stream that crossed the track, he led the horse off the road, then halted. "You can get down now," he said to Nora.

"Why?"

"It's time for a lesson."

For a moment she was suspicious, then realized that he meant a lesson in magic. "Right now? I haven't studied; except for yesterday, I haven't done magic for weeks."

"All the more reason to resume your studies now."

"But we're traveling. And—no books."

"We can manage without books. And I, for one, require a respite on a long afternoon of walking." Aruendiel stared up at her implacably.

"Fine," Nora said after a pause. Possibly her mood would improve after she did some magic. Aruendiel helped her down from the horse, and they went toward the stream, Nora walking at arm's length from him. At the bank, he bent down to pluck a small round stone from the streambed. Straightening, he balanced the rock on his palm, then tossed it gently upward. At the top of its arc, the stone froze in midair, still as a snapshot.

"We shall do some levitation work," he announced.

"I don't need to work on levitation," Nora said. "My levitation skills are fine. I levitated myself up a cliff at Maarikok."

"It is your control that needs improving. Take the rock from me."

With a sigh, she did so, working her own spell to hold it in the air.

"No, no, no," Aruendiel said irritably. The stone had dipped a couple of inches, bobbing slightly. "Hold it steady."

"I am."

"It's shaking."

"All right!" She tried to get the stone to hold still, but she could not eliminate the tremor entirely.

"Very sloppy," Aruendiel observed, placing his hand on top of the stone. With some effort, he forced it downward another few inches. "I should not be able to move the stone at all. The stone should remain exactly where you wish it to be."

"I'm doing the best I can." This precision work was unbelievably tedious. What did it matter if the stone drifted one or two inches out of position?

"Then your best is not good enough."

Nora thought that he could not be any more wearisomely critical and pedantic until they came to the next phase of the lesson, moving the object through the air. It was a childish exercise that she had done before—you directed the stone upward, downward, at right angles, in a spiral, at varying speeds, and so forth. Make-work, really. To her chagrin, though, the stone kept slipping out of her command. Aruendiel's criticisms mounted. "No, too fast—now, too slow. To the left. To the left. Do you not understand what I am telling you? Halt it. Take it a handbreadth lower. Not that low. Now a smooth right turn. Smooth, I said. A drunken finch would fly more evenly. Try it again. Again. Are you drunk yourself? Now bring it back. Back. Do you want to send it all the way to Semr? I have never seen such poor control."

"It won't do what I say!"

"And stop moving your hands," he added. Nora had been gesturing with increasing wildness, as though the stone would respond better to more obvious signals. "It's very poor form. You're signaling to any enemy within eyeshot exactly where you want to send the missile."

"I've seen you move your hands when you work magic. Yes, you do move your hands," Nora insisted, to his dismissive look. "I've seen you."

"I don't wave my limbs like a panicked chicken."

The stone changed direction again. Faster and straighter than it had moved during the entire lesson, it slammed straight at Aruendiel's head. With horrified delight Nora thought: yes, yes.

"This is intolerable," Aruendiel said as the missile bounced harmlessly off the air near his left temple. "What are you trying to do?"

"Trying to aim it properly."

"Well, that was better than you have done all afternoon. What ails you? You are as clumsy as a blind horse."

"I've had enough of this."

"On the contrary, you need more practice."

"No, I can't stand it. This is stupid—boring. And you're just trying to bully me."

"Assuredly not." Aruendiel frowned. "I am trying to teach you. Nora, these are important lessons. True magic—or any magic—is too powerful, too dangerous to be wielded carelessly. I—"

"Oh, can you please stop," Nora said, and then burst into tears. If only he would just disappear, she thought. That would be a spell worth doing.

Aruendiel paused for a split second as though trying to gather his wits, and then stepped toward her. He rested one hand on her shoulder, very lightly. The other hand hovered at his side, as though he were not certain where to place it.

"Nora," he said softly. "Calm yourself. You are out of practice, that is all. You have spent weeks in a world without magic. We will stop now and resume when you have rested, when you are feeling more yourself, and you will see that the magic comes more easily."

Aruendiel raised his hand and gently brushed away a tear with the flat of his thumb. Nora stood stone-still. He stooped, looking into her face expectantly, like a bird seeking out the next place where it will land.

Nora shuddered. Batting away his hand, she wrenched herself out of his reach. "Keep your hands off me," she said.

Aruendiel straightened, she heard his sharp intake of breath, but he said nothing.

"Just don't touch me," she said. "I can't stand your filthy touch."

"My apologies," he said coldly. In a slightly different tone, he added: "Are you well, Nora? I am a strict teacher—you knew that already—no matter how favored the pupil. If I have slighted you or given offense—"

"It's disgusting, that's all, the way you're pawing me. It's—" The Ors translation of the English phrase "sexual harassment" was only approximate, something like "lascivious intimidation." It lacked the bite she sought. "You've been ordering me around as though I were your slave, not your student. You think you own me now because I slept with you."

"Nora—"

"And why I did, I can't say now. I don't know what possessed me last night."

His face was hardening, the black eyebrows drawn together, but still his expression was mostly one of puzzlement. Not good enough, Nora thought. She would have to thrust harder.

"You put some sort of spell on me, didn't you?" she demanded. "Some love spell?"

"Don't be absurd," Aruendiel said sharply. "I would never do such a thing."

"I don't know about that. Otherwise I would never have looked twice at you, that face of yours, never."

She got a strained and crooked smile from him. "I did nothing to ensnare you. Whatever passion moved you—however misguided it may seem now—it was your own."

"Don't use the word *passion*. Insanity would be more like it."

"My apologies again. Obviously I mistook your intentions. As you flung yourself at me, you seemed willing enough."

"Oh, you think you're irresistible, don't you? With those hideous scars. The way you were all over me last night—" She laughed. "Well, it wasn't a complete disaster. You did pretty well for an old man—a dead man. I was surprised." There, she had hit him deep, she could tell from the glacial stillness that had settled into his face. "But another night like that one would probably take you out, wouldn't it?"

"I doubt it, but there is no need to repeat the experiment." He folded his arms. "You have been sulky and short-tempered all day, but I did not realize the depth of your disdain until now."

"You have no idea," she assured him. "And to think I threw away my entire life—everything I'd worked so hard for, my family, my friends—to come back to this dunghill of a world. I hate it. I hate you."

"You were both precipitate and foolish. It is not the first time that I have noticed these failings of yours."

His smugness was maddening. It reminded her of the first time she had laid eyes on Aruendiel's ugly face—the superior tone in his voice as he warned her against marrying Raclin. He must have been so jealous of young, handsome, perfect Raclin, Nora thought.

She said so.

"Hardly," Aruendiel said.

She didn't believe him. "And then you killed Raclin's baby—my baby—and told me it was a monster. You never actually showed me, of course."

"I had more regard for your feelings than that. Why, I cannot imagine now."

"You didn't want me to know that you'd wrung its neck."

"The infant died. It would not have lived."

"You didn't do anything to save it."

"No."

So cold—he showed no shame at all. A sudden thought came to her. "Oh, my God, I just hope you didn't get me pregnant. What was I thinking?"

He looked almost amused. "You have no cause for concern. A corpse cannot father children."

"There's nothing normal about you, is there?" she demanded. "If it weren't for magic, you'd be—"

"A heap of bones."

"It's all so wrong. It's not natural. I fucked a corpse. How did I get mixed up in all this—this magic? And I let you teach it to me. What was I thinking? What was I thinking?"

The question was gnawing, maddening. Aruendiel might have ruined her life, but she had allowed the catastrophe to happen, and even abetted it. "Perin was right, you can't trust a magician."

Aruendiel laughed, the lines in his face like gnarled branches. "So you take Pirekenies as your authority now? The boy does not have enough brains to fill a spoon."

"That's not true. You were jealous of him. I could see that. Well, he was willing to marry me, he was concerned about my future. He cared about me more than you ever did."

"That is not true," Aruendiel said quietly.

"You know," Nora said, groping for her sharpest blade, "out on those marshes, when we were trying to get to Maarikok to rescue you, it was damn cold. So, yes—I know you've been wondering!—Perin and I slept together, those long nights. Sometimes I thought we'd melt our way straight through the ice.

"That's why he wanted to marry me afterward. Because he wanted to do the right thing. It was very sweet of him, don't you think? I don't think it would have worked out, Perin and I, but still, it was sweet."

"You are lying."

"No, it's quite true." She gave a fierce nod. For a moment she almost believed the story herself.

"Pirekenies is a fool, but not a complete idiot," Aruendiel said, calmly and deliberately. "If he had bedded you, he would never have sought to marry you. He would have known you for the whore you are."

"Oh." Nora had thought she was braced for anything, but she still flinched. "Well, you are making your feelings very plain."

"I see no reason to dissimulate just now."

"I'm a whore, am I, because I slept with you?" Nora had found her footing again. "You just hate women, don't you? Yes, you do. You're afraid they'll make a fool of you, the way your wife did—running away with another man. That's what this stupid magic of yours is all about, control. Well, I have news for you—you're already a laughingstock. You couldn't control your wife. You can't control me. And you're a coward, that's what it comes down to. You're afraid of being alive, afraid of being dead."

"You are raving," Aruendiel said.

"I'm just speaking the truth. So I'm a whore, like your wife? Are you going to kill me, like her?"

It was a stupid, reckless thing to say, Nora thought before she had even finished speaking.

Aruendiel, very pale around the lips, said: "Like this?"

A blue-white flash, a crack that emptied all other sounds from the air. The smell of ozone was overpowering. Nora looked around, her ears ringing. A pine tree not thirty feet away had split in half. A smoky orange flame was already flaring along its upper branches.

Nora backed away from Aruendiel, slowly, then faster. "Leave me alone," she said, shaking her head, raising her arms as though she might actually be able to fend him off, if he came after her. He looked at her silently. She could read nothing in his face.

"Just leave me alone," she said again, then turned and ran.

Her footsteps pounded the dirt track, her torn skirt flapping against her legs. Her breath came in frenzied gasps. She did not look back. It seemed to her that if she did see Aruendiel in pursuit, she would be too frightened to move. Coming around a bend in the track, she almost collided with a herd of goats in the care of two small ragged boys. Reeling, she swerved around the mass of animals and children and kept running, while the boys stared and shouted at her in words she could not make out.

A half mile, a mile. She could run farther, normally, but not at an all-out, run-for-your-life kind of sprint. She stopped running because she had to, when she had no more wind left and her legs felt too heavy to move.

For the first time Nora looked behind her. The dirt track was empty, curving away into brush and forest. She could hear nothing except her own panting and the rustle of the wind in the grass and leaves. And from far away, in the woods to her left, the repeated ring of an ax: someone chopping wood.

She bent over for a second, breathing hard, like any runner finishing a race, then gathered herself up and moved forward at a walk, cooling down. Her blouse was soaked, and her heart was pounding. Nora pushed tendrils of damp hair back from her face, feeling the surge of well-being that comes after exercise, and wondered, as she always did, why she didn't work out more often. She thought back to Aruendiel, to what had just passed between them down the road, and wondered blankly: what the hell was that all about?

For the life of her, she could not recall or understand exactly why she had been so angry and so cruel. Launching cheap insults at Aruendiel, goading him until he responded in kind. It was like being an actor trapped in a bad play, a truly ghastly play, mouthing crude dialogue by a first-time playwright who had seen far too many productions of *Who's Afraid of Virginia Woolf*? It had seemed important to provoke Aruendiel, to see how far he would go. And then, yes, the lightning strike, he'd blown up the tree. Evidently she had succeeded.

Nora walked slower now, absorbed in the problem of why half an hour before she had felt it necessary to abuse Aruendiel in every possible way she could think of, when now she felt only surprise at herself and a deepening sense of regret and shame. Gingerly, apprehensively, she probed the wasp's nest that was her recollection of the past six or eight hours. She'd been tired and cranky when she woke up, but that didn't excuse anything, and it didn't explain why a mildly sour mood had mutated into full-blown rage and paranoia within a few hours. Like a head cold turning into pneumonia overnight.

Am I simply the bitch from hell? Nora asked herself. Or just plain loony?

Aruendiel probably thinks I'm both, Nora thought. With justification. Did I really say all those things to him? Yes, I did.

The sun raked the back of her sticky, gritty neck. She kicked at a rock in the middle of the track. "Damn it. Damn it." Without thinking any more about it—certainly without trying to recall exactly what she had said or trying to imagine with any specificity how Aruendiel must have felt hearing it, because that projection was too dreadful—she resolved to face him again. And sort this mess out if possible, though she could not begin to imagine how. Some things you couldn't apologize for. Some things you could never make up for. She hoped this was not one of them.

Nora turned to retrace her steps. She froze.

She was no longer alone. Something was blocking the road, filling the gap between the trees on either side. Her first, fleeting thought as she took in the enormous, outstretched, leathery wings: how could that thing have landed without making any noise?

Then, as it grinned at her with its chainsaw mouth and beat its tail against the dirt, she formed a second, more cogent thought. Raclin. I should have known.

Chapter 9

Aruendiel watched Nora disappear down the road. He made no effort to follow. Better, he thought, that she should get as far away from him as possible.

After a moment, he went to calm Applenose, who had tried to bolt when the top of the tree exploded and was now pulling at his tether in fear. The horse was too high-strung; it was going to be ruined by all these unexpected displays of strong magic. Aruendiel took his time with the animal, clucking to it, stroking its neck. But he could not soothe the horse entirely; it continued to shift uneasily under his touch. Only then did he notice the tremor in his own hand. He addressed himself to extinguishing, with great care and precision, every last spark of the burning tree. Its smoke was dense and resinous. The concentration cleared his head only a little.

The lightning was a terrible mistake. He'd known that as soon as he'd started conjuring it, but some spells couldn't be halted once begun. Destroying the tree was too showy a gesture, too uncontrolled, and it felt false to him even then, with Nora's taunts fresh in his ears.

What had possessed the woman? He'd never seen her so shrewish, so bitter. The poison in her voice. The way she glared and ranted at him, like a madwoman. Perhaps she was mad, and last night's sweet tumble was part of the madness. Did it take insanity to make a woman desire him?

Or was it some sort of pique, some sense of offended modesty, that afflicted her? He remembered how some girls, when you took their maidenhead, would weep and rail afterward, enough to drive you to distraction—one reason that he'd finally sworn off innocent virgins and switched to married women instead. Their regrets tended to be less histrionic. But Nora was no virgin. She'd been married—and had she even been a virgin when she entered that forced marriage with the

Faitoren? How disdainfully she had appraised him, telling him he had done well for an old man. The clear import: she could compare him to any number of men.

Aruendiel clenched his teeth. He'd called her a whore in anger, but maybe she really was a whore. The short skirt, that curiously short hair. Was that prostitutes' dress in her world? He had only her word that she'd been a student at some kind of school. In some neighborhoods in Semr, that would be slang for a brothel.

But all this speculation was beside the point. Why Nora had turned on him was less important than the simple fact that she had done so. And she'd left out nothing in explaining why he was so loathsome to her. Most of the insults she had flung at him were founded in perfect truth. It was only her manner that lacked reason.

In his own life, Aruendiel reflected, he had known what it was like to develop a taste for something enticingly strange, the kind of thing that one would normally find abhorrent, like those maggoty herrings from Lunika, or the entire Olenan episode. Some such fancy must have seized Nora, that she would give herself to him so freely, and then recoil in disgust once her appetite was sated. His filthy touch, she'd said.

Not a single wisp of smoke now rose from the branches of the blackened pine. Staring at it, Aruendiel found that his anger was almost as quenched, at least now that Nora was out of his sight, no longer spewing insults at him. They had quarreled before. It was one of the things he so liked about Nora, in fact—that she would stand up to him as fearlessly as she did.

Now he felt mostly a deep, weary grief, as though he had just found out that a distant friend had died some months past, so that the new knowledge of his loss cast its shadow over the ignorant joys of all the days that had passed in the meantime. He wondered whether he should go after Nora before she came to any harm. She might still be panicked, though. She might run away again when she saw him.

It was better to be patient, let her come to her senses—if she would—and return.

He waited under the burned tree, distractedly watching a raven wheel and dive over a distant hill. Sooner than he expected, Nora reappeared. She approached him hesitantly, keeping her eyes fixed on his face. She was less bedraggled, after her mad flight, than he would have thought. The fragile smile on her face was full of pleading, but it also crossed his mind that she looked as though she expected to get what she wanted.

"Back so soon?" he asked as she came up to him. "I had no idea you could run so fast. I've galloped racing-bred mares that were slower."

Nora laughed softly. "Oh, Aruendiel, I'm afraid I've been a very naughty girl."

How far was she going to have to run today? Nora's chest burned as she dodged forward, another bush whipping her as she went past. That creature—Raclin—was still close behind her, crushing with terrifying ease the same dense undergrowth that was making her passage such a misery. It was loping along, in no apparent hurry, and yet having no difficulty in keeping up with her pace.

She was fleeing toward the place where she had heard the sound of an ax, and she hoped that there would be a whole crew of woodsmen there, armed with an arsenal of hatchets and saws. As she plunged deeper into the forest—not dense enough, unfortunately, to stop the monster behind her—the ax blows started up again, just ahead. She screamed as loudly as she could. A barrier loomed up—a tree that had just been felled, half its branches already stripped away. She scrambled over the trunk, calling for help.

A lone man in a grimy smock looked over his shoulder at her, his face blank with astonishment. He had just swung his ax at the tree in front of him, sinking the blade deep into the wood.

"Help! Please help me!" Nora hurtled toward him, flinging up an arm to indicate her pursuer. "Quick, kill it!"

The man looked past Nora. His mouth dropped open and his eyes grew blank with terror. Letting go of the ax, he backed away, then took off running.

"Wait!" Nora called after him. "Wait! It's afraid of steel, this thing. Your ax—"

It was no use. He had disappeared among the trees. Nora grabbed the ax handle herself and yanked the blade out of the wood. She spun around.

The dragon-thing was mounting the fallen tree in a surge of wings and claws and teeth, wood splintering under its weight. Nora brandished the ax. "Get back!" she said. "Back! I'm warning you."

The thing scuttled closer, head turned slightly to one side so that a single yellow eye remained fixed on Nora. She backed up until she could feel the trunk of the tree behind her. "I mean it, Raclin!" she said, although she was also wondering if the blade of the ax could even penetrate his pebbled hide. "Don't make me use this. Go away! Go! Leave me alone!"

Not an hour ago she had said almost the same words to Aruendiel. Unfortunately, he had heeded them.

The creature's long jaw opened and closed with languid menace, so close that Nora could count every one of the black teeth, and then suddenly it made a feint, as though to attack her from the side. She had to pivot to keep the ax between herself and it. The thing kept sidling to the right, looking for an opening. Nora edged to the right along with it, bark scraping her back, half stumbling on the tree roots because she was afraid to take her eyes off those teeth and claws. Abruptly the monster Raclin changed direction and lunged at her from the other side. Twisting, she just managed to keep the head of the ax pointed at him. At the last instant, Raclin veered away.

So the steel blade did repel him. She gripped the ax handle so tightly that she thought her fingers would cramp. Around the trunk they went again, first one way, then the other, circling the tree, until Raclin appeared to grow tired of the game. He halted and crouched lower, almost flattening himself on the ground. Under the wide staves of his ribs, his torso began to glow, as though there were a pile of hot coals where his liver should be.

Think, Nora said to herself, running through a couple of fire spells in her head. Fire is easy. Fire wants to please. I can handle this.

She cast a fire-dousing spell at Raclin, just as he raised his head and breathed a shaft of flame into the branches above her head. But her magic had no effect on him. The fire kindling inside Raclin's body was beyond her control: she could not get it to acknowledge her at all, let alone obey her commands to extinguish itself.

Once the flames had left his body, it was different, she noted thankfully. The tree's twigs burned with ordinary fire. She could quiet the flames as they tried to thread their way along the branches.

But Raclin reignited them as rapidly as she could put them out. He was using the fire to force her into the open, she saw. In a way, it was oddly sportsmanlike, since he could roast her to a crisp with a blast of fiery breath at any time. "I suppose you like your meat rare," she said.

Raclin hissed at her, wisps of smoke curling through his teeth.

Heat from the burning wood above pressed on her scalp. She was losing the battle with the fire. At any moment a flaming twig could fall and ignite her clothes.

Aruendiel, she thought. Surely he would see the smoke, or sense the magic she was working. No matter how she had treated him, no matter how justifiably he hated her, he would not miss an opportunity to take on Raclin.

But he was probably miles away by now, no doubt doing his best to forget the past twenty-four hours. She felt tears starting and tried to blink them away. Yesterday at this time she had been kissing Aruendiel in the rain—no, I can't think this way, not now, Nora admonished herself. I have to concentrate, stay in control.

Except—

The rain yesterday was an accident. It fell because—as Aruendiel had told her so many times—she needed to work on her control.

Nora turned her eyes to the flames unfurling in the branches above her and began to work more magic. She made the fire burn purple, then changed her mind: hot pink, then teal, then a venomous green. She threw Vlonicl's vision-clouding spell at Raclin, and then followed up with a spell to induce weakness and mental confusion, although she wasn't sure that either spell had any effect on him. His lizard face glared back at her, malign and apparently imperturbable. She did a spell to sharpen her own ax and a spell to try to mend the ripped seams of her skirt. After that, she went back to the flames, turning them khaki, then robin's-egg blue.

She worked this magic with grand, careless nonchalance, doing all the things that Aruendiel had told her never to do: thinking of other matters—she used to have a sweater that color, what had happened to it?—drawing on too much magic or not enough, picturing how she would do the next spell before finishing the one at hand. And as she worked, it began to rain.

It was a light but steady drizzle that gradually intensified. She sensed a cracked pitcher in a village a mile away, and she mended it, and then she tried a spell to shrink Raclin, but it failed. She levitated the felled tree across the clearing a good ten feet in the air before she had to drop it.

The fire in the tree hissed and gradually died. Raindrops sizzled on Raclin's back, sending up small jets of steam. Nora's clothes were drenched. Still, that was the least of her problems. She leaned against the tree and stared back at Raclin, clutching the ax.

They seemed to have arrived at a standoff. He could not come any closer, because of the iron in the ax, and she was trapped.

He squatted in front of her, almost close enough to touch, wings furled, nearly motionless except for the slow movements of his barred eyes. Occasionally he raised his head and showed her his teeth.

Nora worked a spell to keep the ax from rusting and waited apprehensively for the fading daylight to disappear.

Whore or madwoman? Aruendiel wondered gloomily to himself as Nora put her hand on his arm and smiled up at him. He was leaning toward whore: her boldness, the way she came simpering after him not an hour after declaring that he repulsed her, had a sort of calculated, professional finish to it. She had positioned herself so that he could look down into the warm, shadowy fold between her breasts.

"Come, darling, tell me you forgive me. I was only teasing," she said.

What did it signify if she was a whore? Aruendiel argued with himself. He could take his pleasure with her as much as he liked, and then forget her. But rented affection was not what he had hoped for. And there was the vexing fact that—sometimes, not always—he was less of a man with whores. He knew more than he wished to about their wretched lives.

"There are snakes with kinder mouths than yours, madam," he said.

"What can I say to show you how sorry I am? Oh, I won't say anything. Let me kiss away those horrible things I said."

Nora slipped closer to him and lay both hands on his chest. She smelled of something sweet and indefinable—some kind of rose, perhaps—and her red mouth was tilted up toward his. Aruendiel grasped her shoulders, not pushing her away, but not pulling her near, either. Frowning, he said: "It is a charming offer, but insincere."

"You don't believe me? Kiss me, and you'll see."

Aruendiel shook his head. "A few minutes ago those lips of yours called me hideous and decrepit and half a dozen other things—and they were not lying then."

Nora laughed, a throaty chuckle. "But you're so handsome, darling."

"You must take me for a fool."

"Darling, look! In the mirror!" She gestured to the side.

Aruendiel turned and saw his reflection. His own face, unbroken. The pleasing, regular countenance he had taken for granted until it was gone. Instinctively he put his hand to his cheek and jaw. The bones felt straight and fine under his fingers, the skin unscarred.

He glanced away from the oval mirror and saw that he was standing in a bedroom. The hangings of the bed embroidered with dragons and climbing flowers—he knew them well. Through the open window he saw smooth green lawns, raked with early-morning light.

"You see? There is no one handsomer than my husband," said the woman beside him, one hand resting gently, possessively on his shoulder.

He twisted to look at her. "Lusarniev!" he said, taking in the chiseled, pale loveliness of her face. His wife, the way he always wanted to remember her but never could. She wore a white nightgown, her hair loose. He took her hands, not knowing exactly what to think or say. "Lusarniev, what is this? Where—"

"This is our bedroom, darling."

"No, no," he said, wanting to believe her, but shaking his head. "This can't be. You died." Raising his voice, he said: "I killed you."

"Hush." She smiled at him, the placid, gentle smile that she used to give him in the early days of their marriage.

"I killed you," he repeated, feeling the relief of confession pass through him like a storm, "and I have never stopped being sorry."

"But I was a bad wife to you," she said reasonably. "I scorned you, I betrayed you, I ran away. Can you forgive me? I want to make it up to you now," she went on, pulling him toward the great bed. "Come back to bed, it's still early. There's no need for you to be dressed already. We have plenty of time to dally."

Aruendiel allowed himself to be led. "Lusarniev, how can this—"

"Hush, darling, I insist." Sitting on the side of the bed, she unlaced her nightgown. As she pulled the folds of cloth apart, his eyes went automatically to the spot under her left breast where he had thrust the sword. His wife's skin was creamy and unmarked. There was no wound, no scar.

Aruendiel exhaled a long breath that he had not known he was holding. "How can this be?" he asked, but without caring much about the answer. He put his arms around her and kissed her, then leaned down to pillow his head against her breast. She was laughing as he had never heard her laugh. As he began to close his eyes, he caught a sudden movement on the other side of the room.

"Who's that?" he said, lifting his head.

"What? There's no one there."

He had seen something, though. "By the door. There was a woman."

"One of the maids. They're always spying." Lusarniev raised her voice: "Leave us now!" With a shrug, she let her nightgown slide off her shoulders and twined her arms around him.

Obediently Aruendiel kissed the mouth she offered and thought of rose petals, but he could not shed the nagging fear that had just seized him. Somehow he had the fierce conviction that the shadow he had glimpsed—was it really a woman?—had come to menace Lusarniev.

"One moment, sweet," Aruendiel said, releasing her reluctantly. "Let me see what this is about." He crossed the room with hurried steps, vaguely registering that his limp had vanished, and opened the door.

When Raclin changed shape, it was already too dark for Nora to see exactly how the transformation occurred. But his breathing sounded different, and then she saw that his dim silhouette had changed, grown slimmer and more upright.

She tensed, trying to be prepared for anything. Deep in the twilight, Raclin chuckled.

"Now you'd like to see me, right?" he said. "Here, take a look." Two tall silver candelabra, their branches elegantly looped and curved, appeared on either side of the figure before her. Just Faitoren illusion, Nora thought, but the light of their tapers was real enough to show Raclin's silver-screen good looks, his broad-shouldered frame—perhaps a shade beefier than she remembered. The mischievous lock of hair still flopped down onto his forehead.

"You see?" he said. "The monster's gone. It's only me. You can put down the ax now, dear."

"No," Nora said dryly. "Why are you here, Raclin?"

"I'm here to see my long-absent wife. Are you not even a little happy to see me?"

"I'm not your wife," she informed him. "Go away."

"Not my wife? You'd like to think so, wouldn't you?" he said, smiling. "My dear, I knew you'd break your vows sooner or later, but I thought you had better taste than to betray me with that crippled wreck. Were you just trying to insult me? Or was he simply the best you could do, looking the way you do now? I'm afraid you've let yourself go a bit."

"So that's what this is about." The ax's shaft was slippery under Nora's palms. She shifted her grip. "Just to repeat: I'm not your wife.

Whatever I do, whomever I do it with—it's none of your business. Please leave now."

"Why? Are you afraid of me?"

"No, I'm just holding this ax because I feel like it."

He laughed as though the answer pleased him. "I could have easily killed you this afternoon, Nora, but I didn't. Do you know why?"

"Because you're such a nice person?"

"I only wanted to talk to my wife. It's unfortunate, but I don't communicate well during the daytime, when my appearance is so . . . different. You fled, I followed. Unlike your wizard," he went on, "I've never killed a girl for cheating on me."

"I don't know that we have much to talk about, Raclin," Nora said. "Unless it's about this delusion of yours that we were actually married. Let me be very clear. You enchanted me, you took my mind away and turned my body into your plaything. It wasn't marriage, it was rape. And you never mentioned that you turn into a lizard every day. A girl likes to know little things like that before she ties the knot.

"What's pathetic is that I don't think you even wanted to marry me. It was all your mother's idea. Let's stop pretending. Leave me alone, drop the charade, and we'll go our separate ways, all right?"

"What a lovely show of spirit," Raclin said with a graceful smirk. "I would have liked to have seen more of that in the old days."

"You did everything you could to crush it out of me."

"Did I? There's always a trade-off. At least you were beautiful then."

The jibe shouldn't have rankled, but it did. "So what was it you wanted to talk to me about?"

"My dear, I have come to tell you that your little adventure is over. Running away, adultery—it's all becoming very sordid and tiresome. I'm here to take possession of my wife again."

"Didn't I just explain to you that we're not married?"

"As long as you're wearing my ring, you're my wife. Besides, my sweet," he added, "it's not as though you have anywhere else to go. Even that broken-down wizard won't have anything to do with you, after the tongue-lashing you gave him today. You're quite the virago when you try."

Nora stared at him. The sickle-moon smile under his perfect cheekbones was composed, invulnerable.

"How do you know what I said to Aruendiel?" she asked. "And come to think of it, how do you know I slept with him in the first place?"

"You made no secret of it," Raclin said.

"You were spying on us."

"Spying? I have the right to know if my wife is sleeping with other men."

"Aruendiel would have found you out if you were close enough to see or hear us. I know how cautious he is. The ring. It's the ring, isn't it?" Shuddering, Nora raised the ax slightly. "That's how you knew."

"Oh, yes. It told me as soon as you turned whore."

Exactly what the ring had shown Raclin, Nora did not want to know. "You're disgusting." Another revelation came to her. She felt sick.

"And all those terrible things I said to Aruendiel—that was because of you, wasn't it? You made me turn on him. I had one lovely night with this man that I gave up everything to be with, and not only do you spy on us, but you destroy his happiness, and mine. He hates me now, and it's all your fault, you vile, inhuman, degenerate slime—you goatfucker—you—"

Nora's voice broke. She was trying—had been trying for some time—not to remember too precisely the long litany of abuse she had hurled at Aruendiel, but now she found certain phrases were lodged like dark thorns in her memory. *You did pretty well for an old man, a dead man. I fucked a corpse.*

Raclin shook his head, smiling, obviously savoring her distress. "No, I only gave you the courage, let's call it, to say those things. Much as I despise the so-called Lord Aruendiel, you know how to wound him better than I do. Although I think you were too kind to him, even so. There's much more to say about how hideous he is."

"Shut up."

"But what you said to him was true enough. Most of it, anyway. Well, don't worry about the wizard's feelings. My mother will have dealt with him by now."

"Your mother. Naturally she'd be around here somewhere." Nora stared back at Raclin, hoping to hide the apprehension rising within her. "She can't hurt Aruendiel."

"Don't be so sure. She's prepared for battle, and he's not. He's as good as dead. And what about you, my dear? Don't you think it's time to come back to your husband?"

"Of course not." Her arms were getting tired. She adjusted her grip on the ax again.

"Be sensible, Nora. Where else can you go now? And you remember what it was like before. You were blissfully happy. You were madly in love with me."

She laughed at that. "You know that wasn't real. And no love spell in the world could make me fall in love with you now."

Raclin studied her for a moment. "You're right," he said in a careless tone. "But that doesn't matter. You don't have to love me to need me."

"I don't need you."

"Yes, you do. Look at you, all alone. You're terrified. You're weak. You're trembling so much you can hardly hold up that ax."

"That's because I don't trust you."

"But you don't have to be afraid of me. Just give in to me, that's all. Nora," Raclin went on, his voice soft and rich like the humming of bees, "you know you need to be protected. Not just from the outside world. You can't even trust yourself. You thought you loved Aruendiel, and look at how you treated him, all the poison you spewed at him. You cause pain and you feel pain, but you can't control it."

"Stop it," Nora whispered. "Get back."

Raclin had edged closer, his kindly smile overhanging her like a sun. "You're so fragile, like a little child. Give in to me, and the pain will stop. Remember last time, Nora? How frightened you were at first, and then it was all over, and everything was easy?"

"No, I won't," she said, but her vision had blurred with sudden tears, because it was true—she was weak and he was strong. His words were mixing smoothly, inevitably into her thoughts, like sugar stirred into coffee.

"Poor little girl, you don't know what to do. You swore to be mine, remember? And you're still wearing my ring. Listen to the ring. Let it guide you. I'm the only one who can protect you from your own monsters. You can't do it alone, Nora. You can't do anything alone. Put down the ax, dear. It's too heavy for you. That's my good girl. Just close your eyes—you blood-soaked cunt!"

Raclin jumped backward, away from the blunt end of the ax blade that Nora had suddenly thrust toward him.

"I told you to shut up and get back," Nora said, moving to keep the tree trunk between them. "Next time it will be the sharp end."

Raclin said something in the Faitoren language. She could not understand the words, but almost instantly she knew what they signified.

Her left hand, the one with the ring, yanked at the ax handle like a wild thing. It was trying to wrest the ax away from her right hand, Nora realized. With a sense of uncanny helplessness, she felt the muscles of her left hand and arm tensing, and she could tell how tightly her fingers clung to the wooden handle, but she had no say in what they were doing.

That horrible ring again. Nora thanked her lucky stars that she was not left-handed and pulled at the ax with all the strength of her right arm, twisting her body for leverage. Slowly her left hand slipped off the handle, its fingers scrabbling with desperate energy for a fresh grip.

Next thing, that hand will go after my eyes, Nora thought. Or my throat.

She remembered something Ramona had once said. A joke. They'd been talking about how to get the ring off.

"I believe," Nora said through gritted teeth, "that my sister was right."

Immediately, because with even a second's reflection she would lose all resolve, she twitched her left shoulder hard and threw her wayward hand up against the trunk of the tree. Her fingers splayed out against the bark. She brought the sharp edge of the ax down as hard as she could on the crease where her ring finger joined her palm.

Chapter 10

Half closing the bedroom door behind him, Aruendiel stepped into the corridor. It was dimmer here than he expected; the servants must have let the wall lamps go out. He summoned up a light, but the illumination only seemed to multiply the shadows.

Two dozen paces to the right, something stirred in the obscurity.

"Halt," he called out.

But there was another person even closer to him, touching his arm. "Aruendiel," the woman said.

Not Lusarniev's voice. Looking down, he saw the white flash of a smile, dark liquid eyes. Gold glinting at her ears and throat. "Hirizjah-kinis?" he asked, incredulous.

"What do you think?" she asked mockingly.

"What are you doing here? *How* are you here? The Kavareen—"

"Oh, the Kavareen," she said. "Don't worry about the Kavareen."

"But—you're well? Unharmed?"

"Touch me! You'll see." She took his hand and pressed it into the soft swell of her breast. Fragrance bloomed in the air. "Aruendiel," she said huskily. "I never thanked you properly for saving me, all those years ago, from the witch-priestesses of Tlorjika. Let me show you now how grateful I am."

The light of the campfire flickered across her face. He remembered this place: the mountain cave where they'd taken refuge after their flight. Outside, in the sticky night, the insects of the southern jungles were chanting their raucous music.

"No," he said, pulling his hand back. "You told me no. You said you took no pleasure in the touch of a man."

"Bah, I was young, I was foolish. A few kisses between old friends—what is the harm, Aruendiel?"

He hesitated for an instant, then shook his head. "Something is out of joint here, Hirizjahkinis. What afflicts you?" Peeling her away as she tried to cling to his arm, he moved toward the cave's mouth, where moonlight pooled on the rocky floor. He stepped through the gap and found himself in a small, wood-framed room. A young woman in a blue-and-brown dress sat sewing by the fire, her foot rocking a cradle. She stood up as soon as she saw Aruendiel.

"Father, you're here, finally!"

"Blackberry?" She came toward him; he could not stop himself from returning her embrace. "What are you doing here?" he asked.

"Waiting for you—me and the little one." She glanced at the cradle, and he caught a glimpse of a curled fist, a tiny yawn.

"But, Blackberry—by wood and water, what is going on? My wife. Hirizjahkinis. You. I have seen you all just now, but all of you are gone. Dead." The last time he'd seen Blackberry alive, he remembered reluctantly, she had been considerably older, so frail and tired that she could hardly get out of bed. The cough that killed her came just a few weeks later. His magic kept him alive and vital; it could not salve the slow pain of watching Blackberry age and die. "You have come back now. For me." Gazing down at her, Aruendiel shook his head. "What am I to think?"

She smiled at him, her cheeks pink and young as rose petals. "You are tired, Father. Don't you wish to sleep?" Blackberry indicated the wooden bed, piled high with pillows, that occupied a corner of the room.

"To sleep?" Aruendiel stood very still. "What do you mean?"

"You have come so far, all this time, all alone. I can see from your face how exhausted you are. And you've been disappointed, haven't you? Terrible disappointments." Her brown gaze threw back nothing but warmth and concern. "But now you can rest, at last."

"At last?" It was a perfectly ordinary-looking bed, the wool blankets woven in a simple red-and-blue pattern he remembered from his childhood, but he felt his heart begin to pound. He drew a ragged breath. "What do you mean, Blackberry? That I have finally, after all this time, come to the end?"

Was it only yesterday that he had groped for a way outside the world? I am like the young man in the story, he thought—I finally found what I sought, after I had given up the search.

"Hush, no talking. Time to sleep." She gave him a quick but surprisingly forceful push toward the bed. "Make it a long sleep. You can dream about those fine ladies you met," she added, chuckling, "and decide which one you'd like to take your pleasures with."

"I am tired," he admitted, passing his hand over his face. He looked at the bed, thinking that Blackberry jested rather more freely than he remembered.

The white linens on the bed looked very clean and inviting. Despite his fatigue, though, he felt restive, unready for sleep.

Another voice, a woman's, spoke behind him, sounding crisp, faintly annoyed: "She got it wrong. She doesn't know you're not Blackberry's father. But I'm not surprised. You never told anyone, did you?"

"Nora?" Aruendiel turned quickly.

A figure behind him also moved, keeping just out of his direct sight. He caught only a blurred glimpse of her. The woman's hair was too dark to be Nora's.

"Nora's not here," Blackberry said quickly.

"Who spoke, then?" Aruendiel demanded. "Not you. It was someone else."

"I didn't hear anyone. You're mistaken, Father. You're tired, it's time to sleep."

He shook his head slowly, warily. The voice was right. Blackberry had never called him *Father*. "Not now, child."

"No, this is no time to sleep," the other, unseen woman said. Aruendiel wheeled again. "You don't need to see me," she said, still somewhere behind him. "You know who I am."

"Who is there?"

"You know me."

He waited before answering. "I didn't think I would ever hear you speak again."

"Neither did I."

He understood now why her voice reminded him of Nora's. Both of them made the same grammatical slip, using the more straightforward masculine verb form when speaking of themselves. The effect was jarring but not unpleasant.

He sighed. Just one more glance at Blackberry, he thought, but when he looked for her, Blackberry was gone. He was alone with the shadowy woman at his back. For a moment, irrationally, he wished he had his sword in hand. But the blade would do him no good against a ghost.

"She'll be back," said the voice.

He nodded. "Yes."

"Your friend Ilissa, I mean. Not Blackberry."

"I know." Aruendiel grimaced. "Ilissa's tired, all those quick transformations. But she'll be back in a new guise soon enough." He added gloomily: "As some other woman I have known." Perhaps Olenan, he thought uneasily.

"She'll come back as *me*, most likely." The woman behind him laughed.

"You?"

"Why not? You buried me deep, but she'll find some trace of me anyway. She'll know that I'm the first woman you killed. And that you're afraid of me."

"Then she'll be wrong on both counts."

"Oh, come, Aruendiel. Admit it, you are fearful right now, listening to me, knowing that I am here. You wish that I'd never existed."

That was true. No, half true. "It's not so simple," Aruendiel said. "And I have no fear of you." He was bluffing only slightly—he'd had nightmares about her that were much worse than this. "Why are you here, anyway?"

"When your friend Ilissa started digging deep into your past, bringing back all those lovely ladies as bait for you, I woke up. I'm a dream as much as those other women who were running after you just now. But I'm a dream without deception. I'm a dream that tells you what's real."

"You're not being truthful, though," he objected. "What's this slander that I killed you?"

"It's not a lie. I gave my life for you, that night in the sea. If not for you," she said bitterly, "I would have grown old among my children and grandchildren, loved and honored as you have never been. Think of that, what you deprived me of—what you deprived yourself of."

"I had no choice. It was your life or mine." After a moment, he added: "I'm sorry"—What should he call her?—"Warigan." The name felt strange in his mouth from long disuse. "I know what I lost. I have had plenty of time to think on it. But I could not have chosen differently. Do you understand?"

"Oh, certainly." For the first time, he heard some kindness in her voice. "I understand. It was my choice, too, remember?"

Suddenly he wanted very much to look directly at her, even if it was impossible or—he felt this obscurely—somehow forbidden. It seemed to him that he would feel some peace if they could look into each other's eyes for a moment.

He began to turn, but a new shape materialized in front of him. Even though he was half prepared, it was still a shock to recognize Warigan, her hair in tangled curls. She was dressed in the dirty finery that he remembered from the whores' camp.

She advanced, her mouth hard, eyelashes fluttering. From behind him, Warigan's voice said: "Aha! I told you so."

"Aruendiel, it is I," said the new Warigan, her voice throbbing with sentiment—menace or seduction, it was not clear. "Yes, the one you wronged. I haven't forgotten how you treated me. How could you have been so cruel?"

Faitoren magic mined one's secrets, Aruendiel reminded himself, and he wondered how deep Ilissa had burrowed and what strange artifacts she had found. He put his hands on the woman's thin shoulders. "Yes, I was expecting you," he said, squeezing hard. She winced a little. "I haven't forgotten you, not at all. But perhaps you can remind me what it is that I did to you, madam. That part escapes me."

"You abused me shamefully!" she said. "Even now I can't bear to think of it."

"That is not very helpful. Let me think. Did I get you with child and then abandon you? Did I infect you with the pox? Or did I beat you to death because you had become tiresome or inconvenient?" He stared down at her with a crooked smile.

She did not flinch. Her outrage was flawless. "You are playing with me. You know very well what you did!"

Suddenly he'd had enough of this puppet Warigan and her absurd bluff. "Yes, I do know, Ilissa. I had the temerity to throw you over. That's my real crime, isn't it? Let us stop pretending. I want to see your real face."

She squirmed in Aruendiel's clutch, but his hands remained locked on her shoulders. Then she laughed, and Warigan's angular features shifted and recalibrated themselves into Ilissa's honed, luscious beauty.

"You finally saw through my funny little game, Aruendiel! You've been very slow. I thought you were a clever man."

"Your real face, Ilissa."

There were layers and layers of Faitoren glamours wrapped around her, knotted and tangled. He could not even guess how old some of the spells were. Some of them had fused together over time so that he could not tell where they began or ended. Some had rotted away. It was far more magic than she needed to maintain her appearance. She must have been adding to it constantly, perhaps every day, like a bird building a nest and not knowing when to stop, or being afraid to.

Ilissa shrieked as he tore into the matted edifice. Her magic was more fragile than it seemed at first—there was no structure, no organizing principle, and it was riddled with fault lines where old spells had failed. She put her hands to her face, as though that would do any good.

"You brute! You vile, crazed, barbaric lout! I bring your dear ones back to you, the ones you lost, and this is how you treat me!"

It was hard to make out the last sentence. Her voice had soared in pitch and acquired a strangled, almost mechanical stiffness.

Aruendiel looked up at her curiously. He would not have predicted that Ilissa was naturally so tall. Much of that height was neck, though. He tried to decide whether her small head was more avian or reptilian. Despite her fine black scales, he settled on avian, mostly because of her long, spoon-shaped bill. No wonder she could barely make herself understood now.

Her second set of arms was short but equipped with wicked-looking pincers, and her barbed tail was lashing. She got one blow in, the end of her tail striking his arm, before he stepped out of range and put a binding spell on her limbs.

"I'll thank you to let my dear ones rest in peace. You degrade their memory with your antics," he said. "Gods, what Hirizjahkinis would say if she knew what you had gotten up to in her name."

And thank the sun and the moon that he had not succumbed to the false Hirizjahkinis, Aruendiel told himself. If the real Hirizjahkinis knew, she would never let him hear the end of it. Provided he ever had the good fortune to see her alive again.

Aruendiel looked around. The bedroom was gone; he was back in the open air, and it was night. How many hours had passed while he was tangled in Ilissa's enchantments? He conjured a light, and noticed Applenose's foam-flecked bulk sprawled nearby, not moving. Well, it was too much to expect that Ilissa would leave an innocent animal untouched. He glanced down at his arm, the place where she had struck him. The sleeve was slashed. There was some blood—more than he expected, in fact, although he felt almost no pain.

That should have been a warning to him, but now Ilissa was speaking again. Spewing more insults, he determined after careful listening.

"Ilissa, someone who looks like you has no right to complain about my appearance." Reflexively he touched his face; yes, he could feel the old scars and broken places again. Her glamours were gone, all of them. "Now—quickly, because I have wasted enough time—where is Nora?"

A series of wild creaks and hisses poured from Ilissa's open bill. Laughter, Aruendiel guessed. "With my dear boy," Ilissa croaked.

That meant that Nora was likely already as dead as Hirizjahkinis or Blackberry or Lusarniev. The thought would have hollowed him out completely if he had allowed himself to consider it fully.

"I will make Raclin beg for the peace of hell," Aruendiel said, fighting down a malign, ominous vertigo. "But first, what is to be done about you?"

Nora leaned against the tree, keeping her wounded hand curled against her chest. She tried to keep her eyes averted from it. First, because the hand was a maimed and gory mess, with a finger missing, and second, because she had failed—she'd cut off the wrong one, the pinkie, while her bedeviled ring finger, still wearing the ring, hung by a flap of flesh and half-cut bone that she could not bring herself to hack through. She was a rotten coward: one stroke of the ax, it turned out, was all that she had the stomach for.

At least the pain from her wound seemed to have countermanded the ring's magic. She felt blessedly free of any urge to give herself over to Raclin's tender protection, and her left hand no longer obeyed his commands, not that it could do much harm in its current state. Now she was more afraid that she would pass out and drop the ax.

Raclin prowled on the other side of the tree, taunting her. He found her self-mutilation very funny. "Be quiet, Raclin," Nora said wearily. But he kept on.

"Are you going to bleed to death?" he asked after a while.

"No," she said, although she was not completely sure. Her teeth had started to chatter. Blood had soaked the front of her blouse, and she could feel the night chill seeping through the sticky fabric.

"Humans are so weak, sometimes the slightest little thing will kill them," he said, a faint wrinkle appearing on his brow. "I was looking forward to doing it myself."

"What was all that about promising to protect me?"

"I never said I would protect you. I said you needed protecting."

"You should have been a lawyer, Raclin," she said, but he didn't get the joke.

After a while, dizziness made her slide down against the tree. She sat crouched at its foot. Raclin loomed over her—dangerously close—but she left the ax propped up on her knee and hoped that it would be enough to hold him off. Despite the pain in her hand, she wanted more than anything to go to sleep. It was a struggle to keep her eyes fixed on Raclin. He smirked as though he knew what torture it was for her to stay awake. She kept blinking, and each of her blinks lasted longer.

When she heard the baby gurgle, and saw it crawl toward her across the brown leaves, she was afraid for a moment that she had fallen asleep, that she was dreaming. But Raclin was still there, and he also was watching the child. The baby laughed as he crawled, proud of how fast he could scoot along on his hands and fat knees.

As the baby came close, he looked expectantly at Nora, as though he knew without question that she would welcome him. He was naked, with that fine infant skin like the morning sky, and his eyes were blue and infinite. Nora looked into them and felt herself falling hopelessly in love.

"I thought you'd like to see our son," Raclin said.

The baby reared back on his haunches and held out his arms, wanting to be picked up. He babbled something. Baby gibberish, but with the uncanny understanding of parents, Nora knew he was calling for his mother. She smiled at him sadly, willing this moment to last. Then, swallowing, she tilted the head of the ax toward him, carefully, blunt end first, so that he wouldn't cut his fingers on the blade.

He reached eagerly for the shiny thing. Raclin swore, dived for the child, and then recoiled as the baby's hand touched the steel.

What clung to the tip of the ax was a wizened, tiny thing, toothpick bones strung together with scraps of desiccated flesh. As she watched, the little assemblage slid off the steel and crumpled into a heap that could fit into the palm of her hand. One round fragment rolled free. It grinned jaggedly up at her.

Nora gave the skull a long, quiet look. "I've never seen a baby with teeth that large. That sharp," she said.

"What kind of unnatural mother are you?" Raclin asked, as bitterly as though he were truly offended.

"I don't know," Nora said. "I don't know."

"You can't stand to see what you could have had."

"I don't want to be lied to again." That was not quite all of it. "Raclin, it wasn't wrong or stupid for me to want to love, or to be loved. To want a lover—or husband—a child. What was wrong was for you to take that wish and use it against me. Do you see what I'm saying?

"Oh, never mind," she added, as he looked at her—pityingly, she thought. "Never mind. Where did you get the poor little thing? Is that why you came to Aruendiel's castle last summer?"

"He'd buried it in a field, like an animal. My son."

"You should have left it there."

Nora leaned back, feeling the roughness of bark against her scalp. If only she could close her eyes for a moment. Raclin was talking again, something about what a humiliation it had been to marry her.

"—no matter what my mother did to try to salvage your appearance, I could always smell the human stench—"

She tried to make herself interested—anything to stay awake.

"—and now I'll have to go through it all over again with some other cretinous bitch! Because you failed."

"Why don't you just tell your mother no?" she said wearily. "It's not as though you're really cut out for marriage."

"Tell my mother no?" He grinned. "Life is much more pleasant when Ilissa is happy. You must have noticed that."

"You know," Nora said, "women don't like men who are ruled by their mothers. It makes them look weak and childish. Even if the man turns into a monster every day."

Nora was going to add, *Especially if he turns into a monster every day*, but at that moment the ax handle jerked in her hand. For a moment, she had the distinct impression that the ax had come to life. Then, she saw, it was only that she had tiredly, stupidly let the ax slip off her knee.

She grabbed for it. So did Raclin. He was faster, seizing the ax by the handle and then flinging it away as though it were red-hot. The ax landed with a thud in the darkness behind him. Nora looked up at him, shocked. Abstractly she thought, I should run away now. But there was not enough strength in her legs to lift herself her body off the ground.

"And for your information, I don't let Ilissa rule me," Raclin said, squatting in front of her. Nora flattened herself against the tree, pulling in her bent knees as if she could hide behind them. He leaned forward and lifted his right hand with an easy, speculative grace, as though he were going to caress her. His fingers slid around her neck.

"Raclin, look." Was it remotely possible to reason with him? "Please, this is stupid. You don't want to do this. Just let me go. Please."

He laughed, putting his other hand on her neck. "I don't want you to think I'm weak or sissified."

"I won't. I don't."

"Good," he said. His grip tightened around her windpipe. She kicked at him. It only shook his grasp on her throat for an instant. He laughed again and shifted his knee to pin her leg to the ground.

The air in her lungs was burning away. But Raclin's body pressing down on hers brought her to her senses for a moment. There was no sense in struggling physically. He was too strong and too heavy. With a great effort, she forced herself to stop squirming.

"Don't give up yet, Nora," Raclin said. He looked more handsome than ever, perhaps because of the look of pleased concentration on his face. The stray lock hung down, swaying slightly. Nora's chest felt like a bomb that was about to go off. She tried to fight off the dizziness and focus her attention elsewhere.

There was a faint noise from behind Raclin, like something shifting in the dry leaves. He cocked his head, alert but showing no great concern.

Silence. Then a thud, metal against wood. Nora's tree shuddered.

Raclin shouted a couple of brisk Faitoren syllables and let go of Nora's throat. Gratefully she sucked in air. She looked up. The ax had bitten the tree so hard that it stuck there, just above Raclin's head.

"What the hell, you mangy bitch!" Raclin looked blankly from the ax to Nora and back again. Then he began to chortle. "You missed me."

Poor control, poor control. How many times had Aruendiel told her that? Hell, she thought, I almost killed him today with that rock, I should be able to kill Raclin. Working the levitation spell again, Nora wrenched the ax out of the tree and lifted it higher, beyond Raclin's reach.

"Raclin, I'll be your widow if I have to be," she said.

He hesitated. She began to hope. Then his hands clamped around her throat again.

She ran out of air faster this time. For a moment, she fumbled with the spell, not sure how to aim the ax or even which end was which. And then, so quickly it surprised her, she heard a meaty snap and felt the impact of the blow traveling through Raclin's frame. The ax fell sideways. Something changed in his face. He looked even angrier for a moment, then foolish, and then his head pitched forward and thudded to the ground.

Nora would have screamed if she could have. The night was suddenly much darker than it had been. Raclin's body tilted and crumpled. His weight settled on her legs. His hands still clutched her throat.

With her good hand, she jerked his fingers loose. They came away reluctantly, still tensed. She breathed deeply, counting each breath as though that meant something. The air was thick with the smell of blood.

"All right," Nora said. "I'm alive." The urge to scream was still there, but she was ignoring it for now. Urgently she pushed Raclin's body off her own. Even her good hand was sticky now. She wished she had something to wipe it with. *All the perfumes of Arabia will not sweeten this little hand.* She rubbed it in the dirt and on the bark of the tree until it felt slightly drier.

Nora stood up slowly, clinging to the tree. A thought struck her, and she made herself look at her wounded hand. The dangling finger was less horrific in the moonlight, just a shadow that hung too loosely from her hand. No gleam of gold. Very tenderly she encircled the wounded finger with her right hand to be sure. Nothing. The ring was gone.

She was free, but she did not feel free. Nora moved away from the tree, jerking her foot back when it brushed against something hard. Just a root, not Raclin's rootless head. She managed to get all the way across the clearing before sinking to the ground again. Finally, it was safe to cry, so she did. The tears rolled down her cheeks without carrying away any of her grief.

How long she cried, she wasn't sure. Overhead, through tree branches, the moon's white tooth gnawed the sky slowly, and its gray light crawled across the ground, but the darkness around her was unchanging. Aruendiel did not come.

Chapter 11

What finally roused Nora was the memory of Raclin asking pleasantly if she was going to bleed to death. She was not going to give him that satisfaction.

She raised her head and looked blindly into the night. Not too far away was the village where she had discovered a broken pitcher to mend that afternoon. She could sense the hearth fires, banked for the night, dreaming under their ashes. A mile, maybe.

Numbly she made herself get up, start walking. The forest put trees and fallen logs in her way and clawed her with invisible branches. She tried summoning a light from the village fires, but it turned the tree trunks into pale, elongated phantoms, and tiny red eyes winked at her from just beyond her small circle of illumination. After that, she was more conscious of the million sounds haunting the night, the rustles and squeaks and odd sighing noises. She was putting distance between herself and Raclin's body, true, but now the corpse could be anywhere in the vast, shapeless dark behind her. What if she got really lost and went in a circle—she might find herself falling over him again. And who knew if decapitation would really kill a Faitoren, anyway?

Get a grip, Nora told herself. Raclin is dead. Very dead. And if there is such a thing as a Faitoren ghost—well, I'm screwed, that's all.

Leaves slapped her face, and then she stumbled out into an open space, bright with moonlight. A freshly plowed field, she guessed from the feel of the ground under her feet. She followed a furrow to the other side of the field, where the smell of manure was stronger and she could make out the dim, rounded shapes of the villagers' huts. An unseen dog caught her scent and began to bark frantically in a way that suggested that it had lived its whole life with the sole ambition of ripping out Nora's throat. She caught herself expecting the whole place to come ablaze with electric light, like any house equipped with floodlights and motion detectors in her own world, but instead, after a few minutes, a couple of bearded men came out with torches and some sharp, heavy tools she couldn't identify.

Their Ors dialect was nasal and reedy, and Nora wasn't sure how well they could understand her, but she showed them her hand and managed, she thought, to convey that she was a traveler who had had an accident. One of the men kept asking her something. She finally figured out that he wanted to know if she'd seen a dragon in the forest that day. The woodchopper whose ax she had borrowed must have brought back the news of his encounter with Raclin.

"Yes," she said, as brightly as she could. "Don't worry. The dragon is dead. Dragon dead." She should have brought the ax back with her, a goodwill gesture.

After consulting with each other for what seemed like a long time, the men led Nora to the largest of the huts, where they turned her over to an old woman and two younger ones. Their names all sounded the same, a rush of vowels. One gave her a bowl of sour-tasting broth and some parched flatbread. The old woman wanted to bandage Nora's hand with a strip of grimy cloth that she unwound from a lump of cheese. Perhaps it was some kind of folk remedy—homemade penicillin? Nora shook her head. She tried to communicate, in words and gestures, that she wanted to wash her hand instead. The old woman clucked at her but put an earthenware pot of water on the coals. The water was going to take forever to get warm, Nora saw; she did an unobtrusive heating spell, the Calanian protocol.

There was almost no furniture in the hut, just a low platform next to the fire covered with blankets, where everyone was sitting cross-legged. Probably it was also their bed. Nora would have liked to lie down right then and go to sleep, despite the pain in her hand, but she forced herself to keep her eyes open, and smiled at the shaggy-haired children who piled together like wolf cubs and stared at her with round, wary eyes. "What are your names?" The answers came haltingly. She listened harder this time: Amawau, Awau, Yowaum, Clover, Sweet Pig.

The women wanted to know how many children Nora had and where her husband was. It was out of the question to tell them that her ex-husband was lying dead in the forest a mile away, but when she simply told them she had no husband or children, they giggled suspiciously. The old woman mumbled something—evidently a joke, because the other two women laughed again.

Should I ask her to repeat it? Nora wondered, looking uncertainly from one woman to another. In the darkness of the forest, the idea of warmth, safety, human contact had drawn her like a beacon, but now she could not shed a sense of unease. Awkwardly she lifted the drinking bowl with her one good hand to take another sip of broth.

A log rolled off the fire, glowing red, and bumped up against Nora's knee. "Shit!" She flung it back on the fire as fast as she could, then put down her bowl to brush off her knee and make sure that the blankets hadn't ignited.

When she lifted her head, the women were staring at her.

Nora smiled at them, more confidently than she felt. "Is anything wrong?" Some breach of etiquette? In the Uland, even after months there, she'd made egregious faux pas all the time. What the local customs or taboos were like here, she had no idea.

Then she realized why they were staring. She hadn't touched the log when she moved it.

The women muttered to one another, not taking their eyes off Nora. I guess they don't see levitation spells every day, Nora thought. The youngest woman got up hurriedly and went out of the hut.

"It's very basic magic," Nora said. "Nothing to worry about. See—" She made the drinking bowl rise a few inches into the air.

The old woman said something to her companion. Nora caught the word *witch*.

"Magician," Nora corrected. "Don't worry," she said as she lowered the bowl to the ground. "It's perfectly safe."

But the other two women were already on their feet, reaching protectively for their children, backing away from Nora. They shoved the kids through the door and ducked through themselves.

I thought people in this world were used to magic, Nora thought. She'd met plenty of people who were distrustful of magic and magicians, but no one who actually fled when a spell was worked. She stood up to follow the women outside, wondering if she could somehow reassure them, perhaps by working some useful magic. Her studies so far had included a lot of military spells—tracking Aruendiel's own interests— but she knew a few spells for sharpening tools or finding lost animals and the like. And she could always mend more pots.

The door of the hut wouldn't open. Which was surprising, because there was no real lock, just a wooden latch on the inside. Someone was holding the door closed from the exterior. Nora knocked, then pounded with her good hand. "Let me out," she shouted. She could hear voices outside the hut, a lot of them. "Please, let me out. I don't mean you any harm. And honestly, I'm just a student, I'm not dangerous."

The voices outside were louder, agitated. Apparently they didn't believe her reassurances. She kept calling and beating on the door for a while anyway. Then she gave up and turned back to the fire, where the water in the earthenware pot was beginning to steam. She scooped the hot water into her bowl and tentatively began to clean her left hand, wincing as the water touched the wound. What remained of her ring finger looked white, waxy, somehow unconvincing as a finger. I suppose it, too, will have to come off, Nora thought. Oh, fuck, this has really turned out to be the worst day of my life.

Aruendiel must be dead. He had to be. If he were alive, no matter how cruelly she had hurt him, how much he hated her now, he would know somehow—magic or instinct—that she was maimed and exhausted and being held prisoner by crazed peasants in the middle of nowhere, and he would come to rescue her. If only for the satisfaction of killing her himself.

A picture flashed through her mind: the pine tree, so close to her, broken and burning with Aruendiel's rage. The lightning strike had missed her, though. Was that just a mistake?

Suddenly she realized the voices outside were quiet. She listened. Had everyone gone away? She got up to try the door again. Something was not right. She caught a sound like wind above her head; she smelled smoke. Red stars glowed in the roof.

They had set fire to the hut. Obviously they were counting on the roof to burn fast. It was all woven branches and thatch.

"Oh, that's really smart." She felt a sense of tired disgust. "Burn down your own house just to get me? I would have left if you'd asked nicely."

When she ordered the fire to quench itself, the flames overhead died down at once, as though they sensed that she was in no mood to be crossed. A hank of burning straw landed on a blanket and flared up defiantly. Nora dowsed it with a frown.

A new murmur in the crowd outside. Nora could hear their consternation. After a minute, the roof was on fire again, new flames lapping the edges of the holes already burned. Nora killed the fire again.

"Look," she called. "This is stupid. You can keep setting fires all night, and I'll just put them out. If you want me to leave, I'll go. Just let me out. Now."

Silence again, then some whispers. Next they'll send Bill down the chimney, Nora thought. Instead, the door opened. A stone the size of an apple flew past Nora's head. Shadowy figures pushed through the doorway, carrying rocks and cudgels. Outside, people began to shout.

"Wait," she said. "Wait, please, this isn't necessary." A rock hit her side and she almost fell. Another rock just missed her jaw. She backed away until her shoulder blades smacked into the cool earth wall of the hut. "Kill the witch!" someone screamed outside, and then everyone was crying the same thing. In the dimness the men crowding toward her were like a single large animal with a dozen waving arms. Stones thudded into the wall beside her head; they slammed into the soft flesh of her belly, her thigh, her shoulder. "Witch, witch, dirty witch, kill the dirty witch!"

Ducking, raising her arms to shield her head, she remembered the vision-clouding spell, but at this range it didn't help much; they couldn't miss her if they tried. She tried a shield spell from Vlonicl, although it was really designed to protect against arrows. Some of the rocks got through anyway. "Witch, whore, filthy sow!"

She tried using magic to make the stones turn back on her attackers. It was hard to keep up. A blow to her elbow, and her right arm went numb.

"Rotten cunt!" A stone grazed the top of her head. The flying stones, the men with their open mouths and frightened, furious eyes all swirled before her for a drunken moment. If they knocked her out for even a second, her shield spell would falter, she would be lost.

"Fuck the witch, kill the witch! Make the stinking she-cat yowl!"

A rock smashed against her ribs; she grunted and staggered. They would be on her like dogs on meat if she fell. There were too many of them, and too many rocks, and their roaring hatred was a choking fog in her brain. Her bleeding hand throbbed.

She found herself screaming for help, as though Aruendiel might hear, as though anyone at all in the middle of this desolate, alien night might care what happened to her.

"Kill the witch! Kill her, kill her, kill, kill, kill her—"

"Stop," someone said. "Right now."

The stones obeyed, freezing stock-still in mid-flight.

The men kept up their rhythm of throwing, but the stones that they hurled slowed and then halted as though the air had gelled around them. Dizzily, Nora turned to see who had spoken.

"They're always so cruel. It's because they're ignorant."

A woman stood next to Nora. Taking in her ragged gown and the rough gray hood that covered her head, Nora thought she was one of the villagers. But her voice was wrong, edged with a different accent. Nora bent forward to try to see her face.

"And so they're afraid of you," the woman continued. "But fear is no excuse for cruelty." She turned, and Nora met smiling dark eyes under brows that arched like question marks.

"Who are you?" Nora asked.

Before the other woman could answer, one of the men collapsed to his knees, right in front of Nora.

She noticed suddenly that all the men had their mouths open, as though they were still shouting at her, but she could hear only the muddled cries of the crowd outside the hut. A silencing spell of some kind? No, some of the men clutched their throats. Others bent over, their bodies heaving.

Another man buckled, eyes wide, his face purple under his beard.

"What are you doing?" Nora demanded of her new companion. She could feel the slow churn in her stomach that signaled strong magic being worked nearby. "They can't breathe. You're choking them."

"I'm doing justice to them," said the woman calmly. "They wanted to kill you."

"But they're going to die if they can't breathe," Nora said.

"That's right."

"I don't—I just want them to stop attacking me. They don't have to choke to death."

The other woman gave her a friendly, faintly incredulous look. "You don't want them to die?"

"Really, I don't," Nora said. "I just want to get out of here."

The woman in the gray hood paused, as if to give Nora a chance to change her mind, and then nodded. A deep, collective gasp passed through the crowd. The shoulders of the men slumped as they drank in air.

The purple-faced man drew in great shuddering breaths and sat up slowly, bracing himself against the ground.

"Idiots!" the woman in gray said.

The men looked at her with dazed fixity. She made an impatient gesture, like brushing away flies. Although she was at least a head shorter than most of the men, she had the air of looking down at them from a considerable height.

"You are clodheads and criminal beasts, all of you," she said in a cool, sure voice that did not quite lose its sweetness. "You have broken the law of hospitality, and you've raised your hand against the innocent. You should die for that. But I'm giving you justice *and* mercy because this one has pleaded for you."

As she nodded at Nora, her hood slipped down, and Nora got a better look at her face, a pale narrow oval framed by shining dark hair. Her finely shaped features were set into an expression of sternness like a drawn bow. It was hard to tell how old she was.

The men shifted uneasily. Then one said softly: "She's a witch, too." Under a bulbous, balding forehead, his ruddy face was squeezed into a stubborn expression. He glanced quickly at the other men, inviting them to join him.

"That one's a filthy stinkpot witch," he said, more loudly now, facing the woman in gray, "and so are you."

Another collective intake of breath in the small crowd. But it was not shared by the man who had spoken.

He clawed at his throat, gagging. His neighbors stared. Some edged away. His face darkened as he fought for air. One man pounded him on the back, then appeared to think better of it. Nora found she was holding her breath with instinctive sympathy.

"I gave you justice and mercy—and then justice again," the woman said to the crowd, with a rueful half smile. "It was a foolish thing for him to say. The rest of you are wiser, I hope."

She stared hard at them. Their faces were pale, grudging, angry, but none of them spoke.

"Good. I charge you to be more hospitable to strangers in the future." She looped her arm through Nora's.

"You're going to let that man die?" Nora whispered. She could not look away from the balding man. On his knees now, beginning to convulse, he still had some of that look of stubbornness.

The other woman pulled her forward. A twitch of uncertainty passed through the group of men, a half-hearted movement to block the path of the two women, but they fell back as the woman in gray brushed past them.

Outside was another crowd, mostly women. The cool night air reeked of sweat and smoke. The villagers pressed close; the torchlight flickered in their tired, frightened eyes. Nora could sense their confusion: should they try to overcome the dangerous strangers, who had bested the menfolk but were nevertheless outnumbered here, or should they flee for their lives? The buzz of their voices rose higher. Thinking of the gasping man inside, Nora found her own breath tightening.

The woman in the gray hood shook her head. "This is tiresome, isn't it?" she said.

Nora sensed something ominous in her words: any second now, more of the villagers would be rolling on the ground, choking to death in the dust. "Let's just get out of here," Nora whispered. "Now." Squeezing the other woman's arm more tightly against her own side, she worked the fastest levitation spell that she knew and felt her body swing upward. Her companion dragged slightly on her arm but gained enough lift to follow her. They tilted drunkenly over the heads of the people below, who screamed and crouched and clutched their heads.

The woman in the gray hood gave a hoot of laughter. "Well done!" she said, although Nora felt she was being generous about their ragged flight. Anyone below could grab their feet with a good jump. Nora steered a wavering course away from the noise and confusion of the crowds and into the darkness. She pushed the spell as far as it would go, trying to avoid running into invisible trees or other obstacles, until the magic finally ebbed and they fell. The other woman laughed again, more softly.

Nora landed on her side, her wounded hand striking the ground. The pain flooded back, all the stronger for having been ignored before. She whimpered, then swore.

The woman checked her laughter. "You are hurt." Her thin face appeared out of the darkness, although Nora could see no obvious source of light. "It's your hand, isn't it? Show me."

Nora held her injured hand against her breast. "It's not very pretty," she said finally, knowing that her objection sounded absurd but also feeling an odd, primitive unwillingness to let the other see how vulnerable she was.

"I have seen some very ugly wounds," the woman said. "I hope yours isn't as bad as some. Well, let's take a look." Pulling Nora's arm closer, she bent over the hand. "Ah, yes, that must hurt quite a bit!" Her fine dark eyebrows wrinkled sympathetically. "Would you like to be healed?"

"Well, yes." Nora made herself look again at the spongy stump, the flapping dead finger. Seeing the wound diminished the pain a tiny bit, because she was so distracted by how disgusting it looked. "I think—I think my finger has to come off."

With a serious look, the woman folded Nora's throbbing hand between her palms. Her hands felt very smooth and clean, like fresh sheets, but Nora cried out as they pressed the torn skin and muscle.

"Don't be afraid," the other woman said.

Nora was about to say that she wasn't afraid, it just hurt like fucking hell, when she discovered that her hand was somehow empty and quiet. The pain seemed to dribble away through her fingers like water. For an unbelieving moment, she tensed, waiting for it to return, and then yanked her hand back from the other woman's grasp.

The hand looked almost the way it should. The ring finger was reattached, warm and alive again. She could bend it, wiggle it, curl it until her nail touched the top of her palm. Her little finger was still gone, but the stump had healed over with healthy skin, not even a scab to show where the horrible red-meat gash had been.

"Your other finger will grow again," the woman said. "It will take a little time."

"You're a magician," Nora said slowly, distinctly. "What's your name?" Aruendiel had never mentioned another female magician besides Hiriz-jahkinis—or at least not one this powerful.

A simple question, but the other woman appeared to give it serious consideration. "Here, I think they would call me Sisoaneer." She gave a sudden, mischievous grin. "I have had other names in other places."

Her answer wasn't entirely satisfactory. Nora froze with a dreadful intuition. "I know who you are. Ilissa." In a new disguise. It was obvious, Nora thought. Why didn't I see before?

Sisoaneer broke into delighted laughter. With her wide, flexible mouth and sharp brows sketching every expression against pale skin, she somehow looked graceful and clownish at the same time. It was a face that held nothing held back. "You take me for a Faitoren, really? It's the first time *that* has ever happened. My power is greater—much, much stronger—than any petty Faitoren enchantment. I came to help you, not to enslave you."

It didn't sound like something Ilissa would say, but Nora was still wary. "Why did you help me?"

"You asked for help. I heard you." Sisoaneer spoke as though the answer were obvious. More gravely, she added, "You fought well, as you should have. But there were too many of them, and even those halfwits can aim a rock. Besides, this wasn't the first battle you fought today, was it? Your hand was wounded before those idiots attacked you."

"That was an accident," Nora said, stubbornly cautious, although part of her yearned to spill out the whole miserable story of the past twenty-four hours. Something in Sisoaneer's manner, her calm and merry eyes, made Nora think that she'd be a good listener, that it would take a lot to shock her.

"An accident. I see," Sisoaneer said, looking as though she didn't believe Nora but found her reticence amusing, and Nora could not help feeling that she had failed some kind of test.

"I lost my—my traveling companion," Nora said, "and then I met someone who wanted to hurt me. I tried to stop him. With an ax. It just slipped." She registered a slightly jarring note of insistence in her own voice, and wondered if Sisoaneer also heard it.

"But you stopped him, the one who wanted to hurt you?"

"Oh, yes," Nora said, too quickly. "That's all right."

Sisoaneer nodded. "That's good. How will you find your companion again?"

Nora wished she had a better answer, or any answer. "I don't know," she said. She wondered if she could find her way back, through the darkness, to the clearing where she had left Aruendiel. And what would she find there?

It seemed to her that her whole heart was calling out to him in anguish and sorrow—why did he not respond?

"I must go," Sisoaneer said suddenly.

"Where?" Nora asked. She didn't relish the idea of being alone again, of letting go of this thin filament of conversation and kindness. Even if there was something unsettling about Sisoaneer—she'd been so disturbingly casual about killing the villager—she was the only ally Nora had at the moment.

"I'm going to another place where I'm needed." Sisoaneer smiled at Nora. "Will you come with me?"

"What? I don't—" Nora glanced around at the scraps of light from the village fires, at the night forest beyond. "Is it far?"

"Not if we hurry." Sisoaneer's fingers laced through Nora's. "You don't mind if we go on foot, do you? Flying in the dark is dull." She smiled again, turned, and broke into a run, the warm clasp of her hand pulling Nora after her.

Chapter 12

A ruendiel held on to the tree with both hands, shuddering, and waited for the chill to pass. Mentally he cursed the treacherous, black-bleeding, pox-ridden Faitoren hag again. There had been at least three different toxins in her tail venom. One, as far as he could tell, was nearly identical in its effects to the classic poisoner's recipe known as Nuelev's Tears; he had countered it easily with a charm to keep his heartbeat regular. The other two poisons were more obscure, and there was no time to puzzle them out. He'd lost more than an hour in that unconscious fit. Now he was using all the magic at his command to avoid another.

Yet he was cheered beyond all expectation by the sight in front of him: the headless body of Ilissa's son. Nora had been here—Aruendiel knew the taste of her magic—and Raclin was dead. Even if Nora herself was nowhere to be seen, this was more and better than he could have expected. Aruendiel's heart thudded against his ribs with relief, despite the Nuelev counterspell, and he sent up a rare prayer of thanks to the gods.

Although, he reflected with a surge of pride, it was really Nora's own quick wits and the magic he'd taught her that had saved her. Only a few months' study, and she had defeated this monstrous, dangerous Faitoren. Remarkable, hard to credit—and yet why should he be surprised? Nora was remarkable; she would be as brilliant a magician as he had ever known. If she was still alive.

He conjured a light in one hand and moved forward unsteadily, cursing the numbness in his feet, to study the ground around the corpse. An ax lay nearby. Good, Nora had remembered that the Faitoren were vulnerable to iron and steel. There was Raclin's head, matted with blood and leaves. Aruendiel kicked it out of the way. He found a tangle of footprints in the dirt, large bootprints and smaller ones. The smaller boots had stayed near the half-burned tree under which the corpse lay. All around the tree they went, and then she had stood still for a long time. Aruendiel looked up at the blackened branches; Raclin had set a fire, and Nora had put it out. A couple of gashes up and down the trunk, one stained with blood, showed just where Nora had been standing.

At this last sign, Aruendiel's face darkened. He went back to the corpse and its head, and confirmed that Raclin had suffered one wound only, the blow to his neck. He thought for a moment, and then went hunting in the leaves and litter under the tree. At the sight of the severed finger, nestled next to a root, Aruendiel swore again and went cold all over, worse than the chills from the poison. Leaning against the tree for balance, he picked up the finger carefully, if clumsily—his hands felt as nerveless as his feet now—and conjured a linen cloth from the nearest village to wrap it in. He tucked the small bundle inside his tunic.

His head was splitting. Where was Nora now? There were other dangers in the wilderness. Aruendiel worked a testimony spell on the trees of the clearing, but they could tell him nothing he didn't know already. Nora's tree only babbled, half hysterical from the fire; the other trees had paid no attention to the movements of any particular two-legged animal that day. They were merely relieved that the ax that had been felling trees earlier had ceased to bite.

The axman's village—most likely Nora had headed there. Aruendiel located the village hearth fires: southeast, almost half a *karistis* away, he estimated. Faster to fly there, he thought, and then another thunderbolt of pain flashed through his skull. Aruendiel groaned, and found himself lying full-length on the ground.

He could not remember falling. How long had he been unconscious this time? He tried to stand, but there was no feeling in his legs.

Ilissa would be drunk with laughter to see him like this. For a moment Aruendiel thought he could hear that maddening, bell-like laugh. But the real joke was that she had used so much cunning magic over so many years to try to defeat him, when all along she could have killed him with one strike of her tail, if she'd ever cared to show her real form.

Aruendiel raised himself from the ground with a levitation spell, grimacing at the way his legs hung limp and dangling. As dead as they'd been during those long years of convalescence. He could still move his arms a little. If he transformed himself into an owl, would he be able to fly? Nora—he suddenly wanted very much to see her face, her lovely smile. For a moment he thought he caught a glimmer of her magic, not so far away—lifting something into the air—then the trace was gone.

She had saved his life once. It was another black joke that if he reached her now, he might be just as helpless as he had been then.

If he reached her. The headache was starting again. There was no more time.

With almost all of his strength, Aruendiel called the wind to him. It came, roaring at him as though to upbraid him for his stupidity and carelessness, and it wrapped his useless body in its supple power. He told it to take him northward, hoping that he would stay conscious long enough to find the place he was seeking. There were not many magicians who would know how to treat Faitoren poison, and only one whom Aruendiel trusted.

As the rushing wind sucked him into the sky, he set the trees below on fire, to burn away the filth that lay dead under their branches. Hurling through the restless night, he watched the small red glow behind him for a little while, until he could see nothing more.

They ran over dark fields streaked with silver from a setting moon tangled in a skein of cloud. A chilly wind whipped against Nora's face and blew her hair straight back. She could not see the ground properly, even in the moonlight, because they were going so fast, but the other woman seemed to have no trouble finding their way. Nora felt the soft earth of newly turned fields under her feet, and then the slap of grass and brushy twigs against her legs.

A dark, glimmering streak appeared almost under their feet, and they cleared it before Nora could even identify it as a brook. The black trunks of trees loomed and vanished. They vaulted up a slope and raced down the other side.

Where were they going? The question lingered in the back of Nora's mind, but it began to seem less and less important the farther they went. Earlier, in the daylight, she had been running for her life. Now she was running because she was alive. Still alive. Her legs pumped with improbable energy, her lungs filled and emptied. She had never run this fast before. Nora sprinted harder, to see if she could pull ahead of her companion. Sisoaneer laughed. "Faster, faster," she said, like the Red Queen.

They ran on and on. The moon sank behind trees, leaving a sky jittering with stars and a world flooded with a deeper shade of night. They moved into woodlands, taking an unseen path, dodging trees, but hardly slowing at all.

Then the other woman stopped, and after a split second, so did Nora—staggering a little, off-balance. The muscles in her legs twitched, still eager to run.

"That was farther than I expected," Nora said.

"This is the place," Sisoaneer said.

Nora could make out only the outline of treetops against the dim sky. "Where are we?"

"Do you hear?"

The wind rustled shadowy leaves. From somewhere not too far away came the gurgle of a hidden brook. "Hear what?"

"She's calling me. Come on. This won't take long." Sisoaneer's voice receded, her footsteps quiet. Nora caught the whiff of woodsmoke and latrine. Wherever they were, it was close to human habitation.

The vague shape of a small hut materialized out of the darkness, chinks of reddish light around the door and in the walls. Their ragged pattern told Nora how dilapidated the building was. Now she could hear someone inside whispering, a female voice, hoarse and agitated. The woman seemed to be repeating the same words over and over.

"She's a widow. He's her only son," Sisoaneer said. "He has been ill for only two days, but she's afraid for his life. The bloody flux." She pushed open the door of the hut.

The woman kneeling on the floor looked up, her eyes sunken. One graying braid had fallen loose from the tight weave around her head and was unraveling over her shoulder. Her cheeks gleamed wet in the scant light of the fire, but her expression was inert, stony. Nora recognized it. Her own mother had looked that way when EJ was dying, her face eroded of any soft emotion, worn down to bedrock.

The room stank. This was where the latrine smell was coming from. Nora breathed shallowly, through her mouth. Sisoaneer swept into the hut as though she smelled nothing and bent down in front of the woman. Only then did Nora see the stained blanket mounded over a narrow body and the downy face of a teenage boy, looking as dry and fragile as an old man's. Sisoaneer put her hand against his cheek, very gently.

"Don't be afraid," she said to his mother. "I heard your call, and I came."

The boy's mother only stared at her.

"He's close to death, but he'll recover. I will save him because you asked me to. Now"—Sisoaneer's tone grew brisk—"do you have any water? Clean water."

The woman looked at her wonderingly. At first she seemed not to take in what Sisoaneer had said. Then she fell back, huddling against the wall of the hut. Her face crinkled with sudden emotion. "You? Great lady?"

"Some water," Sisoaneer said, "or your child will die."

With a gasp that she tried to smother, the boy's mother groped in the shadows and thrust a pitcher forward. She did not take her eyes off Sisoaneer.

Sisoaneer peered into the pitcher and wrinkled her nose. "I said clean water." She held the pitcher away from her body as bright white flames curled over the top. Nora and the other woman blinked in the sudden glare. The flames sank hissing back into the pitcher, and a new smell filled the air, sweet and sharp. Sisoaneer swirled the liquid inside and angled the pitcher so that a few drops fell onto the boy's cracked lips.

"Drink," she said.

Shyly his tongue appeared. He swallowed. His lips smacked feebly.

"More," said Sisoaneer. She put a hand behind his shoulder and forced him upward into a half-sitting position, holding the pitcher to his mouth. As much water dribbled onto the blanket as the boy took in, but Sisoaneer, imperturbable, kept the pitcher pressed to his lips. After a long minute, he sat up and took the pitcher. Shakily he hoisted it to his mouth. Eyes closed, he gulped with steady greed until the pitcher should have been empty. And still he kept drinking.

Finally the boy lowered the pitcher and let Sisoaneer take it from him. He lay down again. His eyelids flickered as he looked up at Sisoaneer, and then they closed.

The hut was quiet as they all listened to the measured rustle of his breath.

Sisoaneer handed the pitcher to his mother, the water inside sloshing faintly. She looked into the interior, then at Sisoaneer, her eyes wide with questions.

"Have him drink all of it," Sisoaneer said. "It will take him a day."

"A day," the woman repeated. "He will live another day?" Her voice was strangled.

Sisoaneer laughed in a way that was both mocking and kind and made it seem that she had known the other woman for a long time. "Sweet mother, he will live many, many days."

The woman was silent, as though to savor her words. Then she said: "Great lady! He is everything to me. The only one left."

"I know," Sisoaneer said.

"I didn't know if you would hear me. I couldn't bear it, I thought— oh, blessings, blessings and glory upon your head, great lady."

"I always hear those who call me." Straightening, Sisoaneer glanced around the hut. "Wash him now. Clean up his filth." The woman bowed her head. "In three days, invite your neighbors to come feast to celebrate your son's return to health. He'll eat more than anyone, I promise."

The woman looked up, more tears spilling down her cheeks, and reached out blindly as though to grasp the hem of Sisoaneer's dress. Sisoaneer laid her hand lightly on the woman's head, then stepped back. She motioned to Nora to follow her.

Outside the hut, Nora took a deep breath of fresh air. "What did you do in there?" she asked.

Lifting her eyebrows, Sisoaneer seemed to find Nora's question funny. "I healed him."

"I mean, what spell was that? The flames, the water." She knew—she'd read—that people with dysentery could die of dehydration. In her world, they'd be cured by being hooked up to an IV, not by being dosed with magical water.

Sisoaneer regarded Nora more seriously. "Do you know anything about healing magic?"

Nora shook her head. "Not really." She felt some need to explain the deficit in her skills. "Aru—that is, my teacher—thought it was too advanced for me. That I needed better control before I learned any healing spells."

"Healing magic isn't so difficult," Sisoaneer said. Again, she sounded amused. "You could learn it quickly enough."

If I had a teacher, Nora thought. If I ever find Aruendiel again, and if, if—

"Where are we now?" she asked. One section of the sky had lightened. It must be the east. But what did that tell her?

"I'm not entirely sure, but it doesn't matter," Sisoaneer said. "I am going home."

"But it does matter," Nora said, suddenly engulfed by a wave of tiredness, her legs ready to fold beneath her. How far had they run tonight? And before that, she had run from Aruendiel, fled from Raclin, and—

Nora shuddered. Not an hour ago, it had seemed that she could outrun all the pain and fear that had inexplicably taken over her life in the past day. She found herself almost envious of the woman inside the hut for being safe and secure at home with someone she loved, someone who was now also safe and secure. Nora had also been rescued by Sisoaneer, but it had not solved any of her real problems.

"Where do I go?" she asked. "I'm lost."

"You can come home with me," Sisoaneer said. "If you want."

"I need to go back to where I was. I need to find my, my—" The exact nature of her relation to Aruendiel was hard to define right now. And she was oddly reluctant to say his name; it felt unlucky. "The person I was separated from."

"Back to the village of halfwits?"

"No. Near there."

"But you don't know where he is," Sisoaneer said reasonably. "Do you?"

"Well, I don't really know *you*, either. Why should I trust you enough to go home with you?"

"You've trusted me enough to come this far."

Nora quirked her mouth. "Maybe that wasn't so smart."

Sisoaneer gave a low chuckle. "Everyone else you've met today has tried to kill you—but not me. I want to help you, Nora. I watched you fight your enemies tonight, and you showed your strength. You weren't afraid to use your power as you were taught. But even the strongest need to rest. Come home with me."

Nora shook her head. "I *am* tired. Too tired. I can't run anymore."

It was a relief to have a simple, unarguable reason to say no to Sisoaneer's invitation, although what she would do instead was too complicated and exhausting a question to consider properly at the moment.

"We'll go by river," Sisoaneer said.

The sound of the brook was suddenly much louder. A churning whiteness coiled through the trees and came almost to their feet. Cold spray touched Nora's bare legs. Something large and dark drifted toward them on the current.

"Our boat," Sisoaneer said. She took hold of its side. "Go on, get in."

"But—" Nora said. She looked around as though she could discern in the darkness the vanishingly slender thread of fate that would lead her to Aruendiel again.

"Please," Sisoaneer said, already in the boat. "I don't want to leave you here alone."

Nora paused, irresolute. A half-formed thought moved through her mind: that thread of fate is me. If I live, I will find him again. I will.

She waded into the water. It was not very deep. The boat rocked gently as she climbed into it and groped her way to a cushioned seat. She felt polished wood under her fingers, and then a fold of soft woolen cloth, a blanket, was pressed into her hands. Sisoaneer sat behind her.

"I'll navigate," the other woman said. "It will take the rest of the night to get there."

But there's not much left of this hideous night, Nora thought, scrunching down in her seat and wrapping the blanket around herself. The night had already lasted decades. And it was centuries since the morning, when she'd woken up on Aruendiel's cloak in the sunshine and watched him come toward her, smiling.

The tears came so fast that she knew they had been waiting for quite some time for another chance to fall. Nora buried her face in the blanket—an empty gesture, she didn't actually care what Sisoaneer thought—and let her sobs detonate, messy, harsh, hiccuping, until finally it seemed to Nora that she and the blanket both were soaked through with tears and snot and sadness, and she had only enough room left in her exhausted soul for leaden grief. Tired of tears and laughter, tired of everything but sleep.

"Is it so very bad?" she heard Sisoaneer saying wonderingly. Nora closed her eyes. Water slapped the hull of the boat softly, then more softly. She felt the blanket around her shoulders being adjusted. "Yes, I suppose it is," Sisoaneer said.

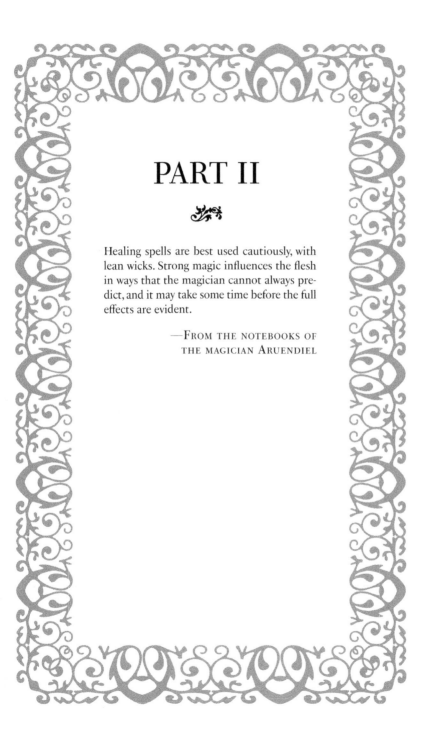

PART II

Healing spells are best used cautiously, with lean wicks. Strong magic influences the flesh in ways that the magician cannot always predict, and it may take some time before the full effects are evident.

—FROM THE NOTEBOOKS OF
THE MAGICIAN ARUENDIEL

Chapter 13

Nora took Raclin home to meet her parents—who were somehow no longer divorced—and the four of them were sitting in the den, on the gray plush sofa and armchairs that her stepmother had thrown out years ago. Her father had just asked Raclin where he worked when it came to Nora that she had already killed him.

Oh, fuck, she thought, how am I going to explain this to Mom and Dad?

She turned to watch Raclin's severed head tumble slowly from his neck as blood soaked through his white cotton shirt and into the upholstery.

Nora opened her eyes. Her first thought was relief: my parents don't have to know.

She was not in her parents' den. She was wrapped in a quilt on a thinly padded mattress that didn't quite make up for the hardness of the stone floor beneath.

There was nothing else in the small, white-walled room, except for a long, blue-gray article of clothing, hanging on the back of the wooden door. Through the open window she could hear water gurgling somewhere nearby. Although the room had a well-scrubbed look, the air held a damp, mossy rankness.

Nora wrapped the quilt around her naked shoulders. They had taken her ruined clothes away early that morning, letting her wash herself in a basin of water that reddened quickly in the gray morning light. Now, looking down, she saw that she had missed a smear under her right breast. She scrabbled at it with her nails, loosening brown specks of dried blood, until the skin turned pink and angry.

Her left hand looked oddly off-balance with the little finger missing. It felt all right, though. No pain. Was the finger really going to grow again, as Sisoaneer had promised? There was a faint white scar where the ring finger had been reattached, and you could still tell where Raclin's ring had been, by the band of paler, untanned skin. Nora resolved to bake her hand in the sun at the first opportunity.

She went to try on the garment hanging on the door. It took some figuring out, like the paper gowns in doctors' offices, and finally she decided arbitrarily that the short sleeve went on her left arm and the long one on her right. There was a long strip of material left over; experimentally she wrapped it around her waist.

On the other side of the door was a second small room, almost as bare. A few cushions on the floor, embroidered with a brilliant zigzag pattern, and an iron brazier. Another wooden door. Nora was apprehensive that it might be locked, but the door swung open when she pushed it.

Stepping outside, she blinked in the slanting sunlight. Late afternoon. She must have slept all day. This morning, climbing tiredly out of the boat, she'd had the impression of being in the center of a large, paved courtyard with tall stone walls. That wasn't right, she saw now.

She was at the bottom of a ravine. A vigorous stream, a young river, snaked along its bottom. Weathered, pale-gold cliffs rose around her. Trees leaned over the rim, leaves shifting in a light breeze. Above, she glimpsed stout, rounded mountains that leaned companionably against each other, their flanks marbled with the bright greens of early spring. Downstream, the gorge widened into a sort of natural amphitheater. A narrow stair descended from the doorway where she stood to a path that ran along the water.

"Praise to Her Holiness! You have rested enough?"

The woman standing on the path waved up at Nora, who recognized her after a second's hesitation: one of the people who'd helped her from the boat this morning. Salt-and-pepper hair; large, slightly worried eyes set in a soft, pouched face. Something about the overly hearty good cheer in her voice gave Nora the idea that she'd been lingering nearby for some time, waiting for Nora to emerge.

"Come down! It's almost time for the evening meal."

Nora edged down the stairs, which had no railing. The rooms where she had slept, she saw, were part of a rambling stone edifice that leaned against the side of the ravine and appeared to have been constructed a few rooms at a time, like shoeboxes piled up next to a wall. Ladders and steeply pitched stairs led up to other doors.

"The Old Dormitory isn't in the best of repair, truthfully. We had some flooding this year when the snow melted—just the lower rooms, but what a mess! Your room was fine, dry as a broken pitcher," the other woman was saying. "But the water almost went into the sanctuary, and Oasme says that hasn't happened for three hundred years."

"The sanctuary?" Nora asked.

"Have you seen it yet? No, of course not, we put you right to bed. You can have a proper tour after dinner, at evening prayers."

"I'm sorry, I don't remember your name from this morning," Nora said. "And what is this place, exactly?"

"I'm the Second Deaconess," the woman said. "My name is Uliverat." She swept an arm through the air. "This is the Deep Court of the Sky, and the sanctuary is upstream a bit. But now we'll go downstream, to the lower complex, where the refectory and sick house and all the other buildings are." Pointing, she started down the waterside path.

"But what is this place? I mean, the whole thing," Nora said, following her slowly, her eyes moving over the ravine. The cliffs were easily two hundred feet tall, turning ocher in the afternoon light. A few trees, looking deceptively small, grew out of fractures in the rock face. Ahead, the stream's braided channels glittered, but the far side of the gorge was already shadowed as the sun moved behind the rim.

She had an intimation that wherever she was, it was a long way from where she had started. A long way from Aruendiel.

"Oh!" Uliverat sounded surprised by Nora's question. "You mean Erchkaii? Erchkaii Oais Ninoes." She seemed to be taking some care to pronounce the words correctly. "Which translates as the Beautiful Secret Mountain Temple of Life, in their old tongue."

"A temple." In the time she'd spent in this world, Nora had seen relatively few religious edifices, except for a few big official temples in Semr. There was a part-time priest in the market town nearest Aruendiel's castle, and many of the villagers had tiny altars in their huts. "What do you worsh—" As an unbeliever in two different worlds, she was not sure how to put this question without causing offense. "Um, what religion do you practice?"

"We honor the mysteries and glory of the great Queen of Holy Power."

Sisoaneer hadn't said anything about a temple or the great Queen of Holy Power. Nora frowned. "I don't think I've heard of her before."

Uliverat gave a complacent smile. "Well, the goddess has many faces, and some worship her by a different name. It is all the same. She loves all who love her."

Warily Nora nodded, mentally edging away. God loves everyone—they said it all the time at her mother's church, but they didn't necessarily act as if they believed it. Although, Nora had to admit, the idea that God was female carried a definite charge.

Uliverat was looking Nora up and down, lips pursed. "Excuse me, dear, your *maran*," she said. "Do you mind if I adjust it a little?"

She meant the doctor's office dress; she was already untucking the long strip that Nora had wrapped around her waist. Nora stiffened as Uliverat draped the material over her left shoulder, then brought it around her body again, and looped the trailing end over Nora's head. The deaconess's dress was draped the same way, Nora saw. The effect was somewhat togalike: full, graceful, perhaps better suited for standing in one spot and declaiming than running very fast or doing any physical task that involved bending at the waist.

"It doesn't feel as though it's going to stay on," Nora objected. "Where are my other clothes, the ones I was wearing when I arrived?" Maybe Faitoren blood could be soaked out.

"Those poor rags!" Uliverat gave an unexpectedly deep, chugging laugh. "We thought you might want to burn them as a thanksgiving offering. You look fine, dear. There's a knack to wearing a *maran*—keep your back straight and your head high—and you get used to it. It's traditional, you know. I never wore one, either, until we came here, and now I like it better than the gown I used to wear. It suits my figure better." She added: "You can pin it, if you have to."

The *maran* felt both binding and precarious. Nora had an urge to shrug the whole elaborately draped affair off her body, but she settled for pushing the scarf end of her *maran* back, so that her hair was partly uncovered. "Where is Sisoaneer?" she asked, but Uliverat was continuing: "And here—these are the Stairs of Healing. Many have been cured here by faith alone, just by praying for the strength to climb these steps. And below, you see the lower courts."

They had come around a broad bend in the gorge, and the stream to their right tumbled abruptly over another tall ledge. The Stairs of Healing had only about three dozen steps, but they were precipitously steep, with no railing to block the sheer drop to the foaming churn under the waterfall. "That climb seems like a pretty strong test of faith," Nora said, "for a sick person."

"The goddess protects those who love her," Uliverat said.

"I see," Nora said.

"And for those who really can't climb at all, we have a litter. The *ganoi* are good for some things," Uliverat added with a shrug and a half laugh.

"The *ganoi*?" Nora asked. Uliverat rolled her eyes and said it was unfortunate, they were more trouble than they were worth, but they'd been here forever and you couldn't run the temple without them.

Below the stairs was a collection of tile-roofed buildings, one or two stories high. Those closest to the water were on stone piers. The deaconess pointed out the functions of the different structures as Nora followed her down the steps—"the New Dormitories; the kitchen; the refectory, where we're going; and the big one is the sick house." Most of the stone buildings with their shuttered windows stood at odd, intimate angles to one another, squeezed into the narrow strip between the cliffs and the water. Uliverat led her across a courtyard and along a winding route among the buildings.

The refectory was one of the more graceful structures in the complex, roofed with a shallow oval dome, arched windows lining the walls. Approaching, Nora smelled something savory, onions and fish, and felt her stomach rumble. When was the last time she'd eaten? "You must be hungry," Uliverat said. "You fell asleep this morning before we could get any food into you." Nora was about to ask Uliverat about what kind of dinner would be served when she noticed that a trio of figures outside the tall double doors, two men and one woman, had turned to look at her.

The woman stepped forward. She was young, taller than Nora, her black hair pulled into small knots. Her dark blue *maran* seemed to hang on her body with considerably more ease than either Uliverat's or Nora's did. "I greet you, Mistress Visitor," she said. "I am Yaioni, the First Deaconess of Erchkaii, Keeper of the Pure Mysteries. Praised be Her Holiness." Her large dark eyes swept over Nora with disdain. Or perhaps that was only her bone structure; she had the kind of bold, sharply modeled features that would always make her look regal and slightly annoyed, Nora thought.

"Praised be Her Holiness," Uliverat and the two men chorused with a precision suggesting long practice. "Welcome to the House of Life and Blessing," the older man said. He was blunt-faced, about forty, with close-cropped hair and small plugs of greenish stone set into his pendulous earlobes. He bowed slightly. Nora copied him.

"It's nice to meet you. My name is Nora." Nora felt her self-introduction sounded slightly curt, with no titles or religious sentiments to rattle off. Indeed, there was a slight awkward pause, as though her companions were expecting her to say more.

"Nora." Yaioni pronounced the name in a way that made it sound as though she were clearing her throat. She stood directly in front of Nora, blocking her way. "I invite you to share our meal, the gift of the goddess."

"Thank you, it's very kind of you," Nora said, and again felt an almost imperceptible chill after she had spoken. Evidently, she had not used the correct polite formula: something-something about how wonderful their goddess was.

"All inside now." Uliverat gave a sort of wiggle, creating the impression of bustle without actually taking a step. "The *ganoi*—we should be keeping an eye on them."

Nora followed the others through the double doors. Inside, the refectory had a worn grandeur, with an intricately ribbed ceiling and massive, scarred tables stretching the length of the long room. As Nora looked to her companions to see where they would take their seats— there were plenty of empty places—the men and women already at the tables stood up abruptly and bowed their heads. Almost all of them had crinkly flaxen or reddish hair, tied back with leather thongs. Something about their heavy musculature, their stained clothes, indicated that they had just come from physical labor. She guessed that these were the *ganoi* that Uliverat had mentioned.

The man with the green stones in his earlobes was now chanting in a clear, pleasant tenor voice. Nora realized with some dismay that she was part of a small procession toward the dais at the far end of the hall.

Whatever she had expected last night, when Sisoaneer offered to take her home, it was not this. She caught a few echoes of Ors in the chant, but nothing she could make sense of. Every few lines, the others chorused a response. Nora was quiet, not wishing to mangle their prayer or hymn or whatever it was, and also because who the hell knew what they were praying for?

On the dais, they took their places at a table that, like the others, seemed to have been designed for far more people. One of the vacant chairs caught Nora's eye. Larger than the others, it was carved with ornate, angular figures—women with jutting breasts, tangled snakes, scowling birds. It did not look especially comfortable. Sisoaneer's seat, Nora surmised.

The buzz of conversation in the hall rose as two women came toward Nora's table, balancing platters on their heads. Their wooden bracelets clattered as they lowered the dishes. Stewed greens, morsels of white-fleshed fish. The others tore off bits of spongy flatbread to dip their food out of the communal dish. As she followed their lead, she was suddenly aware that Yaioni was staring at her again. Mouth full, Nora smiled at her pleasantly, wondering what grievous breach of good table manners she had just committed, then looked away. She tried to make out the figures in the yellowed frescoes on the walls and to figure out what language the men and women at the lower tables were speaking. It was not Ors but something more high-pitched and percussive.

Her companions, though, were all conversing in slightly accented Ors. The man who had led the chant nodded at her from across the table. "I am Oasme," he said. "First Cantor to Her Holiness and Keeper of Her Sacred Books."

His tone was more cordial than Yaioni's. Nora said that she had enjoyed his singing. He gave her a quick, gratified smile. "It is more important that the goddess enjoys it," he said, "but your praise honors me."

The goddess again. Why couldn't he just accept a simple compliment? Nora cast about for a relatively neutral topic. "First Cantor—does that mean there are others?"

"Not at present," Oasme said quickly. "Although Lemoes will likely be a cantor, too, someday. He has a fine voice." He glanced at the other man, as though to prompt him.

Lemoes smiled and ducked his head, the sort of movement that could mean either hello or please ignore me, or both. "I'm Lemoes. First Acolyte."

He was younger than Nora had first thought, a boy of maybe eighteen. A beautiful boy, with velvet eyes, warm brown skin, and an austerely elegant profile—the kind of face that you wanted to look at a second and perhaps third time, just to check if he was really as good-looking as you'd thought at first. Nora reminded herself to feel a purely objective, auntlike admiration, and looked at the empty chair, trying to remember exactly what Sisoaneer had said as they disembarked this morning. Something to the effect of she would see Nora soon. But what did "soon" mean?

Oasme, following her gaze, said: "That is the chair reserved for the High Priestess."

"She's not here tonight?" Nora asked.

It seemed to Nora that Yaioni bridled slightly. "We will see." Her voice was hard, sulky.

"As the goddess wills," Oasme said, his face impassive but his eyes flicking sideways at Yaioni.

"Of course," Yaioni said. "Praised be Her Holiness! She is good to those who love her."

"Praised be Her Holiness," Uliverat said fervently. Half a beat later, the men repeated the same words, Lemoes mumbling through a mouthful of half-chewed food.

How often must they say that, Nora wondered, and how long before it drives me crazy? Sisoaneer had not seemed especially religious last night, none of this Praised be Her Holiness nonsense. This is a waste of time, Nora thought. I'm sitting here trying to be polite to these religious fanatics when I should be looking for Aruendiel.

Something of her emotions must have shown on her face. Yaioni stared at her, unsmiling. "You will not give praise to Her Holiness?" Her Ors sounded rough, faintly stilted, as though she had learned it as an adult. Well, so did I, Nora reminded herself.

"I respect your beliefs, I don't mean to be rude," Nora said. "But I'm afraid I never heard of your goddess before today. Or this place." She summoned all her scant knowledge of this world's geography. "Is Erchkaii near the Kingdom of Semr?"

"Oh, we're far south of Semr," said Uliverat, just as Oasme said: "Semr is many weeks' journey to the west."

Wonderful, Nora thought. *They* don't even know where they are.

"I left my people, my child, my riches behind to follow Her Holiness," Yaioni said suddenly. "Even before that, I worshipped her in my heart. And you have never heard of her?"

"Well, I'd be interested in knowing more about the, um, Queen of Holy Power," Nora said cautiously. These are true believers, she reminded herself, and any sign of disbelief is an attack on their god. "Can you tell me more about her?"

Yaioni looked away, with a sour twitch of her mouth, but Oasme answered immediately, as though he had been waiting for the opportunity. Erchkaii was the chief place of worship for the Lady Healer, as Oasme called her, although she also had lesser shrines elsewhere. A temple had existed here for more than a thousand years, starting with simple underground shrines in the secret caves where the goddess was born, the daughter of an earth goddess and the sun god.

"Erchkaii has long been known as a place of medicine," he said. "People first came to bathe in the river, seeking to be cured, and by the grace of Her Holiness, the waters washed away their suffering. Then Ulausoes, the founder of my order, built the first sick house, and the priests of the Lady Healer have cared for the sick ever since."

Nora decided that it was not the first time that he had given this lecture to a visitor. Oasme was just explaining with some pride that Erchkaii had once been the traditional site for the anointment of the Ghaki Kings when Uliverat broke in.

"Her Holiness is also Queen of Power, you know." Pursing her lips, Uliverat nodded sagely, as though Nora would know what she was talking about. "She is most revered as the Mother of Power."

"Yes, indeed," Oasme agreed. His tone was buttery, faintly apologetic. "We have always honored Her Holiness here for her healing arts. But of course she has other responsibilities that are even greater."

"Let us not forget that," Yaioni snapped, looking up from her plate.

"I do not," he said.

Nora looked curiously at Oasme, but his face gave nothing away. She caught the boy Lemoes's eye, and he grinned at her shyly before turning back to his dinner.

"I thought that Helmis was the god of medicine," Nora said into the silence that had descended on the table. Helmis had a dog's head. That was probably why she remembered him, from some reference in one of Aruendiel's books.

Yaioni muttered something to herself. Uliverat seemed puzzled. "Helmis? Well, yes, he had a shrine in my old village." With more certainty she added: "Some pray to him, but Her Holiness is much greater, of course."

It must be complicated, being a polytheist, Nora thought, always trying to figure out whose god was bigger and badder. "Helmis is a demigod of the western lands, and no, we cannot compare him to Her Holiness," Oasme agreed. "Some say he is the same as our Anies, the son of Ioma." He began a long explanation of Anies's convoluted genealogy. Once he prodded Lemoes to recite a few lines of verse and made a little show of fussing fondly at the boy when he stumbled.

Perhaps too fondly? Nora felt a question form in her mind as she watched them. There were all those church sex abuse scandals, back in her world. Oasme was so much older than Lemoes—and Lemoes was so gorgeous with those big eyes and eloquent cheekbones, not unlike Andy Reeves, captain of the baseball team, who had sat in front of Nora in tenth-grade English and borrowed her copy of *The Catcher in the Rye* and returned it full of penciled underlines that she could never bring herself to erase. Were these clergy celibate?

Lemoes shifted in his seat, eyes downcast, as though sensing

Nora's attention. Maybe her speculation was unfair, Nora thought, but something in this place was off-kilter. And what of Yaioni and Uliverat? The First Deaconess had just leaned over to whisper something to the Second, who nodded hastily, with the air of wanting to please.

Both Oasme and Uliverat were a little afraid of Yaioni, Nora thought. And yet the First Deaconess was very much their junior. Early twenties, Nora guessed. She was still growing into those sharp, striking good looks of hers. Some childish softness remained in the curve of her cheeks, the sulkiness of her mouth.

Now she looked at Nora and smiled with more friendliness than she had before. "You have not seen Her Holiness's sanctuary, I think? I will take you there myself. It is time for evening prayers, to ask for the goddess's protection in the night."

"That would be nice," Nora said, feeling a mild interest in seeing the sanctuary. "There's no prohibition against a nonworshipper going inside?" she asked, to make it clear that she did not plan to join in the prayers.

Something about Nora's question seemed to please Yaioni. "Anyone may enter the Great Hall of the sanctuary." She stood and nodded at Nora. "We will go now," she announced.

Nora rose, snatching at her *maran*—it had slipped entirely off her hair during dinner—and walked alongside Yaioni out of the dining hall, which was almost empty. It was dark now, except for the few torches burning, and the air was already chilly. Nora was suddenly grateful for the woolen folds of the *maran*. Yaioni led her through the complex to the Stairs of Healing.

"What happened to your hand?" Yaioni asked brusquely.

"I cut myself by mistake," Nora said. Involuntarily she touched her thumb to the stump of her missing finger. She wanted to ask if Sisoaneer, the High Priestess, would be at evening prayers, but thought it might send Yaioni off again, for whatever mysterious reason.

They set off up the stairs, which rose even more steeply than Nora remembered. Falling water roared below. Nora kept her hand on the rock face to her right. Then Yaioni said clearly: "You are a witch."

"A witch? Oh, no," Nora corrected, recalling what had happened the last time someone called her a witch. "Not a witch."

"You are a witch," Yaioni insisted. "You know the arts of power?"

The arts of power? Nora hesitated. "I've studied some magic, yes."

"A witch," Yaioni said. "I also am a witch." Her lovely, angry face was suddenly visible in the darkness, a pale flame flaring in her hand. An illumination spell; she must have pulled light from the torches below. "Those who serve Her Holiness must know the arts of power. More than that. They must be very, very skilled"—she almost sneered—"in the arts of power."

"I didn't realize that," Nora said, disturbed, fascinated. It made sense: Sisoaneer was nothing if not skilled in the arts of power. A cadre of female magicians? Nora had not dared to hope that such a thing could exist.

But Yaioni's tone was not exactly reassuring.

"You are completely ignorant of Her Holiness," Yaioni complained. "You are a pagan, a heretic. You practice her arts without honoring her. Why are you here? Why have you come here? You insult Her Holiness's sacred ground by standing upon it!"

"I'm sorry—" Nora stopped, thinking: why am I apologizing? I didn't ask to come here. And Yaioni was beginning to impugn her professional pride. "Magic doesn't come from the gods," Nora said firmly, repeating something Aruendiel had once said.

"Then where does it come from?" Yaioni's words were a taunt.

Nora didn't need to quote Aruendiel this time. "It comes from knowing the world around us—from feeling the true connections among things."

Yaioni's face brightened, as though she were happy to establish the depths of Nora's ignorance. "Lies and blasphemy. Have you no respect? You are foolish to say these evil things before the temple of the goddess, before Her Holiness's most devoted servant."

"I really don't mean to offend you," Nora said. She was a little out of breath. They were at the top of the stairs. "I'm sure your goddess is very powerful and good—and everything a goddess should be. But I learned magic without having to worship any gods. You don't need gods to be a magician."

Yaioni shook her head slowly, an unpleasant smile on her lips.

"Your words are filth, they insult the goddess's blessings," she said. "Her Holiness does not tolerate your insolence."

"Look—" Nora began, intending to say that she was sorry that they had gotten off on the wrong foot, and the last thing she wanted to do was quarrel with another magician—especially a female magician—but just then the air turned thick and frantic.

Soft, bony wings swooped close to her face, small pointed claws caught in her hair. Bats. More bats. Nora shrieked and ducked.

Yaioni was smiling. None of the bats were dive-bombing her.

Slapping at a wing that brushed her mouth, Nora flinched again. "Is this how you treat a guest?"

"Her Holiness has allowed me one challenge," Yaioni said.

"A *challenge*?"

"It was what I prayed for, and Her Holiness listens to the prayers of those who love her."

I've always tried to be open-minded even about the most close-minded people, Nora thought—ducking again, arms over her face—but this is it, now I know that religion makes you crazy. This was a silly challenge, anyway, it was as though Yaioni had watched too many cheesy horror movies. And at the same time you could see why those movies had been made. It *was* ghastly to be swarmed by bats, and that didn't even include the risk of rabies. Maybe rabies didn't exist in this world, Nora thought hopefully.

Can I repel them magically? she wondered. Aruendiel had once said that it was hard to control animals with magic—harder, in fact, than controlling human beings. An animal forced to do something against its will for very long was quite capable of deciding to lie down and die; humans usually found some way to rationalize the loss of autonomy.

She flung a couple of elementary counterhexes at the bats. Nothing very precise, but maybe they would loosen Yaioni's control of the animals. The cloud of bats thinned after the Selvirian counterhex. She sent a meaningful glance toward Yaioni, but Yaioni was looking toward Nora's feet.

Nora followed her gaze. A black scribble on the ground. She jumped back even before her mind formed the word *snake*.

Her foot missed the top step. It found the next one, barely; the jolt of her landing almost sent her down the Stairs of Healing. The snake moved gracefully toward her. The Selvirian counterhex was not working.

"What have I done to you?" Nora demanded of Yaioni.

Yaioni held herself very straight, lifting her arms as though conducting an invisible symphony. "You see how Her Holiness deals with heretics? Her sacred snake comes to punish you. Whose power is greater now?"

"Is that what this is about? You think I'm challenging you and your goddess?" Nora levitated the snake off the ground; it thrashed wildly, obviously annoyed at being dangled in midair.

Leaning away, Nora was intensely conscious of the ski-jump pitch of the stairs at her back. If she fell, could she work a levitation spell powerful enough to save herself? In a split second?

A couple of bats still flitted near her head. She made herself ignore them. Yaioni said something angry in a different language.

It was as though a door had slammed shut. Everything around Nora went black. Yaioni's contorted face, the light she held, the lashing snake, the bats, the moon that had just swum out from behind a cloud—all wiped away.

A stroke, Nora thought. No, a blinding spell.

Staring into darkness, Nora called Yaioni every filthy name she could think of, in English and Ors. Yaioni laughed once, then was silent.

Which was unnerving. Maybe Yaioni was tiptoeing closer in order to push Nora off the edge of the stairs. Nora stopping yelling and listened hard. The bats and their flapping wings seemed closer when you couldn't see them. You'd think it would be the other way around. *Twinkle twinkle, little bat, how I wonder where you're at.*

The snake—she decided not to worry about the snake right now. It was a couple of feet away, last time she'd seen it.

Nora touched her eyes gently to make sure they were still there. They felt fine. They were not bleeding, like poor Gloucester's. They just couldn't see anything. She tried a counterhex to Vlonicl's spell for confusing an enemy's sight, but whatever Yaioni had done, it wasn't the Vlonicl charm.

A flurry in the air right next to her face, needle claws raking her scalp. Instinctively Nora jerked away. Her foot slid off the edge of the step. Arms flailing, she tried to right herself.

Instead, she fell.

That levitation spell, maybe I'll try it now, Nora thought.

A few seconds passed. All she could discern at first was that she had not smashed into the ground. She reached out cautiously and registered only air. A breath of dampness from the waterfall washed over her. The water's roar was louder, she noticed. She must be just above the pool under the falls.

All right, Nora thought cautiously. Not bad. Once before, she'd used a levitation spell to climb a cliff higher than these stairs, but it took a lot more power to raise something that was already plummeting through the air.

A slight noise came from above. A footstep? Nora lifted her head automatically, trying to focus her useless eyes, and felt outrage all over again at being blind. What was Yaioni up to now, in this unreadable darkness? Cautiously Nora extended her arm again to see if she could find the stairs, anything at all.

Her hand grasped stone, and then something cool, dry, supple, and living. The snake wrapped around her wrist before she could drop it.

Chapter 14

How long did it take to die from snakebite, and how painful was it? Nora wondered, trying to shake off the snake as violently as she could, even though that was probably just going to provoke the thing into biting her. The snake squeezed her wrist harder. Any second now she'd feel the prick of fangs.

In the middle of her panic, though, Nora could not help feeling indignant, almost insulted. The bats; the snake; the blindness; Yaioni's maneuvering to get Nora to fall off the staircase, without even considering whether Nora might know a levitation spell or two—it was all so clumsy and stupid.

All at once she saw what Aruendiel would no doubt have seen from the very beginning—that Yaioni was not a very good magician, and that this so-called challenge was jerry-rigged from a handful of rather basic spells. They could be deadly enough, though. Nora knew no spells to counteract snake venom. She allotted a few luxurious seconds to do nothing but hate Yaioni with a rage too pure for words.

Gratifyingly, Yaioni screamed.

Nora raised her head, and this time she saw light. Flames, real fire, not the illusion of it. She blinked.

The world had returned. She could make out the shape of the looming cliffs against the night sky and the glimmering curtain of the waterfall; she could see the churning foam a few feet below her. The bottom of the Stairs of Healing was only an arm's length away. She scrabbled her way onto a step, then ran up the stairs, enjoying the solid stone under her sandals.

A tall bonfire was lit at the top of the stairs, a column of light. The bonfire was Yaioni. Flames were devouring her *maran*, casting a stark, brilliant light on her distorted face. Yaioni beat at them with both hands, roaring. Nora caught the acrid stink of burning hair.

And just a few feet away, the cool torrent of the waterfall. Yaioni turned, and Nora saw exactly what she would do next.

"Yaioni, wait!" she shouted.

Yaioni leaped through the air, bright and blazing as a comet. She landed at the top of the waterfall, swaying in the middle of a hissing cloud of steam and smoke.

Then she was over the edge. Nora threw a levitation spell at her, felt it catch—but she had reckoned without the force of plunging water. The torrent seized Yaioni. She crashed onto the rocks below. The last flames winked out.

Nora pounded down the stairs. Yaioni was a shadow in the moving water, streamers of pinkish foam unfurling from her body. Nora summoned a light and waded into the stream.

"Yaioni! Are you all right?" Yaioni didn't answer. Nora grabbed her arm to pull her to shore. Yaioni shrieked. Nora remembered the burns and cursed herself. "Here," she said. This time, the levitation spell did its work. With all the control she could muster, Nora raised Yaioni from the water and set her down on the bank of the stream as gently as she could.

"You're going to be fine, Yaioni," she said. It sounded stupidly unconvincing.

Yaioni moved her head. "Your Holiness, forgive me," she said. "I failed." Nora began to say she shouldn't worry about that right now, but Yaioni went on: "The heretic lives. Her unholy power was too strong. I failed."

"Don't feel bad, you did your best," Nora said. "Listen, I'll go find your friends—the other deaconess, Uliverat, and what's his name—"

"Goddess, forgive me." Yaioni's voice rose. "I was too weak to serve you correctly. Forgive your unworthy servant." She stared at Nora.

Nora looked down and felt her heart choke. She had forgotten the snake.

It was still twined around Nora's arm, its small yellow eyes only inches from Nora's own. The set of its mouth, like an old man's, gave it a curiously self-righteous look. Nora fought down the urge to scream with an almost physical effort, like throwing her weight on a bursting suitcase.

"Forgive me, Goddess," Yaioni said again, and began muttering something in another language.

The snake's head moved suddenly, as though it was zeroing in on a place to bite. Nora stiffened as it slipped around her rib cage.

But instead, the snake coiled downward along her body with dexterous intimacy, circling her waist, thighs, knees. When it reached the ground, Nora slowly exhaled. Yaioni extended a shaky hand toward the snake.

"Mother of Power! Give me your kiss, and I will be well again. Please. Your holy kiss."

Did Yaioni actually *want* to be bitten? Nora froze. Rearing, the snake faced Yaioni for a long instant. Then it flowed away into the darkness.

That was a deliberate snub, Nora thought. Yaioni dropped her head and sobbed quietly.

"Yaioni?" Uliverat's voice, sounding frightened. A light appeared some distance away, then bounced closer. Uliverat's thickset figure and worried face appeared out of the darkness. "What has happened?" she asked, out of breath. "I heard some—"

Her voice trailed off when she saw Yaioni. Most of the First Deaconess's *maran* was burned away; the skin on her naked shoulders and breasts was splotched red, already starting to blister. One of her legs splayed out at an odd angle.

"She's badly burned," Nora said. "And she fell off the waterfall. Is there anyone here who's a doctor?" Their precious goddess was supposed to be in charge of healing.

"Oh, yes, yes, of course." Uliverat sounded distracted. "Oasme—he'll know what to do. He's very good." Her eyes roamed over Nora, her brow slightly furrowed.

"She tried to kill me, but it didn't work," Nora said. "If that's what you're wondering."

"I angered Her Holiness, Uliverat," Yaioni said softly. "Her serpent would not bless me."

"Oh, dear goddess." In a lower voice, to Nora, Uliverat said: "I told her not to be rash. She wouldn't listen." She sighed.

"You knew she was going to attack me?" Nora tried to keep her voice level. "You could have said something."

"It wasn't the will of the goddess. Would you do me a favor, dear one, and run down to get Oasme? Young legs will be faster. He'll be in the building with the red arch."

Oasme's rather small eyes widened when he opened the door to Nora. For an instant he stared at her, his mouth crimped tight. He was another who'd been expecting Yaioni to triumph, Nora decided; she was in no mood to give anyone the benefit of the doubt. But he only clucked his tongue when Nora delivered her message, his expression turning shrewd and practical. Grabbing a covered basket from a shelf, he called out quickly; when one of the yellow-haired *ganoi* appeared, Oasme addressed him in that staccato language that Nora had heard earlier—even more urgent-sounding now—and then followed Nora to where Yaioni lay on the stream bank.

Without a word, he put wet compresses over her burns with swift, precise movements. Yaioni cried and groaned. At intervals, she implored her goddess's forgiveness. Mostly her voice was a storm of incoherent pain.

Nora looked away, grateful for Oasme's calm competence. She found herself wishing that she knew enough first aid to tend to Yaioni's wounds, then reminded herself that Yaioni had just tried to kill her. But that thought only depressed her more. Yaioni's machinations on the stairs seemed even more pathetic, almost childish. And that was before her fire spell had gone so horribly wrong. Yaioni had no business practicing magic if she couldn't control it better, Nora told herself. With a pang she wondered if Aruendiel had had the same thoughts about her.

The acolyte had arrived with several men in short robes. They began to ease the First Deaconess onto a litter, to be carried to the sick house, Nora gathered, although Yaioni kept making a disjointed appeal to go to the temple: "If she sees me, she'll forgive me."

Uliverat turned to Nora, as though reminded of something. "Did she say the evening prayers?"

"We never got past these stairs." The so-called Stairs of Healing.

Uliverat's mouth pursed. "Then I will say the prayers. You'll come with me, won't you?"

What a thing to worry about at a time like this, Nora thought. Although Nora had her own concerns. "I must talk to Sisoaneer. Right now," she said. Uliverat looked at her oddly, so she clarified: "The woman I came with last night. I have to talk to her. She brought me here, and it was very kind of her, and I appreciate that she saved my life last night, but I think I'm ready to leave now."

Under her *maran*, Uliverat's round face puckered, as though she did not entirely understand Nora's meaning or did not approve of it, but she nodded. "The temple is the best place to seek her."

"Good, then let's go," Nora said. "Unless you're planning to attack me, too, in which case you might as well do it now and get it over with."

Uliverat gave a gasping laugh. "I wouldn't think of it."

They both stood aside as the litter passed. Nora got only a glimpse of Yaioni, her eyes squeezed shut, her face tight and agonized.

"You must understand," Uliverat said, with a faintly admonitory air, "Yaioni is not always so—so foolish and headstrong as she was tonight. I told her she should wait, and let herself be guided by the love of the goddess—"

"Yes, she told me how much she loved the goddess just before she attacked me," Nora said. After a moment, she asked, "Do you think she'll be all right?"

"It will be as Her Holiness wills." Uliverat's voice sounded both quavering and vehement. "We'll say a special prayer tonight for the First Deaconess."

Nora wanted to say, *Fine, you can pray all you want*, but with unwilling respect for Yaioni's pain if nothing else, she held her tongue.

By the light of Uliverat's lantern, they followed the worn stone path upstream. Uliverat kept chattering about the spring flood and the ensuing cleanup. Evidently, she and Yaioni also lived in the Old Dormitory. "Naturally, it was built for many more," Uliverat said. "Praise Her Holiness, those empty rooms will be filled again. But it all needs more repair, and there are always so many other things to do! You cannot depend on the *ganoi*—they only work when they feel like it."

"Mmm," said Nora, more intrigued by their surroundings. Past the Old Dormitory, the path began to climb as the gorge narrowed. To their left, in a sinuous, deep-worn channel, the unseen stream grumbled and churned. The walls of the ravine leaned close, polished by patient water into bulbous, undulating curves that glistened damply in the lantern light. They looked more like heavy flesh than stone. The path felt claustrophobic, but in an intriguing way; you wanted to see what lay behind the next bend.

At intervals, flatter surfaces of stone had been carved with inscriptions in an unknown alphabet and with bas-reliefs that Nora only glimpsed as she passed: rows of tiny figures, dancing or fighting; a snake devouring a man in armor; a woman in a feathered crown, holding flowers and a knife. In the jolting light of Uliverat's lantern, the small forms sometimes looked as though they were moving, heads flicking sideways to watch Nora's progress.

The path turned abruptly, crossing the stream on a small, arched bridge. In the middle of the bridge, Uliverat paused, lifting her lantern. "The Door of Mercy!" she announced.

Across a frothy pool was the grandiose white column of another waterfall, glittering, deafening. This was the tallest yet, its top hidden in the night. The air was chilly with spray; the roar of the falls crashed against Nora's ears. She frowned questioningly at Uliverat, who smiled with sly pride and pointed: "This way."

They followed the path along the side of the gorge and beneath a projecting rock. Nora found herself under the spangled canopy of falling water. Carved into the rock face was a tall archway, flanked by twin statues. A faint light flickered inside.

So this was their famous temple, hidden under the waterfall. Nora gave a grudging smile. "Cool," she shouted over the sound of the torrent, falling back on the English word; it had no real equivalent in Ors.

Uliverat had no trouble figuring out what she meant. "The pilgrims are always surprised, even when they know," she yelled in Nora's ear. "There was a cave here, originally, that was hollowed out. It's beautiful—you'll see."

Nora nodded, and it occurred to her that she might as well treat this temple visit as the opportunity for an art history lesson, the way she'd once toured Chartres and Notre Dame. She squinted critically at the statues guarding the door as she followed Uliverat inside. Something

Egyptian-looking about the two substantial female figures, but it was hard to see very much.

Inside, she wasn't sure she agreed that the sanctuary could be called beautiful. Impressive, perhaps. The builders had burrowed deep into the hillside, opening up a space big enough to give an echoing hollowness to the sound of Nora's and Uliverat's footsteps. Corpulent, smoke-blackened pillars crowded the interior, striping the chamber with shadow. A dim, stiff jumble of figures, carved in relief and tinted with faded paint, covered the walls. The air was chilly, aromatic with incense and a persistent ecumenical mustiness that reminded Nora of those European cathedrals.

The light came from the far end of the sanctuary, where a small fire burned on a round hearth before an outsize statue of the goddess. This one was done in a different style than the sculptures outside: flowing draperies, a more naturalistic pose. The goddess held a knife in one hand and a small flask in the other. One elbow rested on a skull. Her head was garlanded with real flowers, pink and white blossoms, already slightly wilted.

The goddess's feet were hidden under a heap of small objects that looked disturbingly like broken dolls. Then Nora saw that they were miniature clay models of feet, legs, arms, hands, ears, eyes, teeth, noses, heads, torsos—in some cases complete figures of humans or animals.

"You see how many people Her Holiness has cured?" Uliverat asked, indicating the pile. "And this is not all. The more valuable thank-offerings are in the Treasury. Periodically they are melted down for other uses. The previous High Priest had some lovely golden goblets made for himself—which was not proper. Very disrespectful." She shook her head, frowning, as though she disliked even having to mention this solecism. "We restored them to the goddess."

Nora considered this. A question presented itself. "And what happened to the High Priest? He is no longer here?"

"He was unworthy to serve Her Holiness," Uliverat said. "The goddess has decreed she will have no more High Priests, only a High Priestess." She lowered her voice. "There were many mistaken practices being carried on here, when we first came. The goddess has purified Erchkaii of all that blasphemy. Praised be Her Holiness!"

What else besides golden goblets counted as blasphemy? Nora wondered. "Where were you before you came here?" she asked.

"We followed Her Holiness through many lands until she led us here." With some feeling Uliverat added: "Such a long way! I still feel it in my feet."

"'We'? You and—"

"The First Deaconess and I. We were the most faithful. Even when they threw stones at us, we did not desert her. Now I must say the evening prayers." Uliverat took up a position in front of the statue and began to sing in a sweet, thin soprano that wavered a little when she tried to bridge the larger intervals.

Nora found that she could understand snatches of the song, an invocation in a very old form of Ors. "You who see clearly in the night and in all dark places, to whom the waters and the winds pay heed, who commands the fire and comprehends the earth—" She remembered reading a few spells in the same dialect, with difficulty, from one of the frailest, most yellowed scrolls in Aruendiel's library.

Her mind conjured up Aruendiel, so real that her breath caught. She saw him leaning over her table, frowning at the parchment. The ancient grammar was something even he had to pause to recollect. "Is this older than you?" she'd asked, playing innocent. Instead of scowling and saying something about the respect a pupil owed her teacher, he'd laughed. And sounded more happy than rueful, as though pleased that she'd ventured to breach the formal reserve, the invisible fortifications that lay between them then.

Where was he now? He could not really be dead, surely. She resolved that she would not consider that possibility again. It was too black. Another option, only slightly brighter: Ilissa had enchanted him, the way she did long ago. Nora tried to imagine Aruendiel as Ilissa's malleable love-slave. The picture didn't quite come into focus but was still disturbing to contemplate.

Even worse to imagine: the look on Aruendiel's face yesterday as she cursed at him. The barriers refortified, the hopeful light in his eyes trapped and dying. Nora winced at the memory. No matter what, she had to find him again. And then what?

"You make your enemies fall dead at a word, you curse the evildoer with sickness and affliction," Uliverat was singing. "Protect us while we sleep." She paced a slow half circle around the statue and back again, lifting her arms at intervals.

Nora watched her for a minute, then moved away. More offerings were heaped at the perimeter of the room; Nora discovered this when she stepped on a pile of small objects that rolled and cracked under her foot. She swore briefly in English—Uliverat would be scandalized if she understood—and then conjured a light. Dropping to her hands and knees, she searched out the clay shards and began piecing them together.

Under her fingers, she felt the fragments recall their old shapes. She restored a tiny hand and elbow. An ear. A finger. Correction, a penis. A blob that could be any of several different organs. As magic went, this kind of repair spell wasn't very complicated or interesting, as Aruendiel had once informed her. It was, however, restorative for jangled nerves. A few columns away, Uliverat was still chanting. Nora found herself humming along as she worked.

The last of the broken offerings, a miniature leg, was missing its ankle. Nora sat back on her heels and looked around for the lost fragment.

"Here you are." Sisoaneer leaned down, holding out the missing piece.

"Thanks." Trying not to show her startlement, Nora took the small, curved shard and slotted it into the gap between foot and shin. She looked up to meet Sisoaneer's inquisitive dark eyes.

"You enjoy that, don't you?" Sisoaneer said. "Mending things."

It was not what Nora was expecting to hear. "I broke them. I thought I should fix them." She was conscious that she sounded brusque. "But yes, I do like mending things. This was the first spell I learned."

"Really?" Sisoaneer's half smile broadened. "What happened? Did your teacher break a goblet and tell you to repair it?"

"It was a bowl," Nora said, intrigued. "How did—"

"Would you like to mend more than just broken clay?" Sisoaneer's expression took on a new, subtle seriousness, whole histories expressed in the curve of her mouth. "Broken bodies, broken souls?"

"Broken *souls?*" Nora shook her head. "I wouldn't begin to know how to do that."

"Well, you start with mending bodies, and then go on from there."

"I'm not sure what you mean," Nora said.

"Come on, I want to talk to you, and this temple is stuffy. They use too much incense. I keep dropping hints, but—" She gave a resigned, delicate shrug.

"And I want to talk to you." Nora stood up. "I'm ready to leave here. I don't know if you know what this woman Yaioni did to me tonight—"

"I know all about that. You did very well." Sisoaneer was already moving swiftly among the columns.

"If I hadn't, I would be dead right now. I wasn't expecting to be attacked. Last night you said something about how even the strong need to rest, but this evening has been anything but restful—"

Nora noted with some puzzlement that Sisoaneer was leading her toward the rear of the temple, not the exit. They reached the open area in front of the great statue, where Uliverat still sang and paced.

Finishing a turn, the Second Deaconess gave a visible start when she caught sight of Sisoaneer. The fine silk of her song snarled, almost snapped. Uliverat sank to her knees and bowed until her forehead touched the pavement, somehow recovering the melody with a slightly off-key warble.

"Lovely, lovely, Uliverat, your holy queen is very pleased," Sisoaneer said with severe warmth. Glancing at Nora, she pointed behind the looming bulk of the goddess's statue. The giant figure lounged in an alcove in the back of the sanctuary, appearing from Nora's current position to be thumbing a remote while staring at an invisible screen. The back of the alcove was the raw rock of the ravine, slit with a narrow fissure, about the height of a human being. For most human beings, though, it would be a tight fit.

Nora looked at Sisoaneer. "We're going in there? I don't like small spaces, not that small."

"Are you afraid?" Sisoaneer asked with interest. "Truly, you don't need to be. You have nothing to fear." It seemed to Nora that Sisoaneer put undue emphasis on *you.* She remembered the villagers choking last night.

Uliverat was still singing the prayers, lying on the floor, the curve of her back just visible beyond the statue's knee. Nora turned back to the crevice and regarded it somberly.

"What's in there?" she asked.

Sisoaneer's eyes had a way of crinkling that managed to suggest she was laughing with you and at you simultaneously. "There are passages that lead down to very deep, very dark caves—where I was born long ago. But we're going up instead."

"You were born here?" Nora asked. That seemed odd. The thought came to her, not for the first time, that Sisoaneer might be a little mad.

And then—without quite abandoning that thesis—Nora saw what she had missed, what no one had bothered to explain. "You're not the High Priestess," she said. "Are you."

"Oh, no!" Sisoaneer said, shaking her head, smiling. "Wherever did you get that idea?"

"*You* are the goddess." This was a sentence that Nora had never imagined herself uttering without hyperbole or irony.

"Yes." She seemed pleased that Nora had finally caught on.

The goddess. Nora looked hard at her. Her face, her body seemed human enough. No halo, nothing to suggest divinity. Although when you got right down to it, what did goddesses look like? Botticelli's ethereal half-shell Venus; sloe-eyed Isis on the side of a sarcophagus; stern, helmeted Athena silhouetted in red and black. Was that the point, that gods and goddesses were pictured differently at different times and different places, that you always had to fill in the face of divinity for yourself?

The woman beside Nora could pass for one of those dark-eyed, long-necked Italian Madonnas, enigmatic smile and all. (The Virgin Mary wasn't technically a goddess, Nora allowed, but she was close enough.) Sisoaneer leaned past Nora and touched the edge of the crevice. Under her hand the rock flexed like a living thing and the fissure gaped wider, big enough for a normal-sized human to enter, even one wearing a *maran*.

"Go in, and I will show you my home."

Nora thought: oh, well, how often do you get to see where a goddess lives? Her mother always said that that's how you really start to know people, when they invite you over and you can see their furniture, their pictures, the books in the bookcase. For a loony moment, Nora pictured herself and Sisoaneer sitting amid chintz and plants and glass-topped tables—a place not too different from her mother's sunroom, come to think of it—and somehow, keeping that image in mind, she got herself to step into the hole in the rock.

A few feet from the entrance, to her relief, the cave broadened into a passageway tall enough for them to walk upright. It sloped upward, curving to the right. Nora's companion took the lead.

"Do you prefer Sisoaneer or Her Holiness?" Nora heard a tinge of irony in her own words and wondered if Sisoaneer also heard it.

Her companion shrugged lightly. "Either. People call on me with different names. Here at Erchkaii, they are a bit more formal." She gave Nora a sideways glance, the corners of her mouth puckered as though they were trying to tamp down laughter. "Who did you think I was, when we met last night?"

"A magician. A very powerful magician, obviously." That did not seem quite adequate, so Nora added: "Doing good deeds." In the middle of nowhere, in the middle of the night—no, when you looked at it more closely, the theory left much unexplained. But a goddess? "What were you doing there?" she asked.

"I travel from here sometimes. People need my help. Like you."

Nora suddenly realized that although neither of them was carrying a light, she could still see the passageway reasonably well. Some sort of illumination clung to Sisoaneer, as it had the night before. Was this how a halo worked? It wasn't light, exactly, but wherever Sisoaneer went, you could see the things around her. Whereas, a gap in the rock they were now passing brimmed with inky obscurity.

"That's an entrance to the deep places," Sisoaneer said, following Nora's glance. "There are dozens of paths down, but it's not so easy to find your way back."

"Where you were born, you said."

"'Where the last true darkness dwells.' As the hymn says." Sisoaneer raised her eyebrows impishly. "No mortal man or woman has returned from those depths, ever. But along here it's easy to find your way—just keep turning right."

They were still climbing, the passageway tending clockwise. "And where are we going, exactly?" Nora asked, thinking she should have cleared this up earlier.

Sisoaneer pulled her forward. "Here, I want you to see this," she said as they rounded a sudden corner. "I've brought you to the very top."

The timbre of their footsteps shifted subtly, and the dank stuffiness of the cave dissolved as they stepped under a stone lintel and into the open air. Nora found herself standing on rock that sloped downward on all sides. A chilly night breeze washed around her body and fluttered the ends of her *maran*. The moon glimmered dully through a grazing flock of clouds.

Nora stood stock-still, fighting some dizziness. The narrow enclosure of the cave seemed almost comforting in retrospect, replaced now by a disorienting amount of space. She wished that the top of this mountain were wider. She could dimly make out the burly, hunched shoulders of other mountains, surrounding her peak like a gang of watchful henchmen.

"We didn't climb nearly enough to get this high," Nora said. "We were in the cave for what, ten minutes?" A temporary dislocation spell, she thought, or an augmentation spell. But she had never heard of an augmentation spell powerful enough to raise a mountain peak a thousand feet in a minute.

"This mountain isn't always exactly the same size," Sisoaneer said with an air of satisfaction. "It's as I want it to be." She turned slowly, gazing over the dark, rolling ridges, and then raised her face and let the wind lift her tangled hair.

"This is also my sanctuary," she said. "*My* holy place. Down there"— she gestured carelessly—"I take care of those who need me. They come from everywhere to ask for my help, to be cured, to be saved. Like children. So many of them." She was silent for a moment. "Here, it's different. I am free, and no one can find me, and I am as eternal as the mountains, and even stronger than they are."

She gave Nora a sideways glance. "Not many come to this place."

"You brought me here," Nora said.

Sisoaneer nodded. "Do you know why?"

"I have no idea," Nora said. She looked up at the sky. The thin scattering of stars visible through the clouds seemed closer and more tangible—homier, even—than the dark void of the valleys below. "Are you really a goddess?" She hadn't exactly intended to ask the question aloud, because it would be so easy for Sisoaneer, goddess or no, to take it the wrong way, but she couldn't help it.

Sisoaneer's smile stretched like a lazy cat. Her fingertips brushed Nora's arm. "Listen," she said. "Even up here you can hear them." She pointed toward the horizon.

"Over there, over those mountains, there is a boy, the son of a shepherd, calling to me from his tent. His father's leg is injured, the wound is full of disease, he prays for my help. Listen!" She paused, and Nora did hear a boy's voice, very faint, not speaking a language Nora knew, but the tone of desperation was unmistakable.

"And there, to the south, in the city of Nenaveii, a woman prays to me secretly. I have another temple there—built by many kings, larger even than this one—but she can't go, she's afraid to make her petition in public. She gave up her honeycomb to a man who isn't her husband, now she fears her womb is full. Do you hear?"

This small voice was speaking some version of Ors. The woman was asking Sisoaneer for a miscarriage and praying that her suspicious husband would only beat her instead of killing her. As Nora listened, her initial curiosity gave way to a sick feeling. This was real; the woman was sobbing with fear.

"Are you going to answer their prayers?" she asked.

"I always listen to those who call on me with true faith and love," Sisoaneer said.

That all sounded blameless enough, but Sisoaneer's words snagged unpleasantly on Nora's ears. "Your First Deaconess, Yaioni, said she prayed to you before she attacked me."

"Yes!" Sisoaneer's fine brows crumpled together, telegraphing be-mused, helpless concern over Yaioni's foolishness. "She wanted to challenge you. But she is not powerful enough. She has not learned enough magic. I knew you would prevail."

"But you still answered her prayer?" The question felt odd in Nora's mouth. "I mean, did you tell her it would be all right to try to kill me?"

"You are stronger and braver. That is important. I have tried to teach so many, and they were too fearful, or they did not know enough to protect themselves. Yaioni failed."

"The point is, you told Yaioni she could attack me. Isn't that right?"

"She prayed to me, and I gave her what she wished—just as I answered your prayer last night."

"I didn't pray, exactly," Nora said. "I said, 'Help!' I was calling for help."

"And I answered your call. I am the mother of your power, your magic, and I will not let my faithful servants come to harm."

"But I'm not your faithful servant."

"You serve me already, better than you know, and that is only the beginning."

"I don't think—" Nora began, but Sisoaneer held up a hand to silence her.

"Dear child, I brought you here to honor you, to make you more powerful than any other magician in the world. I am Sisoaneer of the Mysteries, Queen of Holy Power and Healing, and I have chosen you to be my High Priestess. You will be my emissary to the world, you will rule Erchkaii, you will lead my worshippers, you will celebrate my name. And in return, I will favor you above all others, I will teach you the secrets of my most holy magic, and there will be no limit to your power."

Chapter 15

"Ligh Priestess?" Nora stared at the goddess. "You're—offering me a job?"

Sisoaneer gave her a luminous smile, and Nora saw that Sisoaneer was not exactly extending an offer; she had already decided that Nora would accept the position.

"Wait—" Nora held up a hand against the swiftly rising tides of misunderstanding. "It's very nice of you to think of me for this, but I'm not interested. I'm exactly the wrong person. I'm not religious at all, I don't believe in God."

She thought Sisoaneer might be offended, but Sisoaneer only looked intrigued. "Do you not believe in me?"

"Well—" It was a good question. If there are gods and goddesses, Nora thought, this woman is powerful enough—and odd enough—to be one. That doesn't mean that I feel any impulse to worship her—any more than if I met Zeus, say, I would feel like sacrificing an ox to him.

Oh, maybe I'd do that for Athena. Or Apollo.

And Sisoaneer was not the unseen, judgmental, omnipotent God that, to the best of Nora's belief, did not exist. "I acknowledge your power—your holy power," Nora said diplomatically. "But I'm sorry, I'm not ready to bow down and worship you. It would be a lie."

Sisoaneer's dark eyes widened. "You are honest. So many people would say anything to be as honored and powerful as you will be."

Nora chose to ignore the implicit prediction. "I don't want to mislead you," she said. "What I really want is to leave this place. Erchkaii," she added for clarity, hoping that she had not missed any vowels.

"But where would you go?" Sisoaneer asked with what sounded like genuine concern. "Where is your home?"

Such a simple question, but an unsettling one. Nora was uncertain how to answer it. "Far away," she said finally. "If you could take me back to where you found me—not the exact village, necessarily—I could find my way from there."

"You want to rejoin your companion?" Sisoaneer asked. "The one you said you'd been separated from." Nora nodded, trying to remember exactly what she had said the night before. "Is he your husband?" Sisoaneer inquired.

"Oh, no!" Nora said, too quickly. "My teacher."

"Ah," Sisoaneer said, her brows lifting slightly. "Aruendiel."

Nora tensed. "I don't think I told you his name."

"I know his magic well. I see its traces in you."

The idea that she carried some recognizable mark of Aruendiel's teaching was a small, unexpected solace, but Nora frowned, partly to hide the comfort it gave her. "How do you know Aruendiel—or his magic? I've never heard him mention you."

"No?" For an instant Sisoaneer's smile grew thin and sharp and dangerous, and then she looked only amused. "I know Aruendiel's magic as I know the magic of every magician. And Aruendiel is a very famous magician in the kingdoms of men, or he was. I do not hear his name as often as I used to, when I travel beyond Erchkaii."

"He leads a quiet life. Most of the time. When do you next leave Erchkaii?"

Sisoaneer shook her head. "When I'm called," she said. "And even I do not know when that will come."

"Well, can you send me back by myself? Tell the boat, or the stream—or whatever it was—where to go?"

"Would you like to know how to do that? The magic to make a stream wander over the land? Or over the ocean—or through the sky itself?" Sisoaneer's voice rose with a happy, teasing, knowing lilt. "It's not so hard. I mean, it won't be, for you. My High Priestess will know that magic and more. You are ready for a new teacher."

"Well, but no," Nora demurred. "I'm what you could call a professional student, and Aruendiel is one of the best teachers I've ever had." If he still cares to teach me, she thought. "I'm sorry. It's just not my nature to be your priestess, or anyone's priestess. This position just isn't a good fit."

She had used the same phrase—in English—several times in her life, to the manager of the slick seafood place in Jersey City that burned down under suspicious circumstances the next month, to hopeful Dr. Hadler, looking for a research assistant for his critical edition of the unedited million-word first draft of *Look Homeward, Angel*. But she had never meant those words more than she did now.

Sisoaneer did not respond at first. Then she said: "Do you see where we are?"

At first Nora did not understand what she meant, and then she did. They were standing in midair, she and Sisoaneer. She was suddenly aware of cold wind under her soles, and she could make out the torches in the temple complex, twinkling far below, no brighter than the stars. Nora sucked in her breath. No matter how good she got at levitation spells, she was never going to be quite at ease with heights, and this was higher than she'd ever been before, except for airplanes. She tried to hold very still in the air, not shifting her weight an ounce, as though that would keep her from falling.

"It's my power that is keeping you alive right now—my will that you don't fall," Sisoaneer said mildly. "Yet you will not worship me?"

"No," Nora said, not very loud. In her mind she began readying a levitation spell. She had never done one at this height before. She could only guess how far below the ground was.

"Conjure a light for me, please."

"What?"

"Didn't Aruendiel teach you how? To take light from fire?"

"Well, yes." It was one of the first derivative spells she had learned. Nora opened her hand to cup the light, and in her mind she reached out to borrow illumination from the flames of the torches below. But she could not seem to get their attention. The distant fire burned on serenely, ignoring her.

"It's not working," Nora had to say, ruefully. She recalled now that something like this had happened yesterday, when she'd tried to douse the fire that Raclin breathed. (Was it only yesterday?) "Those torches are too far away. Or some kind of enchantment—"

"The fire in those torches answers only to me," Sisoaneer said quietly. "There is no magic here but mine."

"But Yaioni did magic, and so did I," Nora objected.

"I lent Yaioni my power, just as I lent you power to meet her challenge. More power, I think, than you had ever wielded before. You did well with it."

"I don't understand. That was *your* magic?"

Sisoaneer nodded, with the kind of patience one shows to a small, not very bright child. "They were your spells, you worked them. But I lent you the power."

"I didn't know it could work that way," Nora said with some confusion. She had to admit, she hadn't thought consciously about where she had drawn power to levitate the snake, to pull herself out of that fall. Very careless, Aruendiel would say. A good magician keeps close and constant track of the nearest sources of power, whether fire, stone, water, wood, or something else, so that he is never unprepared to work magic. (*She* is never unprepared, and I was distracted, Nora told her imagined Aruendiel, knowing that the excuse would carry no weight with him.)

She felt some inquietude at the idea that she had been using Sisoaneer's power unknowingly. And I was so proud of pulling out of that fall, she thought.

"Try again," Sisoaneer said. "I will let the fire listen to you this time."

With care, Nora again worked the spell to summon light. The apprehension she felt did not affect the results: a great plume of light rose from her outstretched palm and showed Sisoaneer looking at her expectantly, her eyes sparkling in the new illumination.

"Very nice," she said. "Now do you see what I mean? My High Priestess will have power without measure. You could make a new sun, if you wanted."

That does *not* sound like a good idea, Nora thought. Another sun, where would you put it? Yet Sisoaneer's manner, as she made the suggestion, had been disturbingly matter-of-fact.

"I'd rather do my own magic, all of it, start to finish," Nora said. "It's more fun that way."

"You would be dead now if I had not lent you my power already," Sisoaneer said. "Yaioni attacked you viciously. But you counterattacked even more fiercely."

"Well—" Nora rocked her hand in an equivocal gesture. "She basically self-destructed, catching fire like that."

"You set her on fire," Sisoaneer corrected.

Surprised, Nora shook her head. "No, I didn't."

"You did. Do you not remember?"

"She did it herself—trying to set *me* on fire, I suppose, and—"

"I saw the whole thing. It was my magic you were fighting with, remember?" Sisoaneer's eyes were grave. "Yaioni is not skilled with fire magic. She knows only a few little spells, like making light. When you ignited her clothes, she could not extinguish the flames herself."

"That can't be right. I didn't mean to *burn* her." Nora's face felt hot, as though she were about to burst into flames herself. She steadied her voice. "It all happened so fast. I don't remember everything, exactly." There had been other times when she had made fire a weapon without meaning to. And now this. Nora tried not to remember the sight of the ravaged, blistered skin on Yaioni's shoulders. Then she made herself remember it.

The magic's not as good if you can't control it. What would Ramona think of her now?

"How is Yaioni?" Nora asked. "Will she survive?"

Sisoaneer pointed downward. "Listen," she said. "What do you think?"

At first, Nora heard nothing. Then a slurred, tired, relentless voice. "Holiness, forgive me. Help me. Forgive me. Have mercy. Mercy." The kind of prayer that was really a symptom of unforgiving pain, a sign that no one could help you anymore. But this time there was a real, live goddess to hear.

Nora regarded Sisoaneer, whose head was bowed, her eyes cast into shadow. "Aren't you going to help her?" she asked. "She's *praying* to you."

"I answered her prayer before. She failed." Sisoaneer sounded regretful.

"She only gets one chance? But she's suffering. She's in pain. Aren't you the goddess of healing?"

Sisoaneer raised her head. "When you cause pain, it will always come back to you somehow. Always, always. Do you understand that?" Her steady dark gaze was an unbearable weight; Nora felt shifty, unreliable, but she forced herself to meet the goddess's eyes. Sisoaneer went on:

"To heal, that is the best use of power. When you heal someone, you are healed, too."

"So, will you help her?"

Sisoaneer said nothing. Yaioni's distant prayers continued, as frail and maddening as the whine of a mosquito.

"She's going to die, isn't she? Because of me." Nora balled her hands into fists. "And you're just going to abandon her? You told me that you hear the prayers of those who have faith—and love."

With a twitch of her head, Sisoaneer seemed to rouse herself from whatever thoughts had been preoccupying her. She smiled at Nora, as though Nora had said something that pleased her mightily, and reached out to squeeze Nora's clenched fist, the same hand she had healed the night before.

"I have not abandoned Yaioni. My High Priestess is a healer, always. I will deny you nothing. Whatever you ask, in my name, I will give you."

"What do you mean?" Nora asked, hoping that she had misunderstood.

"You only have to ask."

Sisoaneer disappeared. The cloud-strewn sky was replaced by a smaller, stuffier darkness.

Nora found herself looking up at the shadowy stone visage of the goddess's statue, still crowned with limp flowers. She was back in the temple, alone. The fire on the round hearth had died down to a few glinting coals. After the cool wind on the mountaintop, the air felt heavy with smoke and damp.

She knotted her hands together and stared hard at the statue, making herself take in the details. It was just a statue. The same tawny rock as the temple. Too dark to see much now. She would have liked to examine the face more carefully, to see if there was any resemblance at all to the woman she had just been speaking with.

She pivoted slowly, scrutinizing the dark forest of pillars. All was quiet. She was alone here, as far as she could tell.

Alone but not ignored, according to Sisoaneer.

Nora took a deep breath. She knelt, trying to cushion her knees somewhat with a fold of her gown, and bowed her head. A fragment of Emily Dickinson came to mind: *My period had come for prayer, no other art would do.* Nora had knelt like this only occasionally in her life, Christmas and Easter when she was a kid, EJ's funeral. The few times she'd gone to her mother's church, they stood up. What to say?

"All right," she said aloud. "Dear Sisoaneer—" Too Judy Blume? She went on: "Please help Yaioni. Soothe her burns, please heal them. Please be merciful."

There, I've done it, I've prayed, Nora thought. Can I go now?

Very faintly, she caught the sound of Yaioni's moaning, persistent, unnerving. Nora looked around, but she was still alone.

"Please," Nora said, raising her voice to drown out Yaioni's. "Please heal Yaioni. Take away her pain." For the first time, Nora wished she had gone to church more often and could rattle off some appropriate prayers. Sisoaneer wouldn't know if they were repurposed from a Christian liturgy. *Batter my heart, three-personed God*—not quite right here.

"Please be kind to Yaioni. Forgive her. Heal her. She loves you— um, Holy Queen of Power. Show her your grace. Ease her pain. For you are merciful and kind." It seemed to her that prayers often seemed to involve some measure of flattery. "You are powerful and loving, O Sisoaneer. Heal your servant Yaioni."

And still, whenever Nora paused for breath, Yaioni's fretful voice haunted her ears and the chambers of her mind.

"I ask you this, because you have been kind to me. Heal Yaioni, the way you healed me. Help her, the way you helped me."

Nora's knees ached. She wondered if Sisoaneer were even listening. What had Herbert said about prayer? *Church bells beyond the stars heard, soul's blood, the land of spices. Something understood.* Not this endless, inadequate pleading.

"Holy Queen, Mother of Power, please soothe Yaioni's burns, heal her broken bones, and fix anything else I did, I ask you wholeheartedly. Please show me your favor and make Yaioni well again."

She was running out of inspiration. "I'm giving you all I can, Sisoaneer. Please, holy—holy you. Only you can save her. Please save her. Please."

When Nora finally stopped speaking, the temple was very quiet, aside from the white noise of rushing water outside. She got to her feet stiffly. Her knees felt bruised and flattened.

At some point, she wasn't sure when, Yaioni's moaning had stopped.

I did what I could, Nora thought heavily. If it wasn't good enough, it's not my fault. *She* could have saved Yaioni anytime.

Even if you believe in a goddess, Nora thought, is that a reason to trust her?

At least Yaioni was no longer in pain. Nora shuffled toward the door of the temple, holding out her arms so that she wouldn't run into any of the columns in the darkness. At the archway, she stopped to let her ears fill with the soothing crash of the waterfall. Her eye caught a bobbing light.

Someone was coming. Nora waited warily. It might be Uliverat, coming to fetch her and tell her that her *maran* was in disarray. It might be the goddess. The light was close now, shedding glints of gold in the river as the person who carried it crossed the little bridge. Now it spilled upward to show that person's face. Yaioni's strong, dark features, looking fatigued and quiet. The skin of her face and arms smooth and unmarked.

As she approached, Nora let out her breath. "Are you all right?" she asked awkwardly, discovering that her feelings toward the First Deaconess were not quite as simple as she'd expressed them in the prayers. But she made herself say: "I'm sorry."

Yaioni hesitated, and then, so quickly that it took Nora by surprise, she went down on one knee, lifting her hands in a graceful gesture. Nora stared down at her, unsure of how to respond. "I thank you, Blessed Lady," Yaioni whispered harshly, her eyes cast down. She rose with the same swiftness, as though not wishing to prolong the encounter, and disappeared into the darkness inside the temple.

After a minute, Nora heard her begin to chant. Closing her eyes, Nora listened to the wavering flight of Yaioni's voice, straining to follow it over the thunder of the falling water.

Thank you, Nora thought but did not say.

Chapter 16

Aruendiel sat upright in the bed, noting with distaste that the effort still gave him a slight vertigo, and resolving at the same time to ignore it. "Well?" he demanded. "What did you find?"

Nansis Abora was looking down at the clutter of scrolls and books on the floor beside the bed. "Did you get up while I was out, Aruendiel? I am quite sure that I told you that you should rest."

Aruendiel scowled. "I have been doing nothing but rest for three days. What have you discovered? Anything?" He added, in a clipped tone calculated to hide his disappointment: "You didn't bring her back, obviously."

"No, I didn't," Nansis Abora said regretfully. He scratched his head, leaving his rusty-gray hair in some disorder. "I'm afraid I couldn't find her at all. I found the place you described without any trouble. The forest is mostly gone now. Was it really necessary to burn so much valuable timber? One of the villagers told me they lost a lovely grove of chest—"

"Nora was not in the fire, was she?" Aruendiel asked. He felt the vertigo again, much worse than before. Reckless, not to consider that the fire might endanger her. The poison had degraded his judgment.

"Oh, no, I don't believe so. You're pale, Aruendiel. I think you had better lie down."

"I'm fine. Where is she, then?"

"I don't know, but here is what I found out." Nansis Abora pulled up a stool to the bedside and sat down. "You were right, she did go to the village nearby. They told me all about it. Dear sun, the place was in an uproar. Nothing so interesting has happened there in a dozen dozen years."

Aruendiel's hand twitched on the blanket, as though ready to drag the story out of Nansis Abora by physical means. "Yes?"

"They said a witch with a bleeding hand had come to the village three nights ago. Some of the fingers on her hand had been cut off, although no one could agree on how many. I heard as many as seven."

"I found only one." Aruendiel gritted his teeth. "They called her a witch, did they?"

"Yes, I'm getting to that part. A man named Pelg saw a witch riding a dragon in the woods that day; he said they chased him, and he barely escaped with his life. Then, later, the witch came to the village and said that the dragon was dead and asked for their help. They couldn't agree on what to do with her at first—some of them didn't believe Pelg, he's known as a tippler—but then she showed she was a witch. So they decided to—" Nansis Abora paused, frowning, and looked shrewdly at Aruendiel. "Now don't distress yourself unduly. I really do believe she left the village unharmed."

"What did they do?" Aruendiel eyed Nansis Aborna like a dog about to snap at a piece of meat.

Nansis Abora sighed and shook his head. "Well, you can imagine, Aruendiel, ignorant folk like that—"

"I don't have to imagine. What did they do to her?"

Nansis Abora took another look at Aruendiel and evidently decided that full disclosure was the better course. "First they tried to burn her inside a hut—they showed it to me, what was left of it—but the fire went out."

One of Aruendiel's black eyebrows leaped. "Good. She remembered something."

"Oh, yes, I think she did well, especially for a young lady. You know, I think magicians as old as we are sometimes forget what it's like for the young ones—how difficult it is to recall the right spell the first time you get into a tight spot. I remember when I was twenty or so—"

"What happened to Nor—to Mistress Nora, Nansis?"

"Lie back, Aruendiel, you should not exert yourself. Well, then they decided to stone her."

Aruendiel's mouth tightened. Of course, knock the witch unconscious, then burn her—that was the preferred method. Nora should have been able to deflect the stones, he thought. But he recalled how clumsy she'd been with the stone at their last lesson.

It was excruciating to remember that episode, and not just because of Nora's lack of skill. He refocused his attention on Nansis. "What happened then?"

Cautiously Nansis Abora said: "They told me they thought they hit her a few times. But then the men who were stoning her began to choke. One of them died."

Aruendiel lifted an eyebrow in appreciation, then frowned suspiciously. "Nora doesn't know any suffocation spells," he said. "She has done nothing with air magic."

"This might explain it, then. The villagers said another witch appeared, and then they flew away."

"Another witch?"

"Yes, is that not curious? I wondered if they might be mistaken, but more than a dozen people saw her."

Aruendiel was silent for a moment. "What did she look like, the second woman? Did she have black skin?"

"You are thinking of Hirizjahkinis." A kind, apologetic smile moved across Nansis Abora's wrinkled face. "I don't believe it was her. I asked the same question, and they said no. A woman with brown hair, in a gray cloak. I thought it might be that troublesome Faitoren queen."

"Ilissa?" Aruendiel shook his head. His recollection of that night was imperfect, fogged by the poison, but Ilissa had been in his presence continuously, tormenting him, until the moment he had taken her prisoner. "No, she can cause no more trouble."

"Then I can't imagine who it might have been. I don't know of any other female magicians besides Hirizjahkinis. Do you, Aruendiel?" Aruendiel shook his head again, his pale eyes narrow and distracted. Nansis Abora went on: "I wonder why there are so few. Women are not suited for the rigors of study, perhaps. I don't believe any of my wives could read. No, I'm mistaken. Pelly could read quite well. She used to read to me in the evenings from the almanac."

"What else did they say about this other female magician?" Aruendiel demanded.

"One of the men said she had horns like an elk, but no one else remembered that. I tend to discount it."

"Did Nora go with her willingly?"

"Oh, they seemed to think so. I suppose the other woman could be a village witch of some kind. There used to be plenty of them in the country. Although I never heard of one flying. Not many country witches could even cure a sick goat, poor things."

"Or work a suffocation spell," Aruendiel said dismissively. He shifted impatiently under his blanket. "Where did they fly? What direction?"

"East, some of them said, but some said south, and some of them said they went straight up into the air."

Aruendiel cursed briefly. Nansis Abora sighed aloud, rubbing the side of his nose with one finger. "I wish I had brought back better news for you, Aruendiel. Or more news, anyway. But at least it is not worse news."

Aruendiel grunted in a manner that indicated that he did not find this observation helpful or reassuring.

"Will you be all right by yourself for a while longer?" Nansis Abora asked. "My neighbor up the road has a wife in labor, he asked me to look in on her. And you had better seek some rest. That is, honest rest, not looking through the books that you should not have gotten up to fetch in the first place." He extended a hand and waved at the nest of books and scrolls on the floor. They disappeared. "How is the numbness in your feet?"

"Virtually gone," Aruendiel said, glowering. "Otherwise I would not have been able to get up out of this bed at all."

Nansis Abora pursed his small, rosy mouth in a way that, for a moment, made him look almost cynical. "You're a very poor patient, Aruendiel. I suppose you have heard that before. Well, in a week or so, if you continue to mend, you may be able to set out yourself to see what has befallen Mistress Nora."

"A week? I would not impose on your hospitality so long, Nansis. A day or two, and I will go."

"We shall see, Aruendiel. It's not a great imposition to keep you here, no greater than having you fall on my thatch in the middle of the night with no more breath in you than a fish has. You were exactly as blue as one of my Pure Lake plums."

Aruendiel grimaced, preferring not to dwell on a moment of weakness that he could not recall anyway, having been virtually unconscious at the time. The opposite wall of the bedroom was lined with green glass jars and clay pots housing part of Nansis's considerable store of preserves. Presumably some of them contained those wretched plums of which the other magician spoke. "I have suffered worse," Aruendiel said, and even he could hear how ungracious his words sounded. He added: "But I am obliged to you, Nansis. There are few magicians who could have made any headway against that Faitoren poison. That is why I came to you."

"Well, it's very nasty stuff, that poison," Nansis Abora said severely, looking rather pleased. "I'd advise you to stay clear of it in the future. And now, that's enough talking. You really must rest."

Frowning, Aruendiel was about to say something else, but changed his mind. "All right," he said. The straw in the mattress rustled as he lay down. Nansis Abora raised his faded eyebrows in some surprise at Aruendiel's acquiescence but elected not to question good fortune. He inquired whether Aruendiel would like some water before he slept. "Only leave me undisturbed," Aruendiel said, closing his eyes.

Still the other magician hesitated. "It may be some hours before I am back. Babies take their time. There is more leek soup in the pot. But if you have some, you must conjure up a bowl. I do not want you getting out of bed again."

"Very well," Aruendiel muttered, trying to keep an edge out of his voice. He listened to the creak of the shutting door and the sounds of Nansis Abora moving about in the other room, probably reshelving the books that Aruendiel had taken down earlier. Those noises were followed by the slam of the kitchen door, as Nansis Abora went outside. Then Aruendiel began to wrap himself in layers of silence.

This was a spell of air magic, one that borrowed power from the vast restlessness of wind and sky. A spell that could reach halfway around the world, if necessary. He made himself deaf to his own heartbeat and the movement of air in his lungs; deaf to the sound of Nansis Abora's retreating footsteps; deaf to the cackle of chickens in the coop and the soft scratch of their feathers rubbing together; deaf to the creaking of tree branches; deaf to the thudding of horses' hooves on turf, on dirt, on the cobblestones of cities; deaf to the gurgle of water in a hundred streams and rivers; deaf to the cries of babies, the shouts and laughter and conversing of men and women—deaf to every human voice but one. He was listening for words shaped and spoken by one particular throat.

He waited. The voice that one sought had to actually say something aloud before it could be detected. The spell was less useful in the middle of the night, when most people were likely to be asleep. Even now, in early evening, if Nora were in some way isolated—imprisoned or wandering alone—she might have no cause to say anything aloud. Or, if she had been shape-changed into an animal or another human form, her voice would be unrecognizable. An injury to the throat or even a bad cold could defeat the spell. And even with the right voice, there was always a delay—for reasons Aruendiel did not understand, sounds from a great distance could take an hour or more to arrive within hearing.

Despite all the grounds for discouragement, he would hear her, if she still had breath to speak. He felt quite confident of that. He waited, ears tuned to the silent air with the kind of patience that he had for few things in life, magic being one of them.

"Aruendiel?" Nansis Abora pushed open the kitchen door and frowned at what he saw. He came inside the house, fumbling at the knot of his cloak. "What are you doing out of bed?"

Aruendiel, leaning over the kitchen table, did not respond at once. Still in his nightshirt, his long, dark hair tangled across his shoulders, he was studying a piece of parchment unrolled across the well-scrubbed planks of the table.

With a sigh, Nansis Abora lowered himself into a chair. "Well, she lost the baby, poor dear. Stillborn, a little boy. Galns, my neighbor—it's his wife—was beside himself. Six girls and no sons. Do you know, he wanted me to do an Eoluthian substitution with one of the daughters? I put out that candle right away. I told him if he wants a son, he'd better get back to bedding his wife instead of sacrificing one of his girls.

"I don't believe that kind of resurrection spell would work, anyway, if the little boy never drew breath in the first place. Poor mite. A very sad business." He shook his head.

"Mmm." Aruendiel did not look up. "It would have been sadder if you'd tried to do the Eoluthian substitution. Do you have any better maps than this one, Nansis?"

"Maps?" Nansis Abora's head swung around, like an old turtle's, and for the first time he regarded the scroll that Aruendiel was studying. "What are you looking for?" he asked, raising his voice. "I told you to rest."

Impatiently Aruendiel shook his head. The other man's voice seemed unnaturally loud after so many hours of silence. "Do you have a map of the Poscan regions? Or Iskii?" Aruendiel asked. Even his own voice was disturbingly raucous. "Anything east of Dor."

"Oh, dear, I gave most of my maps to my friend Polchix's son when he started in the navy. I don't travel much these days. Except for your war with the Faitoren, of course."

"These are all inland regions that I am looking at," Aruendiel observed. He refrained from noting that it was Ilissa, not himself, who had sparked hostilities the previous winter.

"So they are. Aruendiel, please sit down at least and put something over your shoulders. Is this so urgent that it could not wait for morning?" Nansis Abora disappeared into the bedroom and returned with a yellow wool blanket embroidered with spiky blue cornflowers. Aruendiel, still looking at the map, absently shrugged himself under the wrap. Nansis Abora regarded him critically for a moment and then went out of the kitchen again. He brought back a wooden box, which he placed on the table, and extracted a scroll in a leather case.

Aruendiel took the scroll from him and unrolled it. "This is a little better," he said, after a moment's examination. "At least it shows something of the nature of the country. Yes, that's right, it's all mountains from the Casken River to Lake Iskior."

"Do you think you have found Mistress Nora?" Nansis Abora asked, sitting down at the table.

"Not yet," Aruendiel said, but the lilt of excitement was in his voice. He added: "I have heard her, though. I have a better notion of where she is."

"A listening spell—is that why you shooed me out of the room?" Nansis Abora tut-tutted resignedly. "They're a bit imprecise at long distances, I always thought."

"Very," Aruendiel said, his eyes on the scroll. "If you want to understand what someone is saying. But for tracking quarry, they are quite useful."

"Oh, yes, you found that fellow with the invisible army that way. I remember. Well, where do you think she might be?"

"She is to the east of here, and a little south. At least four hundred *karistises* away. Near a temple of some sort."

"A temple?"

"She said something about leaving a temple. What are the temples in that country?" Aruendiel drummed his fingers on the table, then pointed to a spot on the map. "There is a shrine to some vulture god at Tior. The sun's temple near Qu," he added, moving his finger. "And some sort of complex near Ahnamata, is there not?"

"The necropolis," said Nansis Abora. "Oh, I believe there are at least a dozen temples there." He craned his neck to look at the map over Aruendiel's elbow. "Then there is Farlex, Erchkaii, Horba, the monastery at Nuelstona. And you know, Aruendiel, she could have been talking of any little village shrine."

"I have considered that," Aruendiel said, with something like a snarl. "One must start somewhere. And she is certainly somewhere in this region." He drew his hand across the map, indicating a diagonal swath of territory stretching southwest to northeast.

Nansis Abora frowned slightly, his pale blue eyes worried, but he said: "The sanctuary at Horba has been sealed for five hundred years, so I suppose you can eliminate that one. Did Mistress Nora say anything else that might be useful?"

Aruendiel gave an impatient exhalation. "Nothing to guide us to her directly."

"Why, what did she say?" Nansis Abora asked.

"She said, 'I won't do it.' And there was much more that I could not make out. But I heard her say 'almost killed' and 'too dangerous' with perfect distinctness."

"Oh, dear, that is not especially reassuring, is it? Still, there might be some innocuous explanation. Did she sound agitated or calm, could you tell?"

"She was not calm." Aruendiel was suddenly and irritably conscious that he himself did not sound especially composed. He tried to regulate his voice better as he added: "As you say, it is a damnably imprecise spell. But she was speaking with some passion, that was clear."

Nansis Abora sucked the corners of his mouth, considering this information. "What do you propose to do, Aruendiel?"

"I mean to find her."

"Yes, of course, but how? Do you mean to search each of these temples we have named?"

"I will start with that, yes."

"You're still in no state to travel."

Aruendiel thought briefly about disputing this point with Nansis Abora but had to admit to himself that he was unlikely to win the argument. On the way from the bed to the kitchen, he had not actually fallen, but he had been grateful for the walls' blessed steadiness under his hands. "Traveling would take too long," he said. "It would be faster to examine each temple with an observation spell."

Nansis Abora nodded, looking relieved. "That's a much better idea," he said approvingly. "We can start looking in the morning."

"There's no reason not to begin now."

"Except that everyone will be in bed! We'll have a much better chance of finding her in the daytime, while people are up and about."

"There is something to that," Aruendiel said reluctantly, glancing at the kitchen window. No light came through the cracks in the shutters; there were still hours before daylight. He looked back at the other man suddenly, his pale eyes intent. "Do you not have a time spell that would take us to tomorrow morning?"

Nansis Abora was caught off guard. "I do—but heavens, Aruendiel, it wouldn't do any good at all. It would not make time pass any more quickly for Mistress Nora; it would not avert anything that might happen to her between now and then. Not that anything is likely to happen," he added as Aruendiel's face darkened. "We don't know for sure that she is in any danger."

"The odds are great that she is," Aruendiel said. He clenched his jaw, then said suddenly: "She also spoke my name." He had not intended to mention this to Nansis Abora, but now found that he could not help himself.

"Eh? Are you sure? What did she say?"

Aruendiel had to confess that he did not know. His ear had automatically picked out his own name from a series of otherwise indistinct syllables.

Nansis Abora looked at him more keenly than Aruendiel would have liked. "Well, it's natural that you're worried. Mistress Nora is a very delightful young lady."

"She's my pupil and has lived in my household," Aruendiel said. He added, as though anxious to be clear on this point: "I am responsible for her protection."

Nansis Abora nodded. "Yes, yes. Although—forgive me for being forward, Aruendiel—I think you are also rather fond of her?"

Why had Nansis Abora chosen this moment to pry, in his innocent, inoffensive way, into matters that were none of his business? "One always feels some attachment to a good pupil," Aruendiel said.

"Oh, certainly," Nansis Abora said. "Even to the doltish ones, I always found. Some of them try so hard."

"Nora is an excellent student," Aruendiel snapped. Then, carefully: "And certainly, I am—fond of her."

"Oh, yes, I thought so," Nansis said, pleased. "Well, I think that's a very good thing. You've been a bachelor for a long time—getting on for three dozen years, is that right?"

Aruendiel felt some bafflement at the turn the conversation had taken, but he answered: "Four dozen and more."

"That's far too long. Dear me! One of these days, I must marry again, too. There is something very soothing about having a woman around, even if she loses her temper from time to time, as some of my wives did."

Privately, Aruendiel had always had trouble distinguishing among Nansis Abora's successive wives. Nansis had a predilection for generously sized widows in hearty middle age; beyond that, it was hard to recall anything specific about any of them.

"It's not that simple," Aruendiel said with some desperation.

"No?" Nansis had risen from his chair and was hunting among the jars and bottles on the kitchen shelf.

Impossible to tell Nansis how he had already bedded Nora, how she had turned on him. But he found it equally impossible to be silent. "I'm *very* fond of her," Aruendiel said. "It is—unfortunate."

"Why? She is a lovely girl," Nansis said, examining the handwritten label on a medium-sized green bottle.

"Why? Do you even have to ask? Wood and water, I thought I was too old to be such a fool. And an old magician who even thinks of—of passion is a fool. Look at Merlin."

"Merlin?" Nansis made a clucking sound. He poured some pinkish liquid into a cup and handed it to Aruendiel, then poured another cup for himself. "That's only a legend. You've always said yourself that there never was a Merlin."

"A tale can be entirely false and yet tell some truths," Aruendiel said. The idea had occurred to him while Nora was translating that book of hers, the one about the girls seeking to be married. "The point is, Nansis, when a man as unnaturally old as I am falls in love with a girl like that, a duckling right out of the egg, the best outcome he can hope for is to look ridiculous. The best outcome."

"Are you worried that Mistress Nora will shut you up in a cave, like the nymph in the story? I don't know her very well, but I would think it unlikely. Or do you think she will treat you the way your first wife did?"

Aruendiel was taken aback. He had never thought of Lusarniev as his first wife, only as his wife. "I don't know," he said. "Something. She might find my attentions displeasing."

"You never worried about that before with any woman, it seems to me. And Mistress Nora is so plainly enamored of you."

"What do you mean?"

"Well, I've seen her! When we were at Lord Luklren's castle. Like the sun coming out, whenever she spied you. I'm not surprised at all that she decided to come back from her world. I don't think she wanted to leave in the first place."

Aruendiel considered this, frowning. "She has a lovely smile," he said after a moment. Then, with the air of one correcting himself, he added: "She's very young, and therefore changeable."

"Women do change their minds, my goodness! I won't presume to tell you how to manage your affairs. But I wouldn't mind having a young thing smile at me the way I saw Mistress Nora smile at you." A wistful look drifted across Nansis's wrinkled face.

He and Nansis were almost exactly the same age, Aruendiel reflected, and yet to look at Nansis, one would take him for a far older man. Well, Nansis had not been young when Aruendiel introduced him to the study of true magic, and perhaps he had spent more time on his calculations than was good for him. Had Nora noted the disparity in their appearance, Aruendiel asked himself, or did she see them as two old codgers together?

He took a sip from the cup that Nansis had given him. One of those herb cordials that Nansis was fond of. It felt satisfyingly bitter on his tongue.

"We are wasting time on trivialities," Aruendiel told Nansis with a glare. "My obligation is to make sure that Mistress Nora is safe. That is all."

He bent over the map again.

Chapter 17

Gingerly, Nora touched the place where her little finger used to be. No, there was no mistake. The stump was slightly longer. An odd wrinkle had appeared near the top, but there was no tenderness, no sign of inflammation.

She forced down a sudden hopeful impulse. Wait and see, she thought.

There was a different *maran* hanging behind the door this morning, dark blue with a wide purple border dense with embroidery. They had taken away the other, plainer one while Nora slept. She dressed distractedly, still less than certain about how to arrange the various folds of the *maran*, and went outside. A fine lace of spring snow covered the shadowed rocks of the ravine. The mountains basked in pale morning light like great cats.

The sun god is Sisoaneer's father, Nora thought suddenly, recalling what the older priest had said last night. How could the sun be anyone's father? And if it's true, why is she not blond? Or is that just a stereotype?

The lower complex was still quiet. Nora found her way to the refectory kitchen and liberated some flatbread and a couple of discs of fresh white cheese that been left to soak in brine, and then she hurried through the complex until she found the path downstream. She passed through a pillared limestone gate, then an avenue of seated statues. Each showed the same female figure, whose staring eyes and red mouth were crudely painted on weathered stone. Guess who. Nora avoided looking at them too closely, as though one wrong glance might wake them to life.

As she went along, cliffs on either side gave way to grassy slopes. To her left, through a screen of trees, was a scanty settlement of stone huts, their roofs covered with hides. Was that where the *ganoi* lived? Smoke rose; children were crying. Nora walked faster. The snow had already disappeared, and with it, her footprints. Good.

The path curved uphill. Nora followed the edge of the stream instead. The watercourse was shielded by young trees, and she felt as invisible as anyone in a blue-and-purple *maran* on a bright spring morning could hope to be. The day grew warmer. The stream glittered in the dappled light, and in the sunny spots, a haze of gnats swarmed over the water. There were shy pink wildflowers tucked in among the rocks at the edge of the stream.

She began to think that she might get away with it. She did not have any real plan except to walk and keep walking. That might be enough. The stream would lead her out of the mountains eventually, and it would give her water along the way. The priest, Oasme, had mentioned a good-sized city within a few days' journey; the stream might lead her there. She tried an experiment, improvising a spell to trace the movement of the water as it flowed downstream. She could sense that the water heard her, but it would tell her nothing.

There is no magic here but mine, Sisoaneer had said.

All the more reason to leave. And then what? Somehow she would find Aruendiel. Ilissa might find her first, that was always a risk, but Faitoren magic seemed almost benign now. At least Ilissa wasn't a goddess.

She suddenly wondered what Ramona was doing right now. She imagined telling her sister about meeting a goddess, about the job offer to be High Priestess of Erchkaii, and as she pictured Ramona's brown gaze, rapt but appraising, her situation began to seem less unhappy, almost funny. "Really, she wanted *you* to be her priestess?" she could hear her sister saying. "That's crazy."

She couldn't figure out how she'd tell Ramona about what had happened to Yaioni, though, or to Raclin. Ramona would probably say that they both deserved it. But then, Ramona hadn't seen Yaioni's burns. Or heard the wet crack of the ax going through Raclin's neck.

Nora kept walking. She waded in the chilly shallows of the stream when her feet grew sore. She halted only once, for a quick midday meal of bread and cheese in the bright shade of a willow. It was late afternoon when she reached the end of the stream.

A breeze sprang up, and Nora came through a stand of birches to find open water stretching before her. Shaggy blue waves chased each other toward a line of mountains on the horizon. On the shore to her left was a large stone quay that looked as though it could handle a lot of boat traffic, but it was empty of boats.

"Oh," Nora said. She walked across a small strip of brown sand to the water's edge, stuck a finger into the water, and licked it. Fresh, not salt. And cold, very cold.

A lake. A big lake. Nora estimated that the opposite shore was a couple of miles away. Experimentally, she tried a simple piece of water magic, willing the waves to carry a piece of driftwood toward her, but the water sidled slyly away from her command.

Evidently, the goddess reigned here as well.

Nora walked along the edge of the lake. The ground grew wetter and marshier, until she was sinking in rank brown mud that seemed to have no bottom. With some difficulty she pulled herself onto a grassy tussock, then cautiously retraced her steps. In the other direction, she encountered a steep-sided hill, where an indistinct path led her into a maze of thornbushes and then disappeared. She spent some time trying to pick viciously invisible barbs out of her hands and forearms before returning to the quay.

The sky was reddening in the west. Far away, she saw the small, distant silhouette of a boat, its oars crawling slowly over the water. It grew tinier as it receded.

"Pilgrims come to Erchkaii all the time, they said so last night. There's bound to be a boat landing soon." Saying it aloud made the logic sound more compelling, as though she had a real plan.

"Maybe tomorrow or the next day. They don't go out at night."

Nora whirled around. A man had followed her onto the dock. "Hello," she said sharply, "what are you doing here?"

It was Lemoes, the beautiful acolyte. He looked at her solemnly, not speaking, his lovely boy's face giving nothing away. He looked bigger than she recalled, round young muscles filling out the shoulders of his kimono. Nora stared back at him, trying to look fierce. "Did you follow me?"

He slid backward half a step. "I have a message for you. From the goddess."

"I don't want to hear it. Sorry." Nora kept her tone brisk. "How come there's no boat here? What if you need to get across the lake?"

Under his thick brows, the boy's gaze shifted in a way that might have indicated either mild surprise or complete disinterest. "We don't leave the island," Lemoes said.

"You never—wait, this is an island?" He nodded, and Nora sighed. "No one mentioned that," she said. "But all the more reason to have a boat." She gave him an accusatory look.

"The ferry comes on Fourth Day, usually. Sometimes the fishermen come. The pilgrims hire their own boats."

"And you never go across yourself?" Nora asked. He was a teenage boy; surely he wanted to leave Erchkaii, see the world, meet girls— or boys—his own age. But he shook his head. "I would think you'd find it boring here," she said. "I'm leaving, and I've spent less than two days at the temple."

So he could smile, but you had to be quick to catch it. Nora pursued: "If you were going to leave here, how would you do it?"

"Same as you, I guess. A boat."

"You wouldn't try to swim?" It might be a last, desperate option, if only the water weren't so damn cold.

Lemoes looked at her with a trace of pity, she thought. "The lake's full of screwteeth." To her blank look, he clarified: "Screwteeth eels."

"Are those really so bad?" From Lemoes's expression, the answer was apparently obvious. "And you think there might be a ferry tomorrow," she said.

"Maybe."

Nora reflected on the one remaining piece of flatbread that was wrapped in a fold of her *maran*. "I should have brought more food."

Lemoes had the grace not to respond. Instead, he said, "There will be lots of boats once the festival starts next week."

"I'd like to leave sooner." She looked at him narrowly. "You aren't going to try to stop me, I hope."

He shook his head. "The goddess didn't send me to stop you. She just had a message for you."

"And she couldn't deliver it herself?" Nora asked. "All right. Just so you can tell her you did your job. What's the message?"

"There's someone at Erchkaii who needs your help." He spoke as though Nora would know what to do.

She waited, but he did not continue. "Who is it?" she asked.

"That's all she said." Lemoes dropped his gaze, as though looking for an answer on the worn, stained stone of the pier. His lashes were like birds alighting. He sighed. "I think I know who it is, though. The sick woman who came yesterday. On the litter, with her mother."

Nora gave a baffled shrug. "I have no idea who that is. And how do you know she's the one?"

"I just think it's her. She's very sick." A furrow had appeared in his smooth brow; he seemed to be contemplating the sheer impossibility of explaining himself to someone as uncomprehending as Nora. She was familiar with this expression, having taught undergraduates who were Lemoes's age. "I know what she likes—the goddess, I mean," he said.

"How am I supposed to help the poor woman?" Nora asked, raising her voice. She was speaking for the goddess's ears as much as Lemoes's. "I don't know anything about medicine. Magical or otherwise. I told your goddess that already.

"And she may not have sent you to stop me from leaving, but it comes to the same thing—trying to get me to go back to help this sick person. Sisoaneer can cure this woman herself. She doesn't need me to do it. I won't do it. She'd do a better job. And I'm—I'm done with magic, anyway."

She stared challengingly at Lemoes. He squinted against the sunset's reddening light. "I don't understand, Blessed Lady," he said.

"Don't call me that. I can't help her, because—because I'm not sure I want to be a magician anymore." Stating this aloud felt worse than being called Blessed Lady. "I mean, I don't want—I shouldn't do any more magic."

In her mind, Nora could hear Aruendiel beginning a long and furious tirade, asking what insanity had seized her, why would she disown the study of magic, there was no truer way of understanding the world, and involuntarily she hunched her shoulders, as though she could shake off his imagined words like drops of water.

"It's too dangerous. *I'm* too dangerous. You know what happened to Yaioni, don't you?"

He nodded. For the first time, she thought she saw a gleam of respect in his eyes. "She shouldn't have challenged you."

"Well, I didn't even mean to hurt her, I did the magic without thinking about it. I almost killed her. And that's not the first—"

She broke off. Better not let it get around that she'd chopped her husband's head off. People were quick to judge. "Aruendiel—my teacher—used to lecture me about control, how dangerous magic could be. Now I see what he meant. And now the goddess wants to give me even more power. I don't want it." More for her own benefit than Lemoes's, she repeated sternly: "I don't want to be a magician."

Nora had been thinking this all day without wanting to, trying to distract herself with flight and fatigue. Yaioni was healed, but that didn't make it right, what Nora had done to her. I set her on fire, she thought. I would never have done that deliberately, never.

The magic made it too easy. You could destroy someone in the blink of an eye. And there was no way to prevent it, unless you could repress every stray hostile, antisocial thought for the rest of your life. For the first time, Aruendiel began to look like a model of restraint, bad temper and all. At least he only killed people when he meant to. No wonder he was always going on about control.

She had learned enough magic to be dangerous. Not enough *not* to be dangerous. As far as she could see, not being a magician was only one sure way to avoid killing people on the merest impulse. Maybe it was a good thing that she had landed in a place where someone else controlled all the magic.

"Why don't you do it—take care of this poor woman?" Nora demanded. "You're Sisoaneer's priest, or you're training to be one, however that works."

The furrow in Lemoes's brow deepened. "I'd do it if I could. I don't know the arts of power. I've tried, but the goddess hasn't blessed me that way."

"What about Yaioni or Uliverat?"

Lemoes looked unimpressed by the suggestion. "They do a little. Yaioni more than Uliverat. But the people she treats—" He frowned. "A lot of them die."

"Oasme?" Nora suggested. The boy shook his head.

"Why doesn't the goddess of magic have any decent magicians working for her?" Nora thought it was a reasonable question, and a good zinger, but it seemed to be wasted on Lemoes. "So this sick woman came all the way here—for what?"

Lemoes tilted his head gracefully to indicate that the matter was out of his hands.

"She needs help," he said. "You wouldn't kill her. You don't have to help her if you don't want to."

He sounded older suddenly, and Nora saw that the kind of delicious male beauty that he possessed could instantly freeze into something sterner, more judgmental. He turned and walked noiselessly down the pier, toward the shadows of the forest.

Nora clenched her hands and uttered a small yelp of frustration. "How do you know I wouldn't kill her?" she called.

"I just know."

She started after him, quickening her pace as though by overtaking him she could have the last word. "You know, it took me all day to get here, walking along the river," she said. "If it weren't so far—"

"It's not that far, the road's shorter." Lemoes sounded like a boy again, childishly gruff. "You go over the ridge instead of around it."

Nora cast a glance back at the lake's vast crystalline bowl of sky and water, darkening to indigo as dusk fell. The faraway boat had disappeared. The wind whipped her hair over her eyes. She shivered. "Well, how much shorter?"

Nora remembered that she hated hospitals. They were all the same, whether dark and primitive like this one, or clean and bright with kind nurses in rubber clogs and purposeful, blinking machines like the ones that kept your brother alive until you and your parents decided to turn them off.

She moved further into the ward. The thick, flickering light of oil lamps showed her bundled forms on low mattresses. Someone breathed with a sound like feet scuffling through dry leaves. One of the rooms to the left, Lemoes had said.

Shyly she knocked at the first door. A female voice spoke up sharply in a language she did not understand. Nora pushed the door open.

One of the women inside was as brilliant as a parrot in the murky light, her quilted gown shimmering with blue and crimson as she rose and came toward Nora, gesticulating. With her wrinkled, powdered face and her red-painted mouth, she was small, furious, and voluble in her unknown tongue. The other woman crouched in the background, wrapped in dark, dull robes that might have been cut from an old blanket, and her arms were crossed protectively in front of her body. She could not have been more than twenty-five at most, but the blank, defeated expression on her face belonged to someone much older.

Nora's smile felt dry and stiff, like paper glued to her face. This poor woman obviously needed some kind of help; Nora had no idea what kind. Certainly she wasn't qualified to give it. They were burning incense inside the room, perhaps in honor of the goddess, and the smoky air made Nora's eyes sting. She thought, I'll just pretend I went into the wrong room, and leave.

"They have come all the way from Wenhu Nirst."

Nora turned with a start. The priest Oasme was just behind her. "You surprised me," she said.

"My apologies," he said smoothly. The older woman was addressing him, her voice rising interrogatively. He spoke to her in the same language; she frowned at him and said something brusque. To Nora, he said: "This is the Dowager Duchess of Greater Solas, and this"—he nodded at the woman in the dark robes—"is her daughter, the Princess Loku Baniseikinu, the wife of Crown Prince Baniseiki. They have been married three years; she has borne him one son. Now he has taken her son from her and wants to divorce her, because she is unclean. Her mother has brought her here to see if she can be cured."

"Unclean," Nora repeated. "And that would mean—?"

"She bleeds," Oasme said, dropping his voice. "Almost without ceasing."

An open wound? Nora discerned that he meant something else. "Her period won't stop?"

Oasme nodded, a faint expression of distaste flitting across his face.

Nora made a sympathetic noise deep in her throat. "That's no fun," she said, "but I wouldn't call her unclean. Her husband took her son away for *that*?"

"The Lady Healer once cured the river-goddess Selt of the same affliction," Oasme said. "We have had many pilgrims seeking Sisoaneer's help for such bleeding."

"Well, can you cure the woman?"

"The goddess has sent you." He smiled with an irritating assurance.

"I don't have the faintest idea how to help her. I don't know anything about healing spells."

"There is the temple library. I can help you consult the books."

"But I know nothing about medicine. Nothing. I really, really shouldn't even try this." There were so many ways that even the simplest spell could be miscalculated or muddled. People choked on the jewels that fell magically out of their mouths, or their houses burned down because they couldn't extinguish a magical fire, or they had to spend the rest of their lives in seclusion because of an indiscriminately applied love spell.

"Then no one will help this woman."

Nora looked around the dark, smoky chamber. It seemed to have grown smaller since she entered it. The mother stared sternly at Nora. The patient was staring at the floor as though she had already accepted Nora's refusal. She looked so frozen with hopelessness that Nora felt an impulse to put an arm around the woman's slumped shoulders and give her a hug.

Then she would have to explain: I'm sorry, I can't do anything for you.

"I'll try," Nora said.

The temple library was a small octagonal tower near the hospital, its limestone walls dimpled with ancient, illegible inscriptions. Over the generations, the feet of the priests of Sisoaneer had worn grooves in the steps that rose to the door, but when Nora entered, the library was full of a chilly, static silence.

The books were in cages. In the center of the building was a series of alcoves barred with iron, codices and scrolls visible on the shelves within. Small reading tables lined the outside walls of the library, under narrow windows filled with thick glass that blurred all glimpses of the outside world. Oasme went immediately to one of the alcoves, produced a key to unlock the door, and returned with a scroll made of brittle, rather grubby-looking parchment.

"I'd like to make one thing clear," Nora said. "Even if I somehow cure this woman, that's it. I'm not staying around here. I'm not going to be anyone's High Priestess."

With a somewhat reproachful look, Oasme put a finger to his lips. "She hears—not everything, but many things," he said, so softly that Nora could hardly hear him.

"She knows how I feel," Nora said, lowering her voice anyway. "I told her I didn't want to be her priestess."

"That makes it even stranger that you would be chosen. But we mortals can't hope to understand the will of the goddess. Even those who have spent their lives as her priests." He raised his eyebrows.

"Why don't you put in for the job yourself?"

Oasme allowed himself a faint smile, as though amused at her naivete. "I was not chosen by the goddess. My role is to serve the one she chooses. That's part of the vow I made when I came here, obedience to the High Priest—or Priestess. And you will need help in your new office."

"I told you, I'm not—"

Oasme put the scroll down on the table and began to untie the faded red cord that girdled it. "You tried to run away," he murmured. "That is not how you will please the goddess."

"I don't care," Nora said.

"But the goddess's pleasure matters very much. To you, and to everyone at Erchkaii."

There was an odd emphasis in his voice. Nora looked at him closely, but he had the kind of face whose features fit together as tightly as bricks, giving nothing away. "Do you mean that if I left, she would take it out on the rest of you?" she asked.

"The goddess does as she wills," Oasme said. "All praise to Her Holiness."

Nora frowned. "I still don't believe—I can't believe she's a goddess. She seems a little, well, strange, but human."

Oasme pursed his lips. "There's an old tradition that as a punishment for helping Queen Ysto murder her father, the sun god sentenced the goddess, his daughter, to live a dozen lives incarnated as a mortal woman."

"What does that prove?"

"And in the last of those lives, the old scrolls say, she will hold sway at Erchkaii. I'm an archivist, not a theologian. But Erchkaii is the cradle of Her Holiness's power, and only the true goddess could possibly reign here."

His reasoning seemed a bit circular. "What happened to the old High Priest?" Nora asked. "Uliverat said he wasn't worthy. He didn't believe in her?"

"There were other reasons, many of them. The goddess made it known that she'd choose her own High Priestess." He nodded meaningfully at Nora.

"But what happened to him?"

"He made atonement," Oasme said dryly. "Like my other brethren." To Nora's questioning look, he said: "There were more than thirty priests here three years ago."

"Thirty!" Nora thought of all the empty seats in the refectory. "They were all—unworthy?"

The priest cleared his throat. "You see, at first Uliverat and Yaioni came here, on foot, dressed like—" He made a dismissive gesture. "They said they'd come to preach the coming of the goddess. That she would purify her temple and punish the unbelievers.

"We thought they were simply poor pilgrims, a little overenthusiastic in their faith, as sometimes happens. They harangued anyone who would listen to them. No one paid any attention, except—I'm sorry to say—some of the other priests made fun of them."

"And then?" Nora asked, because he had paused.

"Why, then the goddess came. And she purified the temple, just as Yaioni and Uliverat predicted."

That had an ominous sound. "And the other priests—?"

"Officially, it was a sudden plague," Oasme said. His small eyes flicked to Nora's face, as though to see how she reacted. "I hope you never feel her fury. I don't think you will," he added in a brisker tone. "I saw how quickly the First Deaconess healed last night because of your intercession. The goddess favors you, Blessed Lady."

"Please don't call me that. Why would I even want to be the priestess of a goddess who does such terrible things to people?"

"Better to be the goddess's High Priestess than *not* to be her High Priestess, is how I would look at it," Oasme said curtly. "And it is better, it is safer for all of us to have a High Priestess with whom the goddess is well pleased."

Nora hunched her shoulders, trying to ignore the import of his words. "Why can't Yaioni—"

"Yaioni is *terrible*." Oasme closed his eyes for a moment. "I'm not blessed with the arts of power, and I can't tell you what she does wrong, but she has killed as many pilgrims as she has cured. More, even."

"There's no guarantee that I'd be any better than her," Nora said.

"We will discover that soon enough," Oasme said. "Here," he continued, unrolling the scroll carefully, "these are the spells that my High Priest used most often for the princess's ailment. They will tame the disturbance in the womb that is causing the blood to flow."

Nora glanced down. "I can't read this," she said flatly. The scroll was written in an alphabet of tight, square letters that bore no resemblance to Ors.

"I will translate it for you," Oasme said. He pointed to the first line of the scroll, curling his finger elegantly. "When the walls of the womb are lumpy with growths, the blood is agitated, like water moving over stones, and it will not cease flowing." The scroll went on to describe various ways of causing the growths to wither: several different applications of fire magic, all of which sounded painful; a spell using water magic; and one based on wood magic. The author recommended the last method as producing the best, most predictable results.

"I don't know any wood magic," Nora said. "I never got that far."

"What about the other ones?" Oasme asked. "I know you know something about fire magic."

Nora gave him a dirty look. "I don't want to hurt the poor woman." She decided: "I'll use water magic."

"As you wish, Blessed—" Oasme's voice was blandly encouraging.

"Please. Don't call me that," Nora said. The honorific still grated; worse, right now it seemed like bad luck, the deliberate courting of disaster. What if the so-called Blessed Lady couldn't cure the Princess Loku Baniseikinu?

The answer was obvious, Nora thought. *Then there's no way that I'll be the Blessed Lady, the High Priestess—which is what I want anyway, isn't it?*

And the woman in the dark robe would go away uncured and unclean, shunned by her husband. That wouldn't be the worst thing, if he was such a pig as to abandon her. And she'd lose her child forever. Nora sighed.

"Would you read the spell again?" she asked. "The water magic part."

When they returned to the hospital, the Dowager Duchess was eating a small, curlicued pastry from an inlaid bowl and addressing a stream of invective to her daughter, who sat slumped against the wall, eyes closed, a half-eaten pastry forgotten in her hand. The duchess's head snapped around when she heard the door open; she redirected her commentary at Oasme, sounding no more pleased with him.

Raising his hands in placation, Oasme responded to her in ostentatiously soothing tones. He nodded to Nora with a flicker of appeal in his eyes. With a dry mouth, Nora went over to the princess, trying to walk with a confidence she did not feel.

"My name is Nora," she said. The woman raised her head slowly, her dark-fringed eyes half closed. Nora took her hand. "I'm going to try to help you."

Behind her, Oasme seemed to be translating Nora's words, but he went on for quite a bit longer than she expected, and she wondered what sort of flourishes and promises he had added.

The spell needed a lot of power, the scroll had been clear about that. She would have to pull from the stream. Slowly the magic responded, coy, reticent, a shade distrustful—but that was all right. Typical water magic.

Nora began to work through the spell. It was long and somewhat digressive; she could not help thinking how scathingly Aruendiel would critique its structure. When she reached the final step, she waited for a moment, but she already knew that the spell was not working. Nothing happened; nothing happened again.

The Princess Loku Baniseikinu watched her quietly. Her hand rested warm and unmoving in Nora's hand, and she did not return the smile that Nora offered.

She knows this won't work, Nora thought. In a way, that makes it easier.

Mechanically she worked through the spell again, trying to estimate how many more times she should try before giving up.

And then she couldn't hear herself think. The princess was making too much racket.

Blood swishing, breath creaking. The bones full of music. Nerves sparking. The belly roaring, tearing that bite of pastry to molecules.

The princess had said nothing. Her mouth remained a straight line of sadness. Nora found that her own mouth had dropped open.

The big drumbeat of the heart. The twang of muscles. Slow seeps, contented rustles from organs that Nora could not identify. The web of sound had its own harmony, but as she listened closely, she discerned a discordant note. Something wrong, unbalanced deep in the abdomen.

Gotcha, Nora thought.

The more she listened, the more obvious were the disruptions in the princess's womb. She could sense their mass and contours. The body nourished the growths but was fearful of them; they were too insistent, too demanding. One could tame them, Nora saw, by dissolving them in currents of water magic. But when she tried, the growths resisted her efforts. They were stronger than she had imagined, and she could not coax enough magic from the stream to wear them down, the way that Aruendiel no doubt could have done, or the goddess.

"I'm sorry," Nora began to say.

Before she could get the words out completely, another voice sounded in her mind. *I will help you,* it said sweetly.

"Sisoaneer?" Nora's voice was uncertain. The princess looked at her with sharpened curiosity.

I will lend you the power, the goddess said.

Oh, God, Nora thought after an instant. I mean, Goddess. That's enough. That's more than enough. It's too much.

Trying to wield this magic was like plunging into deep, deep water until you could not tell if you were rising or falling. For a moment, she thought the goddess's power would dissolve and destroy her instead of the fibroid lumps in the princess's uterus. And yet she was floating safely, protected; the magic flowed around and through her; it buoyed her up and tore away all fear like rotted rags. Anything was possible, anything at all, and she healed the princess's womb with only a thought.

Nora listened to the sweet relief in the body's song, and it almost made her cry, except that somehow she was beyond all tears. Because pain and sadness and death were negligible, she could see that now. They meant nothing; she was too strong for them. The broken flecks of all the days she had lived swirled like bright dust in the distance. She was alone. No one could ever find her here or harm her. All will be well, she thought. All is well.

All was not well. Nora clapped her hand over her mouth. Her stomach heaved. She groped for the reassuring support of the wall and leaned against it, shuddering.

Someone touched her shoulder. It was the princess, looking concerned. But also looking brighter, less haggard, the strain gone from her face.

"I'm all right," Nora said, forgetting that the other woman could not understand Ors. "Sometimes magic—other people's magic, when it's really strong—makes me feel a little sick." She took a deep breath. The internal commotion was dying down. "How are you?" she asked the princess.

From behind Nora, Oasme's voice insinuated itself, translating what she had said. The princess responded at once, incomprehensible words pouring out of her as she punctuated her sentences with emphatic nods. She smiled at Nora.

The Dowager Duchess broke in, her face screwed up into lines of suspicion. A note of skepticism was clear.

The princess would have none of it. Passionately she corrected the duchess, stabbing a finger toward her own abdomen. Her voice rose into a register of protest that Nora knew well, having used it so often with her own mother.

With a flawless expression of benign helpfulness, Oasme looked from mother to daughter. "The Princess Loku Baniseikinu is feeling much improved," he informed Nora. "The Dowager Duchess is concerned that the improvement might be temporary. A mother is cautious."

In a slightly different tone, he said: "And then there is the matter of a thank-offering. Naturally, she wants to confirm that her daughter is really cured before we attend to that." He looked hard at Nora. "Is she cured?"

"Yes," Nora said curtly. She pushed herself away from the wall to stand up straight. The room seemed more airless than ever, and she felt very tired. "Excuse me, I need to go outside," she said. The princess, seeing her movement, grabbed at Nora's hand and began speaking warmly to her.

Nora tried to remember how to smile, but smiling seemed pointless, when you had experienced a moment of perfect peace and happiness and then lived past it.

She made herself look into the princess's face and saw that it was alive and hopeful again. She kept looking. After all, this is not about me, Nora thought. Her vision blurred with sudden tears.

"The goddess be praised!" Oasme said.

"The goddess—" Nora repeated, her voice shaking. She closed her eyes as though she were praying. A single drop squeezed past her lashes.

Somehow she made her escape from the little room and down the long ward, past the quiet patients on their mattresses. She gave them sideways glances as she went, and saw that they, too, were waiting for her.

Outside, she sat down on the steps of the hospital and let the night air stroke her face like a cool washcloth. Across the small courtyard, a single light burned behind a shutter. It flickered whenever she moved her head.

She was not really surprised to discover, after a while, that the goddess was sitting next to her. Sisoaneer's narrow face bent toward her, glimmering in the darkness like a lily. Her eyes were like black pools. "You did well," the goddess said. "You did very well."

Nora studied her, trying to read her expression. "Who *are* you?" she asked. "What are you?"

"You know now," Sisoaneer said gently.

"I don't know," Nora said. "I don't know anything. I thought I did."

The goddess gave a small chuckle, light as a bird in flight. "You tried to run away!"

"And I still need to go!" It seemed important not to abandon this point, but Nora was aware of something childish in her tone. "I can't stay."

"But you see, there is so much for you to do here."

"I know." Nora looked down at her clasped hands. "It's not why I'm here, though. I mean, I left my home, my family—I came a very long way—to find Aruendiel again, to learn more magic."

"And what will you do with that magic? How will you use it?" Sisoaneer leaned closer.

Nora had no ready answer. She'd always assumed that the pursuit of real magic, like poetry, could be an end in itself, with its own intrinsic worth and satisfactions, but now she began to feel that she had missed something important. What was power if you did not use it? Or rather, if you did not plan carefully how to wield power, would you not be more likely to misuse it?

And magic was useless in so many ways. There were wounds that magic could not heal, losses that it could never make up for. But maybe those limitations obliged you to do as much as you could with the power you had.

"I hope—I'd like to do good." Nora made herself meet Sisoaneer's gaze.

Sisoaneer gave a flicker of a smile that seemed both grave and approving. "I know."

"But I still have to find Aruendiel," Nora added, a little wildly. "I want to know that he's safe. And I need to talk to him. He may not want to see me. But I have to try."

Sisoaneer's long fingers, smooth as eggshell, brushed Nora's cheek. "I will deny my High Priestess nothing—*nothing*—when she opens her heart to me and asks for my help."

Nora thought about this, taking her time, until she was sure she understood.

"Your High Priestess?" she asked. The goddess nodded. "And you would help me? Help to find Aruendiel."

"Oh, yes. Just as when I listened to you last night, when you asked me to heal Yaioni. And tonight, when you asked me to lend you my power. And I did. I let it fill you, and for an instant you made it yours."

Nora shuddered, almost afraid to remember what that short and endless moment had been like. "So every time I want to cure someone, I will have to"—she paused, reluctant to say it, but wanting to be exact—"to pray to you."

"Ask me, and I will give you what you need. In return, you will do my will, to heal and comfort the poor sick and wounded ones who turn to me. As you did just now. There are so many of them! You can't begin to comprehend, not yet." Sisoaneer sighed.

Nora nodded, starting to do a quick calculation in her head—the men on the ward inside, multiplied by a dozen, a hundred—but the numbers felt too abstract. She thought about the princess instead, her suffering, her drawn face. There would be others like that, many others. All of them looking to Nora for relief. And the goddess's power flowing into her like a great river, over and over again.

"You will be healed, too," Sisoaneer said softly.

"And finding Aruendiel?" Nora said his name with emphasis. "When would we get around to that?"

"I will take you with me the next time I leave Erchkaii, soon, and we will look for him together."

"When—"

"When you pray for it, my priestess, my beloved child. When you pray with all your heart. But first we have work to do." Sisoaneer leaned closer, her long hair swaying, and kissed Nora's cheek. The goddess's lips felt soft and precise, as silky as a sun-warmed plum.

And she was gone.

Nora waited for a moment before getting to her feet. She thought she caught a sort of quiver nearby in the darkness, a black shimmer, but it was hard to be sure.

My priestess, my beloved child.

"Healed?" Nora asked the empty courtyard.

"That's the place," Aruendiel said.

"Well, I don't know that you can say so definitely," Nansis Abora said. "But it is very odd." With an abstracted air, he pinched out the flame of the candle he held and sat down at the kitchen table.

Aruendiel was still standing inside the circle they had drawn on the wooden floor. The light from the candle in his hand made his pale eyes gleam gold. "The observation spell failed completely. Three times. There's an extremely powerful protection spell around that temple. What does that tell you?"

"I see where you're going with this, Aruendiel. They have something that they want to protect, and you think it's Mistress Nora. But Sisoaneer is a goddess of magic, after all—it's not entirely unexpected that her priests might have some spells up to make sure that no one steals the temple silver."

"We weren't trying to steal the temple silver. We were trying to take a look inside. None of the other temples have protection spells remotely as powerful."

Nansis Abora picked up the mug of milk from the table, peered into it, then added a small amount of amber liquid from an earthenware flask. "We've looked into a dozen temples in three days—I'd like to think that you've found the right place. But I don't want to see you chasing fleas in the dark, either. Not in your condition."

Aruendiel, who had been ready to sit down, straightened slightly and remained standing. "My condition? I have made a full recovery." With a sudden inspiration, he added: "Thanks to your care."

Nansis Abora gave him a gentle, beatific smile of pure disbelief, then took a sip of his drink. "It is odd, though," he said. "That is Blueskin's observation spell. I didn't think that any modern protection spell would be able to turn it back."

Aruendiel, about to say something, checked himself and looked intently at Nansis Abora. "Yes," he said. "Whoever contrived that protection spell knew the Blueskin spell well enough to come up with an effective counterhex. But the Blueskin spell was lost for a thousand years, until you reconstructed it. Nansis," he asked suspiciously, "did you give it to anyone but me?"

Nansis Abora blinked. "I was thinking of sending it to my friend Puen—he was so disappointed when that other spell that was supposed to be Blueskin's turned out to be a fake—but I don't believe I got around to it. No, I'm sure I only sent it to you.

"Of course, Erchkaii is a very old temple," he added reflectively. "And no doubt there is some very old magic guarding it."

"A counterhex to turn back the Blueskin spell would be very old magic indeed," Aruendiel said. He gripped the back of the chair in front of him—being careful not to seem to be obviously leaning on it—and brooded for a moment. "Sisoaneer. She is of the Ceionian pantheon, is she not? I thought she was a healing goddess."

"Oh, yes, that is her chief aspect, I believe, but she is also a goddess of magic. I used to know one of her priests in Keo, years ago. He gave me a spell to sharpen eyesight that works almost as well as Uelis Nisker's."

"Priests make poor magicians," Aruendiel said.

He was ready to expand upon this observation, but Nansis Abora continued, with an air of equanimity: "Oemo was quite all right with healing magic. And a very learned man. At any rate, he said that there used to be all sorts of little splinter cults here and there that worshipped Sisoaneer as a goddess of magic under different names: Tuth in Mirne Klep; Keersinl in Pelagnia—and I can't remember what they called her in Wor. Nethl? Nenil? No, dear me, that's a kind of fish, isn't it?"

"Keersinl?" There was an odd note in Aruendiel's voice, as though he did not quite take in what Nansis Abora had just told him.

"Yes, that's what they called her in Pelagnia," he said. "Oemo, my friend the priest, said it was mostly the old women in the country who worshipped her. I'd never heard of Keersinl, myself. Do you know of her, then?"

Aruendiel's gaze seemed to have sharpened, but he was not looking at Nansis Abora. "I know who Keersinl is," he said finally.

"Oh? I never think of you as being especially pious. How——"

"I honor the true gods, as any man should," Aruendiel snapped, "and in return I expect them to take as little interest in my affairs as possible. They usually oblige." He released the back of the chair from knuckles that had gone white and bent his head, as though reflecting. "And now—Keersinl. Sisoaneer. Whatever she calls herself, she has Nora."

"We don't know that—" Nansis Abora began again.

"I know," Aruendiel said.

Chapter 18

Nora knelt beside the litter and lifted the patient's hand, wrapping it in both of her own. Not patient, *pilgrim*, she corrected herself. It was a large, rather hairy hand, the palm leathery with calluses that came from hitting other people with a sword, over and over again. Under normal circumstances, his grip could probably crush her fingers. Now his hand lay flabby and exhausted in hers, clammy with feverish sweat.

Beside her, Oasme was interrogating the pilgrim's companions, a serious-faced group of middle-aged men, some in armor, and one very young woman, about six months pregnant. Two men were doing most of the talking in a rapid-fire, irritable-sounding language. When they paused, Oasme hissed the relevant details in Nora's ear. "Baron Tesein of Haariku—abdominal wound, stabbing—his brother, they said. Wound healed up, but the baron continues to weaken. Fever—seepage. Not eating. They're concerned about the succession. Probably internal bleeding, Blessed Lady, and infection. No sign of rot, though."

Good, that meant they wouldn't have to bring out the maggots. "All right, we'll open it up, clean it, and then close it," Nora said. "And then I'll do the strengthening spell. Sound good?"

"Very good," said Oasme, making a note on the wax tablet he carried. "And I wonder—a spell to increase the appetite? Can you manage that? He looks as though he needs some nourishment, and the family always feels better when the pilgrim starts eating again."

Nora hesitated. "Can we wait until we're sure the wound is healing?"

"But of course it will," Oasme said smoothly. "Well, we can wait a day." He turned back to the waiting group and began to explain the treatment in a rat-a-tat of hard-edged syllables.

Oasme kept doing that, pushing her to do more magic, more complicated spells. But then he was usually right about what the pilgrims needed. He had a keen eye for diagnosis, even if he couldn't do magic, and he knew which spells his old Chief Priest had used to treat particular ailments. Over the past two weeks, as pilgrims had arrived by the dozens for the Fifth Moon Festival—feverish, bleeding, covered with sores, crippled, blinded, wasted by tumors, racked by pain—he and Nora had forged a surprisingly workable partnership. She knew very well that she could not help them without his aid.

Or the goddess's aid—but that went without saying.

Nora mouthed the words she repeated each time she began treating a pilgrim: "Sisoaneer, please hear me. Lend me your power." The words were deliberately simple. Nora preferred to think of them as a friendly request, not a prayer—something different from the long, flattering invocations that she recited every morning and evening in the temple, repeating them line by line after Uliverat. At least a few of those elaborate compliments might be truthful or deserved, Nora reckoned. She spoke them dutifully. This was part of the job, she told herself. Keeping the goddess happy.

Wa, the *ganoi* nurse, had already removed the stained bandage from the baron's abdomen; now she carefully washed the seeping wound. As soon as she had finished, Nora leaned closer. She could sense the torn membranes, the troubled flesh in the baron's belly. Carefully she bid the tissue to heal, making sure that the deepest parts of the wound would knit first. And then Sisoaneer's power moved through her, taking her into that blessed place where there was no doubt or death.

This is what it's like to be a goddess, Nora thought, as the exigencies of the ordinary world receded into a vast, potent calm. Sisoaneer herself was somewhere nearby, unseen, coloring the sweetness of the flowing magic with a faint melancholy that Nora always found a little surprising.

Then it was over, and Nora was limp, her thoughts ashen. She was never quite prepared for how far she had to fall after the goddess's magic was gone. At least the nausea had not recurred, thankfully.

There was still the infection to treat. Privately Nora wished for antibiotics at a time like this, but what she did have was a strengthening spell that apparently boosted a pilgrim's immune system to extraordinary vigor. Sometimes—not always—it was enough to fight off the disease. Nora called on the goddess again, savoring the brief taste of divinity before it faded.

"Are you finished?" Oasme asked. Nora nodded, tiredly. He inspected the baron, who moved feebly and half opened his eyes. "Not too bad," Oasme decided. "I'll order that poppy syrup and have one of the women sit with him tonight. What a pity you haven't been able to get that sleep spell to work."

"Who's next?" Nora rubbed the back of her neck. The headache had begun again. It had been coming and going for a week now, a hot, dry band squeezing Nora's skull. Physician, heal thyself, she thought, and did a swift, discreet spell that untied the knot of the pain, at least temporarily. Thank you, Sisoaneer.

"You're done here. More than a dozen pilgrims today, excellent. Now you will need to see Uliverat and Yaioni, and then tonight is Ieona, the midpoint of the festival. You'll be leading the ceremonies."

Nora looked up, grimacing. "Wait. Is that the bit with the dance? I thought maybe Yaioni could do that—"

Oasme arched his eyebrows. "Is it Yaioni who has healed so many pilgrims during the festival? Who has glorified Her Holiness and brought fresh renown to Erchkaii?" In a more pragmatic tone, he added: "Yaioni and some of the women will be in the dance also. Just do what they do. We know that the goddess did not choose you for your dancing abilities."

"Very funny," Nora said. She stood up, straightening the folds of her *maran* automatically. She had found that there was indeed a way of carrying her body inside the gown—waist stiff, steps measured— that kept her looking reasonably unrumpled, but adjustments were still necessary throughout the day. "Tell Yaioni and Uliverat that I'll see them in my antechamber in half an hour."

Nora turned her steps to her quarters, worrying a little about the pilgrim with the arrowhead in his leg and wondering if Oasme was right about the pilgrim with the toothache—did all those teeth really have to come out?

Much of the time she felt like a fraud. She was a fraud. Using borrowed magic to do spells she'd barely mastered. Treating pilgrims with wounds so gruesome that she had to force herself just to look at them, pretending that she knew what she was doing. The thing was, the pilgrims she treated were getting better, nearly all of them. It was remarkable. She felt nearly as grateful for each recovery as the pilgrim she'd healed. She could save lives, even if no one had been able to save EJ's. Nothing else she had done in her life had been so unambiguously good. Could it be that her mother had been right about her vocation, in suggesting medical school?

She felt a surprising and urgent impulse to call her mother and ask her advice. I know this isn't exactly what you meant, Mom, but I *am* helping people.

It would be an awkward call, though. She knew what her mother would say, more or less. If fire magic had freaked her out, the news that Nora was serving a pagan goddess would inspire hysteria of a sort that Nora didn't care to imagine. And being a priestess was the good news— forget about any mention of Raclin's fate or being stoned. Just as well it was impossible to call home, Nora thought grimly.

The other two priestesses were waiting in her rooms. Uliverat, as usual, launched into an account of how she had accomplished virtually every task of the day. The details varied, but the underlying theme was constant: without criticizing anyone directly, Uliverat made it clear that she waged a constant, cheerful, valiant, and underappreciated struggle against the laziness and inattention of most of the temple inhabitants, from the other clergy down to the *ganoi* serving men and women.

Yaioni leaned against the wall, eyes hooded, as Uliverat talked. She had a fashion model's knack for making ennui look fascinating, Nora thought. And perhaps Yaioni had reason to be bored, since she did no healing magic at all now. But she was a surprisingly capable nurse, working side by side on the wards with Lemoes, deftly attentive to the pilgrims even as she glowered at them.

Nora had once dared to compliment Yaioni on her nursing skills. "My husband owned many slaves," Yaioni said dismissively. "And slaves are always getting hurt."

Today, as always, there were a myriad of minor problems. Pilgrims complaining about the food. Some of the *ganoi* not showing up for work. Rats in the storeroom. Another donkey had died, just when all available animals were needed to transport pilgrims from the lake.

Fisticuffs breaking out when the families of two pilgrims who had sworn a blood feud happened to be housed in the same dormitory.

Nora sighed. "No weapons? Good. Then move one family to the other dormitory. If it happens again, they'll all have to leave. Did anyone find out why Tuumo and Nanga didn't come to work in the hospital today?"

"Sleeping off their hooch from the night before," Uliverat said. "Or just lazy."

"Yaioni, could you check on them, please," Nora said. Yaioni's reports on personnel matters were generally more accurate than Uliverat's, because Yaioni showed no more disdain for the *ganoi* than for anyone else. From what Nora had seen, the *ganoi* did backbreaking work in the temple complex for not much in return, the right to hunt and graze their goats and raise their odd, bitter vegetables on temple lands. "Make sure they're all right. And do we have traps in the storeroom?"

Yaioni stirred. "Her Holiness's silent watcher eats the rats, usually."

That was the temple snake, the one that Yaioni had hurled at Nora not so long ago. Repressing an urge to shiver, Nora stared back into Yaioni's black eyes. "Some traps would also be good, " she said. "And check to see whether anything needs to be thrown out." She remembered something Oasme had said. "We should do an inventory on the medical stores; we need to order more unguents from Nenaveii.

"As for the food—" The meals in the refectory did not vary much from the menu Nora had tasted her first night—cheese, fish, greens, flatbread, occasionally goat meat—and the temple cooks used some combination of seasonings that left almost everything with a resinous undertone. If she'd had the time, Nora would have liked to venture into the kitchen to tinker with the recipes, though of course Oasme would have a fit. "Well, they don't come here for the food," she said.

She had never been solely in charge of anything more complicated than a section of a lecture course. What she had discovered in the past few weeks was that people often brought problems to the High Priestess that they could almost certainly solve themselves. What they wanted from her was simply an answer, a decision. She tried hard to make sure that it was the right decision, although sometimes that seemed to be less important than the fact that she had made it.

When Uliverat and Yaioni had gone, Nora went into her sleeping chamber, poured out a basinful of water to wash her hands and feet, and changed into the *maran* with the gold-threaded border. She did not hurry. These preparations had become as much a ritual as anything she did in the temple. She needed time to gird herself before her next duties.

As she dried her hands, she found herself smiling. A week ago, the pinkie finger on her left hand had been as tiny as a baby's. Now the new finger was almost as long as its mate on her right hand. It still had a pristine, unused look. She curled her hand to tap the left pinkie against her thumb, marveling because touching finger to finger felt so completely ordinary.

Cradling the warm glow of gratitude in her heart, as though a stray draft might extinguish it, she hurried to the temple for evening prayers.

Oasme and the deaconesses were already there, along with a scattering of pilgrims. Nora took her place and chanted some of the prayers that Oasme had been teaching her. The short form tonight, thankfully. She only stumbled twice in the liturgy, her best performance yet. When she stopped chanting, there was pure silence for a long moment, then the slap-slap of her sandals as she walked past the great statue with its upraised knife. The cleft in the rock wall gaped wider.

She's expecting me, Nora said to herself.

Behind her, she could hear the temple nave come to life with a wave of rustles, footfalls, murmurs. Class dismissed.

She moved deeper into the darkness of the cave, her hand brushing the rock. The first time she'd come alone, she'd tried to conjure a light, but the goddess wouldn't lend her the magic. You won't be lost, Sisoaneer had said, and so far she was right, but there was always a first time. Nora counted steps until she was sure that she had passed the hole to the deep caves. Now the passage led reassuringly upward.

This was where it did no good at all to count steps, because the distance to the top was different each time. Tonight the passage made at least a dozen twists before she reached the linteled exit and saw the glimmer of stars in the night sky.

It was the meadow tonight, not the mountain peak. Nora walked through the wiry grass. The air here was soft, full of the nighttime spring smells of cool earth and green sap. Clusters of pale petals on the ground showed a moony radiance. Close to the enormous oak at the edge of the meadow, she paused.

"Your Holiness, I am here," she said, clasping her hands and bowing her head. Some kind of reverent gesture seemed to be required, but she was not about to throw herself on the ground, like Uliverat, if Sisoaneer did not absolutely demand it.

"My priestess!"

Two lean, long-toed feet in worn sandals stepped into Nora's field of view. She raised her head to meet Sisoaneer's dark eyes under tilting brows. "How are my people?" the goddess asked.

Nora began to recite the list of pilgrims she had treated that day. She was only halfway through the first case when Sisoaneer interrupted. What of the boy's fever? Had he eaten breakfast? Had he been sweating, and did his sweat smell sour, sharp, or rotten? Nora had to confess that her examination had not been so thorough.

"You had him bathed!" Sisoaneer sounded amused. "And he didn't like it."

"That's right," Nora said. Sisoaneer often knew details about the pilgrims that Nora hadn't mentioned. Some of this information might come from Yaioni, Nora judged, but it seemed to her the goddess had some other means of surveillance. *She hears—not everything, but many things,* Oasme had said. "They'd packed the wound with clay," Nora said by way of explanation. "No wonder it was infected."

"So messy," the goddess agreed. "But it kept him from bleeding to death."

"A clean bandage would have been better." Nora thought of the small plastic miracle of Band-Aids in their tiny sterile envelopes, and marveled that she had ever taken them for granted.

"To avoid the tiny invisible creatures that bring the fever?" Sisoaneer's long smile flashed.

"Yes, exactly!" Nora was not backing away from the germ theory of disease, even if Sisoaneer and her new colleagues had been skeptical ever since Nora had explained it. Shouldn't a goddess of healing know about viruses and bacteria? Nora wondered. But then, Jesus didn't, or if he did, he never mentioned it when he was healing all those lepers.

Sisoaneer seemed to enjoy Nora's vehemence. "Yes, you are right, a clean bandage is better than clay, whether for keeping out the poisons in the air or your little monsters. Well, the bath was good for him. You must keep giving him a strengthening spell, but not more than once a day. If he does not eat tomorrow, then do a spell to reduce the fever. He is past the worst of it now. He will be healed." She spoke the last words as though the boy had no choice.

"Good," said Nora. "I mean, praise to Your Holiness."

They went through the other cases. The goddess was less optimistic about the young man from Bisr with the cough.

"He got out of bed today," Nora said. "Oasme said that he could go home in a wee—"

Sisoaneer shook her head. For once there was no merriment in her face, not even hidden in the smallest crease. "Did he eat anything?"

"A little. More than yesterday."

"Do not be foolishly hopeful," Sisoaneer said. She drew herself up, as stiffly as though she herself were in pain. "I am the goddess of healing, but there are some that are bound for death. You know that already."

Nora thought of the woman who had died the day before, the gray shadow in her flesh, as though she were already turning to dirt. She thought of how quietly EJ had lain in his hospital bed after they turned off the machines, when she kept thinking that she saw his chest rise and fall, because it was impossible that anyone could lie so still. The nurse had to hold a mirror over his mouth before she was truly convinced; the glass stayed clear.

"I don't think hope is foolish," Nora said.

"That is why you are my priestess," Sisoaneer said fondly. "Beloved one, those you can't heal—you will make their last days easier, until finally death comes as their friend."

Nora looked across the valley at the hooded black shapes of mountains against the starry sky. "How—?" She stopped, trying to find a way to ask the question she wanted to ask. "How much healing can we do? How far do we go?"

She saw from a subtle shift in Sisoaneer's expression that the goddess knew exactly what she meant, but Sisoaneer said nothing.

"Aruendiel raised a little girl from the dead," Nora said. "I saw him do it. She'd been murdered."

Very slowly Sisoaneer shook her head, her eyes bright.

"And Aruendiel died once himself—he fell from one of those flying things—and his friends brought him back—"

"He should have stayed dead. Yes, dead! I've shocked you." Nora began to protest, but the goddess smiled tolerantly. "Just a little, I think. Listen, dear one, every pilgrim you heal will die one day, no matter how magnificently you restore them to health today. It's the fate of all mortals. To escape death, as Aruendiel did, or even that little girl, is unnatural, blasphemous, wrong. Only gods are permitted to die and live again, and it is our will that makes it happen.

"That's how you know the true gods and goddesses. If they die, they can return themselves to life."

Nora cocked her head and asked the obvious follow-up: "Have you done that?"

"Oh, yes!" The intensity in Sisoaneer's tone suggested that she was talking about a particularly unpleasant final exam, but one that she had passed with high marks. "And now I love the work of healing even better, because I know what mortals can suffer."

But can she really know? Nora wondered. Sisoaneer had a privileged viewpoint; most mortals don't get to come back from the dead. Not having died herself, however, Nora felt ill-equipped to argue the point. "Hmm," she said. "With all due respect, I'm glad that the little girl—her name is Irseln—is alive, and that Aruendiel is alive. That is," she added more quietly, "if he is alive."

One of the pilgrims Nora had treated that day was a woman with a twisted leg, whose jagged gait had reminded her of Aruendiel's. The leg had had to be rebroken.

"You are still worried about him," Sisoaneer said.

"Of course," Nora said. "Every pilgrim I treat, I wonder if Aruendiel also needs my help."

"Why would Aruendiel need your help? Because of the Faitoren?"

Nora stared hard at Sisoaneer. She was nearly sure that she had said nothing, or almost nothing, to the goddess about her encounter with

Raclin. She preferred not to think about it, and some days she almost succeeded.

"How do you know about that?"

"You mistook me for a Faitoren the first night we met. I still think that's funny." Sisoaneer gave a quick, sidelong grin. "And there was a very dead Faitoren not so far away. *He* was no longer a danger to anyone, but you mentioned another one that night. Their little queen, I think."

"The dead Faitoren, that was self-defense," Nora said quickly.

"I know it was! Well, it would be hard to kill Aruendiel," Sisoaneer said reflectively. "He's crafty and resourceful, from everything I have heard. Whoever killed him that one time was lucky."

Nora made an indefinite sound of polite disagreement—"lucky" was not the word she would have chosen—and Sisoaneer touched Nora's cheek with a light finger. "Let me try to put your mind at ease," the goddess said. "I will seek out the traces of his magic, and we'll get some news of him that way."

She moved away, pacing in a slow circle around the oak tree. A faint luminosity trailed after her. Nora rubbed her arms against the night breeze and looked distractedly at the wall of mountains that lay between her and Aruendiel.

When Sisoaneer returned, her face was sharpened like an arrow. "He's nowhere to be found."

Nora sucked in her breath. "Do you mean—"

"I mean that he is not to be found. He is hiding."

"But he's alive?"

"Oh, yes. He couldn't be dead and use so much magic to hide himself from me. It's very odd. Why is he doing this, my priestess?"

"I don't know," Nora said. Sisoaneer's gaze was suddenly full of dark, glittering facets. It took an effort not to look away. "I don't know what he's hiding from. And how will *we* find him?" She did not want the goddess to forget her promise.

Sisoaneer frowned, then grasped Nora's forearms and rubbed them with hands as cool as green leaves. "I am sure we will find him. Perhaps he will find us. For your sake, I hope he is well. He is quite powerful enough to take care of himself, of course.

"But not more powerful than you," she added, "when I lend you my strength. You feel it when you heal pilgrims in my name, don't you? How do you like it?"

Nora flushed in the darkness. She had told no one what it was like to exist momentarily in that shining bubble of utter peace and power, but Sisoaneer knew. She lived there all the time. "Yes, I feel it," Nora said as neutrally as she could. "It's pure glory." She was afraid that the goddess might hear greed or hunger in her voice, so she went on quickly: "But I wish that I could heal the patients with my own magic. It's how Aruendiel trained me. I know I need to work on—"

"Your own magic is still too weak," Sisoaneer said. "You could never heal so many—or any—with your own power."

"But how will I get stronger if I never—"

"You don't need your own magic. I'll lend you all that you need, and more."

Despite herself, Nora felt a secret thrill. She hesitated, then said simply, "Thank you."

"Well, do you believe in me now?" Sisoaneer asked. There was a silvery current of laughter in her voice, so bright that Nora almost missed the longing underneath. "Do you believe that I am your goddess, your Holy Queen of Power, and all the lovely things you say in the prayers?"

She's still not the God I don't believe in, Nora thought. That God was older and more distant and much more implacable, and sometimes—it had to be admitted—he had a long white beard. But what other gods do I know? Sisoaneer has helped me help all those people. She has shown me what heaven is like.

"Yes, most of it," Nora said gently. She paused to sort through what she meant by her answer. "What I feel in my heart is true. Sometimes the prayers are very long."

The goddess threw back her head and laughed. "Yes, the prayers are very long. I hear them, always, but I listen to what is in your heart. I believe," she said, "you are going to dance for me tonight?"

"Apparently," Nora said, sorry to be reminded of the next duty that awaited her below. "It may not look much like a dance, but that is the intention."

"I'll watch the dance that you make in your heart." Sisoaneer took Nora's hand, the one with the brand-new pinkie finger, and squeezed it. "You will never disappoint me, if your faith is strong."

Torches had been set into sockets in the pavement of the larger courtyard, outlining a square. Their wavering yellow light washed over the faces of pilgrims in the front row, upturned to follow the movements of the dancers. As Nora swayed and circled, she recognized some of the pilgrims: the thin, bald man with the ulcerated leg, the young man from Tima with the bloody urine, the Pernish woman with the tired smile and the sick headaches. All cured now. Behind the faces in the torchlight, the crowd filled most of the shadowy courtyard. Oasme had told her that all of the pilgrims who were not strictly bedbound would be there.

Nora turned and turned again, feeling slightly dizzy, then followed the other dancers into a ring. Clasp hands, make a circuit. Reverse. The throbbing of drums, the quavering notes of goat-horn pipes filled her ears. The *ganoi* music told a story she could not understand, although it filled her bones with restlessness.

Turn, twist. Pick up a line of the chant, throw it to the next dancer. Bend at the waist, sway, twist again without falling over or letting your *maran* come undone. Clasp hands again, another circle. A dancer passed her the hollow silver wand filled with incense, and Nora twirled, wrapping herself in a scented cloud, the crowd dissolving into a rosy blur.

This wasn't so bad. She had reached the point where her feet knew the steps and the rhythms better than her mind did, and she could let herself move freely within the confines of the dance.

The beat of the drums pounded faster, louder. On Nora's left, Yaioni swayed like a sapling lashed by the wind; on her right, a stocky *ganoi* woman rocked on her haunches. She caught Nora's eye and her face creased into deep, gleeful lines. Nora grinned back and thrust her own hips harder.

"All praise to the Mother of Power," Oasme called. "She brings healing out of darkness, she feeds death to our enemies." For a goddess of healing, Sisoaneer was remarkably famous for killing people, Nora thought. The dancers took up the chant. "All praise to the Mother of Power." The words traveled through the crowd in a cresting wave.

Nora stole another glance at Yaioni. It seemed to her that more of the male faces in the crowd were turned toward the First Deaconess— well, no wonder, Nora thought. Even the folds of Yaioni's *maran* could not hide the extravagant swing of her breasts. And she was a better dancer. Her body undulated with flamboyant grace even while her face remained composed, severe, her eyes apparently fixed on mysteries that only she could see. She looks more like the High Priestess of Sisoaneer than I do, Nora thought.

But *I* am the High Priestess, Nora reminded herself. I know magic that Yaioni doesn't know, will never know. She flung herself deeper into the dance, and her heart matched the pulse of the drums. "Guard us, protect us, great goddess Sisoaneer, for we are as children before you, and no knife is as sharp as yours." Twisting, stomping, she let her breasts bounce under her clothes and willed all the men who were undressing Yaioni with their eyes to look at her instead. "All praise to the Mother of Power," she called.

"All praise, all praise," the pilgrims sang back to her.

A man standing a few rows back seemed to be staring at her as intently as she could have wished. He was taller than the other spectators. A torch flared, casting a warm light deeper into the crowd. She saw the grave, scarred face, the angle of the shoulders, and understood why her eye had sought him out.

"Aruendiel!"

Chapter 19

Nora ran into the crowd, almost stepping on some of the pilgrims sitting in the front row. A man squawked something indignant in Pernish.

"Aruendiel?" She scanned the dark ranks of spectators outside the reach of the torches. Her glimpse of Aruendiel's face burned as vividly in her mind as if she were looking at a snapshot, but now she could not reconcile it with any of the shadowy forms and silhouettes around her. "Aruendiel?"

Whispers began to circulate in half a dozen different languages. From behind, Oasme plucked at her elbow.

"Is anything wrong?" he asked in a low tone.

"I saw Aruendiel. My—teacher. I saw him right here." Nora pointed into the crowd.

"That's no reason to interrupt the Ieona observance, Blessed Lady." Oasme looked over his shoulder and made a rapid gesture, presumably to the other dancers: keep going.

"I'm sorry. But I saw him. He's here."

"Then he'll want to see you finish the dance." Oasme's arm had snaked around her shoulders. Somehow, pulling and pushing, he spun her around, away from the spectators.

Nora twisted back, not freeing herself completely, but loosening his grip. "No! I have to find him." She stared hard in one direction, then another, willing—commanding—Aruendiel to come into sight.

Oasme's voice hissed in her ear: "Her Holiness is watching. You must not dishonor Her Holiness."

"Who cares—" Nora began to say, but the angry words dissolved in her throat as she registered something in Oasme's tone that sounded like fear. She remembered the empty seats in the refectory, and a reluctant composure settled over her, like a heavy coat.

She was the High Priestess. She was responsible, in some sense, for everyone in the temple complex, everyone who accepted her authority, and it came to her that it was her duty to protect them from harm, or at least not to expose them to danger if she could avoid it.

She let Oasme steer her back to where the others were still spinning and stamping in the rhythm of the dance. Her absence seemed to have caused little disruption; if anything, Nora thought sourly, the dancers moved faster and with more sureness than before. Only the chanting sounded a little ragged. Her own legs felt jittery, excited, ready to move, but they seemed to have forgotten the shape of the dance. What they wanted to do was run, to carry her away from here in search of Aruendiel. She took her place among the dancers, willing herself to copy them, hoping that her clumsiness was less obvious to everyone else than it was to her.

The drums beat even faster than before, without making time pass any more quickly; it was as though the dance were an invisible cage, and when she tried to look outside it, her eyes only found Oasme, now standing almost where Aruendiel had stood.

Abruptly, the music stopped. Nora, caught in the middle of a turn, staggered a little, then straightened. Oasme was already starting toward her with a purposeful look. Damn. He had said something about a procession to the temple after the dancing, hadn't he?

"Oh, great Sisoaneer!" Nora said, as loudly as she could without actually screaming. She raised her hands and bowed her head. Oasme stopped in his tracks. "You who give life, you who ease the pain of those who suffer, we praise you without ceasing for your power and your mercy. We thank you for all the blessings you shower upon us, O mighty goddess, great lady, wise healer." She went on, stringing together phrases almost at random from the chants she had been learning. Her powers of impromptu prayer had improved in recent weeks. The mass of pilgrims before her swayed and bowed their heads.

"Praise to Her Holiness!" Nora held her arms out to the crowd, inviting it to take up the chant. Her words came back to her in a great swell of sound. Louder, louder, she gestured, smiling. "Glory to Her Holiness, she who lives forever! Death to her enemies!" Again, she motioned, and the pilgrims obliged by shouting her words. The drummers picked up the rhythm; the wave of voices rose higher.

There, Nora thought, as the chanting crested around her, that should do it. She can hear them on her mountaintop, no matter how high it is.

The crowd, meanwhile, was distracted by its own roar. Nora pivoted, avoiding Oasme's eye, and walked rapidly away from the other dancers, out of the courtyard. She plunged down an alley between two buildings, then another, until she was sure she was not being followed.

Now the chant behind her was fraying, breaking down. Her footsteps sounded startlingly loud.

"Aruendiel?" she called softly. She chose her path at random as she passed through the complex, scanning the shadows. "Aruendiel?" There was no answer, not even when she abandoned caution and raised her voice until it echoed off the quiet buildings around her. A *ganoi* woman, hurrying past, looked at her strangely.

Nora closed her eyes, willing him to answer. She could not doubt that she had seen him. The snapshot in her mind was too clear.

"Aruendiel?" Was he hiding from her? Still angry, no doubt, and repenting of whatever impulse had led him to seek her out.

Hiding—of course Aruendiel was hiding. Sisoaneer had said so. He had masked his power with some supercharged shield spell in order to come here, to Erchkaii.

Which left open the question: whom was he hiding from? Aruendiel had no shortage of enemies, but the obvious answer was the most disturbing. It wouldn't be Nora he was hiding from. Even if he didn't want Nora to know he was nearby—and hadn't he more or less deliberately shown himself just now?—he wouldn't need a shield spell to conceal his presence from her. He'd only need the spell to disguise himself from another, more powerful, more dangerous magicworker.

"Aruendiel?" Nora whispered.

She threaded her way among the buildings one more time. By now the pilgrims who had attended the Ieona ceremony were straggling back to the dormitories; Nora scanned the passersby, but none of them were Aruendiel. She crossed the empty courtyard, climbed the

Stairs of Healing, and went up the streamside path. The flowing water winked and chuckled, full of its own secrets. He could be anywhere, really. She glanced up at the darkened sides of the ravine. By now she knew the path to the temple well enough that she didn't really need a light to follow its twisting course, even at night, but she conjured one anyway in case Aruendiel might be waiting in some alcove in the rock.

When she got to the bridge in front of the waterfall, someone came out of the temple, carrying a light that turned the curtain of water to dancing golden fire. Nora felt a surge of anticipation and discovered that she was trembling. She scooped up the skirt of her *maran* and strode across the bridge as quickly as she could.

The person with the light came toward her. Too fat and too short to be Aruendiel. It was Uliverat.

"Good night to you, Blessed Lady!" she said cheerfully. "If you've come to check on the temple, I've just closed it up for the evening. That *ganoi* wretch Olig spilled a flask of oil in the side aisle today and didn't tell anyone, so I had to clean it up. I thought there was going to be a procession tonight! We always have one at Ieona."

Nora caught the implied rebuke. "Not tonight."

"Well, if there had been one, you might have caught me on the floor with sawdust and a brush. Pray to Her Holiness that my knees hold up." Uliverat grunted a syllable signaling extreme exertion.

"Was there anyone else in the temple just now?" Nora asked. "I thought I saw someone heading this way."

"Just me, only me."

From Uliverat's tone, Nora realized her own omission. "Thank you very much for cleaning up the oil, Uliverat. I know that's a lot of extra work for you. Are you sure it was Olig who spilled the oil, though?" she ventured. "If he didn't tell anyone, then how do you know—"

"Of course, it was him, the young liar! He's always spilling things."

"You're sure there was no one else there tonight?"

"Not a body! They were all down watching you dancers. Of course, if there had been a procession, it would have been different."

"Very likely," Nora said. She saw that she would have to come up with a reason for cutting tonight's ceremony short, if only for appearances' sake. Would Sisoaneer want to know why? She had gotten her promised dance from Nora. "Do you know if any new pilgrims arrived tonight, after Ieona started?"

"How would I know that, when I've been up at the temple all evening? Lemoes was supposed to be on duty at the hospital tonight— he would know. He should have told you if there were any urgent cases that couldn't wait until tomorrow. But he's always daydreaming, that boy, away with the birds—doesn't hear a thing I tell him."

She had more to say on the subject. Nora wondered if there was anything one could say that would not somehow provoke a flood of smiling, voluble indignation from Uliverat. Probably not.

The lantern in Uliverat's hand bobbed up and down as they walked downstream; shadows slid around the rocks and quivered among the ferns that grew at the stream's edge; the tawny ravine wall at their side rose steeply into heavy, uncompromising blackness. Over the rise and fall of Uliverat's voice, Nora kept listening for a third pair of footsteps, the scratch of an unseen person's breath. The small circle of lantern light felt like a prison. Somewhere in the night, maddeningly close— she was certain of it—Aruendiel waited.

First she could not sleep, staring holes in the darkness as she lay on her pallet, lying as still as she could so that she wouldn't miss the scrape of a boot on the stairs, the rustle of a traveling cloak, the lightest tap at her door. Once she heard an owl screech across the ravine, and her heart thudded with joy, but there was nothing but silence for a long time after that.

When someone did knock at the door, she was lost in a restless jungle of troubled dreams, Raclin grinning at her as she danced madly in a torn *maran*. With both hands, Raclin lifted his head from his shoulders and tossed it toward her. As the head bounced on the ground with a thump thump thump, still smirking imperturbably, she hoped frantically that none of the other dancers had noticed it, but she could not bring herself to kick it aside with her naked foot—

"What is it?" Nora sat up on her pallet. The knocking at her door was real. "Aruendiel?" she called softly.

Someone outside cleared his throat. "It's Lemoes." He coughed apologetically. "I'm sorry to bother you, but Oasme said to tell you if there was any change with the baron."

The baron? It took Nora a moment to remember what he was talking about. The pilgrim she'd seen this afternoon. Lemoes was saying something about fever, a leaking wound.

Nora dressed quickly and made her way down to the hospital. Over the rim of the ravine, the eastern sky was brightening, layered with clouds. The thought crossed her mind that perhaps this summons was some sort of ploy by Oasme to teach her a lesson for interrupting Ieona and then ending it too soon, but the baron really was worse, flushed and clammy, shivering with feverish chills. He muttered as she examined him, words sliding incoherently from between cracked lips.

She began a spell to reduce fever but almost immediately she knew that something was wrong. The spell felt slack, insubstantial. There was magic nearby, but she could not make it respond. It slipped away, refusing to answer.

Sisoaneer, lend me your power. Nora thought the words, then spoke them aloud. She waited for the surge of magic that would carry her safely into the infinite depths of the abyss and back again.

There was no reply from the goddess. No acknowledgment, no magic. Waiting, then waiting longer, Nora could only feel the staccato beat of her own pulse.

She tried the spell again, knowing that it was useless. She was right.

Lemoes was looking at her expectantly. Nora bit her lip. "I can't do anything," she said. "Not right now. I'm sorry."

She was apologizing to the baron as much as to Lemoes. His eyes were dull slits in his slick, ruddy face. Putting the back of her hand to his forehead again, she registered its heat and grimaced before she could stop herself. Don't Scare the Pilgrims was one of her private rules; she hoped that the baron was too sick, too out of it to see her sudden panic. What to do now? Without magic, she was useless, clumsier and more ignorant in the hospital than even the least experienced of the *ganoi* nurses.

Lemoes gave her a quick, shy smile of encouragement. "The goddess—"

"I tried!" Nora said. "She's not helping. Give him some water, and—and try to cool him off, and let someone take care of him who actually knows what they're doing. Not me." She stood up, rubbing the palms of her hands against her dress.

It was only a fever. People recovered from fevers and infected wounds all the time, even without magic.

She looked down the ward. Most of the pilgrims were still sleeping, but the man in the next bed was awake, coughing quietly. Nora recognized him. Pafagus from Bisr, his name was. He had what they called bloody breath here; as far as she could tell, that meant TB. Catching her eye, he pushed himself slightly higher against his pillow and twisted his gaunt face into something that might have been intended to be a pleading smile.

"Blessed Lady, if you could do something for the pain—it has been bad tonight—"

He was the one who was supposed to go home next week. But Sisoaneer had said no, he would die. "I'm sorry," Nora said. "I'm really sorry." She walked quickly down the ward, trying to step quietly so that she didn't wake anyone else up. Then they would all want her to help them.

Something for the pain. She needed a pain spell herself. Her headache was back, hot and gritty, making her thoughts slow and sore.

Outside, a gray dawn light had spread over the temple complex, turning the walls of the ravine an ashen yellow. The tile roofs of the squat buildings around the hospital shone dully. Some rain must have fallen during the night, although Nora had not heard it. Probably she had slept more than she thought, although right now she felt as though she had not slept at all.

She closed her eyes. Where was Aruendiel? Where would he have gone last night, after his brief appearance at the Ieona dance?

And today Sisoaneer did not answer Nora's prayer, did not share her power. It was because of Aruendiel, Nora was sure. Had he somehow blocked Sisoaneer's magic? Or had he offended the goddess? That was a real possibility.

For the sake of thoroughness, Nora went to each of the pilgrim dormitories and managed to establish, from a halting conversation in pidgin Ors with the *ganoi* porters, that no tall, dark-haired man with a limp had arrived recently or was in residence. She had learned some basic phrases in the *ganoi* language by now, but it seemed to her that a kind of curtain swept across the faces of the *ganoi* whenever she tried to speak to them in their own tongue. Either they saw her as an oppressor, like Uliverat, or she was butchering their language, or both.

Picking a new route through the huddled buildings of the temple complex, Nora made her way to the courtyard where she had seen Aruendiel the night before. The rain had washed away most of the charcoal lines that marked the space for dancing, but she could still pick out the place where he had stood. Aruendiel would never be found unless he wanted to be, she reflected. That was truer of him than of anyone else in the world. So where did that leave her now?

Lost in her thoughts, she did not see Oasme until it was too late to avoid him. He was aiming directly for her, anyway, and he was wearing the expression that sometimes inspired Nora to picture him with a clipboard, a precisely knotted tie, and small, stylish, black-framed eyeglasses.

"Blessed Lady, Baron Tesein—"

"Is he dead?" Nora asked.

"No, but he is in a very bad way. We must make every effort with him. His wife is not yet delivered of his heir, and apparently there is some difficulty with one of the brothers. Haariku is one of the richest provinces in the eastern Empire."

Nora shook her head. "Oasme, I can't help him. Didn't Lemoes tell you?"

Oasme gave her an understanding smile, the kind meant to spread like jam over last-minute jitters. "My old High Priest said that with bad cases, sometimes the only thing you can do is keep them from dying today, so that they can get better tomorrow."

"I mean I can't help any of them." In a lower voice, Nora said, "I can't do magic right now. She's not answering me."

"What do you mean?" Oasme's gaze traveled over Nora in a way that suggested that without budging he could still scrutinize her from several different angles. "Have you angered her?"

"Me? No, I—well, how would I know? She seemed fine last night."

"Mmm. That was before the Ieona ceremony, I believe?"

Nora sighed. "All right. I cut it short. A lot of the pilgrims there last night are still weak; I thought they should go back to bed instead of walking all the way to the temple." Try to argue with that, she thought. "But she'd let the baron suffer because of what I did? Really?"

"Blessed Lady, the ways of the gods are unfathomable." Oasme raised his eyebrows as if to convey that they were not nearly as unfathomable to him as to Nora.

"I don't think she really cares whether we did the whole procession or not," Nora said, although she could see that it was a lost cause.

"Gods are easily offended, not so easily appeased," Oasme said. He lowered his voice: "And if the goddess is truly angry, it is not only the baron—or the other pilgrims—who will suffer."

Nora rubbed a fingertip against her aching temple and felt like saying she knew that perfectly well, she was already suffering. Instead, she asked, "What if it's nothing *I* did?"

The lines of Oasme's frown shifted subtly as he performed a new calculation. It did not take him long. "The man you said you saw, when you interrupted the dance—your old teacher, you said? Did you find him?"

Nora shook her head. "I did see him, you know," she said warningly.

"You think he might have angered Her Holiness?"

"She wouldn't be the first," Nora said.

"Then you must pray," Oasme said, in a voice that almost made her jump, it was so harsh. "Pray for Her Holiness's forgiveness. Pray for your teacher. Pray for the baron and his recovery. Pray for the other pilgrims under our roof, who came here to be helped by you."

"But—"

Before she could get out more than a single word, Oasme's finger flew to his lips. *She is always listening,* he mouthed. He pointed toward the temple. "Go," he said. "You'll be late for the morning prayers."

With its full lips curved in a sinuous smile and its heavy-lidded eyes, the statue wore an expression of beneficent cunning. Incense hung in the air like a veil, blurring the arches of the sanctuary and the bowed shapes of a half-dozen pilgrims small and isolated in the forest of columns. The morning prayers drew the lowest attendance of the three daily services.

"Daughter of death, lead us in the arts of power. Grant that everything we do"—Nora paused in her chant, rummaged for the correct word—"we undertake will be pleasing to you. Hear us when we call upon you. Help us, for we are weak and you are strong."

There was more in the same vein. Her head throbbing, Nora stumbled again, and then again in reciting the prayers. The statue listened with its vacant, unvarying smile. "You who bring death and bring life, it is not for us to understand the mysteries, the mysteries, um—" This time Nora completely lost the thread of the words.

"—of your will," Yaioni prompted from behind her, in hushed tones that were just loud enough so that everyone in the temple could hear. "Beloved child of darkness, the number of—"

"—the number of our days is known to you alone," Nora finished, seizing back the chant.

She was almost at the end. Only a few verses to go, and would any of them do any good? Enough of this, she suddenly decided.

"Sisoaneer! I would like to talk to you." To her own ears, Nora's voice sounded raw and uncertain after the smoothly gliding syllables of the hymn.

She waited. There was no sound except for the low rise and fall of a pilgrim's mumbled, private prayer, drifting from the rear of the temple. She wondered if his request was getting through. Nora stepped closer to the statue.

"Where is Aruendiel, and why aren't you answering when I call to you?" She did not bother to lower her voice; she did not care if the pilgrims heard or what they might think. "There is at least one person in the hospital who will probably die because I can't help him, because you won't help me."

She took a deep breath. "If I have done wrong, I'm sorry that I've offended you. And I don't ask this for myself. Give your power to Yaioni"—she turned to drill the First Deaconess with a sharp look—"or to someone else who can cure those pilgrims, if you want. I don't want them to suffer because of me.

"And, again, where is Aruendiel? I know I saw him. I just want to know that he is all right."

The cloying smoke of the incense felt like sandpaper on the back of Nora's dry throat. For the first time, she noticed that the carved skull that was the statue's armrest was missing a couple of teeth. Perhaps it had been modeled on a real skull. Its grin was manic, pitiless.

"You know, this is why I gave up on religion before. You talk to God, and you never hear anything back." She waited, listening to the silence, then said: "I'm coming up now."

Behind her came a faint, exasperated hiss. "You will only annoy her more," Yaioni said softly, "if she sees you. When she is angry like this, it is easy to make her angrier."

"Then maybe you'll get to be High Priestess after all." Nora sidled around the statue, fitting herself into the crooked gap in the temple wall. It did not yawn any wider at her approach. Apparently she was not expected, not today. Nora took a little more time than she actually needed to clamber through the hole, taking extra pains that her *maran* didn't snag on the rough stone.

Yaioni was probably right; this was a bad idea. However, Nora reflected, she had no better ideas.

Carefully she counted her way past the entrance to the lower caves and followed the twisting passageway upward. In the pure black darkness her aching head felt cooler and less heavy, not exactly released from pain but accommodated to it. Still, it was because of the headache that she sensed the light ahead before she actually saw it. Rounding a turn, she smelled the sharp, warm astringency of pine trees and then stepped outside.

This part of the mountain was new to her. A grove of pines held fast to the mountainside, their roots knotted around cracked rocks, their limbs swaying gently like gallant green plumes. Through the trees she glimpsed the hazy curves of other mountains and a slice of the distant lake, slate-colored on this overcast day. A set of rough steps, cut into the exposed stone, twined uphill.

Climbing them, she noticed recent footprints in the pine-needle loam covering the steps. Some seemed large enough to be from a man's boot. It was hard to tell for sure.

The stairs brought her around a giant, burled tree. She found herself at the edge of an open space rimmed with more pines, their twisted limbs framing glimpses of the overcast sky. The wind murmured in their needles, but the air inside the grove was quiet and warm. The space felt oddly like a shrine.

It also made a nice place for a picnic. Directly ahead, at a stone table in the center of the clearing, sat Sisoaneer, her hair loose and shining around her shoulders. She leaned forward, one slender arm bent, her eyes rapt, somehow expectant, as she listened to Aruendiel.

Chapter 20

He sat at Sisoaneer's left, angled toward her across the corner of the table, so that Nora could see only the back of his dark head. She could hear the rumble of his voice without making out any words. He sounded calm, perhaps even amused. His left hand played with a silver goblet. On the table between him and Sisoaneer was the heel of a loaf of bread, a small jar, a silver bowl half-full of peaches, and another silver goblet.

Sisoaneer saw Nora first. She lifted her head from her hand with the kind of delicacy that one might use to aim an extremely precise instrument, a telescope or a gun. Aruendiel turned. Nora met his eyes, as cool and cloudy as the sky above, and his expression shifted indefinably. Something swift and elusive darted through the harsh landscape of his face and then disappeared, leaving no trace on the bare rock. Whether he was angry or pleased to see her, it was impossible to tell.

Nora approached the table, her heart pounding. "Aruendiel. You're here."

"Blessings of the morning, High Priestess," Sisoaneer said. Something about her was different. "You wanted to speak to me?"

"Yes." Nora looked at Aruendiel instead. She had an awkward sense that she was trespassing, like an insistent waitress bearing down with a check. "I saw you last night, just a flash, and then I looked for you. But I couldn't find you."

Aruendiel gave a clipped nod of acknowledgment. "You were occupied. I thought it better not to interrupt your ceremony, more than I already had."

Nora began to say that it wouldn't have mattered, but Sisoaneer was already speaking: "And then I took him for my own purposes! I am sorry for delaying your reunion. We have been talking, and the night passed quickly." She grimaced happily at her own thoughtlessness. Now

Nora realized why she looked different. She had abandoned her usual rough gray for a blue dress with a silvery sheen, the bodice dotted with pearls and heavy with complicated stitching.

"I see." Nora looked from Sisoaneer to Aruendiel to the breakfast remains on the table. Something about the sensuous pink and yellow curves of the peaches plucked at her nerves. They weren't even in season. What kind of magic did you use to get hold of ripe peaches in springtime? Were they conjured from some orchard to the south, or did you take a flowering tree and make time speed up? Either way, someone had gone to a lot of trouble for breakfast.

"Would you like some fruit, High Priestess?" Sisoaneer asked.

The peaches smelled delicious, but she wasn't hungry. "No, thank you. What were you talking about?" she asked, knowing that the question was intrusive but unable to stop herself from asking it.

"Everything." Sisoaneer's smile was as lively as the breeze. "It has been a very long time since the magician Aruendiel came to do me honor. A mortal lifetime."

Nora raised her eyebrows—composedly, she hoped. "Oh. That long? I didn't know you two knew each other."

Aruendiel's gaze had slipped away from Nora's. "It was longer ago than a mortal lifetime," he said.

"Even so, I remember it very well," Sisoaneer said. She put her hand on Aruendiel's black sleeve and left it there for a long moment. "I have a confession, my priestess," she said to Nora. "I never told you this, but Aruendiel was once my worshipper—and my pupil. I taught him the secrets of true magic when he was very, very young."

Nora gave a politely incredulous smile and waited for Aruendiel to refute this statement.

"And I am grateful for those lessons, Lady," Aruendiel said, turning back to Sisoaneer. "I learned much from you."

"But I thought—you told Hirgus Ext you learned real magic from lost books, old manuscripts," Nora said. The gold and silver threads in Hirgus's beard gleamed in her memory. Hirgus was writing a book; he'd tried to coax a truculent Aruendiel to tell him the origins of true magic. "People had forgotten about all about real magic. There were no true magicians anymore, just wizards controlling demons."

"That's true," Sisoaneer said before Aruendiel could speak. "They loved to order the spirits around. It made them feel so powerful. But—learning from old books? Come now, I'm not an old book." She gave Aruendiel a slanting smile.

"Books have their uses, Lady. But it is true, nothing of what you taught me came from ink and paper."

Nora tried to figure out if Aruendiel had actually returned Sisoaneer's amused, private glance or if she had imagined that. She wanted very much to be wrong about what she thought she'd seen, but ultimately you had to face the truth, no matter how unpleasant.

"How did this all come about, exactly?" Nora asked. "How did you meet? Here at Erchkaii?"

This time she was sure about the swift, rather piercing glance that Aruendiel sent to Sisoaneer. And Sisoaneer's long, delicate mouth flexed as though she wanted to laugh at a shared joke. But when Sisoaneer spoke, her voice was serious.

"I set him free when he was trapped and helpless. I suppose he never mentioned that?"

Nora shook her head. Sisoaneer looked meaningfully at Aruendiel. He pressed his lips together and then said quickly, "An enemy had placed me under an enchantment that deprived me of my powers."

"You mean, like Dorneng—" Nora began, but once again Sisoaneer spoke first.

"He was in a sad state when I first saw him, singing hymns to me at midnight in the forest. You would not have known him—dressed in peasant's rags, hungry, tired, fearful."

She dealt out the last words slowly, one by one, like tossing pebbles into a brook. Aruendiel seemed to be listening intently, counting each splash.

"No more fearful than I had reason to be," he said.

"And you did have reason to be afraid," Sisoaneer said. "You were so weak!" She spoke with amused pity. Aruendiel's face was still but not exactly composed, Nora thought. "I saw that you were hungry for the arts of power," Sisoaneer continued, "even if you hardly knew what they were. I thought, well, let us see what this one can do.

"For seven years I taught him everything I could," she said, turning back to Nora. "There are some things, of course, that even the best pupils are too stubborn to learn. But by and large he learned much, and quickly.

"You remind me so much of him, you know," Sisoaneer added. "The talent, just starting to be honed. The same independence. And you are strong, stronger than women are meant to be." She laughed suddenly, her eyes crinkling.

Nora glanced at Aruendiel, who was not laughing. Perhaps he did not appreciate the comparison. "I'm honored to be likened to Aruendiel," she said. "Although I have to disagree on one point. Women are strong. They don't always realize it."

"I wish you were right," Sisoaneer said, shaking her head. "But I've seen it so many times. Even when I give women power, they're afraid to use it to the full. They practice magic in secret; they do timid, piddling spells. Even against enemies, they don't strike to kill.

"But you did. You're different, dear one. It's why I chose you to be my priestess, to heal the sick. It takes strength to do good. And you will help me make more priestesses, you will show other women how to be strong so that they can wield my power as they should."

I strike to kill, Nora thought. That's my special talent, that's why Sisoaneer chose me for this job. Her head throbbed.

"I can't wield your power if you won't let me," she said, reminded of why she had come here in the first place. "I can't heal anyone. You didn't answer when I prayed today for your—power.

"Oasme thought I might have offended you. If I did, I am sorry," she added stiffly. She found that she was not as eager to apologize as she had been previously.

Sisoaneer's ink-stroke eyebrows lifted, and she drew in her breath sharply. "*I* am so very sorry. When you called on me, I was distracted. As I said, Aruendiel and I talked all night." She offered another rueful smile, like a curling silk ribbon.

But the smile was really for Aruendiel, Nora thought. Was he returning it, ever so slightly? She couldn't tell. His profile, as he watched Sisoaneer, seemed to be chipped out of stone.

"I will hear you next time, Nora, and every time after that, I promise," Sisoaneer said. "You should be quite proud of your former pupil," she added to Aruendiel. "She's healed dozens of pilgrims already. She knows the arts of power like her own teeth."

Aruendiel stirred. He regarded Nora with a chilly curiosity. "I am surprised to hear it," he said, addressing Sisoaneer. "Your High Priestess is still green, a novice magician who is just beginning to understand her craft."

Sisoaneer laughed quietly. "You were green, too, Aruendiel, until I taught you."

"That's true," Aruendiel said. "But she has had nothing like those seven years."

"Seven years! It passed so quickly. I'll give her seven years or as much time as she needs." Sisoaneer tilted her head to one side. "But I think she will be a better pupil than you."

"In the few months I taught her," Aruendiel said, "she mastered a handful of imperfectly controlled spells. She knows nothing of wood magic, air magic—"

"She doesn't need to. She has more power to command than any other magician on earth. My power. That reminds me," Sisoaneer added, turning to Nora. "He has something to return to you. If you want it."

My heart, Nora thought bitterly. Yes, I want it back. Unbroken, please. She had no idea what Sisoaneer actually meant. The only thing she could think of was her handbag; she'd left it behind when she had run away from Aruendiel. He scowled and reached into his tunic as she looked questioningly at him.

"This is yours." He thrust forward a small bottle of bluish glass. Nora held it up to the light, turning the vessel to get a better look at the slender, light-colored object inside.

She drew in her breath.

"My finger!" It seemed smaller than she remembered, but perhaps that was a trick of the glass. Otherwise, her severed finger looked quite normal, except that it ended in a ragged flap of skin instead of her hand. And Aruendiel had been carrying this gruesome relic around for several weeks now. She wondered what to make of that.

"I found it near the dead Faitoren. Rejoining it to your hand would be easy enough—"

"But then I would have six fingers on my left hand," Nora said, lifting her chin. She held her hand toward him and waggled her little finger. "Sisoaneer healed it for me." The goddess gave her a sleepy-eyed smile.

With a short, skeptical utterance, Aruendiel seized Nora's wrist. He ran an index finger along her new pinkie, pressing the nail and the bone, then lifted the finger and bent it, testing the joints. Nora wondered if he could tell how her pulse thudded faster when he touched her skin, and she turned her face away. "I would hope that, in the future, you would have the wit and the magic to tend to your own wounds," he said.

"I could stop the bleeding now. We have a good spell for that." She wanted to show him that she had not wasted her time here. "And I could get rid of the pain, at least for a while. I haven't regrown a finger yet," she added, "but there are spells in the library. A treatise by Tethenisus—"

"Tethenisus? Hmm." Aruendiel pursed his lips disapprovingly. "It's complicated magic, regrowing a severed limb, and it takes a great deal of power. I'd advise you not to try it unless you know exactly what you are doing." He rubbed the finger again, slowly, with a speculative air, and then released her hand. Nora pulled it back quickly, with a muddled, secret sense of loss.

Sisoaneer shook her head, smiling. "She has plenty of power. She only has to ask for it."

"Even if you gave her enough power to blind the sun, she will never learn the full breadth of true magic unless she can draw on her own sources of power."

"You're too stringent, Aruendiel. She will learn faster if she can do more interesting, more important mag—" Sisoaneer broke off, her smile draining away. "Do you hear that?"

"But she is not ready for those spells, or for that much power. She will do harm, to others or to herself, and—"

"Quiet!" Sisoaneer lifted her head and frowned in concentration. "What is that?"

Aruendiel raised an eyebrow. Listening hard, Nora caught only the bright, distant chatter of unseen birds and the lazy whoosh of the wind in the trees. Half a minute passed. "What did you hear?" Nora asked.

Very far away, a crow began to scold. And there was another sound, a faint, distorted straining, so vague that Nora wasn't sure she was hearing with her ears.

Aruendiel remained unmoving, his gaze drifting over Nora and the clearing and the pines. "That?" he asked.

"Yes, *that*."

It was a whole furious chorus of crows now.

"Whatever it is, it is breaking right through your protection spells," Aruendiel said.

"I know that." Sisoaneer rose from her seat and strode across the slab in the center of the clearing. Through a gap in the pines she stared down the side of the mountain. "It is some monstrosity. A demon. What is it doing here?"

No one answered. Two crows flapped up from the valley below, still shrieking. The other birds were quiet.

Aruendiel lifted a hand into the breeze and rubbed something delicately between his fingers that wasn't there. The lines in his scarred cheek grew harsher. "I recognize it."

"Do you?" Sisoaneer wheeled, her eyes slitted. "How do you know it?"

"I've met it before."

"How strange that you would meet it again here."

"Not so strange." Aruendiel stood up, shifting his crooked shoulders. "I expect it has come for me."

"What is it?" Nora asked, but Sisoaneer's voice was louder: "What do you mean, 'come for you'? Is it *yours*?"

"I crossed its trail on the way here," Aruendiel said. "I hunted it for a while, but it seems to be hunting me."

"That was careless of you, or worse." Sisoaneer curled her lip. "You know how much I hate those things—slippery, unnatural. Evil."

Now Nora could hear trees crashing and thrashing, far down the mountainside. She remembered how Raclin had sounded almost the same way, lumbering after her. This thing was bigger.

"Horrible. And you brought it here!" Sisoaneer almost spat the words at Aruendiel, then turned her back. She braced herself between two of the pines, facing outward.

A long, still moment. Then the thwack and groan of splintering wood moved closer.

"Not that spell, you can't attack it that way," Aruendiel said to Sisoaneer's back. "It's too strong." He came around the table, moving quickly despite his uneven stride, to take up a position at the edge of the clearing. With a jerk of his head, he motioned to Nora to move toward the center of the terrace.

"What is it?" she asked again.

The crows had stopped calling. The wind blew through the trees with heightened energy. Nora licked dry lips. There seemed to be too much silence and too much noise, little dry rustles coming from all directions.

"Where has it got to?" Sisoaneer asked. "I'll—"

She spun around, her upturned face white. Nora sat down abruptly without meaning to, because something big and snarling had just leaped over her head, landing on a rock outside the circle of pines.

Its lithe golden bulk loomed over the clearing. Nora stared up into the glassy eyes with sick recognition. It was much bigger than she remembered, the wickedly curved claws as huge as garden scythes. The tawny, black-spotted fur looked improbably soft. Its tail twitched, the same impatient rhythm that a house cat would use to command: feed me.

Chapter 21

It snarled again. Nora drew back, shaking, as the great mouth opened. Beyond it, she knew, there was an infinity of night, enough dark to drown the villages and cities and perhaps entire peoples that the Kavareen had consumed in its centuries of existence. Just as it had swallowed Hirizjahkinis, who'd been bold enough and, in retrospect, deluded enough to call herself its master.

Nora tried to get to her feet. If you met a bear—she remembered the brochure from a long-ago visit to a state park—you were supposed to stand there and back away slowly and calmly, as though you met bears every day and it was no big deal. This had always struck her as risky advice. She reflected numbly that the Kavareen was even less likely to be impressed by a show of nonchalance than the average bear. Especially right now, when her legs were trembling so much that she couldn't get up.

Aruendiel clamped onto her elbow and hauled her upright. "You remember the Kavareen, Nora," he said.

She gave a vehement nod. "Oh, yes."

"You know this thing?" Sisoaneer demanded.

"It belonged to a—a friend of ours," Nora said. "Before it ate her."

Crouching just outside the grove, the Kavareen growled, so loudly that the air seemed to vibrate. A huge paw snaked between two tree trunks; Nora jumped back.

"Disgusting creature," Sisoaneer said, flinging up an arm. The green boughs, the reddish pine loam, the Kavareen's bright, spotted coat abruptly faded to shades of gray. Nora felt invisible pinpricks all over her face and the exposed skin of her arms. With a wild groan, one of the trees split in half, sending splinters and needles flying. The Kavareen yowled.

"Are you mad, to use a rending spell at such close range? You could have torn us all to shreds." Aruendiel's voice sounded raw. Through the settling sawdust, color slowly returned to the world. "Besides, this is a demon—the ghost of a demon," he added. "You can't kill it by ordinary means."

"Do you know how to fight it? Then, pray, show us all," Sisoaneer said. She had sidled to the far side of the clearing. Backed up against the table, Nora could not decide whether to climb over or just hide underneath.

The creature slashed again. The naked claws just missed Aruendiel. The Kavareen rose, tail lashing. It paced left, then right on the other side of the ring of pines.

"Why doesn't it just jump over?" Nora breathed.

"I am holding it at bay," Aruendiel said. "Otherwise it would be upon us."

"Can you do no more?" Sisoaneer asked sharply.

"Not in this place, Lady," he said tightly. "I can pull magic only from afar. There is none to spare for me here; it is all yours."

Nora found his admission disheartening, but Sisoaneer gave a throaty little chuckle. "That's right. All power is mine here. This is my realm, my sacred place. I am Queen of Holy Power, and this vermin cannot stand against me."

It seemed to Nora that the Kavareen was holding its own with little effort, but she decided not to point that out. Sisoaneer moved around the table to face the Kavareen. Pinching her index fingers against her thumbs, she brought her hands together, then jerked them apart as though pulling on an invisible thread. The Kavareen growled and put its ears back.

"You will only irritate it," Aruendiel said. "Remember, it is not alive."

"It can still suffer," Sisoaneer said. She repeated the gesture, yanking her hands apart with greater vehemence.

The Kavareen hissed, the fur on its neck rising. With a furious twist of its body, it lowered its head and raised a menacing paw. The heavy hooks slashed at Sisoaneer faster than Nora's eyes could follow.

Sisoaneer, just out of range, flinched only slightly. "Go, you evil *thing*!" she commanded, touching her hands together again. "Go!"

The Kavareen bared its teeth and tried to lunge through a gap in the trees. There was just enough space for it to fit, Nora observed with disappointment as she dove under the table. Scrambling to her feet on the other side, she was just in time to see the Kavareen recoil, slammed against a tree trunk. Aruendiel's shield spell had thrown it back, she guessed. The creature roared with outrage.

"Leave here!" Sisoaneer said, ripping at her invisible thread.

Another snarl, deep and penetrating, promising all manner of raw, violent vengeance, and then, unbelievably, the Kavareen began to move away. It backed down the mountain slope, its tail whipping the pines, and then it turned and bounded out of sight.

"Well, it understands pain, if nothing else," Sisoaneer said with satisfaction, pushing a strand of hair out of her eye.

"You only maddened it," Aruendiel said. "Where has it gone?"

Sisaoneer seemed to be about to respond, but instead she looked away, frowning slightly in concentration.

That shrill, distant call—Nora hoped it was a bird. She walked quickly across the clearing and looked down the mountainside. Far below, she could see the green thread of the stream and a few square roofs in the lower temple complex. A tiny figure crossed the space between two buildings, moving with surprising speed. Someone running full tilt. She heard the high-pitched scream again and knew that it wasn't a bird.

"It's at the temple," Aruendiel said.

Sisoaneer pushed past Nora to peer down the mountain. "My children—it dares to attack them!"

"It's always hungry," Nora said, knowing it was the wrong thing to say but unable to stop herself.

Color rose in Sisoaneer's thin cheeks. She put a hand on Nora's shoulder. "My priestess, we must save these innocents."

Nora nodded, mostly out of principle, but not sure what Sisoaneer had in mind. What did she mean by *we*? "If you let Aruendiel take the magic he needs, he could—"

"Dear one, you will defeat this monstrosity in my name," Sisoaneer said. Her dark eyes widened with a kind of excited tenderness. "All my power is yours to wield, all of it."

"Ridiculous." Aruendiel pressed forward, his body twisting slightly. "Lady, you can't send this girl to fight the Kavareen. She's too unproven, she cannot—"

"If she fails, she's not worthy to be my priestess," Sisoaneer said. "But she won't fail. She will do this great work for me." She squeezed Nora's shoulder, smiling at her.

Nora staggered. The earth seemed to have shifted under her feet.

Sisoaneer and Aruendiel were nowhere to be seen. The air was humid, full of river smells. All around her were the drab, tile-roofed structures of the temple complex, the long hospital building directly ahead. From all directions, she heard screaming. One of the *ganoi* men sprinted past, almost running her down. He shouted something she couldn't understand, but she heard the panic in his voice.

For a moment, Nora couldn't breathe. Her thoughts stuttered: no. All by myself? You didn't even ask. Even a goddess should know better. Her legs seemed to be making their own decisions as she wheeled to follow the *ganoi*.

Instead she found herself looking up into the Kavareen's stagnant yellow gaze.

She backed away, slowly, just as the bear pamphlet had advised. The Kavareen watched her intently, unmoving. After a dozen paces, she felt the hospital wall at her back. As calmly as she could, she edged sideways until her hands discovered the doorframe of the entrance.

Slipping inside, she slammed the tall doors behind her, then fumbled for a bolt. There wasn't one. Nora vaguely remembered Oasme explaining that the omission was deliberate, because the hospital was supposed to be open to all pilgrims at all times. At the time, it had seemed like a nice idea.

"Blessed Lady." Nora looked up to see Lemoes, the acolyte, coming down the ward toward her. Behind him, she noticed with a sinking heart, almost every bed was still full. They hadn't had time to evacuate.

"No one moved the pilgrims?" she said.

"Some of them are too sick to move," Lemoes said. "And the attendants ran away when the monster leopard came."

"But not you."

With angelic calm, he said, "The goddess told me not to worry, that we would be safe."

"Oh, that's what she told you?" Nora said.

Something pressed hard at the doors behind her. Very hard. For a misguided instant, she tried to hold them shut with her body. She scrambled out of the way just in time as the doors flew open and the Kavareen's head pushed through. It looked to be a tight fit through the doorway, but Nora thought fleetingly of the tiny spaces where her now-departed Astrophel used to hide himself, under the bookcase, behind the dryer—

"It's coming in," she said.

The Kavareen thrust a paw through the doorway, its claws clattering on the hospital floor. Lemoes drew back. "She said we would be protected." There was a new tinge of uncertainty in his voice.

"I guess she meant me," Nora said. Casting the first spell she could think of, Nora set the Kavareen's tail on fire.

At first the Kavareen showed no reaction, and then it seemed to Nora that the blank ferocity of its normal expression took on a slightly surprised cast. The leopard growled, twisted to try to look backward, and then withdrew from the doorway. Through the swinging doors, Nora glimpsed streaming flame that suggested a furiously thrashing tail. Before she could lose her nerve, she followed the Kavareen, closing the doors behind her.

In front of the hospital, the big cat pretzeled itself to lick energetically at its tail with an invisible tongue, or whatever served it as a tongue. The flames smoked and dwindled.

Trembling, Nora mentally leafed through the warfare spells she could recall. They tended to be fairly specialized, which was probably fine in a conventional battlefield situation, but was not necessarily helpful here. She readied her shield spell against arrows and hoped that it would work reasonably well against a dead demon's claws. And she asked for the goddess's aid.

All my power is yours to wield. Sisoaneer hadn't been kidding. As the euphoria of the goddess's magic flooded through her, Nora felt weightless and free, as though her body were made of pure light. It seemed to her slightly insane that she had ever been afraid of the

Kavareen; she almost laughed aloud at the thought. The shield spell, she saw grandly, would protect a dozen battalions against a solid rain of arrows for an entire day. The Kavareen had finished cleaning the fire from its fur, and its tail looked miraculously untouched, but she could not feel disturbed by her failure to inflict any permanent damage. There was nothing greater in the universe than the goddess's strength and goodness. Hail Sisoaneer, kind and splendid, protector of those who love her.

The Kavareen stared down at her, settling itself on its haunches. That feline air of wide-eyed wonder, mixed with scorn—as though marveling at some egregious faux pas you did not even realize you had committed—was familiar to Nora. Astrophel used to look at her the same way. The expression was definitely more threatening when you were looking up at it.

Slowly Nora felt her sense of well-being ebb, and her body tensed again. She still had no idea how to defeat the creature, even if the shield spell was working. How long would it hold?

She returned its yellow stare. Did the Kavareen recognize her? Once Hirizjahkinis had commanded the Kavareen to guard Nora for some hours, and it had spent most of that time dozing peacefully at her side. But that was when the monster was the size of a normal leopard instead of a house. A small house, admittedly.

Hirizjahkinis had been so kind to Nora and so confident in the Kavareen's loyalty, so unsuspecting. And then, one day, the Kavareen had turned on her. The traitor gazed stonily at Nora.

"Where is Hirizjahkinis?" Nora's voice sounded hoarse.

The Kavareen's ears pricked forward. Only the tip of its tail moved.

"Hirizjahkinis! What did you do with her?" Nora's throat felt so tight that she had to struggle to shout, but it was good to be angry instead of just afraid. "She trusted you. That was really stupid—she'd probably agree now—but that's who she was, she wasn't afraid of a dead demon. So where is she now? Inside you? Is she alive or dead?"

The Kavareen snarled. Its teeth were stained, and one of the great fangs was chipped. Nora made herself look hard into the churning, haunted darkness inside the creature's jaws.

"Hirizjahkinis!" she called. "Where are you?"

A massive paw slammed her in the shoulder. It was like being hit with a sofa, the blow slightly padded but not to be resisted. Nora fell backward. Her shield spell was gone. She struggled to rise, but the Kavareen's paw forced her down again. Its black cavern of a mouth gaped wider.

The darkness inside was heavy, suffocatingly close. Nora's eyes found cloudy shapes in the obscurity that vanished as she strained to make them out more clearly. Her ears were full of half-heard noises—human voices; the clash of arms; the cries of animals; the rumble of falling stones.

"No!" Jerking backward, Nora worked a levitation spell.

An instant later, she was balanced on the hospital roof, only a few feet higher than the creature's head. She swayed there, wondering what to do next.

"Vlonicl designed that shield spell to protect against arrows, not demons."

Never had the bite of sarcasm been more reassuring. Nora looked over the edge of the roof.

"Aruendiel! What are you doing? Get away from that thing!"

He was standing not fifteen feet from the Kavareen. It had swung around to face him. Returning to a crouch, it hissed viciously, its ears flattened against its head. Aruendiel folded his arms and stared back at the Kavareen, looking not exactly relaxed but not like a man who feared being devoured on the spot.

"My shield spell is holding, for now," he informed Nora.

Good for him. Good, period. She took a deep breath to calm herself. "I suppose your spell is meant especially for Kavareens?"

"More or less. Most demons can escape any human spell eventually," he said dourly. "It used to be a joke among wizards that the only sure way to defeat a demon is by employing another, larger demon."

Nora squatted on the peak of the roof to hear Aruendiel better. "Is that what Hirizjahkinis did, when she tamed it?" Not that another, more cooperative demon of any size was available right now.

Aruendiel frowned. "Hirizjahkinis was close-mouthed about exactly what she did to enslave this creature. Killing the thing reduced its power, of course."

"I would hope so," Nora said.

"But it also meant that some spells that were used to control it in the past didn't work anymore." For a moment Aruendiel took his eyes off the Kavareen to give Nora a severe look. "Do you know what sort of demon it was?"

"It eats things. Everything."

"True, but what made the Kavareen truly feared was its power to change shape, until death trapped it in the form it has now. Hirizjahkinis was lucky that it chose to attack her as a leopard and not, say, a drove of dragons."

Without warning, the Kavareen leaped. Nora shrieked as the creature rose up over Aruendiel, claws bared, and then she breathed again as Aruendiel's shield spell deflected it. The Kavareen slid away to his left in an ungraceful sprawl of paws and tail.

"Maybe you should move—" Nora began.

"You need not be apprehensive. I can defend myself, unlike some."

Nora felt the sniping uncalled for, and then she saw what Aruendiel had seen and she had not: Yaioni, trying to squeeze into the shallow niche under the library steps, where the *ganoi* sometimes stowed the crutches discarded by pilgrims who no longer needed them.

The Kavareen also saw her. Yaioni emitted a strangled yelp as the monster bounded toward her. Snatching up one of the crutches, she pointed it at the Kavareen like a lance, jabbing at its eyes. She landed a blow on its cheek instead.

The Kavareen recoiled—more in surprise than fear, Nora thought. She remembered another spell of Vlonicl's, To Strengthen a Warrior's Arm, and worked it as quickly as she could to help Yaioni.

At a tilting run, Aruendiel raced toward the library. The Kavareen clawed again at Yaioni, dodging the end of the crutch with a kind of horrible playfulness, and then swiped at Aruendiel.

Nora stepped off the roof, barely finishing a levitation spell in time, and landed hard. She staggered, then looked up.

Aruendiel must have done something to distract the Kavareen from Yaioni. Something unpleasant, judging from the creature's growls, its whipping tail. The great jaws opened. The Kavareen pounced. Aruendiel pulled back, not quickly enough.

His head and shoulders disappeared into its mouth. So much for that shield spell.

Nora screamed. She ran toward the Kavareen, unsure of what to do, wishing she had something to hit it with.

The young, rather scrawny willow growing next to the library twisted suddenly, violently. With a ferocious sucking sound, its roots heaved out of the ground, splattering waves of mud in all directions.

Startled, Nora checked herself, watching as the tree's branches begin to lash madly at the Kavareen. It was as though a small hurricane had seized the willow. Twigs snapped, green wood shrieked and splintered, as the tree bent low, flailing at the huge leopard.

The Kavareen squirmed in a cloud of torn and swirling leaves. It clawed at the whipping boughs. And its mouth remained clamped shut around Aruendiel's body.

Just the day before, Nora had worked a spell, normally used for poisoning cases, to treat a boy with abdominal pain. He'd brought up a handful of pebbles, several buttons, and a rusty key, which his father seized with a look of greedy relief that Nora felt was not entirely related to his son's health.

The willow tree was fast becoming a mass of splinters. Broken branches twitched all over the ground. Nora cast the vomiting spell.

The Kavareen settled back on its haunches. She thought it gave her a disparaging glance, although that was more or less its usual expression. Nora's heart sank.

Then the Kavareen shook its head emphatically. Its mouth opened. Aruendiel's upper torso and head emerged. He slumped forward, eyes closed.

The creature sank into a crouch that she recognized: Astrophel had been prone to hairballs. With an air of fastidious resignation, the Kavareen retched up in rapid succession Uliverat, several pilgrims, two *ganoi* women, a small boat, three horses, an ox, and a flock of sheep. They lay wilted on the ground. Some were trembling. One of the sheep made a croaking noise that did not sound as though it should come from a sheep.

Nora waited; nothing more was forthcoming. She did the spell again, sending the Kavareen into a series of dry heaves.

"It's too late," Aruendiel said, opening his eyes wearily. He sat up and gave his neck an experimental twist, wincing. "It's been too long. You can't get Hiriz back."

"Worth a try." Nora sighed.

Awkwardly, Aruendiel stood up, brushing willow leaves from his tunic. The tree had finally stopped moving. The green sap smell of torn wood filled the air. "That was smart, using the tree," Nora said.

Aruendiel gave her an odd look. "That was your doing."

"But I don't know any wood magic," Nora said.

"She loaned you her power," he said. "And everything here—almost everything—obeys her. So it obeys you."

As he spoke, Nora discovered that he was putting into words something that she already understood to be true. Perhaps she had been afraid to think it herself.

She raised a last objection: "I didn't command that tree—"

"You must improve your control," Aruendiel said, his voice sharper than before.

"My control?" Nora gave a shaky laugh. She looked at the Kavareen, which was sniffing at the croaking sheep. "My control. You mean, like this?"

The Kavareen rose straight into the air. It was by far the largest thing that Nora had ever levitated, but lifting it up fifty, a hundred, two hundred feet took no effort at all. For a moment the Kavareen seemed not to understand what was happening; then it began to paw the air and curl its body as though it could wriggle out of Nora's spell.

She let it hang there, admiring her work. From this distance the creature looked soft, harmless. I'll shake you into a kitten, I will, Nora thought, and swung it back and forth, back and forth. The Kavareen snarled down at her.

She looked at Aruendiel. "Better?"

"Better," he said shortly. "How long do you propose to keep the wretched thing hanging above our heads?"

"Not for long," she said. At her urging, the Kavareen picked up speed, moving in longer, faster arcs, gathering momentum. It writhed more frantically than ever, as though it guessed what she intended. Its shadow floated against the green side of the mountain.

She sent the Kavareen soaring far across the river, as though she were flying a kite. Then she snapped it back fast.

She meant to smash the thing against the mountain's stone flank. The impact might destroy the Kavareen, or only stun it. Both options were acceptable. But as the Kavareen skidded protesting through the air, she saw something else she could do.

The mountain was waiting for her. Like the tree, like her own hands, it was ready to do her will. She could feel its massy strength, its ancient roots, its buried secret heart, as though the mountain were part of her own body. Its slow, vast patience filled her mind until, struggling under the weight of this wonderful, terrifying new intimacy, she had to remind herself to take a breath.

She told the mountain what she wanted it to do.

The rock yawned, opening a deep black seam. Large enough to admit the Kavareen. The creature disappeared inside. She felt it travel deep down through mineral veins into the core of the mountain and then come to rest, a minute foreign particle in the greater body, encapsulated in stone so that it could do no more harm.

The mountain grew still again, returning to its dreams of deep time. Nora felt its heaviness settle into her own being. She could see no obvious way back to her own small, ephemeral, animal thoughts.

Then she became aware that Aruendiel was gripping her by the shoulders. At first his features seemed as small and abstract as a page of arithmetic problems, but gradually she noticed the warm human fear in his eyes and began to hear the words coming from his moving mouth, and the dry, sketched notations turned into a face again.

She discerned that he was asking if she was all right. "I guess so," she said, although she could feel Sisoaneer's power ripping away from her like the tide, and she had never felt so empty, sick, and forlorn in her life. She put her hand on Aruendiel's shoulder, because she needed to lean on something, and he pulled her to him.

She let him hold her. He was saying something about an excess of magic, the intoxication of so much power, only the most foolhardy of magicians, and other things. He stroked her hair. His fingers felt warm and deft and yet oddly vulnerable, transitory. She started to cry.

"You are coming out of it now," Aruendiel said, sounding relieved, although his brows knit as he watched the tear trickle down her cheek.

"You said everything here obeys her," Nora said. "But a mountain—I can't believe a mountain—"

He gave a slight shrug, or maybe a shudder. "It did. It obeyed her, so it obeyed you."

"It was incredible, and I don't ever want to do that again," she said, gulping.

"Not until you have more experience." He studied her. "What gave you the idea to send the Kavareen into the mountain?"

Tiredly, Nora made herself remember. "It was neater than seeing it go splat, I guess. And it was good to see something else eating the Kavareen for once. Why, what would you have done?" she asked.

"Sent the creature to sleep or bound its limbs with a shackling spell." His mouth twisted with rueful impatience. "Either option would require enough power to tame a half-dozen thunderstorms."

Or enough to awaken a mountain, Nora thought vaguely. Then, with sudden interest, she saw what lay under his words. "You haven't given up on Hirizjahkinis," she said. "You don't want to kill it, either."

"It's difficult to kill a demon in the best of circumstances. And it's almost impossible when the demon is already dead." He paused, then added, "In any case, the chance of seeing Hirizjahkinis again is quite small."

His tone was bleak, but Nora had the impression that he was trying to kill his own hopes more than hers. That was very like Aruendiel. Without thinking, she lifted her hand to cup his scarred cheek. Except for the faint prickle of stubble on his chin and jaw, his skin felt tender and unguarded under her fingers. His gaze flickered like a startled bird, and for a moment—she thought—he rested his face against her palm.

Then, gently but firmly, he disengaged. There was no other word for the way he leaned away from her and drew in his arms so that she had to step back as well. She grabbed for his hands.

"Aruendiel, I have to tell you something." Nora took a deep breath, still smelling that faint elusive tang that belonged to his skin and hair. "Um. When we parted, when we quarreled—"

Aruendiel's crooked shoulders seemed to stiffen. "I uttered a vile calumny against you then. It was false. I regret saying it."

"Oh, I said terrible, insulting things to you—"

"Let us not mention them," he said swiftly, like the blade of a skate slashing the ice.

"I would like to forget everything we said," Nora said. "But I want to apologize first. It was the ring, you know, that damn ring. Raclin made me say all those things."

She paused, picturing Raclin again, his face maddeningly delectable even when he was sneering at her. Raclin was saying something in her memory, but she raised her voice so that she would not have to listen. "I think about how awful it must have sounded to you, and I—I'm horrified. I would like to die. I would do anything not to have said what I said. But, Aruendiel, you have to understand, it wasn't really me saying those cruel things. It was Raclin."

She waited for him to respond.

"You did say them," Aruendiel said. It sounded like a key turning in a lock.

"Well, I said them," she clarified, "but I didn't mean them. It was Faitoren magic."

He sighed. "Do you remember the essence of Faitoren magic?"

"It's illusion," Nora said, as though that settled it.

"Faitoren magic," Aruendiel said, more mildly than he usually corrected her, "draws upon your secret wishes. It's illusion that is born in your heart and speaks truths that you would not say otherwise."

She had the sensation that Raclin was choking her again. "No. Not this time. He made me lie. He made me try to hurt you."

Aruendiel's hands slipped out of hers. "You spoke the truth. You said that I'm ancient and disfigured, a corpse unnaturally vivified by magic. All those things are true."

"No. No, they're not. And if they were, so what? I wouldn't care." She was losing him, she could tell. "I love you, Aruendiel."

There was no good, all-purpose word for "love" in Ors. The language had terms for various sorts and degrees of love—illicit sexual infatuation, for example, or the affection between parent and child, or the respect that a chaste and honorable wife owed her husband. Nora used the most powerful word for love that she knew, one that she had read only once or twice and had never heard spoken aloud.

Aruendiel's head jerked back, and she saw a mixture of calculation and raw panic in his face that chilled her even more than what he said: "Then you are doomed to disappointment."

Nora drew in her breath, hoping that no pain showed in her expression. "I can see that." She knew for a certainty that it wouldn't make her feel any better, but she asked anyway: "Is it because you and Sisoaneer—?"

Aruendiel frowned. "The nature of my relations with Sisoaneer does not concern you."

"I think it does," Nora said. "And not just because I'm her High Priestess."

"We have reached an understanding, she and I," he said.

"An understanding? How nice. What does that mean, exactly?"

"It's better you do not know." Aruendiel's gaze swept past her. "It is your responsibility to please your goddess, High Priestess. You will not do so by prying into matters that are not your affair."

"But I *am* very pleased with her." The words came from behind Nora. She felt cool fingers twining through her own, and turned her head, startled, to meet Sisoaneer's dark eyes. "I am proud of you, my priestess. You saved my people! You did even better than I'd hoped." She squeezed Nora's hand.

"I just used your magic," Nora said roughly. She thought, I borrow your magic, you get Aruendiel. Is that the deal we made without my knowing it?

"And you used it with rare cleverness and skill," Sisoaneer said. To Aruendiel she added, "You see? I chose well. Your pupil is not as clumsy and naive as you thought. She even saved *you*. I hope you have thanked her properly."

Aruendiel inclined his head toward Nora. "My deepest gratitude," he said curtly.

"And mine," Sisoaneer said, with another squeeze of Nora's hand. The fine, smiling lines around the goddess's eyes showed nothing but kindness and understanding, too much understanding. How much had she heard of what Nora had said to Aruendiel? She heard many things, Oasme said.

Nora looked away, training her gaze deliberately on a sheep ejected by the Kavareen near the hospital steps. After a couple of tries, the animal staggered to its feet and emitted a faltering *baa*. Nearby, one of the *ganoi* woman was sitting up, her whole body shaking.

"I should make sure everyone is all right," Nora said grimly, pulling her hand out of Sisoaneer's. She moved away quickly before she could collect any more of this excruciatingly unwelcome thanks and praise.

"Give them hot baths and send them to bed with whatever strong drink you keep around this place," Aruendiel called after her. His tone sounded a shade less harsh. He was relieved she was leaving, no question. "It's cold inside the Kavareen."

But *you* won't have to stay cold long, will you, Nora thought. She marched over to Uliverat, still prone on the ground and weeping slightly, to see what could be done.

Aruendiel was right: everyone who had been inside the Kavareen had chills, their teeth chattering, their fingernails purple. One of the pilgrims, an elderly man whom she had treated a few days earlier for a heart ailment, looked as pale as though he had been literally frozen. She conjured a fire. Very carefully—because she had never done this spell with anything out of sight range before—she summoned blankets from the hospital stores and passed them out.

She found Yaioni sitting on the library steps, cradling her left ankle and wearing a sullen expression. "The monster leopard attacked me, and you did nothing to stop it," Yaioni said.

"I strengthened your arm," Nora said, but the First Deaconess did not believe her. "I had to fight it myself, and I sprained my ankle," Yaioni said.

"Do you want me to heal it for you?" Nora asked. "Or are you afraid that instead I'll do a spell to cripple you?"

Yaioni smiled, eyebrows arching, as though she appreciated Nora's line of thought. "I am not afraid of you. You are too soft and weak to hurt me, even though the goddess has given you so much power now."

"Try me," Nora said.

Yaioni looked past Nora and her expression twisted. "She is not angry anymore, is she?"

"No, she's not," Nora said, and then she turned her head to see what Yaioni was looking at. Aruendiel and Sisoaneer embracing.

They were a good twenty yards away; Aruendiel's back blocked part of the view, but there was no mistaking how their mouths pressed together, or how tightly Sisoaneer's long arms were wrapped around Aruendiel's shoulders.

Nora took it all in within a fraction of a second, and then sat down on the steps to work on Yaioni's ankle. She considered doing magic that would tie Yaioni's ligaments into knots or turn her bones to powder or clot the blood in her veins like jelly. It would have answered to her mood, and she would have shown Yaioni just how soft and weak she really was, but after all—Nora reminded herself—it was not Yaioni who had been kissing Aruendiel.

And when, biting her lip, Nora called upon the goddess's magic to repair the ankle, Sisoaneer's power felt sweeter and more joyful than ever, as though she had swallowed a sky full of shooting stars. When the magic receded, Nora discovered that her cheeks were wet with tears.

Yaioni stood up, supporting herself with a grip that dug deep into Nora's shoulder muscles; she put her weight on the ankle slowly and straightened with a faint growl of suspicion. "There is no pain," she said, making it sound like a complaint.

"I can put some back, if you want," Nora said.

Yaioni rolled her eyes and blew a small, cynical sigh from her lips. "I know you would like to." She glanced around. "He is so old and ugly, that man!"

She spoke loudly enough that Nora could tell, without turning to look, that Aruendiel and Sisoaneer were gone.

"Who?" Nora said.

But Yaioni was having none of her pretended ignorance. "You know. He was the one you called to last night when we danced, wasn't he?" She grinned. "You know him. The magician."

"Him? Yes." Nora tried to sound noncommittal.

"I don't see how she could stand to kiss him like that." An edge of anger in Yaioni's voice. "As though she is starving for him." Silently Nora gritted her teeth. "But she knew him long ago, when he was young," Yaioni went on. "He must have been more handsome then. Perhaps she closes her eyes and thinks of what he used to look like."

Nora shot to her feet, feeling a sudden urge to run very fast, as far away as she could. Yaioni had perfectly evoked the scene that Nora was trying not to think of, and behind it the shadowy, secluded past; the tender interlude Aruendiel and Sisoaneer had shared; the unreachable realm to which Nora would always be a stranger. Seven years. It was a long time.

"He had an accident," she said at random and walked rapidly toward the hospital. Her face felt hard and brittle, as though it might shatter. *She knew him long ago, when he was young.* It occurred to her to wonder how Yaioni had acquired that piece of information, and then she realized that Sisoaneer must have told her, probably had been telling her all kinds of interesting details about Nora all along. Or perhaps everyone knew the old story except for Nora. Innocent, ignorant Nora.

That's why Aruendiel came here, Nora thought, to see her. That's why he disappeared last night, why he didn't come to me after I saw him. Just now, when we were facing the Kavareen together, it felt easier between us, almost the same as always, and he held me, and I thought—

But whatever kindness he'd shown then meant nothing, Nora now saw. If his affection for her was unchanged, if concern could still show in his face, it only signified how shallow those feelings had been all along compared to the great love that he must have shared—still shared—with Sisoaneer.

She entered the hospital, shoving hard on the doors, as though they might lead to a refuge from her own thoughts. They barely missed hitting two people passing on the other side: Lemoes and a blanket-swathed pilgrim who shuffled beside him, leaning on his arm. Horrified, Nora began to apologize, but Lemoes shook his head and smiled.

"It's all right. The baron has a good grip on me, and he wouldn't let me fall. Isn't that right, sir?"

The pilgrim lifted up a head of untidy, graying hair, said a sentence or two in his own language, and laughed with a sputter. His jowly face had a deflated look, no doubt from weight loss during his illness, but his black eyes looked unblinkingly into Nora's.

"What does he say?" she asked.

Lemoes smiled awkwardly. "He says I shouldn't let a woman knock me down." The pilgrim added a few words in his own tongue, still chuckling. Lemoes, with a sidelong glance at Nora, did not translate them.

Nora made a couple of private guesses as to what the pilgrim had just said, none of them very pleasing. How satisfying it would be to levitate him upside down for just a moment, say.

Then she registered what Lemoes had first said. "The baron?" She looked hard at the pilgrim. They always looked different when they were up and moving, and their faces were alert and not fever-flushed, not glazed with sickroom sweat. "Baron Tesein?"

Lemoes nodded. "Yes, I'm just helping him get some exercise."

"But, Lemoes"—Nora felt a stab of alarm—"he's really sick. His wound was leaking this morning, he was burning up with fever. He shouldn't be out of bed."

"He's fine," Lemoes said mildly. "Look at him."

The baron stared back with a touch of belligerence. His face was toadlike, Nora thought, but he also seemed to have a toad's solidity. Nora smiled at him with polite goodwill, marveling.

She leaned toward Lemoes to whisper in his ear. "I thought we were going to lose him."

Lemoes nodded. "I prayed to the goddess. She saved him."

PART III

There is always a great demand for spells to make a person invisible. The simplest method is to render the flesh transparent, but such spells require much power and are by necessity short-lived. One can also create invisibility with certain light spells or darkness spells. The subtlest and most powerful invisibility spells, however, affect the perception of observers, so that they do not recognize what is before them or imagine they see something different.

—FROM THE NOTEBOOKS OF
THE MAGICIAN ARUENDIEL

Chapter 22

Uliverat was going on again about the rudeness of the pilgrim from Sasgefao. This was the second time she'd mentioned it today. There was an excited flutter in her voice, and her lips pursed ominously at the end of each sentence as she selected the next round from her stockpile of ammunition.

Nora didn't give a damn if the Sasgefaon had prayed to his own god in Sisoaneer's temple. He had said thank you politely enough when Nora healed his ulcerated leg, and it was entirely possible that his god might be more satisfactory than Sisoaneer in any number of ways. But Uliverat was insistent that a deadly insult had been directed at the goddess.

Across the refectory table, she kept glancing at Nora. But if Nora met her eyes, however briefly, Uliverat looked away.

Uliverat was afraid of Nora. So was Oasme, listening dutifully to Uliverat with a fixed frown. He was more adept at concealing his unease, but he did not like to meet Nora's eyes, either.

It was clear to Nora that the entire temple community had revised its view of her ever since she'd sent the Kavareen hurtling into the mountain. The *ganoi* fell silent when she approached. Oasme chose his words with ever more unctuous care. Even Yaioni now seemed more subdued.

Only Lemoes seemed the same, oblivious to the disturbing if blessed power of the High Priestess. But that was typical of his off-kilter, holy innocence, Nora had decided; either he hadn't picked up on the cues from the others, or he assumed that his beloved goddess would protect him no matter what.

Nora chased a morsel of fish around her plate with a piece of flatbread. Her left hand was in her lap, buried in the folds of her *maran*. Under the table she slid her thumb over the length of her little finger and then wished she hadn't.

It was stupid, absurd, and heartbreaking that they were so afraid of her power. Nora had never felt less powerful in her life, for all that she had healed four dozen pilgrims in the last three days, moved several tons of stone yesterday for repairs to the buildings that the Kavareen had damaged, and lifted the river from its bed this morning so that the *ganoi* could build the foundation for a new bridge. None of it was her own magic; it belonged to Sisoaneer, who had Aruendiel as well.

She had not seen either of them for three days. They were obviously fully occupied.

Nora rubbed her temple. Uliverat was still talking.

"—he must apologize to our blessed High Priestess, may she glorify the goddess forever!"

"May she glorify the goddess forever," Oasme repeated. Nora realized she hadn't heard that particular formula before, just as Lemoes and Yaioni echoed the same words. It took a moment to sink in: they were talking about her.

"You don't have to say that," Nora said sharply.

Uliverat played dumb. Or perhaps, Nora thought, she just was dumb. "Say what, Blessed Lady?"

"What you just said about me. 'May she glorify the goddess forever.'"

A look of disquiet passed over Uliverat's soft-fleshed face. "It is what we all want, Blessed Lady."

"Is it, really?"

Uliverat's discomfiture only seemed to deepen. Nora felt some regret for the sarcasm in her tone. At the same time she could not stop herself from wondering if she could find a spell that would render Uliverat mute. Too bad she knew almost nothing about transformations; Uliverat would be so much more attractive as a rabbit than a human.

Maybe, Nora thought, this is why everyone is afraid of me.

Nora could not stop thinking of dark, cruel magic, all the different spells—some of them very ordinary—that could be used to torment everyone around her. A repulsion spell that would keep a person's dinner—or anything else he wanted to pick up—just out of his reach. An analgesic spell that, if not performed just right, would cause pain instead of soothing it. Any of Vlonicl's more gruesome war spells. Nora kept coming back to the one that would roast your enemy's liver inside his body. It could work for any organ, really, but the liver was a nice big target, easy to find.

She didn't think that she would do that spell, or any of them, but there was evil joy in contemplating the prospect, which made the dull, hot weight in her head easier to bear. It was not really a full-fledged headache, nowhere near as bad as the one she'd had the day the Kavareen came, but it never quite went away, except when she worked magic.

So she worked magic as often she could. The stronger the spell, the better. Fortunately, the festival was still going on and plenty of pilgrims needed attention.

Nora looked up to see Oasme leaning toward her. "When you have finished your dinner, we should go over the order for tonight's service."

She groaned inwardly. For an instant, she imagined Oasme encased in a coffin of ice, eyes glazed over, his mouth frozen open in the act of telling her what she had to do next. It was another Vlonicl spell, slightly modified. "I'm finished now, Oasme, but I'm going back to the hospital. Is this service another long one?"

"Not like some, Blessed Lady." Oasme allowed himself a restrained smile. "This is Falis Woana, the Night of Holy Justice. You will appear for only a few minutes, at the end."

Nora considered this. "Can I just sneak in before it ends?"

"That is exactly what I would advise," Oasme surprised her by saying. "The first part of the ceremony is all about the Ghaki king's justice, a lot of dreary legal business, and it is better that you do not appear at all for that. You come in at the end to represent the divine mercy of Sisoaneer."

"And how will I do that?"

"You will pardon a prisoner."

"All right, I can do that." Nora rose from the table, contorting herself slightly to extricate herself from the heavy High Priestess's chair. "What time should I come?"

Oasme seemed not to have heard her. He was looking at her hands as they rested on the tabletop.

Nora felt her face grow warm as Yaioni followed his gaze, then Lemoes. Uliverat allowed herself a discreet sideways glance. Then another, not quite as discreet. They were all looking at her left hand, probably trying to make up their minds about what they saw.

"Oasme, I'll be there an hour after sunset," Nora said, curling her hand into a fist. The accustomed gesture felt odd, awkward.

Oasme had recollected himself. He straightened. "That should be plenty of time, Blessed Lady."

The hospital was quiet tonight. Most of the pilgrims were sleeping. Nora stopped beside the few who were awake to see if they needed anything. She did some pain-relieving spells and felt the tightness in her own head ease.

At the end of the row of beds, Lemoes squatted next to a pilgrim whom Nora had treated the day before, a middle-aged man with pain in his belly that Oasme had diagnosed as an ulcer. Now he was talking to Lemoes in his own language in short, soft bursts of words. As Nora passed, Lemoes caught her eye and stood up.

"How is he doing?" she asked, tucking her left hand into a fold of her *maran* as unobtrusively as she could.

"He needs a spell to make the blood flow more freely."

Nora frowned. "No, he doesn't. That's exactly what he doesn't need. He had bleeding in his stomach."

"This is different," Lemoes said, irritatingly tall and earnest. It was annoying to have to look up at him to explain a perfectly simple point.

"He already lost a lot of blood. I don't want him bleeding to death."

"No, something else is wrong with him. Not what Oasme said." Lemoes stepped away from the pallet, so that she had to trail after him. "If his blood doesn't flow more smoothly, he'll have a paralytic attack."

It was what they called a stroke. Nora wanted very much to tell Lemoes that he was wrong. She took another look at the pilgrim sitting up on the pallet. A merchant from Nenaveii with a soft, narrow-eyed, agreeably cynical face. Under his stubble of beard, he looked pale but alert. She had done a spell to stop the bleeding in his stomach; his stool had been black with blood for months. It was a pretty strong spell.

"How do you know?" she asked Lemoes.

Lemoes said nothing. She looked hard at him. "Did the goddess tell you?" She couldn't quite keep the pique out of her voice. Lemoes nodded matter-of-factly.

"All right. All right," Nora said. "This is the third time in three days she's given you directions about the pilgrims. It's good that she's talking to someone, I guess. When does she tell you this stuff?"

Lemoes looked at the stones of the floor, his mouth set gravely. "She comes to me at night."

"She comes to you," Nora repeated. "At night." She let her eyes follow the rich curve of Lemoes's lips, the composed symmetry of his strong brows, the deep warm color of his skin. Not just Aruendiel, but also Lemoes? "When at night?" she asked sharply. "You mean, when you're in your bed?"

Lemoes bobbed his head, still looking away.

"And she—talks with you?"

"She doesn't talk, exactly. I mean, she does, but—"

"I don't see how she finds the time," Nora snapped.

"It's not what you're thinking," Lemoes said.

"I don't think about anything anymore," Nora said. "It makes my head hurt."

Lemoes looked even more solemn. "She had a message for you, too. She says she is pleased with you, that you serve her well."

It would be a joy to blow the roof off the hospital, to shake the mountain off its foundation, to make the lake rise up and wash away all trace of Erchkaii and its inhabitants, divine and human. "Great," said Nora. "Thanks for letting me know."

Outside, it was already getting dark. A single bright star shone in the west, just visible over the wall of the gorge. Nora calculated that she was not yet late to Falis Woana. Still, she would have to stop at her chambers to wash and to change into her more elaborate ceremonial *maran*, so she'd have to hurry to get to the temple in time. For the second time that day, she wished that she knew more about transformations. It would be nice to be able to fly straight to the ceremony.

As she passed through the main courtyard, to her right she made out the dim shapes of horses and men and the gleam of torchlight on armor, which puzzled her at first. It wasn't unusual for pilgrims and their parties to arrive with horses or donkeys, but normally the animals were stabled at the far end of the complex, near the path to the lake. Then she recalled what Oasme had said about the Ghaki king's justice, and she guessed that the horsemen in mail had something to do with that.

Nora went up the Stairs of Healing—deserted, was everyone at the temple already?—and followed the streamside path. She climbed the steps to her sleeping quarters, where a single oil lamp had been lit for her. By its light, she stripped off her *maran* and saw that there were bloodstains on the gown that she hadn't noticed before, probably from the man with the leg wound she had treated in the afternoon. She felt tired and grimy for reasons that had nothing to do with the bloodstains. Splashing her face with water, she rubbed her hands vigorously in the basin without feeling any cleaner.

She was adjusting the fresh *maran*, stiff and resplendent with gilt embroidery, when Uliverat called her from outside: "Blessed Lady! I only wish to let you know that Falis Woana is going splendidly, and only requires your presence."

Nora pushed the outer door open to see Uliverat standing in the path below. "How late am I?" she asked.

"Not late at all!" Uliverat said anxiously.

"I'm coming, I'm coming," Nora said, descending the stairs. The slightly dank smell of the stream filled her nose as she stepped onto the path. Something splashed into the stream, probably a frog.

Uliverat took Nora's elbow to steer her toward the temple, then let go as though she had thought better of it. As they went along, she began to tell Nora about some mishap that evening involving a Ghaki prince—evidently the Falis Woana ceremony was not going quite as splendidly as she had said—but Nora found it difficult to concentrate on the details.

Her head was throbbing again. She would have liked to dunk it in the cool, murmuring water beside the path. Absently she slapped at an unseen mosquito. Mocking, shadowy faces appeared and disappeared on the sculpted walls of the ravine, caught in the glancing beam of Uliverat's lantern. A large gray moth floated in the nimbus of light.

Not a moth. A feather. A silky scrap of down.

Nora stared at the gray feather with rising interest as Uliverat droned on. The feather rose in a slow spiral, orbiting the lantern, keeping pace effortlessly with the two women as they walked. Then, as though blown by a sudden gush of wind—although Nora felt nothing—the feather flew over Nora's shoulder and into the darkness behind them.

"Just a moment," Nora said to Uliverat, turning. "I'll be right back."

She had only gone about ten paces down the path when someone grabbed her arm.

"Quiet," Aruendiel breathed in her ear. "Stand still."

"Blessed Lady?" Behind her, Uliverat's voice wavered uncertainly. "Did you forget something?"

With an impatient murmur, Aruendiel let go of Nora's arm. She heard the rustle of his clothes as he knelt, and then came a long scraping, squeaking noise, like chalk on a blackboard. "Blessed La—" Uliverat's voice broke off in mid-syllable. In the sudden silence, a burst of warm yellow illumination showed the rough lines of Aruendiel's face. He rose awkwardly to his feet.

"That will steal some time, perhaps half an hour," he said, slipping something inside his tunic.

Nora looked down to see a thin pale-colored line sketched on the stone path, encircling them both. "What did you just do?"

"First things first," Aruendiel said briskly. "Show me your hand."

Surprised, she started to pull her hand back, but his fingers had already closed around hers. He forced her left hand into the light and clicked his tongue softly as he regarded it.

Nora made herself look at the hand. Worse than she remembered. "You knew about this?"

"I had a suspicion. Not certainty. I didn't wish to alarm you without reason."

"Oh, thank you. I got to worry about it all on my own," Nora said. "Is it ever going to stop growing?"

Her little finger no longer merited that description. It was approximately as long as her middle finger. A casual observer might not notice the disproportionality at first, and then would not be able to stop noticing it. Nora herself had taken a day or so to realize why her left hand looked so subtly wrong—bigger, clumsier, spidery.

"I perceive you've tried to cure it yourself," Aruendiel said.

"I've tried every spell that I could think of—to stop swelling, to heal wounds—everything." Even, in desperation, a spell for ingrown toenails. "It just keeps growing."

Aruendiel snorted. "She used too much magic, and she didn't control it properly. In some months, perhaps, it will stop."

By then, Nora calculated, her little finger might be as long as her arm. "Is there a way to fix this?" she asked, trying to make her voice sound neutral and calm.

Reaching into his tunic, Aruendiel brought out a knife with a short, curved blade of blackish steel and gave it to her, handle first.

"I was afraid of that," she said, regarding the knife bleakly.

He removed a second object from inside his tunic: the blue glass bottle he had shown her once before. She recognized her severed finger inside, slightly distorted by the curve of the glass, as though she were looking at it deep underwater.

"It's been weeks since that finger was cut off, Aruendiel," she said. "It can't be very fresh by now."

Aruendiel, unperturbed, removed the stopper from the bottle and handed it to her. It was an oval gray pebble about the size of an acorn, lighter than it looked, like pumice.

"Do you know what this is?" he asked. "I used it to draw the circle just now."

Nora rubbed the gritty, pitted surface with a probing finger. She was about to say that she had no idea, but what Aruendiel had just said about stealing time snagged a memory of a conversation they'd had, months ago, when she was just starting to learn about magic. He had been talking about resurrection spells and a wizard named Foursheep or Fivesheep who'd brought his brother back from the dead.

"Is it—a timestone?" The word yanked other details to the surface. "It's used to go back in time, right?"

Aruendiel gave her a quick, appreciative glance. "It can be used for that, yes. A timestone is a crystallization of accreted time. Nansis Abora has been experimenting with them for preserving fruit, with some success.

"This is one of his timestones. It's not the best quality, but it absorbs enough time to keep fruit, or fingers, from spoiling. Using it to draw a circle"—he indicated the markings on the path with a gesture—"is a way to release some of that stored time, affording us more leisure for this interview.

"And privacy, as well," he added. "While we are inside this enclosure of secret time, your goddess cannot spy upon us."

Nora gave him a sideways glance, wondering how to unpick what was knotted into his last sentence. Nora's goddess. Also his mistress, Nora felt like pointing out. And why was he so eager for privacy?

"That fruit. Did you ever eat any?" she asked.

"The fruit?"

"Nansis Abora's fruit."

"Oh, the cherries. I did."

"And they were edible?"

"Perfectly edible, three seasons after they were harvested. Nansis believes that he can sell such fruits in Semr in winter for four or five times what they would bring in summer. Well? What is your wish, Mistress Nora?"

Nora would have been pleased to spend a few more minutes discussing timestones before returning to her rebelliously burgeoning finger. She hesitated, remembering the crunch of the ax blade on bone. She thought also of the horrified look on Aruendiel's face when she told him that she loved him. He had already stabbed her in the heart, figuratively; was it really wise to let him cut off her finger, too?

But when she glanced up at him again, his face looked creased and somber, as though he dreaded what the knife would do as much as she did.

Before she could change her mind, she held the handle toward him. "Be quick."

Now it was Aruendiel's turn to hesitate, lifting the knife and then lowering it before touching it to the base of Nora's little finger. She bit her lip, her whole frame tensing, as the blade moved into her flesh, but she felt only a slight tugging sensation as the finger dropped away. She looked at Aruendiel with some surprise.

"It hurt a lot more when I did it," she said.

With a swift motion, he clapped the lost finger back in its old place. "Do I understand that *you* cut off this finger?"

"I couldn't figure out what else to do," Nora said. "Raclin made my hand attack me. So I took the ax and—" She gasped as lightning bolts of pain raced the length of the reattached finger. "Oh, *now* it hurts. Ooh. Is it supposed to hurt this much?"

"The sisterfucker son of an ulcerated whore," Aruendiel said, glowering, "the miserable vomit-eater, the conniving, shit-tongued, pus-blooded bastard. That ring should never have stayed on your finger as long as it did, Nora. I should have freed you, I should have torn Raclin a dozen dozen ways, into wretched bloody shreds of rotten meat and bone."

His hand was locked on hers with a steady pressure. Just to keep the finger in place, no doubt. In a different, more clotted tone, he added: "I am sorry for this pain. It means that the spell is working. Tinl the Mute's annealing spell. More reliable than Drosca's. It will cure a beheading if not too much blood has been lost."

"Those were really good words, what you said just now," Nora said, wincing. "Shit-tongued, pus-blooded. Ouch. Ouch. That spell, it's really strong."

"Not as strong as the one she used on your finger. She uses too much power for healing spells. As do you, although you are more careful than she is."

"I use what I need. And these healing spells take a lot of power," Nora said. The pain was lessening, but every cell of the flesh and bone of her finger still seemed to be vibrating with uncomfortable energy.

Aruendiel snorted. "Yes, if you want to heal someone immediately. Miracle cures take a lot of magic. Your patients would be better off with less magic and slower healing."

"Well, what would happen if I did use too much magic?"

"You saw what happened to your finger. Her spell didn't stop working when it should have." Aruendiel gave her pinkie a gentle pull. "Bend it," he directed. "Straighten it. Again. Good. Good.

"An excess of magic can also be dangerous for the magician," he added, taking Nora's hand again and regarding it with a craftsman's critical eye. With his thumb, he rubbed the fine pink scar at the base of her little finger. Her finger tingled, but in a different way this time. "One can develop a taste for strong magic, as for strong wine," he said. "It can be just as intoxicating."

"I use only what I need." Nora pulled her hand back slowly, made a fist, opened it again. "Thank you for fixing my finger," she said, looking up at him. In the wavering illumination he had conjured, both light and shadow flickered across his battered features. "It seems to be fine, as good as new." To her own ears, her words sounded wistful. Nora frowned.

Aruendiel nodded brusquely, as though to signify that the result of the procedure was no surprise to him. "It's well that your finger is mended before we leave. The fewer distractions we have on our journey, the better."

"Leave?" Nora asked. He did not sound as though he were joking. "Journey?"

"We leave tonight."

"But what about Sisoaneer?"

He did not pick up on the precise meaning of her question—or chose not to answer it. "There is a ceremony at the temple, is there not? She will be distracted."

"I'm supposed to be at that ceremony, too," Nora pointed out. "But—you're just going to leave Sisoaneer?" He gave a curt nod. "Have you quarreled with her?" she asked.

"Of course. We have done nothing but quarrel."

Nora stared at him. Aruendiel went on: "She is as mad as ever, and worse, and she's still angry about what she calls my betrayal, not to mention the one hundred and thirty-six years of neglect that followed. I lost count of the years, but she did not."

This was welcome and interesting news, although Nora also found herself slightly chilled by the savagery in Aruendiel's tone. "Why does she think you betrayed her?" she asked.

"I left her for a time, to settle matters of my own, and when I came back, she was gone. And I did not spend all the years since searching for her, as she would have liked. I believed she was dead, or that she did not wish for me to find her."

"But you did come back for her—here, now."

"I came for you," he said. "To ascertain that you were safe."

It was what she wanted to hear, but again, his answer was not quite satisfactory. Nora lifted empty hands in a half shrug. "And you found me, all fine except for this finger. Which left you free to occupy yourself with Siso—"

"On the contrary, I found you in the service of a barbarian religion, completely reliant on the power of a jealous madwoman who has nursed a grudge against me for a century. You and I have both been in peril from the moment we arrived in Erchkaii, except you were unaware of it. She could kill either of us in an instant, or"—he hesitated—"or do other kinds of damage. Not to mention that you have been practicing complex magic that you barely understand on helpless invalids. I have been as diplomatic as possible to protect both of us.

"But I have played the flatterer long enough," he added. "I spent seven years as a servant to that woman—and now, not another day, not another hour."

"Diplomatic? Is that what you call it?" Despite a strong urge to slap him—punch him—Nora laughed aloud. "Aruendiel, you are absolutely no good at flattery. I've seen you manage courtesy, yes, but not flattery. Either she saw through you right away, or you weren't just flattering her."

Under lifted brows, Aruendiel's eyes widened slightly. He looked at Nora with rueful respect. "It was necessary to be—persuasive. I once had some talent for pleasing women. I thought to make it useful again, whatever little remained."

With a tightly knotted smile, he added: "And an old man, a dead man, must take his pleasures where he finds them."

Inwardly Nora winced at hearing her own words, but she would not let him see any sign of weakness. "Well, you found them all right, didn't you."

"Not as I would have chosen," he said with some sharpness, and then in a quieter tone: "Not at all."

"None of this is what I wanted, either." Again, the words sounded sadder than she intended.

A silence began to grow between them, until Nora broke it: "Well, if I leave with you, what happens to me afterwards?" She frowned up at him. "Where do I go then?"

The question seemed to startle him. "Why, you would go to a place that is safe, and pleasing to you," he said, with some hesitation. "We can talk of that later. If you do not wish to remain in my—"

"Blessed Lady, there you are!" Uliverat's voice floated toward them, and at a little distance, her round face gleamed in the lantern light. "And our distinguished visitor. Are you coming to Falis Woana?"

Aruendiel cursed under his breath. Nora glanced down. Only a faint, broken curve remained of the circle that he had drawn with the timestone.

"We are out of time," he said softly into her ear. "I will turn her into a sparrow—or better yet, a fish in the river—so that she cannot give the alarm, and we will leave now."

A rabbit, Nora thought, and was ashamed.

"They're waiting for me," she said quietly. "*She* will expect me to be there. If I'm not there, they'll know something's wrong."

Aruendiel pressed his lips together, considering. "How long will it take?"

"I'm going to pardon someone. It won't take much time, they told me."

He scowled. "Be quick, then. And be careful. Leave the temple as soon as you can. I will find you."

Nora nodded, trying to look relaxed, confident, and unconspiratorial in front of Uliverat. Before she headed down the path, she looked at Aruendiel again. "Why do you call Sisoaneer a madwoman?" she asked in a low voice.

He smiled thinly. "Her name is Olenan. She used to pretend sometimes that she was a goddess, for a game. Now she believes that she is one. Make haste, Blessed Lady, make haste."

Chapter 23

Oasme was waiting for them just inside the temple door. "Blessed Lady," he said, bowing, and Nora marveled privately at the shades of meaning that he could convey with only those two words. There was just enough of an edge in his voice to let her know that while she had not arrived late, she was not as early as he would have preferred.

"What do I need to do?" Nora asked, peering past him into the sanctuary. At a distance she could hear Yaioni chanting. She could see little except the dark crowd of worshippers and, beyond them, a splash of candlelight on the composed smile and the stony gaze of the goddess's statue.

But she is not a goddess, Nora thought.

Oasme began telling her how they would process through the temple, Lemoes and Uliverat and himself in front of Nora, and which chant they would sing.

Nora listened distractedly. Of course she's not a goddess, she thought. I knew it all along, it's so obvious. She's too—real. Too human. I saw that. But somehow I stopped seeing it. I must have wanted to believe, Nora marveled. Just like my mom, only a different kind of god. Would I have done any of this—worn a *maran*, said all those prayers— if I didn't have some secret wish for *something*?

Oasme was still talking. The Ghaki king's emissaries would bow to Nora as she approached, he explained. It was important that she return the obeisance, but she should not bend as deeply as they did. The Ghaki king must not be encouraged to believe that Erchkaii considered itself to be under his direct dominion.

Nora murmured her agreement, trying to estimate how many minutes this whole affair would last. When she left, she would walk toward the hospital—that would be quite natural, and Aruendiel could meet her en route.

"—then you will pray to the goddess for guidance. 'Let me know what is pleasing to you, let me deliver your mercy—'"

Nora knew the prayer; she had recited it before. But she would never need to remember it again after this night. She was not really High Priestess now, Nora reflected, if she ever had been. She was just performing a role for a few more minutes. Twenty minutes, say. Half an hour at most.

"—then the prisoner you free will lie down in front of you, and you will say, 'Go in freedom and praise the loving justice of Sisoaneer all of your life.'"

"And is that the end?" she asked.

"He will pledge to serve the goddess for the rest of his life," Oasme said. "And you will accept his pledge—"

Lemoes was lighting the tall tapers that he and the others would carry. The light spilled into his serious young face. She smiled at him and looked quickly away. How would he feel if he knew that his beloved goddess was—what? A magician, a human woman. It would be a disappointment for him, probably. He was young, he'd get over it. Or, he might not even believe Nora if she told him the truth about Sisoaneer. He had true faith, which was both lovely and dangerous.

"—and then we will exit, singing," Oasme finished.

Nora realized that she had missed the name of the final hymn but figured that she would pick it up when the time came.

Now Lemoes started forward with his taper. Oasme followed, then Nora. The crowd parted with a slow shuffling of feet as the small procession moved toward Sisoaneer's statue.

"The sun's favorite," Oasme sang, and the worshippers chorused, "The sun's favorite."

"The night's daughter."

"The night's daughter."

"She delivers us—"

"She delivers us—"

"—from suffering."

"—from suffering."

I'll never have to do this again, Nora thought.

"In the darkness—"

"In the darkness—"

"—she protects us."

"—she protects us."

"Do not fear."

"Do not fear."

"You are not alone."

"You are not alone."

Yaioni stood at one side, her eyebrows arched, elegant and aloof. The half-dozen men in red-and-black robes over armor were obviously the Ghaki king's emissaries. They stared at Nora, expressionless behind dark beards. A stout, hawk-nosed man with a broad jeweled collar stepped forward and spoke to her in heavily accented Ors.

"Blessed Lady, holy favorite, pure chalice of power," he said, and then there was more along those lines. Will I miss this part? Nora wondered, and then decided: not really. The Ghaki emissaries bowed from the waist in unison. Nora drew herself up and very gently inclined her head, as instructed. She hoped that Oasme was satisfied with her performance. It would be her farewell gift to him.

Now the Ghaki king's chief emissary was saying something about the offering he had brought on behalf of his lord. Nora couldn't follow all of his murky Ors, but she grasped that all had been done in accordance with ancient custom and that the king prayed for great Sisoaneer's favor. A few sentences came in clearly. "We offer these men to the Queen of Power, who gives life and takes it away. May she bless the king's justice."

Two of the emissaries stepped to one side, and for the first time, Nora noticed the men in chains. Two of them, in white robes, face down, kneeling, polished steel shackles linking their wrists. Their heads were shaved. When one of the prisoners lifted his head, she thought at first that he was wearing a mask. No, their faces had been painted black, a rough red streak drawn down the middle.

Nora turned her head very slightly, meaning to catch Oasme's eye. He materialized just behind her shoulder. "I thought there was only going to be one," she breathed.

"You only pardon one of them," he said, close to her ear.

"What about the other?"

"You choose the one who lives."

The chief emissary was staring at her, some kind of disapproving calculation in his narrowed eyes. Her surprise must have been obvious.

"What happens to the other?" she asked again, loudly enough so that the emissary probably heard her.

"Now you pray," Oasme hissed sternly. "Like this: 'Let me know what is pleasing—'"

Why am I here? Nora thought. If I had listened to Aruendiel, we would be miles away. Distractedly she groped her way through the prayer, following Oasme's prompts.

Both prisoners had raised their heads and were scrutinizing her. She wondered if either sensed her unease. The greasy paint covering their faces was meant to make them look identical, she guessed, but it could not disguise their individuality. The burlier man was older, deep lines carved into his face. The other had sleepy-lidded eyes that gave him an air of mild astonishment at the dire predicament in which he found himself.

She came to the end of the prayer. A strained silence took over, broken only by rustles and coughs in the crowd. They were waiting for Nora: the worshippers, the emissaries, the prisoners, everyone.

"What did they do, the criminals?" she whispered to Oasme.

"You're not supposed to know," he whispered back.

"I need to know."

She felt rather than heard Oasme suppress a sigh. "The one on the left beat and robbed a neighbor and his wife, and violated the daughter, and killed all three; the young one murdered an admiral and several other officers in the course of committing piracy, theft, and rebellion," he said.

The new information did not make her choice easier. "Did they have trials?" she asked. "Do we know if they are really guilty?"

Her hesitation seemed to have emboldened the prisoners. They stared at her. The sleepy-looking one widened his eyes imploringly. The burly man tried a smile that Nora thought might crack his jaw.

"That is the Ghaki king's affair, not yours," Oasme said. "Just pray to the goddess and pardon one, Blessed Lady. Go on!" He joggled her arm. "'Let me know what is pleasing—'"

Nora repeated the words after him, raising her voice. Would Sisoaneer—Olenan—send her some kind of sign? Nothing was forthcoming. When she had finished the invocation, she closed her eyes for an instant. She wished that there really was a goddess she could pray to.

She opened her eyes. "That one," she said to Oasme, pointing to the young pirate. Immediately two of the armored men dragged him forward, then dropped him facedown on the floor in front of Nora, his chained arms extended before him. She had forgotten the formula for the pardon, but once again Oasme prompted her.

The pirate responded in an arcane, salt-tinged argot, pledging his service to the goddess and adding a very long compliment to the lovely and discerning priestess who had freed him from a shameful death. Under different circumstances, Nora might have enjoyed being described as seal-eyed and mackerel-slim, but not now; she wished that he would finish already, so that she would not have to stand facing the other prisoner she had not saved from a shameful death.

She made herself meet the second man's eyes, briefly. Under the stark colors of the face paint, he suddenly looked hollowed out. She reminded herself that he was a murderer who had brought his fate upon himself. The reflection did not make her feel better. She wondered how much longer he had to live.

The pirate seemed to be coming to the end of his endless expression of gratitude, but not quickly enough. "I accept your service," Nora said loudly, cutting him off. "Welcome to Erchkaii. You will, um—well, someone will instruct you in your duties." She turned to Oasme. "Now, we leave?" she whispered.

"Now you strike the condemned prisoner," he said in a hushed voice.

She wasn't sure she had heard him correctly. "What?"

He took something from Lemoes and handed it to her. It was heavy. A piece of polished granite, bigger than her fist, attached to a shaft of wood. Because the thing looked so primitive, it took her a moment to recognize it as a weapon.

"You will hit him with this," Oasme said. "In the head."

The wooden handle had the smoothness of long use. Nora hefted the thing awkwardly. It weighed twelve or fifteen pounds, at least. One side of the granite head narrowed to a sharp, brown-stained edge. An ax. Not again. Did they know?

"But I can't," she said. "I mean, I'm not supposed to kill him myself, am I?"

The prisoner she had freed was gone now; she couldn't see where. The guards dragged the condemned man forward.

"You don't have to kill him yourself," Oasme said firmly. "Just tap it against his temple. Try to draw a little blood. It's part of the ceremony. The Ghaki king's soldiers will execute him later."

"You didn't tell me about this bit," Nora said. Stay calm, she reminded herself. A few more minutes, and she would leave the mad, dank gloom of this temple for the last time.

"I did mention it. Did you not hear me?" Oasme allowed himself to look indignant, the corners of his mouth drawn down.

They were no longer whispering. "You glossed over it, then," she said. "Why don't you do it, if it's so important?" She offered him the stone ax.

"It is your responsibility."

"I don't want any part of it."

Murmurs were beginning to flow among the congregants. Some of the worshippers were close enough to hear what was going on. The lead Ghaki emissary said something to one of his lieutenants, shaking his head.

"Blessed Lady," Oasme said, "this man cannot be executed until you strike him. It can be as lightly as you like, but you must strike him."

"It's fine with me if he can't be executed," Nora said. "Oasme, why are you going along with this? We're healers here, not killers."

"'She gives life and takes it away,'" Oasme said. "And the life of this man belongs to the goddess."

"Then the goddess can do her own dirty work," Nora said. "I won't."

Oasme looked horrified. "Recollect yourself, Blessed Lady!" But Nora turned away. Out of the corner of her eye, she saw the Ghakis exchanging more glances; the lead emissary shrugged. The soft tide of voices in the nave of the temple rose higher, pilgrims asking each other if they had just heard what they thought they had heard.

So much for making a quick, discreet exit, Nora thought, scanning the crowd. Still, if she left now, there might be enough confusion over the interrupted execution for her to get some distance away from the temple and meet Aruendiel before someone came to look for her.

The wave of sound in the temple faded suddenly. The crowd shifted, then parted, letting a slight figure in a black robe pass through. Nora drew in a dry, startled breath, although she was not completely surprised.

This is Olenan, Nora reminded herself. Human, like me. But it was hard to stop thinking of her as Sisoaneer. She came straight toward Nora, her bare feet making no sound on the floor. Her dark eyes were steady, her mouth unsmiling.

"High Priestess, you will not strike at this man?" Her voice was like a flute in the cool silence.

Nora shook her head. "I won't."

"Why not?" Olenan asked.

"I can't. I don't want to be a part of this."

Olenan regarded Nora with somber patience. "Some are bound for death. I told you that."

"I don't have to send them there," Nora said. "You also said that it's better to heal than to kill."

"Yes, and you've already brought one man back to life tonight. In the eyes of men, this other one"—she nodded at the condemned prisoner without looking at him—"is already dead."

"He's not actually dead, though," Nora said. "And I don't want any part in killing him. I've had enough of that."

"My priestess, I must have my sacrifice. It is my right, my due."

There was something almost trusting in the way she looked at Nora, as though she knew that Nora would understand finally and do the right thing.

But you're not a goddess, Nora thought wonderingly. *As mad as ever, and worse*, Aruendiel had said.

"I can't do it," Nora said. "And I'm not your priestess. Not anymore."

Olenan nodded slowly. "You will no longer serve me?"

"No. I can't."

Olenan's mouth quivered, then made a straight line. "I understand, dear one." She held out her hand; Nora thought she saw tears shine in her eyes. "Then I will make the sacrifice," Olenan said.

Nora hesitated, wondering if there was anything else she could say. She had no reason to apologize, nor any real wish to, but at the same time she was troubled by an oblique sense of loss. She handed over the ax.

The prisoner watched them unblinkingly. Nora steeled herself for what would come next for him.

When the stone struck her temple, she heard it before she felt it. Delicate bones cracking under the granite's bite.

Nora tried to get her balance, shuddering. The second blow made her teeth chatter. She lost count after the fifth. She could not focus her eyes; the world was spinning too fast. Her cheek lay against the cool hard smooth floor, which was unexpectedly wet. I have to get up, she thought. A brilliant red light bloomed inside her skull, so bright that it was painful to look at, and then it started to fade.

She had the confused idea that a bell had been rung, one long rich note reverberating through the whole world. Dissolved in it were voices she recognized: her mother, reading a number off the thermometer and saying you are not going to school today, sweetheart; her father telling her to give it some gas when you let the clutch out. Ramona and Leigh shrieked that the water was really cold, are you coming in, Nora, come on. EJ told her don't throw like a girl, keep that shoulder loose. Aruendiel said make haste, make haste.

She could have listened to the bell's sweet cry for her entire life, but it ended.

Aruendiel fought his way through the crowd of worshippers who milled about, chattering inanely, gaping at the spectacle that had unfolded before them. He used not only his own crooked shoulders, but also a spell that Tiretus Copperhand had devised for clearing a path quickly through the infantry ranks of an enemy. If some of the pilgrims who found themselves slammed against the wall of the temple suffered broken bones—well, those injuries would heal, unlike some.

In truth, it would have suited him better to use a sword on the interfering mob, but that would have slowed him down too much.

Olenan, in front of the statue of the goddess, turned to look at him. Her cheeks and forehead were flecked with dark spots, as though flies had settled on her face. More wet stains covered the front of her black robe and her hands.

Blood puddled around the dumb, inert tangle of cloth and limbs on the floor.

Aruendiel dropped to his knees beside the corpse. Gently he lifted her wrist and felt for a pulse, feeling the stillness of the flesh, the skin's dwindling warmth. He made his eyes trace the contours of Nora's kind and lovely young face under the mask of blood, trying not to look at the splattered gray matter, the pieces of her wrecked skull. It was her—he would know her anywhere, always—but she was gone all the same.

"I won't let you bring her back," Olenan said. Only then did he realize that she was weeping. "The way they brought you back. I smashed her brains to mud. Only the worms will enjoy her now."

She should die for that remark alone, he thought. He lifted his head and saw her face crumble into fearfulness and malice.

"You should have struck at me," he said.

"I did," she said.

Chapter 24

As she walked, Nora knew where she was without having to think about it. She had been in this hall too many times in real life, and sometimes in dreams, not to recognize it. Lockers lined the walls, and automatically she recognized some of the numbers. Her friend Vicky's locker was 379, just past the drinking fountain. Locker 431, with the Mets decal, that was Andy Reeves's.

Her sneakered feet squeaked faintly on the linoleum. The classrooms she passed were quiet and shadowy, biding their time in the spooky secret life of school buildings without students. Was this a weekend or a holiday, or had school let out for the day? She glanced at the hall clock. Unhelpfully, the hour hand was missing.

In the next classroom, the lights were on, although it was as deserted as the others. "B47" was stenciled on the outside of the half-open door; under it someone had taped an index card with the symbol for infinity drawn in blue Magic Marker. She regarded the card for a moment, then pushed at the door and went inside. The desks were lined up neatly with a precision that suggested that school was not in session, although half of the blackboard was dusty with scrawled equations. The other half was clean and blank. Behind the teacher's desk was a poster of Mr. Spock, gaunt and solemn, aiming a phaser at some unknown enemy.

Ms. V's classroom. Was this one of those dreams in which she was going to have to take her geometry final without having gone to class or done any of the homework all semester?

It didn't feel like that kind of dream, though. She felt no particular anxiety about taking the test. She didn't feel much of anything.

—except that she was supposed to be somewhere else, wasn't she? Where?

She looked around with a sudden sense of urgency. It came to her now that this classroom and the rest of the Sidney M. Kriegsman

Academic and Administration Building had been demolished some time ago—three years after her high school graduation, in fact—to make way for a new performing arts center. Nora touched the laminate top of the desk nearest her. It felt solid and dully smooth, undreamlike.

"Ms. Vorys?" Nora lifted her voice. "Are you here?"

The silence felt mournful. She noticed that there were no textbooks, no papers on the teacher's desk, only a thin black rectangle that was immediately recognizable as a grade book. She had never seen Ms. V's desk so neat, even at the very beginning of the school year. It must be summer vacation.

But what was she doing here in the first place, in a building that didn't exist anymore? When she was supposed to be somewhere else. Where? It came back to her, finally. She was about to go away with Aruendiel, any minute now, he was waiting for her—

"Good, I thought you'd be able to find your way here." It was a very young man's voice, oboe-bright, still finding its way in the lower registers.

Nora froze, then cocked her head warily. She had heard that voice before, so many times. Most recently in a video that her mother had insisted they watch together, one that had turned up in some relative's ancient stock of tapes. The video ended after just five minutes, and then it seemed to Nora that she and her mom sat in silence for at least twice that long.

"Who said that?" she demanded.

"It's me," the voice said. "I picked this room because you had Ms. V for geometry, too."

"Who is this?" Her heart was pounding. "And where are you?"

"C'mon, Nora. It's not that hard."

Nora whirled, scanning the quiet classroom. "If this is a trick, whoever is doing this, I will curse you and kill you, because this is just cruel. Where are you?"

"Try outside."

Hesitantly she stepped toward the squat casement windows. From here, if she remembered correctly, she should have been able to see the cafeteria roof and a wedge of parking lot, but the view seemed curiously indistinct.

She came closer and found herself staring into her brother's brown eyes. She knew him immediately, even though she couldn't quite make sense of what she was seeing. EJ was either unnaturally large or she was impossibly small.

His cheeks were still soft with a little baby fat. He wore the wire-rimmed glasses that someone found smashed in the road after the accident and sent to the family; they were still in a drawer in New Jersey. He smiled at her in that half-serious, half-goofball EJ way. But somehow he seemed to be part of the sky as well, as immense and distant as a constellation.

"EJ?" she asked. "EJ, is that you?"

He nodded. "It's me."

"It's really you?" She closed her eyes and opened them again. He was still there. "Why are you so big?"

Her brother looked slightly self-conscious. "I'm still growing."

"Oh, my God. Are you OK?" Nora steadied herself against the window frame. The metal was cold and dusty under her fingers. "Damn it! We missed you so much. Are you really real? Is any of this real?"

"I'm fine, I'm just fine," he said. "I'm real. The classroom, it's not exactly real. Just a memory. I thought you'd feel more at home."

"Here?" Nora laughed shakily. "Geometry class? Ms. V gave me a C-minus, and that was generous. She felt sorry for me because you died."

"You had the concepts down," EJ said. "You just didn't do the homework."

"You weren't there to help me. I mean," she added, "it wasn't your fault. You were gone. You were—oh, why did you have to be such a fucking idiot?"

"Nora?"

"You died," she said. "You left us. Everything fell apart. Mom got weird and she joined this awful church, Dad just hid, I was a mess, I did stupid things. It felt like we were just three miserable people, not a family anymore. And they got divorced, and that was a relief. I thought we could all start over, except you can't. Not really. Fuck, I'm so sorry." Her voice was trembling. She blinked hard. "After all this time, all I can do is yell at you."

"I missed you yelling at me," EJ said, and Nora began to cry in earnest. "Listen, particle brain," he went on. "I can't tell you how often—well, if I could go back and *not* get into Kevin Weiss's car that night, I would. He couldn't drive straight when he was sober."

Nora gave a strangled sobbing laugh. "He totaled his brother's car on the way to school six months later."

"But now *you* get killed?" he asked. "That was dumb, Nora. Even dumber than riding with Kevin."

"What?" In the middle of wiping her nose, Nora lifted her head to stare up at EJ. "I'm not dead. I think I'd remember dying." Thinking back, she could summon only cloudy impressions: a memory of lying on the floor, trying to raise her impossibly heavy head; a sense of perplexity and betrayal. And then the skein of narrative in her mind ended abruptly, ominously. "Oh, crap," she said.

"She hit you on the head, remember? She faked you out. It's so frustrating, Nora. All this time—what, seventeen years?—at least I could tell myself that *you* were alive. That you were doing things, meeting people, learning new things, being happy, being sad, whatever. And now it's over."

Nora ran a tentative hand over her head, searching for fractures, dents, fissures, and found none. Her flesh seemed solid enough. She touched her neck and found a pulse. "I'm breathing," she said in protest. "My heart is beating."

"That's only habit, you're used to having your heart beat," EJ said. "After a while, you'll forget."

"But you don't even have to think about your heartbeat," Nora said. "It's just what your body does. The, um, autonomic nervous system," she added, because it was EJ she was speaking to, and you always had a better shot at convincing him with science.

EJ said nothing, but he wrinkled his brow at her in a way that made her suck in her (remembered?) breath because his expression was so familiar and yet had been lost for so long. *I'm sorry, sis,* it said, and also *Grow up.*

Everyone dies, Nora understood that all too well, but still, in her experience death only happened to other people. Death would come for her someday, but not today—not already.

"You mean I really don't have a body anymore?" she asked. "Or, rather, my actual body is somewhere else, dead?" Perhaps already rotting. She tried to thrust that thought away.

EJ nodded, like distant cloudy galaxies shifting.

"What do you mean—'it's over'?" she demanded. "You're here, I'm here. Even if I'm—dead—we're talking, we're doing things. The story hasn't come to an end."

"It isn't the same," EJ said.

"Well, no—"

"It's harder here. You have to work at it. And I've been lucky. I had math. That's my story now." EJ shrugged slightly. "You had a good thing going. You traveled to a different world, you learned magic—who knew? I didn't see that coming."

"How do you know all this?"

"I've kept up. You're my sister. Hey, you remember the Cartesian formula for a sphere?"

"The what? Oh." Nora gave her brother a long look. "Yes. I do. Well, not really, but strangely enough, I thought of it not too long ago. It just came back to me."

EJ's voice was teasing, a little proud: "That was me."

Nora frowned suspiciously. "Aruendiel was trapped in a kind of bubble, and I needed to open it up—"

"That's right. I helped you with the formula."

"That *was* you." She looked away, and found herself staring at Mr. Spock, frozen in an attitude of chilly skepticism. "I did wonder. Because it wasn't something I would have thought of, normally. How did you know, at that moment—?"

"You needed help," EJ said simply.

She tilted her head back to look her brother full in the face. It was hard to tell how far away he was. "I didn't know you were there. I didn't know you could *do* anything." Something was unfolding in her heart, a green shoot making its way through thawed earth.

"Well, when I could," EJ said quickly. "Ms. V isn't the only one you should thank for passing that final. Too bad you didn't take more math, Nora. I could always reach you that way." He gave a rueful smile. "I try with Mom and Dad, too, but they keep thinking of me as a little kid, even a baby. That makes it easier in some ways, but there's a lot that doesn't get through."

"You always assumed I liked math as much as you did," Nora said.

"Equation boy. No one liked math as much as you." She felt like crying again, but there were no tears. Had she already forgotten how to shed them, being dead?

"What happens now?" she asked, trying to keep her voice level. "Do I get judged? Do I meet God? Although frankly I've had enough of gods lately."

"I don't know, Nora. I think it's a little different for everyone, just like when we were alive. You figure it out as you go along. Like I said, I have math. It's very cool stuff here, really exciting. You can divide by zero, and that blows everything up in ways I'm just starting to understand."

There was a new authority in his voice. All these years Nora had been thinking of him as frozen in time, sixteen years old forever, but he seemed older than sixteen now.

"Is that why you're so big?" she asked.

"Sort of," he said.

"I can't spend eternity doing equations," Nora said.

"You'll need something else, then."

"What would that be?" Nora glanced around the classroom as though she could find the answer pinned to one of the bulletin boards. Mr. Spock frowned at her.

The memories were clearer now. She could picture the crowded temple moments before her death: Sisoaneer's stricken, triumphant stare; the packed, gawking pilgrims; candle flames fluttering in a web of darkness. In comparison, the orderly rows of empty desks in Ms. V's room looked more and more unconvincing.

"This can't be right," she said, more to herself than to EJ. "I have a life, or I had one. I was about to go away with Aruendiel. I'm learning to be a magician. I was a High Priestess although not anymore. I've cured the sick. I can speak four languages. Well, three and a half. I know almost every sonnet John Donne wrote by heart. I've had boyfriends, I've been married although it ended badly. I had a life, not perfect, but it was interesting, I liked it, and now it's over, and I'm back in high school for eternity?"

"I'm sorry," EJ said sadly. "I know this isn't easy. You don't have to stay in this classroom forever."

"Oh, I'm not going to," Nora said. "I'm going back somehow—I'm going to find Aruendiel, even if I have to wear a sheet and haunt—"

"Nora," someone said behind her, loudly enough to startle her. There was something experimental about the way this person, a woman, pronounced her name, as though she had not spoken it aloud before. "Nora?"

The person who spoke looked oddly, vividly out of place in the fluorescent-lit classroom. She wore a long, shabby gown, blue-gray, the kind that peasant women wore in Aruendiel's world. Her black hair was piled on her head in an untidy nest. Her feet were bare. Her smoke-colored eyes, set in a handsome, bony, anxious face, peered at Nora with a slightly unnerving intensity.

"That's me," Nora said carefully. "Who are you?"

"You might call me Warigan, but my name really doesn't matter. I'm here because of Aruendiel."

The sudden, wild surge of hope she felt was like being alive again. "He sent you?"

"He doesn't know I'm here." Warigan gave a private, lightning grin. "But I have some license in the kingdom of the dead, not being alive myself. He wouldn't have thought to send me, but I'm here on his behalf."

"He's not dead?"

"Well, not at the moment," Warigan said. "*She* is trying to kill Aruendiel. Unless he kills her first."

"Oh, it's not worth fighting her," Nora said. Aruendiel's life, any life, seemed almost infinitely precious and fragile from where she stood now. "Tell him it's not worth it. Except," she finished sadly, "he would never listen."

"Probably not," Warigan said. "I don't know who will prevail. She's stronger than he is. But it was foolish to kill you. She lost all influence over him."

She added, with some severity, "Aruendiel should have told you sooner that she's not a goddess. *I* knew she wasn't, from my first glimpse of her. He was too cautious, and he is no good at being cautious. He was afraid of what she knows." She smiled again with abrupt fierceness. "And afraid of what she might do to you."

"With good reason, as it turned out," EJ said. The window framed one clear brown eye so large that it looked almost inhuman, like something from deep under the sea. "Who are you? You're not a kind of ghost I've ever seen before. And I've never seen you in the lives touching Nora's—"

"But I feel as though I should know you," Nora interjected, staring at the other woman. "There's something—"

"Oh, I was long gone and safely buried. Aruendiel woke me up—not meaning to, of course," the woman said with a jerk of her head. A strand of dark hair fell down. "And here I am. But I must be quick now. Aruendiel has a timestone. Do you know what that means, Nora?"

Nora gave a quick, excited gasp. (Still haven't forgotten how to breathe, she noted.) "He's going to go back in time to save my life."

"That's not how a timestone works," Warigan snapped. "It reverses time. When all the stored time in a timestone is released at once, everything close at hand is pushed into the past."

It seemed counterintuitive. "Why not the future?" Nora asked.

"Huh." EJ's giant eye squinted with concentration. "That's really interesting. I mean, it could theoretically go in any direction in time. Forward, back, up, or down. But the whole thing is so unstable. It actually takes less energy to go back in time instead of forward. That's really wild."

"Up or down?" Nora asked.

"Holy shit, Nora, this could really work. You could go back."

"You're missing the point, both of you," Warigan said. "Once Aruendiel uses the timestone, Nora will find herself in the past—"

Nora felt a qualm. "How far back?"

"A few hours at most," the woman said. "Portat Nolu said no more than one, in most cases."

That sounded manageable, not like getting zapped back to ten years ago. "Great. I'll know not to go to the temple. Or if I get there later, I can duck when Sisoaneer swings.

"I mean, it's not as though I'm irremediably fated to die, right?" she added.

"But, Nora," EJ said, frowning again, "she's right. All this—your death, this conversation—it won't have happened yet. This isn't like jumping in the TARDIS to go back to 1890. When all that energy is released, the intervening timeline will be destroyed. Everything starts over again. Everything."

"Oh." This was the kind of convoluted chronological paradox, she remembered, that she'd always found rather tiresome in fiction involving time travel. "Will I remember what happened?"

"The difficulty with timestones," Warigan said, "is that so often people don't remember what happened. Most people do exactly what they did before."

Olenan smiled at him through the smoke. "You're still afraid of me."

"No," Aruendiel said, stepping aside as another chunk of the temple roof crashed to the floor. He nodded grimly toward the pile of rubble that buried Nora's body. "I have nothing to fear now, Olenan."

"I'm Sisoaneer now. And it's not too late, Aruendiel. You were unfaithful, you tried to leave me yet again, but I will forgive you, if you ask. Sisoaneer is merciful to those who fear her."

Aruendiel found that he could not breathe. His chest felt as tight as a locked door. He gagged, coughing up a spume of saltwater, and recognized the spell, an ancient one from Rrosl. It had once been used to kill rats, then thousands of the best warriors of the Pernish cavalry. Probably she'd learned it from her father.

"You could be my High Priest," she said. "Pray, and I will forgive you."

He reached the end of the counterhex and took a shuddering breath, then another. His shield spells had turned back her primary attack, the obvious one, but she could still find ways around them for lesser assaults, spells that might only kill him.

Aruendiel fumbled inside his tunic. His fingers closed around the smooth cylinder of Nansis Abora's preserve jar. He drew it out and pulled the stopper. The timestone lay in his palm. It seemed almost weightless, smaller than he remembered. How much time was stored there? Would it suffice?

He dropped the stone on the floor, then crushed it with his boot.

"I'll remember," Nora said.

Chapter 25

Nora followed the swooping glow from Uliverat's lantern, her feet finding their way on the familiar track to the temple, and told herself that the darkness would help her and Aruendiel elude pursuit later on. She was starting to regret that she had insisted on going to the temple. Time seemed suddenly precious.

Oasme was waiting for them just inside the door. "Blessed Lady," he said, bowing, and Nora could hear the faintest shade of irritation in his voice, like a cat letting you feel the prick of its claws as it purrs and leans closer to you. She was almost but not officially late, she concluded, and again she had the disturbing sense of time passing too quickly.

"What do I need to do?" Nora asked. She squinted into the darkness behind Oasme. The temple was packed. She could hear Yaioni chanting, but she could not see her. The blank, slightly slanted eyes of the great statue stared over the crowd, and Nora thought again how little it resembled Sisoaneer in real life. But then, she thought, it would be strange if the statue did look like Sisoaneer—Sisoaneer not being a goddess.

Olenan, she corrected herself.

She had to force herself to listen as Oasme started giving her directions for the procession through the temple.

"—and I will walk in front of you," he was saying. "We will sing the hymn that starts 'The sun's favorite.'" Oasme hummed a few notes. "But only the first three stanzas."

The sun's favorite. Ha. Did I really believe, even for a moment, Nora wondered, that that woman was actually the daughter of the sun? Somehow I did, she thought. It seemed true, on some level.

Oasme was talking about the Ghaki king's emissaries, some question of precedence. This has nothing to do with me anymore, Nora thought.

Oasme looked at her expectantly, and she nodded, chancing that she had gleaned enough to get through the ceremony without incident.

Then to find Aruendiel again! She'd have to give Oasme and Uliverat and the rest of them the slip. Would there be time to change out of this ceremonial *maran*? She would never need to wear it again, thankfully.

Oasme was reminding her of the prayer she would have to chant. She recognized the words. And then she would pardon the prisoner. It was the only part of the next few minutes she was looking forward to, despite some qualms. What if he had committed a truly unforgivable crime?

"—then he'll lie face-down on the floor, and you'll say, 'Go in freedom and praise the loving justice of Sisoaneer all of your life.'"

"And then we'll be done?" Nora said.

"Not yet. He vows to serve the goddess," Oasme said. "You acknowledge it and—"

Lemoes was lighting the tapers for the procession. Nora saw the reflected flames shining in his eyes. She smiled at him. He looked calmly back at her with none of his usual shyness. For a moment Nora had the distinct impression that they shared a secret, some knowledge that she couldn't have put into words.

She gave herself a mental shake. He did look a lot like Andy Reeves, that was all. I used to think that Andy and I had some sort of secret sympathy, too, she thought. Andy Reeves with his big hands and quick smile. She had a sudden memory flash: the blue-and-orange Mets sticker on his locker, drawing her eyes every time she walked down the hall. I hadn't thought about that for ages, Nora thought. They made him scrape it off, eventually.

"—and then we process out of the temple, singing," Oasme finished. Nora had to ask him to repeat the name of the hymn.

Lemoes raised his taper and began to pace forward. Uliverat and Oasme moved into place behind him; Nora followed. The pilgrims fell back to let them pass, a crowd of jostling shadows. Oasme sang, "The sun's favorite!" and Nora chorused with Uliverat and Lemoes, "The sun's favorite!"

"The night's daughter."

"The night's daughter."

"She delivers us—"

"She delivers us—"

"—from suffering."

"—from suffering."

The chanting sounded sweeter than it ever had before. It's the last time I will ever do this, Nora thought.

"In the darkness—"

"In the darkness—"

"—she protects us."

"—she protects us."

"Do not fear."

"Do not fear."

"You are not alone."

"You are not alone."

Nora found herself unexpectedly moved. The candle flames swirled. She blinked hard to clear her vision as they reached the open area in front of the statue where the sacred fire burned.

A small knot of men stood there, their black armor glinting under their red-bordered robes. The Ghaki king's emissaries, Nora guessed. One of them, his neck swathed in jewels, came forward to address her in a thick, sibilant Ors that buzzed in her ears. She could make out only a few words: "Blessed Lady, holy favorite." Nothing she hadn't heard before.

Yaioni, watching from the other side of the fire, stifled a yawn. Look lively, Nora thought, you might have another chance at this job. She ducked her head hurriedly because the Ghakis had just bowed.

Then she saw the two men in chains, kneeling behind the Ghakis. Their faces were masked—no, blackened with a red streak. Their shaved heads looked pallid and vulnerable. The Ghaki king's emissary was saying something about the offering he had brought on behalf of his lord.

Nora looked around for Oasme and found him at her elbow. "Two?" she whispered out of the corner of her mouth. "I thought it was one."

"You pardon just one."

"And the other?"

"They are both condemned criminals," Oasme said. "You choose the one who lives. Now, your turn. The prayer."

The emissary had finished speaking. Behind his close-trimmed beard, his face was weathered, serious, and slightly impatient, as though he had better things to do elsewhere. Some of his colleagues moved aside so that Nora could have a better look at the prisoners. Their black-and-red faces were oddly distinct to her. One blinked with a hapless air; the other prisoner looked so sunk in gloom that he seemed not to notice what was going on.

"What did they do?" Nora muttered to Oasme. "Their crimes."

"That doesn't matter. Whomever you choose will be the right one."

"I have to know."

Oasme gave a small sigh and leaned over to mutter in her ear. "That's bad," Nora whispered when he had finished. "Both of them."

"It's none of your concern. Just pray to the goddess, and pardon one of them, and tell him he has to serve the goddess from now on." With an aggrieved look, he added, "Don't worry about having him around here. They almost always run away. Now, 'Let me know—'"

"Let me know what is pleasing to you," Nora recited. Oasme gestured at his throat: louder. "Let me deliver your mercy," she said, raising her voice. "Let me speak truthfully for you, let me do as you would do."

She closed her eyes, but almost immediately opened them to look hard at the condemned men again. They were both murderers. From what Oasme had said, the older, more muscular man was also a rapist. The younger man with the heavy-lidded eyes might actually be a political prisoner, she thought; one of the charges against him was rebellion. She could see a case for sparing him. But he had butchered the officers and most of the crew of one of the Ghaki king's ships. Oasme said that he hadn't been charged for the deaths of the sailors, since they were slaves.

There was no way to make this kind of calculation work out neatly or comfortably. I've killed, too, Nora thought. I had far better reasons than these men did, but still, I did much the same thing. I saw my chance, and I took a life because it suited my own purposes. Why am I passing judgment on them?

She found herself looking at Lemoes again. He stood to one side, facing the prisoners. His taper was guttering with a flapping noise like a flag. In his other hand was an odd implement, a piece of stone with a wooden handle.

She wondered idly what the stone was for, and then she understood. When she pardoned one prisoner, the other wouldn't live much longer. No more appeals, no reason to delay. I hope they wait until after I leave, Nora thought, and then was chagrined at her own selfishness. It came to her that she was not saving one man as much as she was helping kill another.

Death comes to everyone, she argued to herself. And people die for far more senseless reasons. In car accidents, for example. That idiot Kevin Weiss. She wished she could go back in time and find him and take his goddamn keys away.

Nora took a deep breath, then cleared her throat. "In the name of the goddess, these two men are pardoned. Both of them."

A short, incredulous pause. "I beg your pardon, Blessed Lady, what did you say?" Oasme asked.

"Free them both," Nora said. "It's the will of the goddess." She thrust her open hand toward Lemoes. "Give that to me." Obediently he gave her the stone tool. An ax, ancient and well-used. Its dead weight was powerful and disturbing.

"No one's going to die here tonight." The words rose easily to her lips. "The Queen of Power doesn't need human sacrifice."

"She never objected before," Oasme said.

"I don't know about before," Nora said. "I know what she wants now." It was a lie—anything to buy time—but saying it gave her a strange sense of peace. Her glance fell upon Lemoes; he offered her a small, luminous smile.

The lead Ghaki emissary spoke quickly to one of his lieutenants, forehead furrowed. The other man bobbed his head. Under his beard, the emissary pressed his lips together and stared at Nora. In the dimness of the nave, whispers were beginning to flow among the congregants.

"'She gives life, and she takes it away,'" Oasme hissed to Nora, with a significant look. "Blessed Lady, are you sure? Because this is a grave offense to the Ghaki king, to reject his justice, and—"

"I don't care about the Ghaki king's justice. Tonight we're giving life, not taking it. Justice is nothing without mercy."

"That is true, my priestess. But am I to have no sacrifice at all?"

Sisoaneer's voice was low but clear and penetrating. Abruptly the tide of murmurs inside the temple ebbed. .

Nora turned, feeling a kind of dread at what she was about to say. Sisoaneer—no, Olenan—came toward her, very pale in her black gown. The embroidered blue finery was gone.

"No," Nora said clearly. "No sacrifice. And I'm not your priestess. Because you're not a goddess."

As Olenan stepped closer, there were all kinds of fine, taut lines in her face that Nora had never seen before. "Did he tell you that?"

"I always knew," Nora said. She was fairly sure that was true.

"You turn against me, after all that I've given you? Foolishness. I am the goddess Sisoaneer, and I will have my sacrifice." For a moment she looked almost sad, then she squared her shoulders. "Give me that." Her hand shot toward the ax.

Instinctively, Nora yanked it free of her clutching fingers. Olenan made another grab, but Nora brought it down on her elbow, the nearest part of her, and it must have hit the funny bone, because Olenan's face twisted, and she yelped.

Someone grabbed Nora's other arm, not in a friendly way, and Nora swung the ax again. It hit something that was partly soft and partly rigid. Nora jerked around just in time to see Oasme drop to his knees, hand to his face, blood streaming from between his fingers.

She had to get out of here, find Aruendiel. But there were a hundred worshippers between her and the temple door. Some were shouting for the goddess, pushing forward. The closest pilgrim was familiar, a balding, thickset man whom she'd cured of a skin disease. For a moment he hesitated, and she could read confusion in his eyes; then he snatched for the ax. She felt some reluctance to strike a patient. When he made another grab, Nora feinted, then shoved him away.

She spun, but her shoulder hit something unyielding. A Ghaki breastplate. A bearded face looked down at her. Black armor on all sides. It clattered like machinery as the soldiers crowded around her.

Nora raised the stone ax again, aiming at the man right in front of her. With insolent ease he caught the handle and wrenched the weapon from her hands.

She dived under his lifted arm, twisting between him and the next soldier. Someone tried to grab her, but she was too quick, too desperate. Armor makes you clumsy, she remembered Aruendiel saying. Dodging, she nearly slammed into the prisoners, still in their chains, but the pirate winked at her as she slipped around them. Behind her she heard a curse, a metallic crash and thud. More cursing.

Ahead, the roiling crowd of pilgrims. She moved swiftly along its edges, looking for a way through.

Then, Olenan again. Nora almost bowled her over. Olenan laid a hand on Nora's arm with an air of casual gentleness, as though she were about to invite Nora to have a cup of coffee, but her grip was steely. She steered Nora into an alcove between two columns.

"I heard you tonight," she said. "I know you were planning to leave with him." Nora stared back at her, trying to give nothing away. "I should never have expected anything better from him," Olenan said. "You were different, though." Over Nora's shoulder, she spoke sharply to someone: "No, no, leave us alone."

Nora tried to pull her arm away. "I don't know what you mean."

"I shouldn't blame you. I should not. You're so young. Naive. You don't know what he's really like. *I* should have known better, this time." She shook her head. "What I mean is, I'm not angry at you for wanting to leave with him—I'm really not. He could fool anyone. He almost fooled me." Olenan sounded increasingly distraught.

Nora couldn't resist. "How did he fool you?"

"He sought *me* out, and then he lied to me. Every kiss was a lie, every embrace, every caress."

Nora thought: Well, I don't need that much detail. "If he's that bad, you should just forget about him," she said. The standard line, but it was still good advice.

"It was all false. He was trying to distract me. Because of *you*, I could tell. As though I would want to hurt you!" Olenan's mouth drew tight in a way that made her suddenly look querulous and old. "Don't think I didn't know what he was doing! You can't trust him at all."

"It's hard to know whom to trust, sometimes," Nora said, not very sympathetically. "I've had that problem quite a bit recently."

"Is that why you hit me just now?" Olenan touched her elbow. "You really thought I would hurt you?"

Nora gave a single nod. "Yes." Behind her she could hear the Ghaki commander roaring at the crowd to get back, to be quiet.

"I'm very sorry, this is not what I wanted." Olenan's slender brows tilted, weighted down with contrition. "I was angry, and then you said what you said, in front of all these people. I can't let that go. You must see that. It's painful for people to lose their faith."

"I think it's worse for them to be lied to, *Olenan*," Nora said, pulling away. Unexpectedly, the other woman released her.

"I don't want to do this," she said. "I really don't. But blasphemy must be punished. You understand that, don't you?" She brought her hands together in a pinching motion that Nora recognized, then yanked her hands apart so hard that it seemed that the invisible thread would break.

Nora tensed. The spell hadn't killed the Kavareen, she reminded herself.

But still she screamed, every nerve popping, sputtering, burning, as a white storm of pain flashed through her body. There was no refuge. Even the fine threads of her *maran* were razor blades on her skin.

Nora opened her eyes to discover that she was lying curled on the floor, staring at her clenched hands, fingers bent like claws. Her body felt as though it were made of sand: one touch, and it would crumble. Carefully she breathed in and out, then straightened her fingers, marveling at the absence of pain.

Probably the whole thing had taken less than a minute. Much longer and that kind of pain could kill you. Slowly she got to her feet.

Olenan was still there, smiling. From the look on her face, she was about to say something. And then, with what felt like the faintest of breezes, a sigh rippling through the air, darkness flowed through the temple.

Olenan, two feet away, was suddenly invisible. From somewhere nearby, Uliverat wailed that the sacred fire had gone out. The sooty, pungent smell of extinguished candles filled Nora's nose. She took some experimental steps in a direction opposite to where she calculated Olenan lurked. All over the temple, people were shouting in a cacophony of languages, in a frantic way that meant that no one was listening to anyone else. Someone large and soft barged into Nora, almost knocked her down, then panted away into the obscurity. Staggering, Nora bumped into another person, who smelled strongly of onions; this time she went down.

When she got up again, she had lost her bearings completely. Her outstretched hand touched curved stone. She clung to the column for a moment, as though it might hide her.

"Nora!" It was Olenan, not far away. Nora held her breath. "Are you all right?"

Nora almost replied automatically, Olenan sounded so concerned, but instead she slipped around the pillar as quietly as she could, moving away from the sound of Olenan's voice. Striking out into the darkness, within a few paces she found herself against another column. She tried to work out where in the temple she was. Under the tumult of raised voices and hurrying steps, she could hear the steady roar of the waterfall outside, but it didn't sound particularly close.

"It doesn't last long, that pain spell, so you must be feeling better." Olenan's voice was coming nearer. Nora backed away. "That's good. I don't want to torture you. I only want you to understand that you can't mock the gods without paying a price."

I wasn't mocking you when I said you're not a goddess, Nora wanted to say, *I was just stating facts*. She bumped into another column and veered left. Was the temple door this way?

"And you don't have to leave Erchkaii, you know. I mean that. You're better off here with me than with him. I'll think of a suitable penance for you—"

Nora stepped on a small, round thing that broke with an audible crunch. Silently she cursed. One of the small ceramic offerings to the goddess. They were always getting scattered all over the temple.

Olenan's voice brightened. "There you are! Will you speak to me, Nora? You can't keep hiding in the dark."

It was strange, Nora thought suddenly, that the temple was still pitch-black, that no one had relit the candles, that Olenan had not conjured a light. With a flutter of hope, she wondered if this was Aruendiel's work, a spell for persistent darkness.

She touched stone again. Something bulky, blocking her path. Long smooth ridges under her fingertips, like the folds of a dress. The big statue of the goddess at the back of the temple. And Olenan was between her and the exit.

Olenan was still speaking. "—one of the gods. Yes, I am. How could you doubt it? Those who have no other help, they pray to me. I hear their prayers, I answer them. You know better than anyone how great my power is, because I shared it with you. And I will never die, not ever again.

"I must have my sacrifice," she added reasonably. "But it doesn't have to be you. It could be anyone, except for those prisoners that you pardoned in my name. We can hardly kill them now, it would look strange—and you are right, justice is nothing without mercy. You understood that, you understood everything. Almost everything. My beloved priestess!" She was wistful now. "You were better than any of the others, all of them. It wasn't just the magic. How good it has been to talk to you.

"Will you say something? You are still hiding." A note of irritability now crept into her voice. "I can always do the pain spell again, and then you won't be able to be silent."

Nora groped her way around the statue. It seemed larger in the dark. She trod hesitantly, trying to avoid crushing another offering. Yes, here was the crack in the rock wall. Still open. She wedged herself through the gap. It was a hiding place of sorts; she could retreat a short way into the caves if she had to.

"You could still be my priestess, Nora. Yaioni could be my sacrifice. Would that please you? She still prays for your death, you know. She could die in your place."

Crouching in the cave entrance, Nora felt perversely outraged. The enmity between Yaioni and herself was a private matter; Olenan had no right to exploit it that way. "No! Absolutely not!"

Olenan laughed, pleased that Nora had finally spoken. "Or it could be Aruendiel," she said slyly. "That would be appropriate."

"He's gone by now," Nora said quickly. "He said he would leave Erchkaii if I didn't get back from the temple in a few minutes. You won't find him."

"Liar," Olenan said. "He's not fifty paces behind me, trying to break through the wall of power I made." She laughed again. "You stay there while I deal with him."

Nora was suddenly aware of how quiet the temple seemed. The noise of the crowd had completely died away. "Aruendiel?" she called through cupped hands. "Aruendiel?"

She thought she heard him answer. The syllables of her name, then other words that she couldn't make out.

She started forward, but the echo of his voice was already gone. By a sort of instinct she halted, just before she would have cracked her forehead.

Groping for the opening that she had passed through just a minute before, her panicked hands found nothing but rock.

Chapter 26

Nora locked her arms around her knees and leaned back tiredly against the chilly, obstinate stone. Her hands stung and were slightly sticky from small abrasions she could not see. Her throat felt like sandpaper. She was sick of the sound of her own voice battering her ears, with no reply. The mustiness of the cave air filled her nostrils, but by now she was hardly aware of it.

She'd been trapped here half an hour? An hour? Time seemed more elastic in this absolute blackness. She could discern more noises underground than one might expect: the distant drip, drip, drip of water; an occasional rustle. Once, a musical echo from a falling stone. But she could hear nothing from outside, where Aruendiel was presumably engaged in some kind of negotiation or argument or all-out combat with Olenan.

On the face of it, the stillness meant nothing. Stone could muffle sound. Magic could work silently.

The longer she had to wait here in the dark, though, the more likely that Olenan had prevailed.

Nora's head ached. She should have left Erchkaii with Aruendiel right away, as he'd wanted. Skipped that absurd, barbaric ritual. She'd wanted to play the merciful High Priestess one more time. The wrong choice, yet again. It didn't bode well, she thought, that she and Aruendiel seemed to be perpetually out of phase, blundering past each other. Make haste, he'd said. Make haste. He knew, he had lived long enough to understand that there was never enough time, never, to do all the things that you thought were important and also the things that really were. She could see that now, too late.

Nora stood up, groping the walls to orient herself. Yes, the passage stretched this way. She moved forward with small steps, counting each one, staying close to the right wall to avoid the entrance to the lower caves. She'd come this way in the dark so many times to see Sisoaneer—Olenan—that doing it again now was vaguely reassuring.

Sixty-nine steps, seventy. She was definitely walking uphill now, the passage trending clockwise. Did the air seem slightly fresher? Olenan might have closed the exit to the mountainside already, just as she'd sealed the entrance to the temple. Or she might have forgotten. She had a lot of distractions. Ninety-nine, one hundred. Nora quickened her pace.

One hundred nineteen. Something was wrong. She was no longer climbing. The passageway leveled off, then began to descend. She went a few more steps to be sure, then backed up in confusion, trying to imagine where she had taken a wrong turn.

Her shoulders slammed against something hard, uneven, damp. With a gasp, she reached back and felt stone, and then more stone everywhere her hand touched.

She could not go back. The tunnel behind her was gone.

She ran her sore hands all over the rock again, in case she had become disoriented in the darkness. One tiny crack exhaled a stream of cool air, as if to mock her.

"So that's how it is," Nora said to Olenan, as if she could hear. Maybe she could. Nora stood there for a while, considering. Then she started down the passage ahead.

This downhill part was steeper. She kept having to brace herself against the walls to find her footing. It made her conscious of how horribly narrow the tunnel was. She was still counting steps, as though it mattered. Two hundred five, two hundred six. The only sound, except for the numbers she whispered under her breath, was the scratch of her sandals against the stone.

From time to time, she reached an exploratory hand backward. Each time she found rock, as though a door had swung shut after she passed. She never had to reach back very far.

Her toe throbbed; she'd stubbed it somewhere. The numbers mounted. Three hundred eighty steps. Five hundred fifty. Six hundred fifty-seven.

"Well, Ramona, I've had better days than this one," she said aloud. "It is not working out the way I'd hoped."

The stone underfoot felt greasy and slick, except when it was so uneven that she stumbled. Going down is always harder than going up, she thought. She came to sections so steep that she had to sit down and lower herself from perch to perch. The passageway was so tight now that her elbows and shoulders kept scraping the rock. The ceiling was a few inches above her head.

Her cramped muscles trembled, but there was also a certain calm, Nora found, that came with knowing that you were moving in the only direction you could. It seemed important to stay in motion. If she stopped, she might end up swallowed by the wall of rock that followed her implacably, and as long as she kept sliding, bumping, clambering, groping her way along, she did not have time to fully appreciate how terrified she was.

Suddenly she stepped into empty space.

Nora flailed, one foot in the air, then lost her balance entirely and sledded downward in a shower of loose pebbles. She opened her mouth to curse just as she plunged deep, deep into black chilly water.

For a moment the shock felt as though it would crush the breath out of her, and then she thrashed her way to air. In a blur of panic, she dog-paddled until her knee brushed something hard, an underwater ledge, and the water grew shallow enough to let her crawl. The bottom of the pool was bumpy with small rocks or possibly bits of wood that rolled and scattered as she moved.

Shaking, Nora tried to sort out whether any of the various pains she felt in her legs, back, and arms were serious injuries. Everything seemed to be functional, if cranky. She exhaled and listened. Nearby, water lapped against rock. Cautiously she followed the sound through the darkness until her fingertips found what seemed to be the edge of the pool.

Behind her, a gentle splash. One final pebble falling? Maybe. And then, from another direction, a different noise. A faint crunch, a rustle. Something moving, unseen.

Nora tensed, waiting for another sound. Even so, she started when someone spoke not far away.

"You would have done better to come down more slowly, little one." A woman's voice, accented, with a quick, musical rhythm. "But I am glad to see you."

"Who's there?" Nora called sharply.

"Someone you are not expecting, I think."

Nora sat as still as she could, hushing her own breath to listen. She wanted to be absolutely sure. "Tell me who you are!"

Footsteps, light and assured. "You would be more comfortable out of that water." A gleam of light appeared in the blackness. Nora caught a flash of gold, a white robe. A bright, steady gaze in a dark face.

"Hirizjahkinis!" Nora shot to her feet. "It's you?"

The flickering light, shining from the twisted strands of the woman's necklace, showed her features more clearly. Hirizjahkinis was smiling, although the lines around her mouth held a certain fierceness. "You are surprised? You thought I would stay inside the Kavareen forever? Let me tell you, it was very dark and very dull in there. I was glad to make my exit. Here, give me your hands," she said. "Easier to fall down the well than to climb out again, as we say in my country."

Hirizjahkinis's grip was surprisingly strong. Nora scrambled out of the pool. "We thought you were dead, Hirizjahkinis!" she exclaimed. "Although Nansis Abora said you might not be." She was ready to embrace Hirizjahkinis, then checked herself, remembering her wet clothes—not only wet but filthy, a downward glance told her. She raised a hand for the ceremonial palm-press that was Hirizjahkinis's usual greeting, but Hirizjahkinis gave her an amused look, then a quick, powerful hug. When she released Nora, the pleated linen of her long dress was still a pristine white. She had always been fastidious, Nora thought.

"Certainly I am not dead. And you are not dead, either, I see."

Nora laughed shortly. "Not yet. Some people have certainly been working on it."

"Oh, but you did die," Hirizjahkinis said. "Although it was a short death. Or I should say that Aruendiel undid it quickly." She pursed her lips to expel a small puff of amusement. "For all his grumbling about how he would much rather be dead, he is very fond of bringing people back to life."

"That's not right." Nora shook her head. "I think I'd remember dying." As she spoke the words, she had an unsettling sense of déjà vu.

"It was all so quick, I would have missed it myself, but the Kavareen saw everything." Hirizjahkinis touched the leopard pelt draped over her shoulders.

"The Kavareen!" Nora had not noticed the leopard skin before, but there it was, just the way Hirizjahkinis had always worn it. The empty claws dangled like the ends of a tatty scarf. The golden-eyed head resting on Hirizjahkinis's chest wore an expression of dull menace. "You made it go back to being a—a shawl!"

"It is not a shawl," Hirizjahkinis said. "It is the Kavareen. We have made peace, he and I." She stroked the skin again. "He does not regret it, exactly, doing what he did, but we have resolved our differences."

"But he ate you," Nora said.

"He won't do it again!" Hirizjahkinis laughed. Then she looked more serious. "We understand each other better now. He does not like to be alone, he does not like having to decide everything for himself, he does not understand the purpose of human beings. He needs a master who protects him and does not let him do foolish things."

"Like eating people," Nora said. "How did you get out? What happened in there?"

"What was it like to be dead?" Hirizjahkinis asked. "Aruendiel would never tell me."

Nora was unsure how to answer. This conversation felt a little like hearing from someone else about the wretched things you'd done when you were drunk the night before. Except she hadn't been either drunk or dead. She shook her head. "I really don't know what you're talking about."

Hirizjahkinis's smile was skeptical. "Well, the next time you die and someone takes the trouble to bring you back to life, you must remember better. But for now—" She looked past Nora, across the pool. "We must find a way out of here. I am very tired of these caves. They are damp, which is bad for the lungs, and they are not very friendly, not at all. Look at those bones in the water, ugh!"

Nora looked down. The light from Hirizjahkinis's necklace glittered on the surface of the pool. Underneath was a chalky tangle of pale, oblong shapes—curved, straight. Now she saw what they were. The shadowed, vacant eyeholes of a human skull stared up at Nora. With an effort she kept herself to one small shriek. This talk of dying had affected her nerves.

"I guess I'm not the first person she's sent here." Nora looked up and was not much surprised to see that the cave wall above the pool was unbroken stone.

"It is a good trap. Who is *she*?"

"Olenan. She's a magician who claims to be a goddess, but she's not. I was her, um, priestess for a while—it's complicated—but I resigned, and she didn't like that. And things got ugly. I hid in the cave entrance in her temple, and just as Aruendiel was arriving, the rock slammed shut." She added: "You're right about this place not being friendly."

"Well, that is just what you did to me. That is, to the Kavareen and me, when you crammed us into the mountain."

Nora grimaced. "Oh. I'm sorry. It seemed like a good place to put the Kavareen. Is that how you got into the cave?"

Hirizjahkinis nodded. "It was very cramped! But I found my way here, and I have found you. Now we will seek for an exit together. Aruendiel will be too occupied for some time to come looking for you. I hope that he is not so busy that we will have to rescue him."

"You don't have a spell that would get us out?" In the back of her mind, Nora was flipping through images of Aruendiel wounded, unconscious, dead by Olenan's magic. There was an alternate vision, Aruendiel and Olenan suddenly reconciled, reunited in each other's arms. (Why do I torture myself like this? Nora wondered.)

"Do you have a map spell, maybe?" she asked Hirizjahkinis. Aruendiel had an entire shelf of books on map and direction spells, but Nora had only begun to learn the elements of orientation magic. There was a lot of precision involved; you had to have the angles and distances just right. It all came back to control. Nora sighed.

Hirizjahkinis shook her head. "I told you, these caves are not friendly." For a moment she looked weary, her eyes shadowed, the few lines in her face stark and deep.

"That's probably because the fake goddess keeps all the magic around here for herself," Nora said.

"That is very greedy of her. And not clever. Like the little boy in the story, who killed the antelope and tried to eat it all himself." Turning her back on the pool, Hirizjahkinis moved toward the opposite wall of the cave and indicated a cleft in the rock about five feet high. "This is where I came in. And here, there is another."

Her light skittered over the cave walls, glinting on the wet stone; Nora glimpsed surrounding stalagmites like robed old men. Behind a column of fused rock was a long, crooked gash in the wall, taller than Nora, full of darkness.

Nora felt a chill emanating from the opening. "There's a draft."

"I have been frozen to my bones over and over again, going through these drafty caves," Hirizjahkinis said, pulling the Kavareen's hide tighter around her shoulders. But she moved closer to the gap. By the light of her necklace, Nora saw that the new passageway widened farther in.

"Do we try this one, or go back the way you came?" Nora asked.

Hirizjahkinis pursed her lips. "The way I came is not so easy. There are holes that are very deep—and odd. Well, let us see where this one goes." With a silky motion, she climbed through the opening. Nora followed.

The new chamber was shaped like an irregular gallery that angled away to the left. Limestone had flowed down the walls and dripped from the ceiling like candle wax, like caramel, like cream. Nora could not resist touching the rock to see if it felt as malleable as it looked; her finger slid on the moist, glossy stone. Hirizjahkinis only made a soft grumbling noise and moved forward. They began to pick their way through a lush hanging forest of stalactites.

"What about the little boy who tried to eat the antelope alone?" Nora asked.

"Why, there was no one to help him chase the lions away." Hirizjahkinis glanced back with a slightly mocking smile. "And they ate him. You know, when I was a witch priestess, long ago, *my* goddess was truly a goddess."

"How did you know?" Nora asked.

"Oh, we knew. We prayed to her and sacrificed, and she did what our spells asked her to do. Most of the time. Sometimes she did not listen. That is one reason we knew that she was a goddess."

Nora laughed rather bitterly, but Hirizjahkinis was unperturbed as she climbed deftly over a tilting, broken log of stone. "No, it is not a joke. The gods have their own ways, they are different from men and women. There is no knowing what they think or feel. What is the name of this false goddess of yours, again?"

"She pretends to be the goddess Sisoaneer, but her name is Olenan. She's one of Aruendiel's former mistresses. I seem to keep running into them."

Hirizjahkinis chortled, her dark eyes gleeful. "Well, they are not rare, his old loves—or at least they were not rare once upon a time, before he decided to hide himself away in his dreadful castle and let his heart dry up like an old apple."

"Mmm," Nora said, wondering what to say next. There was quite a bit to explain—including parts, she thought, that Aruendiel would rather Hirizjahkinis not know. But her silence had already lasted too long. "You are very quiet, little one!" Hirizjahkinis said. "You are keeping something under your tongue."

"Oh—" Nora began.

"Ah!" The beads in Hirizjahkinis's braids rattled as she gave Nora a grinning sideways look. "Tell me, has my old friend recovered his senses and taken you into his bed?"

"Oh, well, yes and no—"

It took a long time to tell the entire story, especially with frequent interruptions from Hirizjahkinis, pressing for more details as the tale wended its twisting path from Micher Samle's apartment to Erchkaii. Under her questioning, Nora found it impossible to be fully discreet.

"You said he was old, that he was dead!" Hirizjahkinis gave her a look of mock horror. "I am sure that he has never thought such things to himself, never."

"But that makes it worse, for me to say awful things he was already thinking—"

"You were not polite, no," Hirizjahkinis said. "Aruendiel is not always very polite himself, have you noticed that?"

That reasoning did not entirely assuage her own feelings of guilt, Nora found, but the conversation itself had given her at least a momentary sense of release.

"And you say that this woman taught him magic, as well as bedded him. For seven years! He has never, never named her to me," Hirizjah- kinis said. "Why not, I wonder. I would not have tormented him about her more than some other things." She gave a deep, satisfied chuckle, like a strutting pigeon's coo. "But I am pleased that my friend Aruendiel has suddenly become so amorous again. Taking a goddess as his mis- tress! Even if she is not really a goddess. That is the old Aruendiel, the one who seduced the queen.

"Don't look so crestfallen, little one," she added, catching sight of Nora's face. "It is because of you. You have been good for him; you have roused the sap in the cold wood."

"Not so that he could sleep with other women," Nora said gloomily as they rounded a cluster of stalagmites melted together into one immense trunk.

"But he was ready to leave his false goddess, you said—and to leave with you."

"And then what? It's confusing. He's still convinced that I secretly despise him, because Faitoren magic is all about suppressed desires."

"Whenever Aruendiel talks about the Faitoren, he always feels a little sorry for himself," Hirizjahkinis said. "He cannot forget how Ilissa tricked him. Well! My advice is to tell the truth." She was still smiling, but a new kind of gravity had come into her face. "If you despise him, you must tell him that. You have a mouth and a tongue and a brain— you do not need Faitoren magic to say what is in your heart."

"I don't despi—" Nora began.

Hirizjahkinis interrupted with an impatient cry, stumbling and splashing. "Dear night, it is wet! These puddles!" she said, righting herself. "I fell into a dozen yesterday. Or the day before. It is hard to know how much time passes down here."

Three days since Nora had buried the Kavareen inside the mountain—and how many weeks or months since the Kavareen had swallowed Hirizjahkinis in the first place? "You must be starving," Nora said.

"I am famished," Hirizjahkinis said with a flash of her white smile, an unsettling intensity in her tone. "But I am still strong."

Nora herself was beginning to feel empty, not just cold. "If we could use magic here, could we turn a rock into food?"

"I have done that, once or twice in the desert. And afterward!" Hirizjahkinis grimaced. "Transformations do not last forever—most of them. Here is more water to step in, take care. This one is deeper. At least we will not die of thirst."

"No." The moist stone around them glistened diamond-like in the light of Hirizjahkinis's necklace. The wet skirt of Nora's *maran* clung clammily to her legs. She was regretting that they had been so quick to choose the passageway with the chilly draft. "I wish I could dry off a little," she said.

"What, are your clothes still wet?" Hirizjahkinis laid a hand on Nora's shoulder, then pulled it back quickly. "They are soaking! Did Aruendiel not even teach you a simple spell for driving water out of your clothes?"

"He did, but Olenan controls all the mag—"

"Water likes to change its mind! If you are kind to it, it will not be so loyal to Olenan. She is not here; it is only us. Go on, tell the water to leave your garments."

"I've tried to do my own magic before, I can't tell you how many times, since I got here," Nora said, but dubiously she began to address the water soaking her clothes, asking for its attention, listening for its silent response. At first, nothing, the water not even acknowledging her presence. But it knew her already, a little. It could not ignore her entirely. She kept calling to the water softly, calmly, and she felt its interest quicken and grow stronger. Do you know me? she asked, and the water said yes.

Will you do this for me? she asked.

Water dripped madly from the folds of Nora's clothing; rivulets streamed down her legs. The wool fabric began to feel lighter on her body. After a moment, she found that she was standing in a small puddle, and her *maran* was still grimy and creased but was now completely dry.

"Better?" asked Hirizjahkinis.

Nora laughed, surprised by a new sense of well-being. "Oh, yes."

"You were freezing all that time, and you did not even think of trying a water spell! Aruendiel would be beside himself."

"It's not just the dry clothes." Nora put her hand to her head. The heaviness, the sense of constriction, had dissolved. She had become so used to having a headache that she had stopped noticing it, until it was gone.

She felt more present, more alert, and even the stale darkness that surrounded them seemed fresh, nuanced, almost dazzling in a way that she would not have suspected a minute ago. It was like having your ears finally unblock after a bad cold and rediscovering the ordinary musicality of the world.

"Ah, you have found the magic again," Hirizjahkinis said. "Isn't that better than asking your goddess to give you some of hers? Although, I warn you, you will not throw the Kavareen into a mountain with magic from that little trickle of water."

"I don't care," Nora said. "And she didn't give me her magic as a gift. There was a price. Which I was stupid enough to pay."

Hirizjahkinis's smile carved deep lines in her face. "I do not think you were stupid," she said. "When someone offers you such great power, it is not foolish to take it. Sometimes you do not have a choice."

"I gave up too much for it, though," Nora said. In her mind, she sought out the water again and was reassured to find it still listening to her. And it was not just the water that had run out of her dress; now she could sense the droplets clinging to the walls of the cave, the slow dribble from a crack behind them, a shallow pool hidden in the shadows.

"I suppose I will miss all that power," she said slowly. "But real magic isn't just about power. It's about knowing the world around you."

"Yes, but that is not why most people become magicians," Hirizjahkinis said. In a slightly different tone, she asked, "Do you know the water light spell? No? It would be useful now. Water has a good memory, for all that it is so changeable, and even in a dark, nasty cave like this one, water remembers the sunlight. If you ask politely—very politely—it will show you what it remembers."

What the water remembered, Nora decided after working the spell, was more like moonlight than sunlight, a fitful, silvery sheen on the cave walls and floor that was brightest when you caught it out of the corner of your eye instead of looking directly at it. In the new light, Hirizjahkinis looked like a hollow-eyed ghost of herself, and Nora guessed that she looked the same. But now they could see more precisely the shape and dimensions of the passage that they had been following.

Hirizjahkinis clicked her tongue in annoyance. "It goes down and down! That is not the right way."

"But look!" Touching Hirizjahkinis's arm, Nora pointed. "Aren't those stairs?" The cave floor ahead sloped down in a series of flattish planes that certainly resembled steps, although they were not entirely regular in size, and their edges had a rounded, eroded quality that—Nora had to admit—gave them a natural rather than a man-made appearance.

"It is a trick of the stone," Hirizjahkinis said. "And if anyone went to the trouble of carving a staircase here in the belly of the world, it is because they wished to go up, not to go down." She did not laugh when Nora did.

"I think it's artificial. Someone has been here before sometime," Nora said. She felt a flutter of expectation. "It might be a way out. Just a little further, all right?"

"You are as stubborn as Aruendiel, little one," Hirizjahkinis said. "And no, that is not a compliment."

They began to descend. Here and there, Nora thought she saw chisel marks, but when she pointed them out, Hirizjahkinis was uncharacteristically silent. Once she said, "This is a cold place." The cave narrowed as they went along; it curved to the left, then back to the right. They passed a ledge with a large, flattish animal skull posed on a pile of bones.

"Ribs and vertebrae," Hirizjahkinis said coolly. "I do not see any leg bones." Nora reached out to touch the skull, but Hirizjahkinis's hand closed around her wrist. "Let the dead rest."

"Are these bones here because a big snake died here, or are they here because a big snake lived here?" Nora asked. There was a subtle but important difference between the two possibilities; she hoped that the answer was no longer relevant.

"It is a very good question," Hirizjahkinis said. "A snake that big would need to eat a lot. There are serpents in my country, not so large, that can eat a whole cow."

"There is nothing to eat in these caves," Nora said, starting forward.

"There is you," Hirizjahkinis said. "And me."

They went on. Another bend to the left. Nora was trying to remember what Olenan had said about the caves. She'd claimed to have been born there. A lie, obviously. And she'd quoted a hymn, one that Nora had sung several times since. *Where the last true darkness dwells.* That was certainly true. No shortage of darkness here.

They came around another curve, and abruptly the stairs ended. The passageway continued for a few yards and there, Nora saw, was unmistakable proof of human agency, an archway framed with twisting pillars, an inscription circling the top. She went up to read it, but the letters were from an unknown alphabet.

"Can you read this?" She looked back. Hirizjahkinis had paused some distance behind her.

"Something here is very—old," Hirizjahkinis said. "And it is not pleased to see me."

"What do you mean?" Cautiously Nora looked through the archway. Something about the quality of the darkness and the draft that touched her face told her that on the other side was a much larger cave. Her eye went to a spark in the darkness. "There's a light," she said hopefully.

She was concerned by the expression she read on Hirizjahkinis's dark face—lips pressed together, eyes fixed stoically, as though she were in pain. It was out of character for Hirizjahkinis, and a strangely intense reaction to the vast vacant silence of the cavern beyond the archway. "Do you think we should leave?" Nora asked.

"Yes, I do, little one. I cannot go any further, and you should not."

Hirizjahkinis's words, spoken so emphatically, almost drowned out something else that Nora wanted to hear. She waited for a moment, concentrating, breathing as quietly as she could.

"Listen, do you hear that?" Nora said wonderingly. "Someone's calling my name."

She walked through the archway.

Chapter 27

Whispers clung to her ears, too low for her to understand, and then dissipated like smoke. Her footsteps sounded small and light on ground that was more level than any other surface she'd walked on in the cave. She moved steadily toward the light, which was tiny but seemed uncannily bright after all this time in the dark. It wavered, casting a pale yellowish haze into the air.

A candle flame, not a chink of daylight. Oh, well. She went closer.

The candle stood at one end of a long, squared-off piece of stone, about waist-high. It was a hollow box, Nora saw as she approached. Its sides were crudely worked into a crowded design: leaves, flowers, a snake's sleepy curves. She looked inside.

The candlelight fell on a face, very still, that she did not recognize at first. Then she did. It was like looking into a mirror—although, she thought, your eyes are always open when you see yourself in a mirror, and these eyes were closed.

The corpse had brown hair, matted, spiky, and wore a purple *maran* that was stained even darker with blood. Its mouth hung agape; the tongue inside was unmoving. The skin had a dull, sickly cast. There was a blackish, dried smear on one side of the forehead, and something misshapen about the head. The hands were crossed neatly on the chest.

Nora stepped back. Her own body felt frantic, as though she were about to vomit. "Not possible. That isn't me. No."

Priestess.

Nora stood still, listening hard. Had she imagined it? The candle flame guttered, and shadows whirled overhead. Let the lamp affix its beam, she thought madly. It took her a moment to place the line of verse. The only emperor—

I know who you are. Priestess.

She glanced around, seized with an apprehension that the voice—if it was a voice—was coming from the corpse in the sarcophagus in front of her. But it was hard to say where it came from. It was a low, inhuman vibration that pulsed through the rock around her. She had the sense that she was hearing it with her bones, not her ears, tap-tap along her spine and into her skull.

I have been waiting for you. You are mine. You see.

Nora was trying to look everywhere but at the crude, broken figure inside the coffin. It was impossible to look anywhere else.

Your death belongs to me, child. Have you come to pay your debt?

Nora's throat was tight, but she forced out a few words: "I—I don't owe you anything." It would be best to leave now, she thought. She could not move. On the cave ceiling, shades of dark and light fluttered and circled in huge, restless, shifting patterns.

You have taken life, you have given death. You are mine.

"That's not right," Nora said, but it was as though an arid wind blew through her. Everything I have ever done, everything that has ever happened to me, has been leading me to this point, she thought, and there is no way out. She thought of Hirizjahkinis, just a few dozen yards away, of Aruendiel. They seemed infinitely far away.

A second sarcophagus appeared next to the first.

"No," Nora said again, recoiling. Somehow she found the strength to make her frozen legs move. Shakily she took a few steps toward the exit—toward where she thought the exit was. But the archway through which she'd entered was gone.

Nora found that she was facing the two stone coffins again. Either they had moved or she had, or she was losing her mind. "What do you want from me?" She could hear the hysteria in her voice.

Look.

"I don't want to. I can't."

Look, child, at what you have made. Do you not owe the dead that courtesy?

Nora swallowed, smoothed her tattered *maran* with quaking hands. Hesitantly she moved past the sarcophagus that held her corpse—it looked pathetically vulnerable from this angle—and came close enough to the other coffin to see inside.

As she'd expected, the second sarcophagus held Raclin. Raclin's body, that is, laid out so carefully that you would not know that his head had been sliced off until you saw the slim white gash just above his collar. Although the corpse filled the coffin, big shoulders touching each side, Raclin seemed oddly diminished, the bulk of his body somehow unconvincing. His mouth was slack and pouting. One eye was open, a cold blue marble, and Nora found herself holding her breath for a moment in case it might start rolling in its socket to meet her gaze.

It occurred to her that always before she had regarded Raclin with desire—induced by enchantment, and therefore myopic at best—or with fear. She had never simply looked at him. Now she did. The fine, manly nose had begun to seem pinched; the stalwart jaw was loosened; but you could still marvel at the cruel, exquisite lines of his face, even as they began to soften with death. Beauty is dangerous, Nora thought, not for the first time. There is so much it can hide.

"Why isn't he in his monster form?" she asked sharply of the shadows above.

This is what he was when you chose to kill him.

"I didn't choose—" She dropped her eyes to the corpse again. "To do what I did."

And Raclin's beauty had so much to hide. Maybe he would have liked to be a dragon all the time. Nora had never asked him about that. Ilissa preferred him to be a man, or a simulacrum of one, and perhaps he was secretly afraid of being a despised, lonely monster. So he had worn his polished mask faithfully, with aplomb and evil brio. Now this shell was all that remained of him, now it would rot away, and whatever it had concealed was gone forever.

Good riddance, Nora thought. At the same time she felt a deep, secret, impersonal sorrow, as emphatic as a judge bringing down a gavel, that she knew she would never quite forget for the rest of her life.

"I killed him," she corrected herself.

Very gently, without a sound, Raclin's body began to dwindle. His limbs shifted and crumbled. Withering, his face collapsed into unrecognizable dust. For a moment Nora caught a glimpse of something intricately formed, the grinning puzzle of a dinosaur skeleton, and then that was gone as well.

The sarcophagus was empty.

Involuntarily Nora glanced at the other coffin. Her dead twin still lay there, unchanged.

Nora raised her head, scanning the darkness. "Who are you?" she whispered. Then: "No, wait, I know who you are."

Do you? The voice sounded almost sad. *I am she who was born into darkness, but always I remember the light.*

"I sang hymns to—to someone like that. She wasn't who she said she was." Nora wet dry lips. "But now I think it was supposed to be you."

Yes. They pay tribute to me, above, but they do not understand who I am. In the beginning they called for me because they needed me, and I came.

Nora considered this. "What did they need from you?"

They had learned death, and they were afraid. I helped them make death their servant, so that it would come or depart at their bidding. I am their teacher and their companion, I protect them, and I chastise them, and I walk with them in darkness, wherever their path leads them. As I have walked with you, priestess, when you took life and when you sought to save it and when you finally gave up your own life to save another's. I was there, I was with you.

"I don't remember that," Nora said, very softly.

You did not know me, but you knew me better than the others. You protected the weak, the guiltless and the guilty, in my name.

Nora shook her head. Too many riddles. (The guilty—did that mean the condemned prisoners?) "I don't think I've protected anyone. Not really."

You found the light in the darkness. The truth among the lies.

"What truth?" Inwardly she shuddered. "Why me?"

Priestess, I am hungry.

Oh, dear, Nora thought.

My house is defiled with blood and lies. Do they think they can feed me with the death they make? Blood is not enough. It will never be enough.

"But what you just said about death—"

I do not wish them to make death for me! I am tired of blood. They blind themselves with the blood they spill. Let them come to me with their eyes seeing and their lips speaking truth and their hearts grieving for the death they have dealt, that I may chasten and cleanse them. Always, always I remember the light. I am hungry for the light.

Through dry lips, Nora said: "What do you want from me?"

My house has been stolen, polluted, filled with lies. You will purify my house so that the truth dwells there again. Let my people know me truly.

What if they are better off not knowing you? Nora thought but did not say.

Purify my house, priestess! I am hungry for the light. The voice revved to a grating, subterranean roar that for an instant blurred everything in Nora's sight with strange tremors.

"I'm not anyone's priestess," she said, her teeth chattering only slightly. "Not anymore."

You are mine. You died into my service, and I claim your death.

Nora shook her head. Her body felt tight and brittle, as though it might break at any moment, but she forced herself to survey the dim expanses of the cave to see if she could find the archway again.

"You know, even the gods can be wrong."

Nora flinched with shock, a yelp caught in her throat. A woman— not Hirizjahkinis—stood next to her. She had dark hair, some of it escaping from the knot on her head, and taut, strong-boned features that gave her a fierce look.

"And frequently the gods are wrong," the woman continued. "It's not as simple as she makes it out to be. Not quite."

Nora drew back. "Are you—" She swallowed hard. "Are *you* Sisoaneer?"

"No!" The woman frowned. "You've met me once, although you don't remember, because it never happened. Just as *that* never happened." She pointed to the sarcophagus where Nora's corpse lay. "Don't trust everything she says or shows you. You are alive. You must realize that, surely."

One more task, priestess. Purify my house. And then you shall rest with me forever.

"You can leave here anytime you wish," the woman said.

"But the door is gone," Nora said, hearing the hysteria in her own voice. "And that's—that's me. She has my body."

Her gaze was locked on the coffin. The pale figure inside was so precisely detailed—not lifelike, that was the wrong word, but it had a horrible verisimilitude that made her wonder, against her will, whether the voice in the darkness was right, whether the warm flesh in which she moved now was a dream, a mistake. She had a sudden urge to stroke the cold, quiet hands.

"Don't be foolish." The other woman's eyes were like flecks of sky, chilly and kind at the same time. "Go! Just go. Now!"

One more task, priestess. The air grew dimmer, full of twisting shadows.

"What about you?" Nora asked.

"Run!" The woman stabbed the air with a long finger, pointing behind Nora.

Nora stepped backward once, twice, keeping her eyes on the sarcophagus, and then turned and ran on trembling legs that could not even keep to a straight course, but she veered and staggered though growing darkness until suddenly her left side banged into something hard, knocking the breath out of her. She edged around it, touching carved stone; it was one of the columns framing the archway through which she'd entered. She hoped.

"Hirizjahkinis! Hirizjahkinis!" No answer. Running, Nora tripped on the first, invisible stair step and went sprawling. "Hirizjahkinis?" She ran her hands over the steps as far as she could reach, in case Hirizjahkinis had fainted or collapsed or died where she had been waiting, but touched nothing that might have been warm or even cool skin. "Hiriz-jahkinis?" The name came out as barely a whisper.

She was suddenly aware of the archway yawning behind her in the darkness. No sound came from the room beyond, no disembodied voices speaking into her brain, nothing from the woman who thought that gods could be wrong, but the silence was not enough to reassure her. Nora went up the stairs, scrambling on her hands and knees because taking the time to stand up would slow her down too much, and also because she had the confused idea that she would be less of a target if she stayed low.

Then she stopped, straining to hear. It was the ghost of a sound, a faint scrape-scrape, and it seemed to be coming from somewhere far ahead.

"Hirizjahkinis?" Nora waited until she could not bear the darkness any more. The water-magic spell streaked the walls with a bluish glimmer that was almost spookier than no light at all. She listened again, and this time the silence around her seemed infinite.

Straightening, she continued up the steps. The way back seemed to take longer than she'd expected, probably because she was climbing, and because she was alone now.

She kept an eye out for the snake bones, but they never appeared. Perhaps she had passed them in the dark. She called Hirizjahkinis by name every few minutes, more and more out of a sense of obligation than from any hope of a response. She made the water light as bright as she could, feeling some comfort in having the water respond to her. In her mind she began to ask it simple questions and puzzled over its oblique and shifting answers.

The steps ended, and the cave floor leveled out. She splashed through an ankle-deep puddle, maybe the same one that Hirizjahkinis had stepped into on their way down. How long ago had that happened— an hour? Two hours? Six? She had lost her sense of time down here, away from the sun.

What would Ramona say if she could see Nora now? So, this magic thing isn't quite working out the way I hoped, Nora told her sister.

The Ramona in her head, though, was undeterred. You'll find your way out, she insisted. And you met a goddess! A real one, this time.

Nora almost laughed at that. She was glad that Ramona had not seen the dead Nora in the coffin, though.

That scraping sound again, dry as a finger riffling the pages of a book. She was not imagining it.

The passageway was wider now, thick with stalagmites. Nora walked cautiously, straining to listen for even the slightest noise. The water light was showing her details of the cave she had not noticed before. A shaft angled downward to the right, under an overhanging ledge like a balcony. A rock formation bulged like a pile of pillows.

Ahead of her was another mass of stone, black and dense, eroded into sinuous curves. As Nora approached, she watched beads of reflected light slide along its surface, broken into tiny facets—like scales—and she heard the light, papery sound of rock scraped by something smooth and supple, and in that instant she made a wild, fearful, lucky guess. She stopped.

The snake raised a sleek, black head, improbably massive. Nora got a good look at its flat eyes, the pair of round nostrils, the neat vampire fangs tucked into the sides of its mouth, and she began to back away. With another slow dry rustle, the long dark body unspooled itself effortlessly to follow her.

She watched its leisurely tracking grace with a kind of fascination. The weaving head was almost level with her eyes. Was it a venomous snake or the strangling, crushing kind? Why had she never learned a spell that would destroy giant snakes? Or turn them into something smaller and harmless. A pencil, maybe.

Nora tried a paralysis spell that she had once read, but she could not pull enough magic from the water nearby. She fell back on the levitation spell that had once worked on a normal-sized snake. Again, not enough power; she could not budge the creature. Still—

The surest way to defeat a snake, Aruendiel had once said, is to tie it in a knot. Nora tried the levitation spell again, this time aiming at the snake's tail. The tip rose precipitously into the air. Taken off guard, the snake turned to see what was happening to its opposite end; Nora thrust the tail under its chin—if snakes had chins—and pulled it up to make a loop.

But the real problem, she saw now, was what sort of knot to use. It had taken her an entire summer of Y camp to learn to tie a bowline. Out of the hole, around the tree—but the snake, now thoroughly suspicious, cracked its tail like a whip. Its coils slid free from her precarious magical hold.

Nora turned to run. And instead slammed into something bigger than she was, heavy and muscled, covered with cool, silky fur. It gave a low growl. Nora recognized the topaz eyes and the spotted muzzle just as the Kavareen tilted its head sideways and its jaws closed around her waist.

It felt like being jammed into a freezer. Nora twisted madly, thrusting her shoulders against its jaws, kicking to try to find the ground that was no longer beneath her feet. The Kavareen growled again, the roar filling her ears. The snake hissed, uncomfortably close.

Were the two monsters working together? At the edge of her vision, the black reptilian head streaked toward her, just as the Kavareen's leap jerked her upward. She shrieked.

The Kavareen landed with a jolt, its claws ringing on stone. It bounded forward, carrying Nora through the darkness. She squirmed, but the icy points of the Kavareen's teeth held her in a delicate, powerful grip, and she was afraid of what might happen if it bit harder.

Abruptly the Kavareen halted. With a shake of its head, it let Nora drop to the cave floor. The hard, luminescent eyes looked down at her. It raised a paw, batting at her like any cat playing with a half-dead mouse. She rolled away and scrambled to her feet.

Reaching out blindly, she found a cave wall, and scrabbled along it until suddenly her hand discovered an opening in the rock. She pushed herself through. The aperture was barely wide enough for her. The Kavareen would never fit. She wasn't sure about the snake.

The water light spell took less time now, the water in the cave responding more quickly to her call. The pale light told her that she was in a new passageway, rising in a different direction.

A furious hissing seeped through the gap behind her. Actually, two different hisses, she decided after a moment, but she couldn't tell which belonged to the snake and which belonged to the Kavareen. She edged away from the opening. A snarl. More sounds of muffled tumult. Then a loud cry, raw, deep, and piercing. Oddly, it seemed to be coming from deeper in the caves. Like a baby's howl, it was almost physically painful to hear, full of vast anger and desolation.

Nora clapped her hands over her ears. She felt herself quivering, then realized that the rock she stood on was also shaking.

The long cry died away. The cave steadied. Nora took a deep breath, tried to prepare a couple of spells that might be useful—the vomiting spell, in case she was swallowed—and waited.

A minute passed with no giant snake slithering through the gap in the rock. Another minute.

Nora stepped closer to the opening. Her throat felt dry. She hoped that her voice would penetrate into the far chamber.

"You'd better come through as Hirizjahkinis," she called. "It's too narrow for the Kavareen."

She wondered if her words would be understood. Hirizjahkinis used to speak to the Kavareen in some language other than Ors. It sounded rather lovely, Nora remembered. She waited.

On the other side of the hole in the wall, there was a flutter of white linen. Then a brown hand gripped the side of the gap. Hirizjahkinis slipped through the opening, her beaded braids swinging, the Kavareen's spotted hide draped neatly over her shoulders.

She straightened and faced Nora, head balanced high with the ramrod posture that usually made her seem slightly taller than she was. Right now, Nora thought, it made her seem more fragile. But a smile played over Hirizjahkinis's lips. "I am here," she said.

"Are you all right?" This time Nora's inclination to greet Hirizjahkinis with a hug was more stilted. She folded her arms. "How do you feel?"

"I am well indeed! I am no longer hungry. Well, not very hungry." Her voice hardened slightly as her dark eyes searched Nora's: "How did you know? About—us?"

Nora gave a tight shrug. "The Kavareen came to my rescue. It picked me up in its mouth, and I didn't even get scratched. Well, my clothes, maybe"—she plucked at her muddy, torn skirts—"but nothing else. That seemed strange."

Hirizjahkinis nodded. "But it could have been that I commanded the Kavareen to help you, to fight that very ill-mannered serpent."

"And then there was the magic," Nora said, frowning. "You had me do the water magic. You didn't do any yourself, even after spending days in this cave." She wondered whether Hirizjahkinis would take offense at her next question, but asked it anyway: "Can you still do magic?"

"I am Hirizjahkinis, but I am also the Kavareen, and he is a creature that is made up of magic, mostly. I am still learning all the things that he is capable of. More than I knew." She smiled in a way that made her look both proud and chagrined. "But real magic, the kind of magic that Aruendiel taught me? I do not know. Whenever I try a spell, I am clumsy and slow-minded. It is like a tune that I cannot quite remember. No, it is a tune that I hear perfectly well in my head, but it will not come to my lips."

"I'm sorry," Nora said.

"It is better than freezing for a black eternity in the belly of the Kavareen," Hirizjahkinis said. "I made a bargain, and so far I do not regret it. Well, and how are you, little one? What did you do in that evil room to bring that monster snake after us? I waited, wondering what I would say to Aruendiel if you did not come out—I knew exactly what *he* would say—and then I heard the ugly thing slithering about upstairs. So the Kavareen went to investigate. I do not mind snakes so much, myself, but they do not improve with size. I liked this one better when he was only bones."

"I'm not completely sure what happened there." Nora was still turning over in her mind how much she could say to a Hirizjahkinis who was also the Kavareen. "But I think we should get out of here as soon as possible."

"I will not disagree. If it takes a giant serpent to keep you from dawdling in dark caves that smell of death and old angry magic—then I am pleased we met that snake."

"I didn't notice any smell," Nora said.

"The Kavareen did," said Hirizjahkinis.

Chapter 28

Through caverns measureless to man, Nora thought, not for the first time. They were walking again, after crawling, climbing, sliding along twisting passages that burrowed through the limestone with magnificent indecisiveness, leading only to more winding caves. Trudging behind Hirizjahkinis, Nora flexed her tired shoulders and tried to work the gritty taste of clay out of her mouth, not quite succeeding. Even Hirizjahkinis's magically snowy linen was now streaked with yellow mud.

Rounding a thick, waxy curtain of stalactites, Hirizjahkinis paused. "We are descending again. We should go back to that fork we just passed and try the other way."

Nora considered the corridor ahead, which indeed sloped abruptly downward. "Let's try this one just a little farther."

"You wish to meet more giant snakes?"

She shook her head. "No giant snakes, I swear. I just have a feeling there's air and water moving down there—" She edged forward. The sloping rock was slick with moisture, but uneven enough to yield some footholds. Hirizjahkinis did not move until Nora looked back at her. "Please come. Does it smell bad?"

Hirizjahkinis sighed. "Very damp." Taking small, cautious steps, she followed Nora with no visible enthusiasm.

When their path finally leveled, they were ankle-deep in water. "So, yes, it is damp," Nora said, wading ahead.

Hirizjahkinis gave an unexpectedly demure sneeze. Like a cat, Nora thought. "Just because I am part demon now does not mean I cannot catch cold, I believe."

"A little bit farther, all right? Just around this bend." As Nora followed the curve of the passage, she kept an ear tuned for the slosh, slosh of Hirizjahkinis's footsteps behind her own. If there were four paws moving through the water instead of Hirizjahkinis's two human feet, Nora thought, would I be able to tell?

"Careful, little one," Hirizjahkinis called. "Do you hear that?"

"Hear what?"

Hirizjahkinis, not the Kavareen, came around the curve, her head lifted with focused attention. "I heard something ahead."

A small, flat, darkish something floated near Nora's shin. Leaning down, she recognized the rounded lobes of an oak leaf. "Look, look, look!" she said triumphantly, plucking it from the water. "A leaf, and it's still green. And there's another." She pointed.

"Shh." Hirizjahkinis lifted an imperious hand for silence. After a moment, she gave an impatient shrug. "Now I hear nothing. But you have found a leaf. I suppose you mean that this nasty wet hole leads somewhere where there are leaves, and even trees?"

"It seems like a good sign." Nora smiled archly.

"And I was about to insist that we go back to the dry ground." Hirizjahkinis blew a puff of air out of her lips, then cocked her head to listen for another minute. Nora waited, unmoving, hearing the patter of dripping water, the slurp of water against stone. Was that wind hissing somewhere far down the passage?

"Go slowly," Hirizjahkinis said finally. "Quietly. There is no sign of anyone, which is all the more suspicious, because the sweet moon knows I heard someone there a little while ago. I think we should see who it is, don't you? I will not introduce them to the Kavareen, not unless I must—he is shy. Tell your kind water thank you, and no more light, please."

In the new darkness they waded forward. Nora tried the only silencing spell she knew, one intended to muffle the clinking of armor, and found that it worked surprisingly well to hide the splashing of their steps. The silence was disconcerting, though. And her feet were getting numb in the cold water. But yes, the air was definitely fresher in this tunnel than in any of the others she had passed through.

Looking ahead, she thought she saw a patch of darkness that seemed less dense, almost silvery. At the same moment, pushing through a slick of leaves, Nora realized that the water was nearly up to her knees.

"There is a current," Hirizjahkinis said suddenly. "You feel it?"

"Oh, yes." The flow was suddenly pushing against Nora's thighs, tugging at the torn ends of her *maran*. She turned sideways, trying to find better footing on the cave floor. The water was moving so quickly that it gave only passing acknowledgment to her magic. She sensed its rising excitement, a new, wanton strength, as the air filled with a heavy rumble, like approaching traffic.

"Hold on to the walls," Nora began to say, reaching out to find Hirizjahkinis in the dark, and then an onrushing wave lifted her off her feet and flung her backward.

Nora twisted and kicked, choking, paddling with all her strength. The murky torrent was thick with a rolling, silty slurry of pebbles and sand. She thrashed upward in search of air and managed to suck in a couple of breaths as the current bullied her along. Then the crown of her head bumped against rock, and she had to go under the lightless water again. Her lungs burned.

Enough of this, Nora thought. I need to breathe. Make way, make way. I said, *make way*.

She tilted her head back and felt her mouth and chin emerge from the water. Nora let out her breath, then inhaled greedily. Raising an exploratory hand, she found she was in a small air pocket carved out of the flood. Water hung over her head—slightly aggrieved, she sensed, at the urgency of her demand, but also secretly proud of how quickly and neatly it had assumed this unusual form.

Kicking to stay in place, Nora thanked the water profusely and told it how clever it was to divine her wishes so quickly. Then she asked for something else. You know the other one like me? she said to the water. The one that's warm. Moving like me. Bring that one to me.

Then she waited, flexing her limbs against the current and wondering if the element would understand what she meant.

She felt very alone in the freezing dark. If Hirizjahkinis did not surface again, what would she do? Keep doing what we were doing, she thought. Try not to drown, try to get out of this cave. She tried not to dwell on the possibility that the water might return a cold, silent unmoving Hirizjahkinis. If the Kavareen came back instead, that would be all right, probably.

The current pushed hard against her numb limbs. She paddled hard er, afraid of being ripped away from her small refuge. Suddenly bubbles erupted near her, and she felt the swirl of movement in the water. Something bumped her. Next to her ear, someone took a long, sputtering breath. Nora reached out instinctively.

The shoulder she grabbed seemed too large, too solid to be Hiriz-jahkinis's. Urgently, she asked the water for light again.

"Nora? It is you?" She recognized Aruendiel's deep burr, roughened, gasping.

Was he real? In the gray light, his face appeared, pale and intent, looking oddly naked with his wet hair slick and streaming in long, dark fronds.

Nora gave a cry and took in a mouthful of water, some of which got into her windpipe. She dug her fingers into Aruendiel's shoulder, coughing.

"You must not drown, *nefle*, not now," Aruendiel said, taking hold of her arm and steadying her. Her voice was a hoarse fragment, but she choked out some words to ask if he was all right.

He gave a dismissive nod, his gaze traveling methodically over her face, looking for something. She could not tell what. In the dimness, the water pressing high around them, it was hard to read his expression, but she thought she saw the thin, graven lines of his mouth quiver.

"You're alive," he said.

So are you, Nora thought. Her tongue felt as though it were locked inside her mouth. She nodded. "So far, so good," she got out, but she was dissatisfied by her own flippancy.

"Where did you come—?" she started to ask, then sputtered as a new rush of water nearly pulled them both under. Aruendiel grabbed at an overhang, curling his fingers tight against the rock as the current dragged them downstream.

Holding fast to Aruendiel—she would not be separated from him again—Nora kicked against the surging water as hard as she could. Her little air pocket was almost spent. She craned her neck, trying to keep her nostrils in the air.

"We have to swim," he said.

All those years of swimming lessons, all those badges, Nora thought, but they never taught you how to navigate fast-moving currents of black water underground. She nodded and tried to smile confidently.

"Don't be afraid," he said as he pushed her underwater, harder than she would have expected.

Her mind went blank with fear for a moment, as the current carried her away, and then she made a conscious decision to swim as hard as she could and not to panic until she ran out of air, probably thirty seconds from now.

And in fact she was swimming easily, not feeling the cold. She nosed her way forward, riding the flow, almost enjoying herself. She could see very little in the murk, but tiny eddies and vibrations told her how to avoid the cave walls, and she steered her way through the flood with delicate motions. She tasted different scents as she swam, the dank tinge of algae and riverweed; the saltiness of human skin; the acrid, disturbing, unmistakable smell of blood.

Aruendiel swam past her, a long, dim, swiftly moving shape, and then with a splash he leaped out of the water. Maybe he had spotted a fly or something else that was good to eat. Curious, she went closer.

An instant later, light flared above, and a wavering silvery mirror overhead showed her the alarming border where the water ended. Beyond it, a looming dark creature with long appendages.

Fear rippled through her body. With a flip of her tail, she darted downward.

The water suddenly felt much colder. Nora's hands and knees scraped rock. She pulled herself upward, her body feeling heavy, unusually clumsy, and then her head broke the surface. Blinking, she took a long breath of air. It felt rough and warm in her throat.

Aruendiel was crouching at the water's edge, his bent arms and legs looking incongruously long in the narrow cave. Taking her hand, he hauled her onto dry land. A pale, conjured flame burned at his side, weirdly bright after so much darkness.

"I apologize, Nora, involuntary transformations are not pleasant," he said, "and usually reserved for one's enemies, not one's friends."

Nora nodded, her teeth chattering. She looked down at her arms and legs, and for an instant she could see only an alien tangle of gawky extremities. Then she recognized the familiar shape of her own body.

"I was a fish," she said wonderingly. "I could breathe underwater. And I didn't even really notice—" Abruptly she remembered: "Hirizjahkinis! I almost forgot."

Aruendiel raised his head with a grunt of surprise. "Hirizjahkinis?"

"She was with me. Before the water rose."

"Are you sure?"

"Of course!"

The black eyebrows knit in concentration. Aruendiel dabbled his hand in the water and stared into the depths from which they had just emerged. After half a minute, he shook his head. The flickering light drew stark lines on his face as he glanced at Nora. "There is no trace of her magic anywhere near here. No trace of *her*."

"Well, she was here." It occurred to Nora that perhaps the Kavareen could survive underwater for some considerable time, and that perhaps it could hide from Aruendiel's magic. The thought hovered on her lips, and then she said: "Maybe she found another way out."

"Maybe. She has had plenty of practice in escaping snares, having been caught so often. She escaped the Kavareen?"

"Yes." Nora was not sure what else she could safely say.

He regarded her, frowning, and pushed the wet hair away from her face. His fingers were surprisingly warm against her forehead, considering that he had been a fish minutes ago. His frown deepened. "You are chilled," he said, more gently than before.

She remembered that she could at least dry their wet clothes. The water began to drip from her *maran* and Aruendiel's tunic. "What kind of fish were we?"

"Trout."

Nora nodded. Previously she had only encountered trout on a plate, with a fork in her hand. She wondered if she'd ever be inclined to do so again.

"You must have been doing a lot of magic," Nora said, looking at Aruendiel. His eyes seemed brighter, his battered face fresher and less worn—almost handsome, from the right angle. That was to be expected, she supposed, given that he'd been working magic against another magician powerful enough to give a reasonable impersonation of a goddess. But his expression was new to her. His gray, luminous gaze, which did not leave her face, was honed to sharpness, yet seemed almost painfully unguarded.

"How did you get here?" she asked. "Into the caves?"

"A sinkhole, upriver."

"Can we get out that way?"

Aruendiel shook his head reluctantly. "It would be a long swim in that tunnel, and Olenan might be waiting at the other end. This is her flood, you know—she conjured a storm, and it's raining snakes and sticks up there. She wanted to drown me. And you," he added, his mouth twisting. He put his hand against her face as though to brush the hair out of her eyes again, although Nora had not noticed any stray hairs in her field of vision.

"Nora, I am greatly—I am—" He appeared to be rummaging with some anxiety for the words. "I am very well pleased to find you."

"I am so happy to see you, Aruendiel," Nora said with a small sigh. "I didn't know if I would ever see you again. I should have listened when you said we had to leave. We would have had a head start, we would have escaped all this mess."

Aruendiel shook his head. "I should have—"

"I was wrong. I wanted to do one last good deed, to save that prisoner. Only it turned out that someone was going to die no matter what. I pardoned both of the prisoners, and no one was happy about that. Except the prisoners, I suppose. And—I don't know." *You protected the weak, the guiltless and the guilty, in my name.* Sisoaneer. The real one. Nora found that she did not want to say the name even in the silence of her own thoughts.

"Their life was not worth yours, but you have a kind heart. It does not bear—Nora, I did not know what to think." Aruendiel's voice sounded raw. "I had the conviction, as soon as we parted, that some great evil had happened to you. That you were—lost. I could not shake it, even when I followed you to that vile temple and heard your voice, even when I found traces of your magic in these caves. Even now, I almost can't believe I see you here."

"Oh." Nora felt oddly chastened. "Well, I am fine. I really am." There was plenty more to say, the whole story in her throat, ready to be told, but looking into his face, his searching eyes, she saw something there that she was afraid her words would injure.

"And there is this," Aruendiel went on, reaching into his tunic. He pulled out a blue glass bottle that she recognized. Removing a twist of cloth from the opening, he tilted the bottle so that the small object inside slid into his palm.

The timestone looked different from what she remembered: wizened, smaller, and darker, like a fossilized raisin. She gave Aruendiel a puzzled frown.

"When I was exchanging salvos with Olenan up there, I thought to use the timestone, and I found it like this. Burned out."

"Burned out?" Nora asked. "You mean—"

"It had been used already. When you smash a timestone—"

"—all the stored time is released at once, and everything nearby is pushed into the past. The recent past," she added. "Portat Nolu said you couldn't go back more than an hour." Where had she learned all this? From Aruendiel, surely, although he looked slightly surprised at her answer.

"Correct," he said. "You see how blackened this stone is, and dense? Now it holds time that never was. A history that never happened."

"And if you smashed it now—"

"It would take us to a different present."

"A different present," Nora repeated. "So we might not be here, we might be somewhere else?" She wondered: would I be anywhere? Feeling a new tension in the center of her body, she asked: "And you think you were the one who used it?"

Aruendiel set his jaw, and his face grew harsher. "I don't know that for certain, although that seems most likely."

"And you don't remember why you used it," Nora said. "Most people don't." It was remarkable how much she knew about timestones. Taking the stone from Aruendiel's hand, she rubbed it between her fingers, feeling its dry, roughened surface.

"Be careful with that!" he said sharply.

"I know," she said.

It was strange to hold her own death so compactly in her hands.

Like a book that someone warns you not to read: "It's terrible, so depressing, you won't like it." You already know how it ends, but you still feel a nagging curiosity to know exactly how the plot unfolds to the grim conclusion.

Aruendiel reached for the timestone. "It is of no matter. I should have said nothing of this."

Nora did not give him the stone. Keeping her eyes on Aruendiel's face, she said carefully, "When I met Hirizjahkinis, she told me that I'd died, but you undid it. I had no idea what she meant. What if she meant you used the timestone? That I died, and then you reversed time and prevented it?"

"This is merely supposition." He sounded pained. "There is nothing to prove—"

"But then Hirizjahkinis and I went to a deep cave, very deep, and I saw myself there. Dead, in a coffin. And a voice said I belonged there. And—other things."

Aruendiel's expression was stormy and fearful. "What other things?"

"The voice, it showed me Raclin. Also dead. The voice said I belonged to her because I'd killed him. It told me I had to purify her temple, and then rest with her."

He gripped Nora by the shoulders. "What voice?"

She grimaced, feeling an obscure embarrassment. "She called me her priestess. I think it was—you know—"

"No. Ridiculous." His tone was unyielding. "This is not worth a shred of your attention. You were hallucinating, or you encountered some crazed, forgotten monstrosity of a demon. Not a real god. And even if—well, I tell you, even gods can be wrong."

"That's what the woman said. Funny," Nora said, as Aruendiel gave her a hard, questioning look. "Not the voice. Not the—goddess. This was someone different. She just appeared, this woman, and spoke to me."

He seemed to be considering various possibilities, all of them somewhat troubling. "A dream, another demon?"

"I don't know." Nora shook her head. "I felt as though I should know who she was, but I couldn't quite place her. She said that I was alive not dead, and that I shouldn't listen to the voice, and I should leave right away."

"She was right, whoever she was. You did not die," Aruendiel said. "It is not true, it never happened."

Nora held up her fist with the timestone in it. "Except maybe here—" She stopped at the look of clouded desolation in Aruendiel's eyes.

Almost blindly, he touched her cheek, then leaned toward her. Nora let herself rest against his shoulder, feeling his breath in her hair. This closeness was not quite enough to calm the secret, fearful sense of urgency that had seized her, now that she knew for certain of that other destiny, erased and written over like a chalkboard but still not entirely illegible. Aruendiel had given her back her life, but she wondered if it would ever feel completely hers again.

"Thank you for saving me," she said.

"It should never have happened."

"It never did happen," Nora said, and Aruendiel gave her a shadow of a smile. Then he pulled away, his black brows knotted. "Olenan. This was her revenge. She's a madwoman. I was too cautious. I should never have tried to—to placate her." His mouth twisted.

"Well," Nora said dryly. "She's your old flame. I'm sure it was nice for a while."

"I thought I would find some sweetness, I own that," Aruendiel said, hunching his shoulders, "but there was only sour wine in that bottle. I thought I could beguile her. In the end it only made her angrier and more dangerous. I should have moved against her from the start."

"Why didn't you?" Nora could not keep some bitterness out of her voice.

The question seemed natural enough to her, but it appeared to take Aruendiel aback. He gave a slow sigh.

"I feared for you," he said at last. "She had you in her power. And I had some weakness of purpose. Even as I faced her just now, out there"—he nodded upward—"several times she was exposed, at a clear disadvantage, and yet I could not make the killing stroke." He glanced away, frowning.

"You still have tender feelings for her, then," Nora said. Killing stroke, indeed. She felt it herself, right through the heart.

"No, that is not right." He spoke with more characteristic sternness. "It is this: in all my life, I have killed one woman, a woman I shared a bed with, and I do not wish to do so again. No matter how she has wronged me."

He was talking of his wife, that shadowy girl, who would always be both stained and immaculate in his eyes. Nora felt a sudden shyness, but she said, "Even if that woman might be trying to kill you?"

Aruendiel gave a dry and rusty laugh. "There would be no satisfaction in it." He stood up abruptly, almost hitting his head against the rocky ceiling, and nodded toward the darkness that lay beyond his light. "We have dawdled here long enough," he said. Dimly Nora could make out a narrow passageway that twisted upward.

He gave Nora a sharp look. "Mistress Nora, you have been clever enough to dry our clothes and light your way with water magic. Do you know how to find our way out of these caves?"

She was glad to have some happier news to discuss. "I do," she said.

Chapter 29

"Hirizjahkinis told me the water would remember the light," Nora said to Aruendiel as she scrambled onto a muddy shelf of rock. She examined the sloping limestone in front of her, looking for her next handhold. "Then I discovered the water remembers other things."

Behind her, Aruendiel grunted approvingly. Or perhaps it was simply the exertion of hauling himself up the slick stone face. They were making the climb under their own power and not with magic. Levitation spells were tricky in tight, crooked confines like this one.

"Water knows all these caves. It made them in the first place. Honestly, I can't follow everything it's telling me. Water is weird—it doesn't think the way we do, does it?" Nora found a new grip and pulled herself upward. "But I can tell there are places where water gets into the caves, and where it goes out, and I can get an idea of what's in between. It's not perfect, but it's something to go on.

"I wish water's idea of a direct route was a little more direct, that's all," she added.

"Vresk the Navigator had the same problem with his water mapping spells," Aruendiel said. "Water is a poor judge of distance. But your basic spell is sound—wait! Pray do not kick me in the face."

"Sorry," Nora said. "Are you all right?" She peered down over her shoulder but could only glimpse the top of Aruendiel's head and the splayed, grimy fingers of one hand grasping a knob of rock.

"Keep going. The water mapping spell was not Hirizjahkinis's suggestion?"

"No, it was my idea." Just too late, Nora saw that the conversation was straying onto dangerous ground.

"She knows at least a half-dozen map spells. It is odd that she did not employ any of them herself. And how in the names of all the gods did she get out of the Kavareen?"

Nora was relieved that Aruendiel could not see her face. "She said they came to an agreement."

A snort from below. "Has she not learned: never trust a demon?"

Nora said nothing. Hirizjahkinis and the Kavareen, that was not her secret to tell. Trusting a demon, though—wasn't that exactly what she was doing? With an exhalation that was theatrically louder than it needed to be, she attempted a sort of push-up to mount the ledge in front of her, but only got herself halfway over the brink. Her dangling legs scrambled for a foothold. "Pigfilth," she said under her breath.

Aruendiel's hands closed around her hips, pushed her smoothly upward. They rested on her thighs for a fraction of a second more, and then released her. She missed the pressure of his hands as soon as he let go. It was odd, Nora thought in some confusion, not for the first time, how Aruendiel's body could give a general impression of brokenness and dilapidation and yet move with such sureness when he wished.

"Are you up?" he asked.

"Yes, thank you." Nora found that the passage had narrowed but also leveled out. She crawled forward to give him space to follow, although she had to keep contorting herself to avoid the drooping stems of stalactites.

From somewhere ahead came a sudden, sharp clap. Small echoes resonated through the darkness. A rock falling, maybe. It was hard to tell how far away. Nora, pausing to listen, was aware that Aruendiel had also stopped.

"Does she—does Olenan have some kind of invisibility spell that she likes to use?" Nora asked softly.

"Oh, yes." Aruendiel's tone was knowing, slightly caustic. "It's quite powerful."

"Do you think she might—?"

He shook his head. "She didn't make that noise. I do not discern her magic so near."

Another minute passed. The sound was not repeated. They began to creep forward again, both moving more carefully this time. "Did she tell you about the spell?" Aruendiel asked.

"I just guessed. She knew things. Sometimes she would just appear. People told me she heard everything."

"She would use the invisibility spell often, especially when we traveled," Aruendiel said. "She enjoyed watching without being seen."

"Just like a goddess," Nora said sardonically.

"Perhaps. Although in my experience the presence of a true god is hard to disguise."

Nora thought back to the dry, relentless voice in the deep cave. She wondered suddenly if she would ever hear it again, and if so, what it would say to her. The idea was both unbearable and strangely attractive.

"You said—you were talking about what it's like to kill a person you'd shared a bed with," Nora said. "Um, I did kill Raclin, you know."

"And it was a job well done," he said at once. "I saw the viper's carcass. I fault you only in that it was a quicker death than he deserved. And as for the notion that you are somehow bound to the service of a—some long-buried voice, simply because Raclin is dead," he went on with some energy, "well, whatever you encountered in that cave was both greedy and deluded."

Nora rolled on her side to squeeze between two stalactites like upside-down beehives. She was hoping that the water map didn't lead to a tiny fissure in the rock passable for liquid but not for humans, and she was also thinking hard about exactly what she was trying to say. "Even if he deserved killing, even if I had no choice—and I think both of those were true—it doesn't make his death go away. It happened, and that knowledge will be there, somewhere, for the rest of my life."

She could say this to Aruendiel. He would know what she meant, the enormity of what she had done. There was silence for a moment, except for the scrabbling sounds of their progress over the rock. "Yes, that is true," he said. "It's a burden you should not have to carry. It should have been mine. I would have enjoyed killing Raclin more than you did."

"I didn't enjoy it, but I didn't not enjoy it, either. It was so easy," she said. "That's what scares me. I almost gave up magic afterward. It seemed so dangerous to have so much power."

"But you didn't give up magic," Aruendiel said, not entirely able to tamp down the apprehension in his voice.

"No, I thought I could use it to help people." She sounded an ironic note in the back of her throat. "Well, for a while I did."

"It *is* dangerous to have so much power, and in your case, I am glad that you are dangerous. I would rather you felt some grief and regret because you used magic to kill someone, than to see you guiltless and dead. As for using magic for philanthropy," he said, "that can be more difficult than it seems. Even if you don't pretend to be a goddess."

"Sisoaneer—Olenan said that if I healed people, I would be healed, too. Watch out, there's a drop here. Ouch."

With a faint curse, Aruendiel lowered himself over the edge. "And? Were you healed?"

Nora reflected for a moment. "Not really. It made me feel better, treating the patients. I don't think it made me a better person or washed away my sins or anything like that." It was ironic that she would fall back on a concept like sin, although she was not sure it translated properly into Ors. The word she'd used had a religious connotation, but it meant something like an infraction of the rules. Crime, dereliction of duty, blasphemy? Those Ors words were more powerful, but none of them were quite right, either.

"The best reason to heal people—with magic or no magic—is because they need healing," Aruendiel said dryly. "Olenan has played goddess for I don't know how many years, she has treated a dozen dozen dozen patients and more, and yet I would not say that *she* has been healed of whatever plagues her."

Nora decided to voice a question that she had been wondering about: "Have any other magicians played god?"

"Certainly, it happens from time to time, but they're rarely successful for long. Old acquaintances turn up, spells go awry. Olenan was clever to hide herself in this backwoods temple."

Nora pushed herself under a row of skinny stalactites and discovered more headroom beyond. Cautiously she got to her feet. "It seems like an obvious temptation. Did you ever think of it?"

Aruendiel's pale, scarred face emerged from the gloom behind her. He gave a crisp laugh. "Me? What sort of god would I make?" Unfolding himself from the space they had just crawled through, he added, more reflectively: "I knew a magician, Jornanit Longnose, who set himself up as an agricultural demigod in Pernia for a few years, but he gave it up. It was arduous to keep track of all the prayers, he said, and he found it lonely."

They were now in a gently sloping gallery, where even Aruendiel could stand upright. The walls were streaked with flows of sugary white stone; Nora thought of melting ice cream and wondered how many hours it had been since she'd last eaten. Aruendiel held up his hand for silence, and she heard, very faintly, the rustle and burble of unseen running water somewhere up the passage.

"I think we're getting close," she said.

Aruendiel did not move. Head cocked, he listened for another minute. Dripping water pattered down somewhere nearby, like footsteps.

"Show yourself!" he called suddenly.

A white quiver in the darkness ahead. A clatter of rocks.

"There you are!" Hirizjahkinis said. Her smile lit the cave like a sliver of daylight as she came forward. "You did not drown, either of you."

Nora scrambled forward and looped Hirizjahkinis into a hug. Aruendiel did not move at first; Nora caught the scrape of his indrawn breath. Then he stepped forward with brusque swiftness, his face creased with an uncertain smile. "Hiriz? It is really you?"

Hirizjahkinis raised her palms in greeting, and he intertwined his long fingers with her finer, darker digits. She winced playfully at his grip, laughing. He frowned slightly as he studied her upturned face.

"You are solemn, Aruendiel," she said.

"Once again, after I'd given up all hope—" Reluctantly he let her hands go. "You are well and whole? I did not believe that I would see you again."

"Then you were too gloomy, as usual." Hirizjahkinis shook her head. "Nora, did you not tell him that I had found you? And that I am quite well, aside from the nasty chill here?"

"I did." Nora had a fairly good idea of what Hirizjahkinis was really asking. "I told him you were fine. I was worried after losing you in that flood, though."

"So many weeks inside the Kavareen!" Aruendiel said roughly. "I never heard of anyone escaping its maw after so long a time."

"All these years that we have known each other, you and I—then one little mishap, and you assume so easily that I am doomed? I am disappointed, Aruendiel. You have so little confidence in me, who was your own pupil?"

"I did not teach you well enough, evidently, or you would never have trusted that filthy demon." Aruendiel's narrowed eyes raked her with fine, frustrated bafflement. "You are still wearing its hide?"

"Certainly, these caves are freezing," Hirizjahkinis said calmly. "I will not be truly happy until I see the sun again."

"That will not be long. You look more flourishing than I would have thought."

"And you also, Aruendiel. You have been fighting and doing strong magic, I can tell, and that always makes you happy. But something else has warmed your blood as well, I think." Hirizjahkinis's smile flicked toward Nora. "I am glad of it."

"There has been plenty of fighting," Aruendiel said, his eyebrows snapping upward. "And I—well, by every god it is pleasant to see your face again. How in the name of the sun did you get out of that vile creature's belly?"

"I am not so easy to digest," Hirizjahkinis said. "Even for the Kavareen. And in the end, when we were both lost under this mountain, he was ready enough to let me out again."

Nora found that she had tensed; now, this was the moment for Hirizjahkinis to tell Aruendiel the truth of how she and the Kavareen had negotiated a new existence together. But Hirizjahkinis was talking about encountering Nora in the cave; she was even boasting gently about Nora's skill in coaxing magic and light from the moisture in the caves.

"You should be proud of this one, Aruendiel," she said, her hand on Nora's shoulder. "It is not just the magic she has learned. She has good eyes, and the wit to know what she is seeing."

"I have seen evidence of it," Aruendiel said. "From time to time." Nora met his eyes with some difficulty. It had just occurred to her that Hirizjahkinis might be laying on the praise a bit thick to keep Nora allied with her, to buy her silence.

On the other hand, Nora thought again, it's Hirizjahkinis's secret, not mine. She decided to hold fast to that thought. It seemed to her that she might be protecting Aruendiel as well as Hirizjahkinis, although that reflection did not make her feel much better.

The sound of water grew louder as they went farther along. Eventually the gallery they were following crossed a passage whose floor was a shallow stream rushing over round stones.

Aruendiel knelt at the edge of the water. He let his fingers play in the stream for a moment, then rose and touched his wet finger to Nora's. "What does it tell you?" he asked.

Nora rubbed her fingers together and picked up a kind of shimmering excitement that she had not found in the cave water elsewhere. "It's coming from above ground," she said.

"Yes. You hear how many small, light voices there are? How scattered they are? This water was rain not an hour ago."

"You said Olenan was trying to flood the caves. To drown us."

"Or flush us out," Aruendiel said.

"Then she is foolish, she is wasting her time," Hirizjahkinis said. "As though we would stay here any longer than we have to."

They waded upstream, single file. The cave walls here were worn smooth, the little stream curving through grottoes that yawned like enormous shells. Hirizjahkinis took the lead, as though determined to be the first out of the cave. Aruendiel came after her. Somewhat to Nora's surprise, he and Hirizjahkinis did not speak much. From time to time, Aruendiel glanced back to make sure that Nora was still following, but he said almost nothing to her, either.

Abruptly, the stream grew noisier, and they came around a bend to see several strands of water pouring straight down from an opening in the cave ceiling. Flowing toward them, the water churned and foamed around their feet. Hirizjahkinis said something under her breath about the dampness of caves and wrapped the Kavareen's pelt a little tighter around her shoulders.

Aruendiel's gaze rested on her for a moment, and then he turned to Nora, who was staring upward. The hole was perhaps two feet in diameter. Small but not impossible.

"That's it," she said. "That's the way. And then we're almost out." She could feel sunlight on water, so close.

Aruendiel gave a nod. "Very good. And above, is there enough room for us to pass?"

"I think so," Nora said. She had a clearer sense now of how flowing water filled the space available to it. It seemed to her that there was air as well as water in the cavity above.

"Are you not sure?" Aruendiel said, one eyebrow cocked.

"I'm sure," Nora said, hearing the challenge in his voice, and she launched herself upward with a levitation spell and a kick. He was definitely smiling, almost grinning, as she rose.

She made it all the way into the hole before her spell began to falter. There was just enough time to wedge her foot against the side to halt her slide, and then Aruendiel's more powerful spell tugged her higher. She wriggled up through the gap, sputtering as water splashed over her face, until her head emerged into dry air and she found herself in a new chamber.

Hauling herself out of the water, she found a perch on a flattish rock beside the hole she had just exited. "I'm up! And there seems to be some space here." Nora took a deep breath. The air here smelled of river and smoke instead of the dull clay reek of the lower caves.

"Well done." Aruendiel's voice sounded hollowly from below. "We will follow. Hirizjahkinis? It is your turn."

"Yes." There was a pause. "There is no gentlemanly assistance for me?"

"Do you need it? It is only a simple levitation spell."

"It is not so simple! Your friend the false goddess does not like to share the magic here."

"That didn't stop Nora, and she is only a child in magic compared with you."

Child, really? Nora thought. As the water light spell gradually spread its faint illumination over the rock, she glanced around, trying to estimate the dimensions of the new cave. A gleaming streak of water traveled a jagged path across the floor before it plunged into the hole from which she had just emerged. She was trying to see where the streamlet came from when a brighter light flared in the dimness. It showed a face as pale and startled as Nora's must have been.

"You!"

Nora almost didn't recognize the speaker, her expression was so different from usual. But the arched eyebrows, the fierce cheekbones were unmistakable. "Yaioni?" She doesn't look bored now, Nora thought.

"You are alive?" There seemed to be genuine astonishment in Yaioni's voice.

Nora was getting tired of the general presumption that she was dead. "Are you disappointed?" she asked.

Yaioni gave an infinitesimal shrug. "I am surprised. No wonder *she* is so angry." She turned to call over her shoulder: "Come, over here!"

"Wait, who are you calling? Who else is here?" Nora angled herself to look back through the gap she had just passed through. What was keeping Hirizjahkinis and Aruendiel? She caught only a glimpse of his black-clad shoulder, but over the sound of splashing water she heard his voice.

"—traces of Nora's magic all through these caves," he was saying, "and none of yours. You have used no magic at all. It's curious that you managed to escape the Kavareen and subdue it. Did you simply persuade it to let you go?"

Hirizjahkinis's voice: "You know I have a lively tongue, Aruendiel."

"I have never known demons to be amenable to persuasion."

"Perhaps you are not very persuasive. Even demons do not like to be scowled at. As you are scowling now."

Nora crouched to shout through the hole. "Aruendiel!" He had waited until she had gone up the shaft to say these things to Hirizjahkinis. That was ominous.

"I beg your patience, Nora," he called back. "One moment."

"Who is there?" Yaioni asked, with some alarm. She lowered her torch slightly, peering at the crevice where the water disappeared.

"My friends," Nora said warningly.

From behind Yaioni came another voice, indistinct, hollowed out by the cave echoes. "Over here!" Yaioni flung over her shoulder. "Look, your High Priestess is here." Catching sight of Nora's face, she laughed. "Do not look so afraid. It is only Lemoes and Piv."

"Lemoes?" Nora said dubiously as another light appeared. "How many people are wandering around these caves?" A man's arm held the torch; she made out the curve of his shoulder, a dark head. Behind him, a shorter figure with light hair. She recognized one of the *ganoi* attendants at the hospital.

From the cave below, Hirizjahkinis's voice drifted up, musical but guarded. "What are you thinking, old friend?"

"That you are not really my old friend," Aruendiel said. "That the Kavareen has managed one last transformation."

"Aruendiel, you are never happy unless you can be full of suspicion and mistrust. If you cannot find an enemy that suits you, you will make one. I have said this many, many times."

"Hirizjahkinis has said it. I do not entirely agree with her, myself."

"I am Hirizjahkinis." There was the shade of a cool threat in Hirizjahkinis's voice.

"No," Aruendiel said blackly, "I wish it were true."

Nora discovered that she was holding her breath. "Aruendiel, listen to me," she called down. "I know it doesn't look good. But she's telling the truth, I really think so."

Glancing up, she found Yaioni, Lemoes, and the *ganoi* called Piv staring at her curiously. Piv carried a spear with a stone point. Lemoes's face was smudged, tired, but oddly tranquil. She nodded curtly at them.

"You were right, she is not dead," Yaioni said to Lemoes, just as Hirizjahkinis said, in a more subdued tone, "It is not untrue."

Lemoes cleared his throat. "The goddess told me that I would find you," he said to Nora. "Priestess."

Nora gritted her teeth. Still under the sway of his goddess. Did that mean Olenan–Sisoaneer would appear next? She shook her head warningly. "You haven't found me," she said. "You haven't seen me at all, in fact." With a wary glance at Piv's spear, she bent down closer to the gap in the rock, straining to hear what was happening below.

"—more complicated than you think," Hirizjahkinis was saying. "The Kavareen could not have done what it did without me, and without the Kavareen's help, I would not be speaking to you now—"

Lemoes began to speak again. Nora slashed with her hand for

silence. "Quiet," she hissed. "I don't want to hear about your crazy fake goddess."

"—we live through each other now, he and I," Hirizjahkinis said. "Yes, I am the Kavareen, but I am also Hirizjahkinis. I know it."

Aruendiel said something that she could not hear clearly. He had moved out of Nora's line of sight. She found that his disappearance increased her agitation.

"I did not want to tell you these things," Hirizjahkinis went on. "But there is no sense in lying about any of this, either."

"I told Hirizjahkinis, again and again"—Aruendiel had raised his voice—"that the Kavareen was too dangerous to be an ally, let alone a plaything."

"And you were right!" Hirizjahkinis said. "That is another thing I would rather not have to say. But I will say it. You were right."

Would that be enough to pacify Aruendiel? Vaguely Nora was aware that, nearby, Lemoes had stooped to try to catch her eye.

"My goddess is not crazy, not fake," Lemoes said, smiling, determined.

Nora shook her head. "She's not a real goddess, your Sisoaneer. You should know that. She's a woman named Olenan. I'm sorry, but it's true. Now quiet, I'm listening." She frowned downward into the hole in the floor.

"—jakinis is gone." Aruendiel's voice was scathing. "Her mind and memory stolen by a vicious demon whose only interest is to feed and destroy."

"I don't mean *her*," Lemoes said. "I mean *my* goddess."

"I said, be qui—!" Nora looked up. "Wait. *Your* goddess?"

"And yours," Lemoes said.

Nora felt herself flinch involuntarily. She sat back on her haunches and stared at him. "No!"

Lemoes nodded, his eyes meeting hers gently, almost regretfully. "You know her now, too."

"But—" Nora shook her head. This new realization felt inexplicably like a wound. "It was—it was *that* one who came to you? All this time?" she demanded. She mouthed the name: "Sisoaneer?"

He nodded again, and she shivered.

"—at my side all those years," Hirizjahkinis was saying. "I had no secrets from him. And you know, he is not without love. He is not as destructive as you wish to believe. He grows more like me every day."

"Not a week ago, the Kavareen attacked me savagely—and Nora, and a dozen other innocents," Aruendiel said. "If you are truly Hirizjahkinis, where were you then?"

Yaioni, her head cocked, was also trying to follow the exchange below. She gave Nora a suspicious look. "The Kavareen? Does he mean the monster leopard? That tried to eat me?"

With some reluctance, Nora nodded.

"What does he mean? Is the monster leopard down there?" Yaioni demanded.

"Not exactly—"

"He was in pain then, and angry," Hirizjahkinis said. "I will be honest with you, Aruendiel, he does not always heed me perfectly, not yet. There is much for me to learn."

"Yes, you will grow more like him every day," Aruendiel said.

Their conversation was growing too painful to overhear. Nora swung her legs into the hole in the floor. The water draining through it slapped her with a fresh chill and reminded her of how cold she was. "I have to go," she said to Lemoes and Yaioni.

"The monster leopard will eat you," Yaioni said, almost sorrowfully.

"I hope not," Nora said, lowering herself carefully, triceps burning. She used a levitation spell to slow her descent, then dropped the last few feet and stuck a wet, wobbly landing under the sluicing water.

Wiping her eyes, she found the other two facing each other, Aruendiel holding himself with wary economical tension, Hirizjahkinis standing with her head high, one arm akimbo, looking almost relaxed until you noticed how tightly her hands were clenched. Both sent sidelong glances at Nora; she could not help sensing some impatience at her interruption.

"Are you two going to fight, or get out of this cave?" Nora said. "I'm sorry, I couldn't help overhearing—"

"That Aruendiel has decided I am a wicked, dangerous monstrosity who must be destroyed," Hirizjahkinis said.

"That's wrong, that's not true," Nora said, but Aruendiel's glare was like the north wind scouring a frozen lake.

"Oh, he is not wrong. I am a dangerous monstrosity." Hirizjahkinis smiled.

"Nora, you shouldn't be here. This matter is between this creature"—Aruendiel nodded at Hirizjahkinis—"and myself."

"You mean between *Hirizjahkinis* and yourself," Nora said. "But that's not correct, either, because she's my friend, too, and no matter what, she has been nothing but good and kind. And nonviolent," she added. "She is still Hirizjahkinis. And when she *was* the Kavareen—not for very long—it saved my life, it rescued me from a giant snake. She—the Kavareen could have eaten me then, but it didn't."

She could tell her words did not have the intended effect on Aruendiel. "You were fortunate," he said coldly. "I am sorry your life was in her treacherous power for even an instant."

"You are the treacherous one, Aruendiel. Pretending to greet me in friendship, and then turning on me."

Nora tried to sound calm: "It doesn't make sense to be fighting when—"

"It is you who will turn on us," Aruendiel said. There was a sword in his hand; where it had come from, Nora wasn't sure. A faint wisp of smoke drifted off the blade. She tried to step between him and Hirizjahkinis, but he pushed her aside.

"If you are enough of an idiot to do this, I won't make it easy for you." Hirizjahkinis lifted a hand to her shoulder and clenched her fist around a fold of the Kavareen's hide.

"Stop it, both of you!"

"This is not easy." Aruendiel ground out the words, but he raised the sword. It sang through the air. Hirizjahkinis drew back with agile grace.

Nora grabbed at Aruendiel's wrist, trying to force the blade down; she could feel its heat on her skin. "You don't want to do this, Aruendiel. Not again. Remember?"

She felt him recoil, as though she had bludgeoned him. "Nora, it's not her," he said.

"Close enough." Nora stared up at him, willing him to meet her eyes.

The Kavareen's fur brushed against her arm like thickly falling snow. But when they looked up, it was gone.

Chapter 30

Aruendiel lowered the sword, and it disappeared from his hand. He glowered down at Nora with a kind of incredulous intensity, as though he could burn away her misapprehension with a stare. "I won't tolerate this fraud," he said.

Nora folded her arms. "She's not lying."

"If she believes the lie, that doesn't make it true."

He called Hirizjahkinis *she*. That was progress. "But I recognize her," Nora said. "She talks like Hirizjahkinis. She acts like Hirizjahkinis—and what I mean by that, she helped me and protected me and generally behaved like a good, caring, friendly person. A human person."

"She is a clever simulacrum." Aruendiel shook his head. "Do you not see? If you accept her as Hirizjahkinis, it's no different from being beguiled by a Faitoren enchantment."

Nora drew in her breath. "No! It's completely different."

"To embrace a falsehood courts your own destruction," he said, with an edge of bitterness that made Nora suspect that he spoke to himself as much as to her.

"Since you mention Faitoren enchantments, Aruendiel!" Her own quivering fury took her by surprise. "You were tricked before, and you're falling into the same stupid trap again."

"I prefer not—"

"Remember all those terrible things I said to you—that you're old, and dead, and I don't know what? You know what? They were *true*. I admit it. I thought them, and then the ring made me say them." She shook her hand with its now-naked ring finger in his face. "Ilissa and Raclin made me spew up every mean, fearful, dark, evil thought I ever had about you."

These were things that she hadn't quite told herself yet, but she went on, stone by stone across a raging river.

"There's more in my heart than just fear, though," Nora went on. "So much more." She resolved not to say "love" again, she would not make that mistake. "You should know that. But you couldn't see it then, and you can't see it now, with Hirizjahkinis."

"This is completely different," Aruendiel said, white around the mouth. "It is not the same magic. The danger is greater—"

"Is it?" Nora snapped, then made herself speak more gently. "You're worried about falsehoods? It would be false to say that Hirizjahkinis is *not* in there. She said she is, and you can see it. Look, I wonder, too, I have doubts, but in the end I think we have to trust her, until—unless she gives us some reason not to trust her. If you have a friend who has a—a terrible accident, and she recovers, and maybe she's not exactly the same, maybe she's very different, but still, she's your friend, you try to stick with her. And if we don't do that with Hirizjahkinis, then we're not truly her friends. Are we?" She frowned up at Aruendiel.

"That blind loyalty is exactly what the demon is counting on."

"It's not blind! It's about seeing things as they are. Recognizing someone even if they've been changed by magic, or anything else."

Aruendiel's mouth was pursed to reply, but he checked himself, his brows lifting almost uncertainly, as though Nora's words had caught him off guard. "It's a rare kind of sight," he said after a moment.

"Not so rare. It's called affection," Nora said. "Friendship." What the hell, she thought. "In my language, 'love.'"

"Affection can cloud the sight as much as magic," he said, but some of the conviction was gone from his voice. "One sees only what one wishes to see."

"But that's true of any emotion. Fear. Anger. They can cloud your perceptions, too. Come on, Aruendiel, we're talking about Hirizjahkinis. She wouldn't give up on you or me, if the situation were reversed."

"Perhaps—not," Aruendiel said, his mouth twisting. "Unless she already has." Nora had to strain to hear him.

She was suddenly aware that the churn of falling water had grown much louder—because, she saw, the flow from the gap in the ceiling had thickened and intensified. Foaming water now covered the floor of the chamber.

"I completely forgot—there are some people from the temple up there," Nora said, her eyes following the white column of water upward. "Yaioni and Lemoes and Piv."

"They are loyal to Olenan?"

"Yaioni, definitely. The others, maybe not."

Aruendiel glanced back the way they had come, then looked up at the gap in the cave ceiling again. "We should not delay," he said. "If she warns Olenan, we may have a lively reception. You have the water's favor, Nora. Make a path for us." To her questioning look, he added, "Give the water a different shape, that is all. You don't need to interrupt the current, only to redirect it."

It was not so different, she decided, from the spell she had done before in the flooded tunnel to make a breathing space. After some coaxing, the falling water offered them a series of footholds, the approximation of a ladder. "It's slippery," Aruendiel called over his shoulder, but it sounded more like a warning than a critique. Nora climbed cautiously, feeling the liquid churn and bubble under her soles, and was glad to reach the cavern above.

She pushed the damp hair out of her eyes and did the water light spell again. The floor of the chamber was now completely flooded to a depth of several inches, with a noticeable current flowing from the far end. Lemoes and Yaioni were gone.

"That way." Aruendiel pointed, and Nora nodded. They splashed toward the source of the current. Gradually the cavern narrowed to a passage that twisted in one direction and then the other.

"The spell I just did—is that how you held back the raindrops?" she asked. "Remember, when I first—"

"That also required some air magic. We must start you on that next. You will enjoy air magic, I believe, after the moodiness of water."

It was the first time that he had made any clear reference to the continuation of Nora's studies in magic, or indeed to any kind of further association with her. Did he intend for her to become his pupil again? Only his pupil again?

A draft of milder air touched Nora's face. She noticed that the shadows where her water light spell didn't reach were not as absolute

She and Aruendiel waded faster. They rounded a bend, and suddenly the cave seemed to expand in the streaks of grayish, splendidly mundane daylight that filtered through a slim crevice in the cave wall.

Nora gave a tired cheer. "Finally!"

In the new light, Aruendiel was grimier than he had seemed before, his tunic caked with mud, but the tired, wary look on his face crackled into something warmer. "A welcome sight," he said. "And these are your friends?"

Nora turned quickly. In the shadows at the rear of the chamber, people were crowded onto a ledge just above the water. She recognized Lemoes, taller than the rest, and then Yaioni. The others were pilgrims and *ganoi*, jammed together like refugees on a lifeboat.

"Why are all of you here?" she asked. A harsh, weary snicker erupted from someone in the rear of the group. Nora felt reproved. "You're hiding, is that it?" she asked.

"Of course we are hiding," Yaioni snapped. "It is not safe, she is too angry."

"Angry at you?"

"At everyone in Erchkaii," Lemoes said.

"But—the pilgrims, too? That makes no sense."

"Nora, come here." There was urgency in Aruendiel's tone. He was stooping over the opening in the rock, looking outside.

Nora waded over to him. Water poured into the cave through the bottom of the fissure; this was the origin of the flowing water they had been following. Through the opening, she saw tree trunks, a mosaic of green leaves, sodden cloth tangled in branches. Beyond that, an enormous sheet of sullen gray water, lightly pocked with raindrops. Was it the lake? Had they made it that far? Then she recognized the tawny wall of the ravine opposite. Far to the left was a squat brown building—the second floor of the hospital, protruding above the floodwaters.

Her eyes went back to the tangle of bushes and young trees that screened the cave opening. The brush had trapped a bundle of floating debris. Something about the color and proportions was troubling to her.

She looked more closely. A shoulder, a sloping belly. Gray hair floated around the lolling head like a wreath. Nora sucked in her breath. She knew those heavy features.

"It's the baron. One of the pilgrims. I treated him." A day or so ago, she had seen him on the ward, walking shakily on his own. "He's dead."

"His throat was cut," Aruendiel said. Nora looked away from the white gash under the baron's chin.

"But he was getting better," she said. "He was going to live."

Aruendiel pulled her gently away from the opening. "That was why he died."

She didn't know what he meant. "He was my patient, my responsibility. I was, I—was she trying to get at me somehow?"

"That wasn't why she killed him. It was only his life that she wanted. His and others', I suspect." Aruendiel looked across the cave at Lemoes. "How many did she kill?" he called.

"Dozens," Lemoes said flatly.

"Do you think we had a chance to count?" Yaioni said, curling her lip. "All we could do was run away." She nodded at Lemoes. "He knew about this cave, the *ganoi* told him about it the other time she was so angry. We brought the ones from the sick house who could walk, before the river was so high. Lemoes says she does not know about this cave." Yaioni's voice rose, trembling. "I am not so sure. And now the water is rising, we will drown anyway."

A fish had smelled blood in the water, Nora remembered, but it did not guess where the scent came from. "Why?" she asked. "Why would she do this?"

Aruendiel did not respond at once. When he did, his tone was dry and ruminative. "To save her own life, what remains of it," he said. "It's a very old, primitive kind of magic, but it survives because it's the easiest way to raise someone from the dead, as long as you're willing to kill and kill again.

"Mefransk Redhand reigned two hundred years after the wizard Eoluthias brought him back to life on the battlefield, and they say a thousand people died in those years to keep the king alive—although the records are incomplete," he added. "The toll could easily be higher."

"You mean, he killed a thousand people to stay alive?" Nora repeated. "And she did the same magic here?" Not a thousand people, surely, but over time it would add up. "She said something, something—" The echo of Olenan's voice in Nora's memory seemed to come from another age. "She told me once that she had brought herself back from the dead. It proved she was a goddess."

"She said that?" Aruendiel seemed grimly amused. "Well, yes, I suppose she could have worked the spell herself, if she found a victim just as she was dying. The timing would be tricky, the first time. But then she would be at leisure to find more sacrifices."

"The prisoners from the Ghaki king," Nora said, frowning.

"Or the occasional death of a patient," Aruendiel said.

Yaioni shifted impatiently, frowning. "There were always enemies," she said. "She has many enemies."

Nora gave her a hard look. "You must have known what she was doing. All the priests she killed here—"

Yaioni drew back her lips, unsmiling. "They were heretics! And she was angry with them—that is all that I knew. She was my goddess, my life, and I did everything she commanded me to do."

"Everything?" Nora asked. "What do you mean, 'everything'?"

The other woman's shoulders twitched. "Yes, everything. Even when she told me, 'That pilgrim, this pilgrim, they must die.' I let her have them, and they died. Everyone said I was a bad healer, but it was her wish, she wanted them to die.

"*I* would have died for her," she went on. "She only had to say to me, 'Yaioni, you must die,' and I would have done it and been happy. But she said it to you. 'Yaioni will be my sacrifice.' I heard her."

"That was not my idea," Nora said. "And I was against it."

"It was an insult to me," Yaioni said broodingly. "As though I were a goat or a chicken for a New Year's offering. She did not ask me. And then he told me"—a sidelong glance at Lemoes—"that she is not even a goddess."

"She's not," Nora said.

Yaioni gave an unexpectedly joyous peal of laughter, her face brighter than Nora had ever seen it. "Good! Well, you are welcome to be High Priestess. I have had enough of trying to please the gods, real or false."

"Gods are pleased or they are not pleased," Aruendiel said with a lift of his eyebrows. "And it is difficult, even foolhardy, to try to change their mi—"

Black wings beat the air like an explosion, blotting out Aruendiel's face. Nora felt a blow to the bridge of her nose, a sharp pain. Raucous shrieking, a stabbing beak.

Birds, but where had they come from? She ducked, shielding her eyes with her hands. Through her fingers she saw that there were two of them, crows, ravens, she couldn't tell the difference.

Aruendiel was swearing. They were attacking him now, bloody streaks on his face. He raised a hand to beat them away.

But the birds grew out of his wrists; they could not be shooed away.

He lowered his arms with an effort. The birds flapped their wings and thrust their beaks at his face, squirming, croaking angrily. Abruptly one of them shrank into Aruendiel's right hand. He took the second bird by its throat and squeezed.

Its wings fanned wildly, spilling black feathers, and then they became Aruendiel's fingers and thumb. He flexed them, made a fist.

After the hoarse scolding of the birds, the cave seemed weirdly quiet. Nora became aware of the horrified stares from the pilgrims on the ledge. She daubed at the bridge of her nose. Her fingertips came away wet and red, but the beak had missed her eyes.

"It is nothing, a distraction," Aruendiel said, still breathing heavily. "Olenan is taunting us."

"Olenan." Yaioni pronounced the name experimentally. "That is *her*, you said?"

"It's her," Nora said.

"Then she knows where we are," Yaioni said.

Chapter 31

Thigh-deep in the river, Lemoes helped the last of the pilgrims, a thin, dark-skinned Enlite woman, step over the gunwale. She gasped as the boat rocked under her weight, then gave a quick, nervous chuckle; the other passengers squeezed together to let her pass to a space in the bow.

The wooden boat had been a floating oak branch, leaves still attached, not ten minutes ago. Aruendiel surveyed his craftsmanship critically, a small crooked frown lurking in the corner of his mouth. "It's riding low in the water," he said. "I should have used the Rgonnish spell."

"Mmm. There won't be room for anyone else, once Lemoes climbs in," Nora said to him, arms spread against the rock behind her. They had a precarious footing on a skinny ledge outside the fissure that led into the cave, their feet just above the lapping water of the swollen river.

"They'll stay afloat long enough to get down the river a *karistis* or two. And I'm putting an anti-drowning charm on all of them." Giving Nora a sharp look, he added: "You would be safer if you went with them."

Lemoes, holding the boat's side, looked up. "I will stay, sir, and the High Priestess can go with the others."

"No, Lemoes, that's all right. Go," Nora said before Aruendiel could answer.

"But the goddess—"

"I don't care what the goddess told you. I'm telling you, you need to look after the pilgrims. And Yaioni," Nora added. Lemoes still hesitated. "I mean it," she said.

Lemoes nodded, and she thought he looked slightly relieved. Only then did Nora glance at Aruendiel. "I'm safer with you," she said.

"I hope that is true," he said.

The boat shifted uneasily as Lemoes climbed inside. Taking a seat in the stern, he grabbed the steering oar. "The goddess's blessing goes with you," he called. He guided the craft through a strait of half-submerged trees and into the main current; it picked up speed as it moved downstream. Nora lifted a hand in farewell. Lemoes was too busy steering to notice, but someone in the middle of the boat waved back. Nora wasn't sure, but she thought it might have been Yaioni.

She turned back to Aruendiel to find him gazing upstream, toward the temple. Very high up, a dozen small shapes drifted in the cloudy sky, as fine and black as letters on a printed page.

"Carrion eaters, over the temple. They smell a feast," he said. "Well, you must do exactly as I say. If I tell you to remain in a place, or to leave it, you must do so at once. I will give you a protection spell that will shield you from most direct attacks, but you must not engage Olenan yourself."

His hard, pale gaze dropped to the makeshift pouch, knotted from a strip of Nora's ruined *maran*, that hung from her neck. "Then there is the timestone to consider. You will not let me safeguard it?"

She put her hand over the pouch. "It feels as though it belongs to me," she said.

He gave a reluctant nod. "And I understand, I need to stay out of trouble," Nora went on, "but what can I do that's actually helpful?"

"Against an opponent like Olenan? I cannot imagine," Aruendiel said. "But you have surprised me before this. Truthfully, you are a more careful, conscientious magician—in some ways—than Olenan. She can be clumsy; she has always been more interested in having great power than in wielding it skillfully. Now—"

He cocked his head as though listening, while his gaze swept the wrinkled surface of the floodwaters and the pale yellow flanks of the ravine. "Yes, she is still at the sanctuary. Using a fair amount of magic. She has chosen a highly defensible redoubt—upriver, underground, narrow entrance through a crevice. A battalion could not storm it."

Nora's dismay must have showed in her face. Aruendiel unsheathed a quick, fierce grin. "You must remember, a fortress is always potentially a prison. I have locked her in with constraint spells and counterhexes.

Fasguin Nock, Nusindr, even one of Turl's. Puny, modern rubbish, but it will puzzle her long enough for us to pass her defenses. From what I can tell, she has not learned a single new spell in the past one hundred and thirty-six years."

"How will we get—?"

"I hope you do not object to another swift change of shape? We will fly. Follow my lead, and let your wings move naturally. You will be tempted to flap them excessively, this first time, for fear of falling, but it is not necessary."

Nora turned to see the sleek gray hawk beside her fling itself upward, arching its wings, flaying the air. Without giving herself time to think, she opened her own wings and followed.

It was much like going off the high dive, although she was moving up, not down—the same vertigo, the rush and speed, the escape into a new, liberating element where she moved as lightly and easily as thought. And then the recollection of diving boards faded, and she simply flew, pumping her wings, gliding. The flat, glittering expanse of water passed under her, then the leafy edge of the cliff.

A flash of brown on a branch, an unwary sparrow—she could see the sunlight glinting on its streaky wings. She flashed downward, claws reaching for the fat warm meat.

Her feet closed on air, as the sparrow fluttered away and disappeared among the leaves. She lifted again, with hunger that felt like anger driving her wingbeats, and scanned the trees for the sparrow. Stupid, fearful thing.

A gray streak—the other hawk. Hunting the sparrow, too, she thought. But it flew straight at her with a scream, jostling her and then veering away, and then she remembered confusedly that they were on a different kind of hunt. She set herself after the other hawk, the exact nature of their prey somewhat vague to her.

High above, the carrion birds were still drifting on the wind. She had a confused recollection that a human woman and man would be waiting at the end of their flight, and she wondered if it would be safer to keep flying. But she was bound to follow the other hawk, circling down into the cool shadows of the ravine, down to a perch on a rock next to the waterfall.

Aruendiel's scarred face looked stern. "We have no time for daw-dling," he said severely.

With both hands, Nora grabbed the branch of a shrub growing out of the ravine wall; the rock underfoot was slippery. "I keep forgetting who I am, when we change. And I never was a bird before." She could not entirely stop herself from smiling.

Aruendiel's eyebrows snapped, but his mouth softened, as though rediscovering that it was not, after all, a hawk's scimitar beak. "Your memory must improve, or you will never be able to change your own shape. Will you open a door for us?"

"A door?" Now Nora took in their surroundings through human eyes. The flood had rendered the exterior of the temple almost unrecognizable. The waterfall was a continuous white explosion. Below, the muddy stream churned and fretted; it had swallowed the path at the bottom of the ravine and the arched footbridge at the far end of the pool.

Nora guessed at where the temple door stood behind the great wall of crashing water and made her request. The waterfall parted—with unexpected enthusiasm. Perhaps flooding had put it in a good mood. Through the gap in the streaming water, she could make out the twin seated statues of the goddess that flanked the entrance to the temple.

As she watched, the statues rose from their stone thrones and stood at attention, their wide eyes unblinking in the spray. With a twist of his body, Aruendiel edged down from their rock, then held out a hand to help Nora. She gave the statues a dubious look. She had never liked dolls or toys that moved by themselves.

"She knows we're here."

"They cannot hurt you," he said, "while our protection spell holds."

Apparently he was right. The statues remained motionless as he and Nora passed.

The temple nave was shadowy, but a bluish, flickering light came from the far end of the sanctuary, showing them a path through the massed pillars. For a mad, reassuring instant, Nora thought of the cool glow of television glimpsed through a neighbor's windows at night, and then that comforting illusion dissolved.

She'd thought that she was at least somewhat prepared for what they might find, having seen the baron's body in the river. But there was really no way to steel yourself for stepping over one slumped, quiet body after another, for the still hands and feet protruding like pale, heavy flowers, for the stickiness underfoot, for the ripe, metallic smell of blood hanging in the air.

There was almost no sound except for the plink-plink-plink of liquid, like a dripping faucet, coming from somewhere in the temple.

The sickly, wavering light made the corpses look as though they had been dead forever. Nora recognized most of them. Pilgrims, *ganoi*, even one of the Ghaki king's emissaries. She found herself reciting names under her breath in a kind of horrified greeting.

Aruendiel touched her arm. "There will be time for proper mourning later," he said quietly. She hoped that he was right about that.

They came into the heart of the sanctuary, and Olenan, sometimes called Sisoaneer, looked up to greet them.

She was sitting on the floor beside the giant statue, her toes pointed, one thin arm draped over her knees in a graceful, contemplative way, as though she had been daydreaming. Her features were as fine and cool as marble. Her dark hair hung in secretive curtains around her face; her eyes, rimmed with purplish shadows, were bright and enormous.

Her hand caressed the spotted fur of the Kavareen, her fingers buried in the loose scruff of its shoulders. Uncharacteristically, the Kavareen pressed itself to the floor as though to make itself as small as possible, tail glued to its side. Around its neck was a collar of blue fire, illuminating the cavernous space.

Olenan followed Nora's gaze to the Kavareen. "Your abomination attacked me," she said reprovingly. "Foolish." She smoothed her skirt. Her black gown was wrinkled and chalky, dust clinging where the cloth had been soaked and stained.

Only now did Nora notice the downy gray feather drifting in the air near Olenan, moving perhaps a little faster than one would expect.

"Greetings to you, apostate," Olenan said. "And Aruendiel. I am surprised to see you both. Why are you here? I gave you a chance to flee, when you came out by the river."

Her tone was light, matter-of-fact, which did not obscure the threat behind her words. Nora eyed the wisp of pale gray, which seemed to have embarked on an irregular circuit around Olenan. Aruendiel's binding spell would seem more reassuring if his token did not seem so fragile, she thought.

Meanwhile, the wet-iron stink of blood still filled her nose. "How many people did you kill?" Nora asked, ignoring Aruendiel's warning frown.

"Everyone I could," Olenan said. "There are a few others hiding here and there. They think I don't know where they are."

"Lady, an Eoluthian substitution requires victims but not a massacre," Aruendiel said, his lip curled.

"It was my sacrifice. It was necessary." Tilting her head, she looked from Aruendiel to Nora with an appraising air. "You don't understand, do you? I am truly a goddess now. And it's thanks to you."

A sharp, derisive syllable broke from Aruendiel's throat. "Olenan, no more of this mad—"

"I am not mad. I never was. I know what I am, and I am not human anymore."

The Kavareen snarled, a deep, aching note that startled Nora because she heard so much yearning in it, and she wondered whether Olenan knew that the Kavareen was also Hirizjahkinis. Olenan gave it another fond scratch behind the ears, and then stood up with a fluid motion.

"You're right," she said. "The trivial spell that has kept this body alive doesn't need so many deaths, not at the same time. An Eoluthian substitution, you said? Of course you would know what the books call it, Aruendiel. It's not really important, though.

"I started being a goddess long ago, but it was not complete until now. This time, I took what I needed, and then I kept taking. Those people died for my divinity. They died to glorify me. If you could hear how they cried for mercy, one after the other—" Her mouth twisted gently. "Only a goddess could bear such a sacrifice. That is how I know I am truly divine."

"No, that's just insanity," Nora said, wishing that *sociopath* translated more precisely into Ors. *Megalomaniac. Serial killer.* She remembered the hawk's pure, unmediated, not quite innocent lust to fill its stomach. But that was hunger, and hunger could be sated.

"You don't know what it's like," Olenan said. "I am alone, more than alone. Now and always. I took you to the mountaintop, but you don't understand—you can't understand—what it means to live there."

"And when we were there," Nora said, "you told me that healing was the most important thing."

"Oh, it is!" Olenan's eyebrows arched. "I will heal more people than ever before. They will come to worship me and be healed, thousands and thousands. Some of them I won't even need to treat. Their faith will cure them."

"Olenan, you are mocking the true gods." Aruendiel's voice was calm, as though he were describing something as obvious as the weather. "They will not be pleased. They will act against you."

"It's funny to hear you say that. I never thought you had much trust in the gods."

"Very little trust. I respect them, however."

"Then you should respect me." Her voice rose suddenly. "I am one of the true gods. Maybe I'm the only one. It's very hard, becoming a goddess. But I had to do it."

"What's wrong with being human?" Nora asked.

Olenan began to laugh, but in a disturbingly quiet manner, as though determined to keep the joke all to herself. "There's nothing wrong with being human, not for most people. But ask *him* what's wrong with being human."

Aruendiel raised a quizzical eyebrow. "The various laments of the human race, well-founded or not, fill a dozen dozen books."

"No! You know what I'm talking about. You know. Trying to live among ordinary men and women when you're not one of them—when your power can fill the sky and the sea, when you live on and on without dying. Like a god but not a god. *That* will drive you mad, eventually."

"Very few magicians have such power," Aruendiel said.

"Some do. You do, now."

Aruendiel gave his head the barest shake, his eyes fixed on Olenan.

"Ah, you used to be so young!" Olenan added suddenly, her voice lilting. "Do you know what a child you were, when I first knew you? You can't imagine—well, now you can, since you have this one," she said, glancing at Nora.

"You were afraid of me, and repelled—yes, you were—but you were greedy, you were desperate, you wanted to learn what I could teach you.

"And you did learn, and when you had learned enough, you went back and used your magic for little kings and princes, you fought their wars and did their bidding, you whored and schemed and spent your gold and plowed your lands as though you were an ordinary man. But you are not an ordinary man, you are a magician, and I never taught you the hardest lesson of magic.

"You know it now, though. That you can't live in the world. There is too much time in it." She smiled. "All the things you love die or disappear, or what's worse, you discover you don't love them anymore."

The Kavareen's tail twitched. Its whiskers trembled with a silent snarl.

Nora found that she was dreading to hear what Aruendiel would say. She spoke up instead: "That might be true for you—"

"I'm a goddess. I am free of such trivial things; they mean nothing to me now. But what will you do, Aruendiel? You've already started to hide yourself from the world. How long before you decide to leave it entirely?" Olenan's brown gaze studied Aruendiel's face with caressing attention. "You've already thought about it, haven't you?"

He took a deep breath, as though gathering strength. His eyes found Nora's, then slid away. "Thought and action are two different things." His voice was unexpectedly gentle. "Is that how you died, Olenan? You decided to leave the world behind?"

"Why would you care? And I did not die, not really." Olenan's slim brows dove down, angry arrows, like a child's drawing. "I am divine, I overcame it. Death has no power over me."

"As you say. But you chose it once, I think."

"Once. Just once. You will, too. You won't be able to bear the loneliness. I was born before the Thaw; do you know that?" Her voice rose with what could have been either anger or yearning. "We wore fur all year round. When I was little, ice bulls ran past our house, like an earthquake. It's now underwater, the valley where I grew up—a lake. No one else remembers. There is no one left but me. Is that what you want, Aruendiel? *She'll* make it even worse, eventually." A nod at Nora. "You'll be alone even when she's there, and then one day she'll leave you. As you left me."

"I did come back, you know that," Aruendiel said. "I looked for you."

"You didn't look hard enough."

"No. I did not." His voice held both a faint tinge of regret and a heavier finality, the bones of a shipwreck settling gently on the ocean floor.

Olenan seemed to be waiting for him to say something else. Then she said, flinging the words: "I didn't die because of *you*."

He nodded. "Good. How did you do it? I have wondered." A crooked smile. "Magicians are not easy to kill."

She smiled at him. "You want to know so that you can do the same, is that it? Don't deny it."

"I would like to know what happened to you. That's all."

"It was simple enough. I let someone else do it. That's how the old ones did it, my father's friends, when they grew so tired they knew they'd come to the end." Her thin face tightened for an instant, before she grinned. "But you're right, it isn't easy to kill me. Then or now. My power is too great, it protects me before I know it.

"I found a way, that time. A couple of men, idiots and cruel. I let them make me very, very drunk. And I found some way to annoy them, I believe. I'm not sure. I don't remember very much. I looked down, and I was naked and covered in blood. There was a knife—here." She indicated a spot on her right side, just above the waist. "I wasn't afraid. All I could think of was how much I hated them, brutes, the evil clods. I lay on the floor. I closed my eyes, cursing them with all my heart.

"The next thing I knew, I was getting to my feet. The tavern was deserted. Two dead men were lying next to me.

"It was the first time I knew I was a goddess. Not a magician, a goddess. My wound had healed." Olenan touched her side again. "It opens when I need a new sacrifice, but it always heals." A new thought struck her. "I wonder if it will still come back now, now that I'm completely divine, not human at all?"

"You never told me anything about this," Nora said, her voice prickly. It was a horrifying story, and Nora resented having to hear every piteous word. How was Aruendiel taking it? She was apprehensive about his chivalrous streak—also about something in the way he addressed Olenan, and the fact that they were having a conversation with Olenan instead of fighting her. Aruendiel's face was drawn into somber lines but was otherwise unreadable.

"You never asked," Olenan said, kinking one corner of her mouth. "It's not the worst thing that ever happened to me, child."

"Lady, I regret that you suffered these evils. They are unspeakable," Aruendiel said with deep seriousness, and Nora's heart sank a little.

"It doesn't give you the right to kill all these people," Nora said, more for Aruendiel's benefit than Olenan's, in case he was feeling too much sympathy. He gave her a canny sideways glance.

"I wouldn't have killed them if you'd let me have my sacrifice," Olenan said.

"You're already trapped, Olenan," Aruendiel said. "Locked inside this temple with half a dozen spells to bind and blunt your magic."

Olenan looked up at the tiny gray plume, still circulating aloft on its oddly purposeful course. "Your magic won't hold me," she said. With an air of lazy curiosity, she reached for the feather; instantly it twirled upward. She gave a half shrug. "You put such trust in the spells you learned from books, Aruendiel, you always did. But you should know by now"—her voice hardened—"that I'm stronger than any spell of yours."

The stone floor buckled; Nora staggered against Aruendiel. The columns of the temple seemed to shudder as the air vibrated with a deep, calamitous groan. Olenan laughed as Nora's left foot dipped into empty space. Aruendiel yanked her back. Her other foot toed the edge of a new, ragged gash in the temple floor, a chasm brimming with darkness. There was no telling exactly how deep it was. She heard the tinkle of falling stones far below, like someone fingering an out-of-tune piano in the house next door.

"I'll break out of any prison you try to build," Olenan said from the other side of the rift.

Aruendiel thrust Nora back another step. He did not move from the edge of the crevice. "Olenan, I'll give you a choice," he said. "Stop these murders, stop this pretense of being a goddess, and live out whatever time the deaths you've caused have already bought you."

"Or, what?"

He shrugged slightly. "Very much the same, except that you will have much less time."

"You can't kill me. I will never die," Olenan said, but this time, Nora thought she heard something bleak in her tone. "Anyway, I don't think you really want to kill me, do you?"

A long moment before Aruendiel spoke. "I won't enjoy it."

"Ah." Olenan laughed again, not happily. "Well, that's something new for you. I thought you enjoyed killing." She paused, provokingly. "Like that unfortunate woman who was your wife."

Aruendiel's voice was steely and polite. "You are correct. She was unfortunate."

"She made a bad choice in her husband."

"I must agree."

"I should have warned her. How you hate female weakness, and how ruthless you can be. Remember poor Warigan? Of course you do."

"I don't need you to remind me. This grows tiresome," Aruendiel said, just as Nora repeated, "Warigan?"

She thought she recognized the name, but it fluttered away, maddeningly. Aruendiel gave a half glance at her before turning back to Olenan.

"Did you tell Nora about her?" Olenan said mockingly. "I feel most sorry for those children, left without a moth—"

Olenan doubled over, clutching her chest, retching. Her thin frame convulsed, straining; her head snapped back; she gasped for breath.

A mass of thorny tendrils erupted from her mouth, dark leaves unfolding. As Olenan gagged, the brambles lengthened, wrapping themselves around her neck and her arms, tangling in her hair. Blood dripped from the thorns and smeared the leaves. Nora winced in involuntary sympathy. She had read about silencing spells like this one. They would kill an ordinary person, but probably not a powerful magician with a ready command of healing spells. Or a goddess.

Olenan ripped at the vines, tearing them out of her mouth. They withered at her touch. Dry leaves flew. Olenan coughed and spat red.

From her knees, she looked up at Aruendiel, very white, blood smearing her mouth. She giggled. "No, you didn't tell her, did you?"

In a sterner tone, she added: "What you just did was rude. And impious." She lifted her hand casually, one finger raised.

Nora felt deep cold wrapping itself around her limbs, making her skin burn. She had a sudden, convincing intuition of something unknown and very large prowling nearby, just out of sight.

Aruendiel clapped his hands and rubbed them together. Abruptly, the air warmed again; Nora felt her internal equilibrium return. "Did you think we came here unprotected?" Aruendiel said.

Olenan had turned away, extending her hand toward the Kavareen. The creature was crouching, ears flattened. "Come here, beast," Olenan said. Ears still pinned back, the Kavareen slunk over to where Olenan knelt. She gave it a rough scratch on the top of its head. The Kavareen submitted, tail twitching.

Nora tensed. One quick gulp—that's all it would take, she thought. *Now.* She did not entirely look forward to seeing the Kavareen devour Olenan, but she could live with it.

The Kavareen turned its empty eyes toward Nora, then with quick violent affection rubbed its cheek against Olenan's head.

"This is my abomination now," Olenan said fondly.

Nora shot Aruendiel a horrified, questioning look. He shook his head gravely.

"I thought—instead of destroying the monster, why not tame it?" Olenan let the Kavareen nuzzle her, then pushed it away, smiling. "That's enough, you. Are you hungry?" she asked, scratching its chin. "Soon, soon, my dear."

The Kavareen yawned, giving a glimpse of infinite darkness, then butted its head gently against Olenan's shoulder. Nora had never seen it quite so friendly, even in the old days with Hirizjahkinis, before it ate her.

"I didn't know you liked cats," Nora said.

"I don't. Just this one. It's big enough to be useful." Olenan looked directly at Nora. "And now, what shall I do with you? You rebelled, you defied me—"

Aruendiel shifted slightly; Nora sensed the spell he was wielding silently without being able to identify it.

"—you broke my trust," Olenan said. "Is that another binding spell Aruendiel?" She smiled, her brows wrinkling apologetically, as though she were ever so slightly embarrassed for him. "Oh, no, my mistake

Melting my flesh into mud—what an unkind thought." She shrugged. "I have my own protection spells, you know."

"Your quarrel is with me, Olenan, not her," Aruendiel said quickly.

"That's not entirely true," Olenan said. "But don't worry, I won't hurt her. That protection spell of yours won't even know what's happening. I'm going to hurt *you*, Aruendiel."

She pointed at Nora.

Nora's field of vision constricted, until all she could see was Olenan's face, intent, no longer smiling. The other woman's eyes were dark gems. Nora felt a sudden shift in all her perceptions, as though a camera shutter had clicked. Then the impression dissolved, and she could not have said what, if anything, was different.

Next to Olenan, the Kavareen gave a quiet snarl. Aruendiel whirled with an urgency that should have been a warning.

"Nora?" Then, shouting: "Nora?"

His face was not even a foot away. His gray eyes went past her. She could not get him to meet her gaze. "I'm right here," she said.

He said again: "Nora?"

Chapter 32

Nora waved a hand—hello, hello—in front of Aruendiel's face. "Can't you see me?" She stared at her hand. It seemed perfectly normal: solid, opaque, grubby. Nails ragged and black from scrabbling through the caves.

"Where is she?" Aruendiel wheeled, glaring at Olenan.

Olenan's wide mouth flexed as though she would like to laugh. "Oh, she's not far away. But you can't see her, can you? Can't hear her, can't touch her."

He scowled. "Your invisibility spell."

"You won't find it in any book. And I never taught it to you," she said reflectively. "I knew I should keep some secrets for myself."

Aruendiel turned back to where Nora had been standing, although she was now a foot to his left. "Stay near me—I will work out the counterhex directly," he instructed, raising his voice.

"All right," Nora bawled back, the way you did on a bad cell phone connection. Did he hear her at all? She grabbed for his hand, but somehow her fingers glided past his. He seemed unaware of her touch.

Olenan was laughing outright now. "I should have done this earlier. You can't break this spell, Aruendiel. My father taught it to me—he and Nagaris worked it out. Yes, that Nagaris. They were real magicians in those days. Not like now.

"Well, what next? Your magic isn't doing very well, is it? But I know you're proud of your swordplay."

She lifted one arm, fragile looking but straight as a pencil. And the big stone statue of Sisoaneer—the one that Nora had always admired for its lifelike quality, the vaguely baroque fluidity of its lines—stood up.

A wilted garland drooped over one blind stone eye. The offering that had been piled at its base crunched under its feet. In one hand the stone goddess held the sculpted skull; in the other, the curved stone knife. The blade looked sharper, more like a real knife, than Nora remembered.

The statue cleared the crevice in the floor with one long stride and swung at Aruendiel's neck.

Rocking back on one leg, Aruendiel parried the statue's weapon with the sword that had materialized in his hand. The knife skidded down his slanting blade. Stone screeched against steel. The statue reversed and slashed downward—excellent backhand, Nora noted—and missed his sternum by an inch.

A sword wasn't going to do much damage to a limestone statue. Why had he not tried a shielding spell? Nora began a spell, missed a step, had to start again. The weapons met with another grating shriek. This had to be hell on Aruendiel's blade. He manipulated it with practiced deftness, even as his long, rickety frame seemed to teeter with every hit.

Nora's shielding spell was in place. Before she could draw a new breath, the stone knife cut straight through it. The spell was meant for arrows, not a weapon wielded by a piece of stone that probably weighed several tons, and she wondered if Vlonicl had a spell against living statues.

She shadowed Aruendiel as he fell back. If he could see her, he would probably tell her to get away, she was too close to the battle. Some combination of noises behind her—rustling, a dull slapping sound—made her spin around.

She blinked, made herself look again.

"Dear god, fuck no," Nora said in English. "No. No. Aruendiel, look out!"

He couldn't hear her.

Out of the shadows of the columns came a low, scuttling shape, groping a path across the floor.

Another followed, oddly humped. It was crawling toward the combatants, although facing backward. Its pallid toes gleamed like dirty pearls. In the darkness that stretched to the back of the temple she sensed other furtive movements.

"Aruendiel, the dead people," Nora said, this time in Ors, her voice quavering. "She got the dead people to move. All those dead people, they're moving."

The statue swung again at Aruendiel. He diverted it with what seemed to Nora to be agonizing deliberation.

"Aruendiel!" Nora shouted uselessly. His back was turned as he lifted his sword again.

The foremost of the corpses moved closer, pushing itself along on knees and elbows. Its long hair, matted with blood, dragged on the pavement. Nora shrank back a few steps. Could zombies see through an invisibility spell?

Now she recognized the dead person. It was a pilgrim, an older woman, who stretched out a scrawny, yellowish arm. Nushka, her name was. Nora had treated her for a liver ailment. Nushka didn't weigh more than eighty pounds or so, and when she was alive, Nora would have no more been afraid of her than of a kitten.

Now it was different.

Nushka's body crept forward. It was less than a yard away from Aruendiel's bootheel. Two more of the dead were close behind her, crawling stiffly, and other bodies were stirring behind them.

Aruendiel thrust his blade forward at the statue, then feinted sideways, letting the stone goddess bring the knife down on empty air. He almost seemed to be enjoying this match, Nora thought—a chance to demonstrate his swordplay. Absorbed in the fight, he still hadn't noticed the zombies.

Unsure what to do, Nora yanked Nushka's body upward with a levitation spell. At least she could stop its advance. The corpse felt slippery under her magic, a drunken marionette, arms and legs jerking violently. Nushka's head rocked back and forth, eyes fixed. Her jaw moved mechanically as though she were trying to get out the same clogged syllable over and over again.

Aruendiel glanced back in time to see Nushka's clawed hand sweep through the air inches from his face. Recoiling, he frowned. "What—? Nora!"

"Here!" she said, out of habit.

Aruendiel gave Nushka's body a hard look. "That's your levitation spell, on top of her spell—" He whipped his attention back to the statue as the stone blade slashed toward his head. He ducked. "What has she done here? They're not alive, and no, it's not an animation spell—" He parried a blow from the statue, then another.

"Definitely not alive," Nora said, keeping an eye on the two corpses that had been trailing zombie Nushka. The one that was crawling backward she couldn't recognize from this angle; the other was the weathered, muscular body of a *ganoi* man named Gelm, making unsteady progress on his hands and knees. "What I want to know is, are they going to eat my brain?"

"Nora, if you're still near, don't let them touch you," Aruendiel said, just as Gelm sideswiped the other corpse, which immediately grabbed for Gelm's arm. In a second, the two bodies were rolling over in a ferocious embrace, shoving, kicking, groping blindly for a handful of the other's flesh.

"And don't just hang them in midair," Aruendiel added, watching the statue narrowly as it raised the knife again. "It's untidy, and disrespectful to the dead."

A wet, sickening crack: Gelm had bent his opponent's elbow forty-five degrees in the wrong direction, and now he was trying to twist it off.

"What do I do, then?" Nora said, lowering Nushka's body, but not all the way. She noticed again that her levitation spell seemed clumsier than usual.

The stone goddess slashed at Aruendiel again. Staggering a little, he deflected the blow with his sword.

"Counterhex them!" he shouted. As he edged to one side, his hand darted out to touch the statue's left hand, the one cradling the sculpted skull. The knife came down just as the stone hand crumbled into powder. Aruendiel winced visibly as he retracted his arm. The skull crashed to the ground.

Nora called out to Aruendiel, apprehensive about his injury, but he was lifting his sword again.

A counterhex? The Selvirian countercharm had worked on the bats. She tried it now. It didn't help against zombies. Or was her spellcraft off, somehow? First the levitation spell had felt balky—

Down at her feet, another wriggling zombie, a Ghaki soldier, was about to bang into her shin. Without thinking, Nora jerked herself into the air.

Nothing wrong with that levitation spell. And why, she wondered as she landed behind the soldier and watched his body crawl away, armor scraping the pavement—why were none of the moving dead actually walking upright? Zombies weren't known for being graceful, but it was as though these zombies didn't know how their bodies worked on the most basic level. By comparison, the movements of the stone goddess were almost human in their agility.

She glanced at Aruendiel. He retreated a few paces, but most of the statue's left arm was gone, leaving an uneven stump. His touch seemed to be dissolving the stone, a little at a time.

Olenan hadn't used a classical animation spell on the zombies, Aruendiel had said. "Did she do some kind of weird levitation spell to get them moving? And it's interfering with my spell?" Nora spoke aloud, half hoping for some kind of response from Aruendiel. She heard him grunt, and saw that the statue had landed another hit, this time on the side of his rib cage. Aruendiel wrenched away, staying on his feet but looking more unsteady than Nora had seen him yet.

There were lots of different levitation spells, because people so often needed to move things. Usually you applied a magic pull or push from outside. But there were a few rare levitation spells that could make an object budge itself. . . . Nora closed her eyes, willing a half-forgotten page from Aruendiel's library to come into focus.

A thud, a curse from Aruendiel. She opened her eyes to see him on the floor, rolling sideways. The statue stomped at his kneecap, missed. He scrambled to get upright, yanking hard against something that held him back.

Behind him was the Ghaki soldier, empty-eyed, loose-jawed—one hand wound tightly in a fold of Aruendiel's tunic.

Nora rattled off a levitation spell counterhex, quick and crude. She could tell right away it wasn't a perfect hit, but it wasn't terrible, either. Her spell found a precarious grip on the magic binding the Ghaki soldier's body and began to unravel it.

The soldier wavered, then collapsed with a slow clatter of armor. The dead face never changed expression.

Aruendiel pulled himself free, just in time to dodge as the statue aimed its foot at him again.

"Good! Try something more precise, Nora. The Loedan variation," he said. "It's faster. And—thank you." His sword caught the edge of the stone knife.

Under his raised arm Nora glimpsed the Kavareen some yards away, ears pricked forward, yellow eyes fixed on the duelers. Resting her chin on one hand, Olenan scratched the Kavareen behind its black-tipped ears, watching the fight with a faint smile. Then the statue moved into Nora's sight line, blocking her view, although its left arm and shoulder and most of its head had disappeared—

A scream, very close. It sounded as though it came from a living throat. Nora spun around. Along the wall of the temple came an advancing tangle of arms and legs—corpses swarming around someone who was staggering forward and trying to beat them off simultaneously. Without being able to see the person's face, Nora recognized the swirl of glossy black hair, the slender neck and shoulders.

"Yaioni?" she shouted. "What are you doing here?"

Yaioni, falling to her knees as a burly dead man wrapped his arms around her waist, did not answer. Nora recollected again that she was invisible and inaudible. This was hard to get used to.

The Loedan variation. What was Aruendiel talking about? She racked her brains, and blessedly, it came back to her.

He was right, this spell was faster. A suddenly limp body in a *ganoi's* gray robe let go of Yaioni's waist and slithered to the floor. The dead man's name came to Nora: Goatfoot. One of the other zombies tugged at his arm in an appraising way, as though testing to see how firmly it was attached.

Yaioni's head jerked back as a third zombie grabbed her hair. She screamed again. Nora flung a Loedan counterhex, and watched it sink to the ground.

The other corpse, a young woman, was still occupied with Goatfoot, busily dislocating his shoulder. Nora was in the process of hitting it with the Loedan when another figure lurched into sight, bent almost double.

It was Lemoes, with a zombie on his back, its thick arms dangling over Lemoes's shoulders. Nora cried out a useless reassurance—damn, she'd forgotten again—and sent the counterhex at the piggybacking corpse. It slid downward, cracking its skull on the pavement.

Yaioni got shakily to her feet. "I told you we shouldn't have come back here!" she cried at Lemoes, who shook his head. "And what about those?" she added, pointing.

Nora's gaze followed her finger. More of the dead were coming. They crept out of the shadows, advancing in a sullen, motley mass. At least fifty, Nora guessed. Maybe more. It was the rest of Olenan's body count.

Am I going to be able to keep up? she wondered. She could only work the Loedan counterhex on one zombie at a time. I need more power, Nora thought.

Yaioni suddenly ran forward and kicked the foremost of the advancing cadavers right in the face. A pilgrim from Pernia. Nora had treated him for kidney stones. The corpse toppled sideways, then tried to right itself with spasmodic motions. Before it succeeded, two other dead men scuttled closer and began a tug-of-war with the Pernian's neck. Nora used the counterhex to neutralize them both before one of them won.

This piecemeal spellcasting wasn't fast enough. If she could only wipe them out all at once—

Thunder rumbled ominously in the distance.

But we're underground, Nora thought. Still, somewhere near she could hear what sounded like the patter of rain. She glanced upward at the dim, coffered ceiling of the sanctuary, and saw the tinsel flash of dripping water.

All the magic she was doing—it was water magic still, coming from the underground streams and trickles that had begun listening to her as she passed through the caves and had kept up a skittish trust in her all this time. But there was even more magic nearby, in the swollen river flowing overhead and down the waterfall outside. She had a sudden intuition that it was looking for her.

As she thought this, a small area of the ceiling between two of the columns began to bulge.

Control, control, Nora told herself desperately.

Too late.

The ceiling ballooned, then ripped. Down poured a sludge of roiling water and debris, splashing thunderously against the pavement and sending dark waves surging through the temple.

Nora clung to a column, water swirling furiously around her ankles, and she let the Loedan counterhex flood outward, too.

As the water surrounded the moving dead, they seemed to relax into its embrace. The arms and legs of the corpses stopped their spastic agitation and fell into the rhythms of the spreading current. Water puddled in their open eyes and mouths. They let themselves be tumbled between the columns, dashed against the sanctuary walls, even swept into the great crack in the floor.

Slowly the torrent subsided, draining away through the sanctuary entrance or into the broken floor. Nora looked around to see Yaioni disentangling the now-slack corpse of a red-haired pilgrim—treated for an infected arrow wound, prognosis formerly good—from its grip on Lemoes's ankle. On the other side of the crevice, Olenan was perched on the deserted pedestal of the stone goddess, looking up at the hole in the ceiling with a rueful expression. The Kavareen shook itself, hissing.

The statue itself was no longer moving. Aruendiel's spell had eroded it to an almost shapeless lump. And Aruendiel himself—

Nora ran over to where he curled against the wall. His arms were cocked at an odd angle, pressing against a spot on the left side of his torso. Then she saw the handle of the stone knife squirming through his fingers as the blade dug into his flesh.

A diaphanous red cloud was unfolding in the puddled water around his boots.

Grim and pale, Aruendiel wrenched the knife out of the wound. It twisted wildly in his grip, then melted into dust. He sat down heavily.

"No," Nora moaned. Red bubbles appeared in the ragged gash in his side. The blade must have reached the lung. Not his heart, she prayed.

As quickly as she could, she did the spell to stanch bleeding. Was it strong enough? She pressed her hands over the wound, but they couldn't seem to find a grip. Aruendiel frowned, his gaze searching, then coughed up a gobbet of blood. "Nora?" he whispered.

Someone clucked next to her ear, and she found herself being pushed aside. "It is his lung," Yaioni said.

"I know—" Nora said. The sound of tearing cloth. "Here," Lemoes said from behind, passing a long strip of his robe to Yaioni. She folded it over the wound and held it down tightly. Almost instantly the gray cloth turned red.

Aruendiel brought up more blood. His lips were blue.

"He needs air," Yaioni said, shaking her head.

"I don't know any air magic," Nora said. She found that she was trembling. What had happened to the calm that usually settled over her when she treated a pilgrim?

"That's too bad," Olenan said. Yaioni looked over her shoulder; Nora saw her cringe. "Get away, I want to see him," Olenan said.

"Your Holiness, he is badly injured—" Yaioni began.

"I know that," Olenan said impatiently. "Out of the way."

Yaioni hesitated, her hands still applying pressure to the wound. Nora tried again to take hold of the makeshift bandage. Turning his head, Aruendiel put his hand on the cloth to keep it in place. "As she says," he said softly. Yaioni drew back.

"I didn't mean for you to die, Aruendiel," Olenan said.

"Funny way of showing it," Nora said. She laid her hand directly on top of Aruendiel's, but she could feel it only distantly. Once again, she went through the spell to stop the bleeding.

Aruendiel's smile was like a slash of ink on crumpled paper. "I would not—have chosen to kill—you, Olenan," he gasped.

"I almost believe you." Olenan's voice was subdued. "You know, all those years, I never missed you, not so much. I suppose I knew I'd see you again."

"You could save him," Nora said. "With all your goddamned power."

She spoke only to relieve her own feelings, but to her surprise Olenan looked directly at her.

"I could save him." Olenan frowned. "But I think it's better if I don't. It is not fitting that I should—that is, I am stronger than whatever pang this will cost—"

"*Pang?* Is that all you'll feel? If he dies, it will tear my heart out."

"Good," Olenan said, with a bob of her head. "You should be punished, Nora. You betrayed me."

"Leave her out of this," Aruendiel said, more crisply than Nora would have expected.

It was the wrong thing to say. Olenan's pale face was suddenly as brittle as eggshell. "I will do as I please! I will punish her—and you—and your death will mean nothing to me and my divinity."

"I don't believe you," Nora said. "You can't escape your own pain by pretending to be a goddess. Maybe even by being one." She was less angry at Olenan now than at herself for having been distracted from Aruendiel for even a moment. His gray eyes looked upward so fixedly that she felt hope draining away; then she saw the quick rise and fall of his chest. Her turn to exhale.

"Aruendiel, tell me what I need to do. Don't just die. I need to talk to you. I need you to stay. No one else, no one—" Her voice felt strangled in her throat.

He closed his eyes. Nora thought, I will never see them open again.

Behind her, voices were volleying maddeningly. She tried to tune them out.

Olenan sounded tart: "Don't mock me, little boy."

"She'll forgive you all of your crimes, if you ask her." It was Lemoes, almost mumbling, but resolute. Of all the times to start proselytizing, Nora thought. Shut up, both of you, but especially you, Lemoes. For your own good. She'll strike you dead on the spot.

"How dare you say that to me?" Olenan said.

"The true goddess is greater than you," Lemoes said, and then yelped with pain.

Aruendiel stirred, moving his shoulders as though trying to sit up. That was encouraging, but shouldn't he be resting quietly? Nora made a movement as though to push him back gently. Again, her hands slipped numbly from his shoulder.

"That's enough, from all of you," Olenan said. "Beast! Take them now."

Surprisingly, thankfully—Aruendiel's eyes were open again. Nora leaned toward him. "Aruendiel, can you breathe? Are you still bleeding?"

His gaze slid frustratingly past her to focus on a point above her head. The back of her neck prickled with deep cold.

Nora turned her head. She was not entirely surprised to find the Kavareen's muzzle inches from her face. What struck her was that for the first time she thought she saw some trace of feeling—a quizzical, undefended look—in the Kavareen's lantern eyes.

"Oh, it's you," Nora said, although she was not entirely sure whether she was speaking to the Kavareen or Hirizjahkinis. "Are you going to eat us?"

Chapter 33

"Yes, that's right. Eat them, Beast," said Olenan. "They're yours. The one you can't see is right under your nose," she added helpfully.

The blue flames encircling the Kavareen's neck flared with a hot, whistling sound, like a whip. The Kavareen shuddered, rolling its head uneasily, and then squatted, tail twitching. Under the faded leopard skin, its powerful forelimbs and haunches tensed. The golden eyes narrowed. Its growl seemed to come from all directions at once.

With a muttered expletive, Aruendiel hiked himself to his elbows.

"No, wait," Nora said. She was more afraid for him than for Hiriz-jahkinis—the bandage he'd been pressing to his chest fell to the wet pavement—but she said: "Remember, it's Hirizjahkinis. It is."

Even if he could hear her, she wondered, would he pay any attention?

Aruendiel's eyes narrowed in concentration. Nora felt the queasy internal agitation that meant that a rip current of powerful magic was passing nearby, and the Kavareen tumbled backward, paws splayed, twisting and yowling as it tried to right itself. It crumpled against the far wall of the temple.

Olenan made an impatient noise. "Come, Beast," she said. "Time for your dinner."

The Kavareen rolled to its feet. Glaring across the length of the temple, ears back, it stalked toward the small group of humans.

Just then Nora noticed that the restraining collar of blue fire was gone.

Olenan saw the same thing. She put up her hands, forefinger and thumb pinched together, and jerked the invisible thread tight. The Kavareen screamed, convulsed, and then gathered itself into a stiff but purposeful crouch.

It gave the pavement a few quick, anticipatory kneads with its fore claws, as though it could not wait to sink them into something. Olenan pivoted, and her gaze fell on Nora. She stepped toward Nora, yanking her to her feet with a grip that was preternaturally strong, and thrust her toward the Kavareen as the giant beast pounced.

Nora felt the black gate of its descending jaws, deep cold raking her exposed skin. She had the sensation that she was falling, falling, with the ghosts of a million voices rising to meet her.

"Hirizjahkinis?" she called urgently. "Spit me out right now."

For good measure, she worked the vomiting spell.

Nora landed sprawling on the stone floor, with a thud and a groan that she felt must be audible to everyone, invisibility spell or no invisibility spell. She rolled away from the Kavareen. It was still gagging, head bent. The big cat swiped at its mouth with a paw, then heaved again. A long black tongue slipped out of its open jaws.

Not a tongue, Nora corrected herself. The shining jet curves reached the pavement in a slow, meditative shimmy.

A snake. The snake from the caves. It looked as big and muscular as a river. Its reddish eyes found Nora. The black head reared up, swaying gently from side to side, its forked ribbon of a tongue darting almost playfully between its fangs.

Nora shoved herself backward, but the snake moved so quickly that all she registered was a dark flash of motion, a sharp jab just above her heart. She gasped. Her pulse rattled, unnaturally loud.

This is the end, she thought clearly. There were spells for snakebite she knew none of them.

The snake looked down at her with what seemed like an intolerably smug expression. Nora took deep breaths, wondering how many she had left. Her body felt numb. The sting of the bite had already faded.

She looked over at Aruendiel, struggling to sit up. His eyes were intent fixed on the spot where she lay. For a relieved moment she thought that the invisibility spell had lifted, and then she realized that he was only trying to see what the snake saw. He had seen it strike, probably.

She thought that she felt his healing spell pass nearby, soft a smoke, just as useless against the venom in her veins. He should save for himself, she thought painfully.

"Faugh! That's better," someone said. "I have not been so sick since that Daovestian idiot tried to poison me."

It was Hirizjahkinis, adjusting the Kavareen's hide around her neck with shaky hands. Nora wished that she could tell Hirizjahkinis how good it was to see her again instead of the Kavareen. There were a lot of things she would like to say, actually. How could it be that she would never talk to Aruendiel again? Or feel his arms around her, or find the tiny lines of tenderness in his face that he thought were so well hidden? Her parents, her sisters—they would never know—

Physically, though, dying was not so bad. She felt remarkably comfortable, warm, and relaxed. The place on her side where she'd hit the floor didn't hurt at all.

To her right, the snake was moving, rippling past her. An instant later, the flat black head reappeared to her left and stretched to meet the curving wall of its own tail. Its body made a ring, and Nora was in the center.

As the snake curled to face Nora again, its stare was like cracked stone, infinitely old. Now she could see that there were markings on its skin, deep black on black. Curling lines that shifted and recombined. The flowing script of an unknown language.

It came to Nora slowly that her own name was written there.

"Another monster!" Olenan's voice startled Nora. Glancing back, Nora saw that the other woman also stood within the circle of the snake's body. "Suddenly this place is teeming with them," Olenan said, sounding bitterly amused.

"It's from the caves," Nora said dreamily. "You never saw it before?"

"Of course not."

Nora almost laughed, but only managed a kind of hacking gasp. "Did you ever go down into the caves? I mean—deep, deep?" Olenan didn't answer. "You of all people should know what this is, this snake," Nora said. "Who sent it."

"Aruendiel's joke. A poor—"

"No, no." Nora still felt blissfully warm. Almost sleepy, but she kept her eyes open. The snake watched her, unblinking. "There's a special cave down there. A sacred place. I went into it, and—well, the snake followed me later. Where's Aruendiel?" she added, as a sudden fearful thought made her glance around; Olenan made a derisive noise. "Oh, I see him," Nora said.

He was still half sitting, half lying on the wet stone floor. Hiriz-jahkinis squatted next to him, examining the wound in his chest. They seemed to be addressing each other with some intensity.

That was good, better than she'd hoped. Hirizjahkinis would look after him, even if he didn't want her to.

"This snake is your monster, then?" Olenan prodded.

"No, it's hers. Sisoaneer's. Or maybe—" Nora paused to consider the snake's sleek black immensity, its sinuous patience. Had it grown even larger? Its bulk seemed to fence out the world. "Maybe it's really *her.*"

"That—? No!"

"I'm not sure it matters. But it's kind of funny," Nora went on, "that you're finally getting to meet Sisoaneer, or her snake."

"Funny, funny?" Olenan repeated the word as though she did not understand what it meant. "Why is it here? After all this time, why?"

"What do you think, Olenan? Do you think she's happy that you tried to take her place? Lied to her worshippers, co-opted her temple?"

"It bit *you,*" Olenan said. "You must be dying now."

"Not at this exact instant," Nora said.

"Those worshippers came for my sake—I brought them here," Olenan said. Nora gave an involuntary start as Olenan pressed a cool finger against the side of her neck. "It was my power that healed them. She should thank me for bringing more pilgrims, more tribute, to a temple that was dying, filled with corruption. All this time, she never harmed me, or sent a single evil omen."

Nora felt obliged to point out the obvious: "Until now."

"Your pulse is still strong," Olenan said with an air of dissatisfaction. "How do you feel?"

"Not so bad," Nora said, after a moment's consideration. "All things taken into account." She touched the spot on her chest where the snake had struck, then looked at her fingertips. No blood. That seemed strange. She frowned.

"The venom must be numbing the pain," Olenan said. "You're right there was no sign from her until now. But is that so odd? She should be pleased with everything I did to glorify her.

"And now, is this visit really an evil omen? Look at how the serpent is watching me." The snake's blunt nose undulated from side to side with a quiet, lulling rhythm. "It's here for me. It's a message," Olenan said. "She sent her sacred monster to me. To recognize my divine nature. To do me honor."

Nora sighed. "Do you know who Sisoaneer is? What she's actually goddess of? 'She gives life and takes it away.' Hint, hint."

"Sisoaneer is a healer," Olenan said. "As am I. It's why she's here. We have an affinity, she and—"

"She's the goddess of murder," Nora said.

A sudden intake of breath. "Now this is true blasphemy," Olenan said.

"She's called 'daughter of death.' I sang that to you every morning. All those hymns were like that. 'You make your enemies fall dead.' 'No knife is as sharp as yours.' What did you think they meant?"

"Those are just words." More confidently, Olenan added: "It means power—power to protect her people."

"No, it means she's in charge of death. *Some* deaths. Because for her, healing is just the other side of murder. Anytime a person decides that someone else is going to live or die, she's there. That's what she told me. I think. So, anyway," Nora added, "I'd say you do have a real affinity with her."

"Speaking of dying," Olenan said. Nora felt a caressing hand on her hair. "You don't have much time, do you? You're delirious from her sacred poison."

"I feel some tingling," Nora allowed. "But nothing awful." She struggled into a kneeling position, then stood up carefully. "Might as well die on my feet."

The snake's eyes were ancient and unyielding. There would be no escape, they said. Only endless, arid rest.

"I don't know which came first, the murder part or the healing," Nora added. "I'm guessing murder. Human nature."

"Myths," Olenan said dismissively. "Legends. What matters is power and how you use it."

Mine. Mine. The whisper was as soft as scales scraping rock.

"Did you hear that?" Nora asked.

"Hear what?" Olenan said, too quickly, and Nora knew she was lying.

"The legends tell you about the power," Nora said. "She's here for you, Olenan. She asked me to purify her temple. You murdered a lot of people—"

"I had to!"

"—and you did it in her name. She's goddess of murder, but she doesn't like it when people lie. She's tired of blood, she told me that. She has come for you."

Mine.

Olenan pushed past Nora and stared up at the snake as it swayed gently back and forth. Its forked tongue appeared and disappeared mockingly. There was something weirdly inviting about the rhythm of the snake's movements, as though it were coaxing her to dance.

"This is a trick, a demon. Something to frighten a child," Olenan said, clenching her hands.

"It's not too late," Nora said. "Lemoes is right. She'll forgive you. She judges murderers, and sometimes she forgives them. But you have to ask. You have to own up to what you did."

She had a momentary impression that the space around them was suddenly full of shadows, half-seen faces and limbs quivering with sorrowful echoes. Some of them, Nora knew without understanding how, were the same bodies that Olenan had stolen and forced into a clumsy imitation of life not so long ago. But there were many more.

Olenan also saw them, her mouth twisting unhappily as she glanced up.

"Justice and mercy?" she asked. "I always tried to give both."

"You said that the first time we met," Nora said. "When you choked a man to death."

Olenan looked puzzled for a moment, as though she had trouble remembering what Nora meant, and then she smiled briefly. "That's right, I could have killed all those villagers, and I didn't. Because you asked me not to."

Nora remembered how one night two women, hand in hand, had raced the setting moon across darkened fields, so fast and free that it seemed that they would never stop. Only their shadows could keep pace. Where were they going, so wild and happy? Somehow they had both come to this place instead.

"Ask for mercy now," she said gently.

Olenan hesitated. Her eyes met Nora's, full of questions. Then the tender lines of her face hardened and grew austere.

"I can't," she said dismissively. "There's too much for her to forgive, and my heart is too dry to care. You took the last drops, you and him."

Olenan looked back at the snake, then lifted her hands. Thumbs and index fingers together, ready to yank on an invisible filament.

The snake reared up in a black wave. Olenan cried out. She sounded more angry than afraid, it seemed to Nora. The open mouth struck downward.

Olenan twitched and crumpled like a rag as the snake's jaws closed around her. Nora wanted to avert her eyes, but she could not. With fastidious movements of its mouth, the snake gathered Olenan's struggling bare feet into its maw.

There was no sound but the low rumble of falling water. It was not enough to fill a sudden silence.

The great snake lifted its head and bent toward Nora. Its tongue flickered. One could see only the slightest hint of distention in its long throat.

Priestess, you have done well.

Nora said nothing. Her mouth felt dry. It would be gracious and good politics to say, "You're welcome," at this point, but she could not bring herself to utter the words. The black tower of the snake's head looming before her blurred. A giant snake, she thought. A giant snake. This is not the God I ever wanted to believe in. It's not my wise, deceitful, wry, murderous friend Olenan, who was not really my friend any more than she was a goddess. But she tried to be both, in her way.

Rest. Come to me and rest.

"No," Nora said, as loudly as she could. "With all due respect—no. I did what you wanted, didn't I? The false goddess is gone. You have no claim on me. Let me go."

Snakes had an inherently shrewd, calculating expression, she thought. Probably because they had no lips. It told you nothing about what they were really thinking, of course.

Your death belongs to me.

"No, it doesn't," Nora said. "And even gods can be wrong."

The snake peered down at her, swaying very slightly.

I gave you my kiss. Give me your death.

"You ask too much."

Nora turned, startled, as Aruendiel's strained voice sounded closer than she would have expected. On the other side of the barrier that was the snake's body, he was standing up, barely, not quite leaning on Hirizjahkinis, who scowled up at him with what might have been either concern or annoyance.

"Nora does not belong to you," he said. "Her life, and her death"— Aruendiel grimaced—"are her own."

She owes me a death.

"If you touch even Nora's shadow, I will tear down these mountains to bury your temple, I will fill your caves with mud, and any tongue that praises you will dry and burn, until you are utterly forgotten."

"And I will eat you again," Hirizjahkinis said. "If I must."

The snake elevated itself a yard higher and opened its mouth to show tidy rows of pointed teeth. It hissed.

Enough. Give me your death, child. It is mine, I will keep it safe.

This time, Nora understood.

"All right," she said.

Chapter 34

Nora fumbled at the pouch around her neck until the knotted cloth loosened. The timestone fell into her open palm, small, malign, unyielding.

Abruptly she raised her eyes to the snake again. "I want something in return." She gestured behind her. "All the dead people here. Can you—"

The snake flexed its neck impatiently and bared its fangs again. Involuntarily she flinched.

Priestess, you have my kiss. Use it wisely.

She rolled the timestone between her fingers once, twice, and with a fierce, silent prayer, she tossed it to the snake.

It darted faster than she would have thought possible. The snout snapped shut around the timestone. The muscles in its throat rippled, very slightly.

Nora let out a breath that she hadn't realized she held. The snake's eyes shone like dusty jewels now. It lowered its head and gave Nora another long, unreadable look. She felt an unexpected sense of regret. Now she'd never know exactly how the fate encoded in the stone would unspool. How she'd died, once upon a time that never was. And what might have happened after that.

But it was not her story now, not anymore.

The snake curled away from Nora with an air of graceful boredom, like a fellow guest at a cocktail party who has spotted someone more interesting to talk to. Its long, curled body shifted, and suddenly the creature was no bigger than any ordinary snake. It whipped across the pavement, a scrawled signature in black ink, and disappeared into the crevice in the temple floor.

A slow tremor shook the ground. More pebbles rattled down. With a long, unhurried, grinding rumble—of contentment, Nora thought— the rupture closed. Only a hairline crack remained, and then it was gone.

Snakes are misunderstood, the nature documentary narrators always said. Nora thought that was mostly true, although not in the way the films meant.

"Nora, are you here?" Aruendiel's voice was harsh and tense; the snake's disappearance had been no relief to him at all, Nora realized. He was looking around, in all the wrong directions. So was Hirizjahkinis.

Nora moved toward them, waving her arms with spastic motions, as though that might fix their attention, but it only made her feel foolish. It would have been nice if Olenan's invisibility spell had worn off with her death, she thought.

"Whatever the big snake swallowed just now, it wasn't Nora," Hirizjahkinis was saying. "The thing it swallowed was much, much smaller, and full of very clever magic."

"The timestone I gave her," Aruendiel said. "But where is she? That wretched goddess's pet snake bit her. Is she here somewhere, injured, or did the thing take her underground with it?" His gaze swept over Nora without finding her.

"A timestone—ah, I see now! Nansis's, I suppose. Well, if Nora was well enough to feed it to the snake, that is a good sign. If the snake took her into the caves, the Kavareen can find the snake."

"And what is to stop the Kavareen from devouring her, once it finds her?" Aruendiel demanded.

"Myself," Hirizjahkinis said calmly.

Aruendiel scowled. "I'll go after her."

"Not alone, Aruendiel. No—" She raised an admonitory finger. "Don't shake your head like that. I do not leave my friends unprotected. Not Nora, not you."

In the set iron of his face there came a flicker of ruefulness. He gave her a long look. "Then I'd rather have your sharp wits on my side, Hirizjahkinis, than the Kavareen's vicious power, no matter how—"

He broke off, looking up. Pebbles were falling from overhead. And rocks bigger than pebbles. They hit the pavement with an accelerating rhythm.

From the break in the ceiling, a new crack extended. It grew darker and wider and longer—the rock above unzipping. Dust billowed down.

ward, and then a new flood poured through the entire length of the fissure, forcing its edges apart.

Nora yelled a useless warning to Aruendiel and Hirizjahkinis. Blinking hard against the dust, she made herself keep looking up, so that she could aim her levitation spell better, try to hold up the dead weight of falling rock and water to keep them all from being crushed.

But the unwieldy mass overhead slipped away from the grip of her magic—too heavy, too fluid for her levitation spell. In desperation, she tried something else. A new shape for the water. If she could not stop the temple ceiling from collapsing, she could at least tell it how to fall. Olenan was gone, and the magic she had hoarded for herself was unbound and ready, fresh for the bidding of another magician.

Nora pushed the slurry of rubble and water away from the center of the temple, toward the walls, and found that her spell was not alone. Aruendiel must have had the same idea. His magic shifted the debris with the assurance of long practice; she tried to match his workmanship. Her spell overlapped his and twined through it, both spells growing stronger and richer, chiming and rhyming, it seemed to Nora, as their shared magic carved a refuge in the mayhem that crashed through the air and made the mountain shake.

In a moment, it was all over. Nora's ears rang. The sanctuary was suddenly much brighter, daylight filtering through clouds of dust. Slabs of broken stone as big as cars lay aslant. Water tumbled down the rear of the sanctuary and churned through the debris. Half of the huge columns had snapped or fallen; the others stood uselessly above the wreckage.

Aruendiel and Hirizjahkinis were dusted gray as statues, and Nora supposed that she would look the same if anyone could actually see her. Aruendiel brushed impatiently at his eyes. "Did you catch that?" he asked Hirizjahkinis.

"Half of the mountain falling on our heads? Oh, yes, I did notice that," Hirizjahkinis said. The dust coating her face cracked as she smiled. "Peace, Aruendiel. That was some of Nora's magic in your spell, was it not?"

"I'm here," she said, right to his face. "Here. Talking to you."

"Nora?" Aruendiel's voice sounded hoarse, unusually hesitant. He looked around, then closed his eyes. He held very still, head lifted. Listening.

"Here," she said, reaching for his hand again. Her fingers slid away, unable to connect.

He was working powerful counterhexes; she could actually feel them near her, like weak hints of breeze on a humid day. He opened his eyes, and his gaze swept right across her again.

"No?" Hirizjahkinis said.

"It's as though she has gone out of the world again," Aruendiel said grimly. He turned his head sharply as voices sounded behind a pile of rubble. "Who's there?" he called.

A dust-streaked figure appeared, then another, splashing through the ankle-deep water. A man and a woman. Aruendiel took a step forward, and then his crooked shoulders sank slightly as he recognized Yaioni and Lemoes.

"Lord magician," Lemoes said quickly, "I pray for your help. There are injured people here—"

"I have other concerns," Aruendiel snapped.

"You will not help them?" Hirizjahkinis asked, as Yaioni said, "Please, we can't take care of them all by ourselves." Her voice shook. "There are so many. I don't understand it but—"

"What do you mean, so many? You do not mean the dead that she revivified—"

"They are not dead anymore," Yaioni said. "They are alive now, they're not dead. But they're badly hurt, bleeding, all of them."

"Aruendiel, it's what I asked for, that she'd bring all the dead here back to life," Nora said, and something in his harsh expression shifted For a moment she was sure that he had heard her.

"I should have asked that she heal them, too," she added contritely You had to be careful, when you asked for something, whether it was a spell or a wish or a prayer. Gods could be as legalistic as demons, she thought.

"Nora is here—somewhere—and she is awake, and I do not thin she is dead," Hirizjahkinis was saying. "I am sure she will not min waiting a little while to be visible again."

Aruendiel gave another impatient glance over the rubble before rounding upon Lemoes. "Show me the ones who can be saved," he said. "Be quick."

With some surprise in his expression, Lemoes nodded, and began wading toward what had been the rear of the temple. Aruendiel plowed through the water with a jerky, purposeful stride. "And, Nora, if you are here," he added, raising his voice, "come and make yourself useful."

The wounded were everywhere. A few corpses remained—those whom Olenan had beheaded had already died again—but most of the bodies that had been dead, undead, and then dead again were now struggling to sit up, rolling over, bleeding, groaning, and Nora could tell at a glance from the variety of their movements, from the individual lines of pain on their faces, that they were alive and not zombies, not this time. Nushka, the old lady, held her bloody head with one hand, face scrunched, as she tried to crawl on her knees out of the swirling water. Nearby, Aruendiel was giving directions to Lemoes and Yaioni, passing out bandages, needles, and thread that he must have just conjured.

Nora splashed over to Nushka. Gently—more gently than with zombie Nushka—Nora lifted her out of the water with a levitation spell and placed her safely on piled rubble. She did a spell to slow the bleeding, another to relieve the pain. Nushka, eyes closed, moaning, still looked like the hollowed-out husk of a human being, but Nora couldn't ask her what else she needed, so she moved on to the next injured person, and the next, until she began to lose count.

She worked frantically, even on those who were already almost dead a second time from wounds that bled out too fast, from internal injuries, from drowning. She wanted to save them all. That they were alive and in pain—in a way it was her responsibility.

How much good she was doing, though, she wasn't sure. She could only summon a small fraction of the power that Olenan had once lent her. But when she had a moment to watch Aruendiel work on a pilgrim's stab wound, she was struck by how little magic he used, just enough to patch a wound quickly—battlefield first aid. She wanted to ask him about that; it felt strange to hold her tongue, knowing that he could not hear her question.

When she next looked up, he had worked his way around to Nushka and was examining her head wound. He looked more pleased than the situation warranted, and Nora wondered if he had found the trace of her magic. Meanwhile Nushka was smiling and talking to him and looked about a hundred years younger. Well, Nora thought, it's far more satisfying to be treated by someone you can actually see.

Lemoes was leaning over a man half buried in debris, his face blackened by blood and dust. When the man's eyes fluttered open, Nora recognized Oasme.

"I can't feel my legs."

"Your spine is probably broken." Lemoes's tone was almost casual.

Oasme moaned. "I can hardly breathe."

Lemoes sat back on his heels, saying nothing.

"Help me!"

Lemoes shook his head. "I know what you did," he said.

There was something clean and stark in his expression, his angel's face now sculpted in a more adamantine stone. Oasme blinked up at him with a faintly furtive air and wriggled as though he were trying to sit up.

"You knew she was going to kill them," Lemoes said. "You emptied the hospital. You brought them here for her."

"No, that's not right. Ah, that breath, like a knife—my ribs, broken." Oasme groaned again. "I saved the ones I could. Told them to leave."

"And the rest?" Lemoes nodded at the wounded pilgrims. "You let her have them, the way you did before."

"She was mad." Oasme licked his lips, frowning weakly as he tasted the blood dried on his skin. "Horrible. Wouldn't stop. I didn't know she'd kill them all."

"What did you expect? She killed almost everyone before, except for you and me."

Oasme turned his head away from Lemoes's cool prosecutorial gaze. His eyes fell upon Yaioni and her patient nearby, a *ganoi* woman named Three Finger. "Wait. *She* was there, I know. They're not all dead, look. Look!"

"The goddess brought them back," Lemoes said. "The true goddess

"Ah, the true goddess. Your goddess. Your protector." Oasme laughed shakily. Nora remembered how he had seized her arm when she was fighting for her life with Olenan and reflected that she herself was probably responsible for at least some of his injuries.

"You never believed in her, did you?" Lemoes asked.

"I served the goddess that I had." Oasme's smile was wry and sad. "You were lucky."

"You will know the true goddess now," Lemoes said. "She gives life, and she takes it away. Bless this sacrifice, Lady."

With one hand he pinched Oasme's nose. The other he clamped across Oasme's mouth.

Oasme's eyes widened. He tried to move his head; his mouth worked as though he were trying to speak. His upper body squirmed and trembled. Lemoes's shoulders clenched as he pushed down. It seemed to Nora that he looked almost as frightened as the other man.

"No," said Nora. Her levitation spell knocked Lemoes ten feet, throwing him against a column. Oasme took an abrupt, honking breath.

Hirizjahkinis raised her head from the patient whose gashed chest she was stitching. "Please try not to injure yourself," she called to Lemoes. "We are very busy at the moment."

Lemoes glanced around, as though trying to measure his own trajectory. "I slipped," he said.

"Help me!" Oasme managed a surprisingly resonant cry. "Save me—"

"Oasme." Yaioni glided toward him, one eyebrow cocked. "You are safe now." She gave Lemoes an unreadable look, then knelt next to Oasme. "The wounded will always find succor at Erchkaii," she said calmly. "We do not need to kill anyone anymore."

I'm so tired of people dying, Nora thought. And I'm pretty sure the goddess is, too.

Wearily she looked around her. Lemoes had gone over to help Hirizjahkinis with her patient. Aruendiel, frowning, was bandaging a head wound.

Behind them, about where Sisoaneer's statue had once stood, water cascaded down to what had been the temple floor, blossoming into pure foam, then flowing sweetly, unhurriedly through the wreckage. It lapped at the limbs of the dead and the living alike, washing away dust and blood in its cool oblivion, before making its way outside into the wider world. The river had found a new course, Nora saw. The realization made her almost happy.

She had undertaken, as part of her duties as High Priestess, to cleanse the goddess's temple. A different High Priestess might have done it more neatly, Nora thought, but in the end she had finished the job.

Chapter 35

Over the days that followed, as Nora moved invisibly through the temple complex and observed the activity around her, it seemed to her that almost every able-bodied person was perpetually busy—tending the injured, mostly—and yet there was a sort of desolation imbuing the whole place, a stunned, collective anomie. The daily rhythm of prayers and work and meals and more prayers had been broken, and there was no particular shape to each day.

More people had survived Olenan's killing frenzy than Nora had first guessed. Many of the *ganoi* had escaped into the hills. Oasme had warned off a few dozen pilgrims. The survivors drifted back to the temple gradually, cautiously.

As the floodwaters receded, there were funerals for the dead, who in the end numbered more than twenty. No one could tell whether Nora was at the ceremonies or not, but attending them felt like an obligation she owed. The Ghakis built a long, boatlike pyre in the muddy main courtyard for their dead soldiers; a group of Pernish pilgrims constructed another down the river to their own specifications. The smell of burned flesh and wood lingered afterward.

The *ganoi* removed their dead without a word to anyone. Following them deep into the forest, Nora watched them tie the bodies to the branches of oak trees, crooning long, quavering songs that might or might not have words. She felt more like an intruder there than at the other funerals, but something in their cryptic, wild music helped unbind the sadness that was still knotted into her heart.

Aruendiel came to some of the funerals. More than once, she turned to see his long, angular figure on the other side of a crowd of mourners. By the time she made her way to where he had been standing, he was always gone.

The hospital was beginning to empty out. Having come for a cure and lived through a massacre instead, the remaining pilgrims had no wish to linger at Erchkaii. If they were well enough to walk or ride away, they did; the sicker ones were bundled into donkey carts by their family members and bumped down the path to the lake.

Nora patrolled the half-deserted wards, sometimes working spells to relieve pain or fever, although she was more cautious now about the risks of magical healing. She always seemed to arrive shortly after Aruendiel or Hirizjahkinis had finished their rounds, in time to overhear the patients gossiping about the magicians and what they had done or said. Hirizjahkinis was a favorite; Nora had the impression that the patients were a little afraid of Aruendiel but that they preferred it that way.

Oasme occupied one of the private rooms—officially because of his status as a priest, but also to protect him from revenge attempts. He was not doing as well as some of the other survivors, but he would live. It was general knowledge—Nora learned from eavesdropping—that he had convinced the pilgrims to return to the sanctuary in the middle of the night, promising them an audience with the goddess, and then handed them over to Olenan.

Nora slipped into his room one day.

"Did you do it just so that she wouldn't kill you like the others?" she asked Oasme. "Or did you really believe her, whatever lies she told you?" Oasme lay quietly on his pallet, his eyes half closed. "Did you ever believe in her?" Nora demanded.

She didn't expect an answer, even if he could have heard her question.

Later the same day, sitting alone by the river, she had an imaginary conversation with her mother that followed a less predictable course. For the first time, Nora told her everything—almost everything—about what had happened over the past year or so. Her mother was silent for a long time, staring into her coffee. (They were back in the sunroom, as Nora pictured it.) "They're all false gods, if you ask me, Nora," her mother finally said, her eyes red. "Not just the big snake. This magic you're so excited about, too. I'm still so worried about you."

"To be honest, I'm a little worried, too," Nora said. "I'm sorry."

"I know you're doing the best you can, sweetie," her mother said surprisingly. She sighed, and her face took on a more resolute expression. "I dreamed about EJ last night. Usually he's little, or it's that horrible night, but this time he was all grown up, a man. And he seemed—happy. I was so comforted."

Nora said she was glad to hear that.

"I felt God answered my prayers, He really did," her mother said. "I'm going to keep praying for Him to look after you, Nora. It's all I can do."

"Thank you, Mom," Nora said, and discovered that her own eyes were wet.

"Am I ever going to see you again, Nora?" her mother asked.

She wasn't talking about the invisibility spell, whether it would ever wear off. "Yes, definitely," Nora said. Her mother smiled severely, clearly unconvinced, and took a long, ruminative sip of coffee.

"I mean, I think you will," Nora said. "I hope so. I don't know. I'm sorry."

Her mother nodded. After that, neither of them seemed to be able to think of anything to say, but somehow it didn't feel as awkward as Nora would have expected.

Being invisible made you a little weird, no doubt about it.

The spell showed no signs of weakening. She could see her own body, but no one else could. Nora spoke to every person she met and brushed against people until it began to seem creepy; no one ever responded. Sometimes, forgetting, she fought down a sense of hurt that everyone around her seemed to be ignoring her on purpose.

She had no shadow, which was more troubling than she would have expected, and she had no reflection in either water or a battered silver tray, rescued from the wrecked temple, that she peered into hopefully. Several times she tried to attract attention by splashing in the river and then leaving wet footprints on the path. It made her happy to see them, but the pilgrims and the *ganoi* passing by seemed to be looking anywhere but where she wanted them to look.

She thought for certain that when she sat down in the refectory to eat one of the sporadic meals that were still being served, other people would notice her bowl floating through the air or her chair pulled out or her food vanishing, but everything she handled seemed to share her own obscurity. She was not quite sure whether the objects truly became invisible, or people simply didn't notice anything that seemed unusual, or some combination of the two. She even tried walking around naked one day, after discarding the rags of her *maran*, on the theory that nudity would trigger some kind of subliminal recognition, but the obliviousness of everyone she passed was so disorienting that after an hour she gave up and stole a *ganoi* gown from the hospital storeroom.

This is what being a ghost is like, she thought.

Her current state was worse, in some ways, than being caught in the nothingness between worlds, where thinking of Aruendiel had brought her to him. Now, perversely, it seemed that the more she wanted to see him, or anyone else, the less likely they were to cross paths. Wherever she was, he was not. He was staying in one of the visitors' rooms near the hospital, and one night she sat at his door for hours, determined to catch him. Near dawn, not seeing him, she dragged herself back to her own room to find the oil lamp empty, the window open, and on the floor a long gray feather, as from an owl's wing.

When she did encounter Aruendiel—and it was always by pure chance, when she least expected it—she was struck by the dry, tense watchfulness in his face and the hunch of his shoulders. Instinctively she would go to stand where his pale eyes were searching, for the momentary satisfaction of meeting his gaze.

She said inane things, like "I'm still here!" and "Can't you hear me at all?" and "How many years before this spell wears off?" There were much more important and complicated things that she needed to say to him, but it was too hard to speak them to unhearing ears. What she really wanted was to hear the deep burr of his voice speaking to her and only to her.

In the end, she came back to Donne, who—she now realized—had thought a lot about invisibility, albeit in a slightly different context. In poem after poem, he had considered the elusive relation between the flesh and the soul. *Twice or thrice had I loved thee, before I knew thy face or name.*

Still, you needed more than what Donne called some lovely glorious nothing. *Love must not be, but take a body, too.*

Nora's outstretched hand slipped numbly from Aruendiel's arm as he moved away, his eyes somewhere else.

Six days after the killings at the temple, a delegation arrived from the Ghaki king, some thirty soldiers in uniform and their commander, accompanying a red-faced nobleman in armor and two shaved-headed men in yellow robes and oval pink caps, worn at an angle, that to Nora looked distractingly like Mrs. Kennedy's pillbox.

As they progressed into the central courtyard, the bald men looked around with a proprietary air, casting an appraising eye on the hospital buildings and the sparse crowd that had gathered, and Nora suddenly realized who the two visitors were: priests from the other temple of Sisoaneer, the one at Nenaveii.

Lemoes went to greet them, looking very young and slight next to the armed men. He accompanied the priests and the noblemen as they inspected the ruined temple, taking in the new waterfall and the stream merrily plunging between the topless columns and broken statuary. On a flat stone in the middle of the rubble, someone had set up a new, makeshift altar, covered with flowers and a couple of dishes of food.

Nora, too far away to hear what anyone was saying, could still read disapproval in the older priest's stiff mien and his abrupt pivot from the little altar. Curious, she followed them all back to the refectory, where, she was pleased to discover, Aruendiel and Hirizjahkinis joined them. Whatever repulsive force was keeping Nora apart from him, it seemed to be lessened when they were part of a group.

The older priest, who had sturdy features and a slight paunch, spoke first—since, as he made clear, he was now in charge of Erchkaii. A few days before, some of the pilgrims whom Oasme had saved had reached Nenaveii, where the chief clergy were already concerned about the provocative rumors that the goddess Sisoaneer had appeared at Erchkaii. Obviously some kind of appalling fraud and sacrilege had taken place, the priest said now, and his mission was to restore order. He pulled a scroll from inside his robe.

"We have an order from His Gracious Majesty for the arrest of the woman who led the criminal heresy against the true religion of Sisoaneer and the Ghaki throne, resulting in the death of many innocents," the priest said. "Styling herself High Priestess, she spread the false rumor that the goddess herself had returned to Erchkaii. She is to be taken into custody and removed to Nenaveii for the disposition of her case."

"What!" Nora squawked. "Are you talking about me?" But of course they were; they needed a scapegoat.

She glanced at the others. Lemoes was wide-eyed. Something about the set of Hirizjahkinis's mouth suggested that she could not decide whether to laugh or be furious. Aruendiel's black eyebrows lifted interrogatively.

"On what grounds have you determined that this woman is responsible for the criminal heresy, as you put it, and the murders here?" he asked.

"Oh, there has already been a trial," the priest said. "There was testimony from several witnesses, and the High Priest rendered his decision."

"With His Gracious Majesty's approval," interjected the nobleman.

"Yes, exactly," said the priest.

"I have always heard that the cardinal virtue of Ghaki justice is its swiftness," Aruendiel said.

The priest bowed. "That is our particular pride."

"But we cannot turn over the woman you seek. The onetime High Priestess of Sisoaneer has disappeared."

"Disappeared?" The priest frowned.

"Completely vanished," Hirizjahkinis said.

"And you don't know where she is?"

"She has not been seen since the day of the killings," Hirizjahkinis said. "The day the great serpent appeared." She nodded encouragingly at the priest.

"The great serpent?"

"The black snake that had pursued the High Priestess from the bowels of the mountain," Hirizjahkinis said.

"A serpent is one of Sisoaneer's totems, I believe," Aruendiel said.

The priest exchanged glances with his yellow-robed colleague. "That is a local legend," said the younger priest.

"Very local," Aruendiel agreed. "I saw the snake myself. It seized its prey, and then the creature went into the earth again."

"You mean this snake devoured the heretic priestess?" The older priest turned to Lemoes. "Did you see this, boy?"

"I was too far away to see very much," Lemoes said. "But I have not seen the High Priestess since, and neither has anyone I've spoken to, either." He cleared his throat.

It would be just my luck, Nora thought, for the invisibility spell to wear off right now.

"'High Priestess' is a false title," the priest said irritably. "That is another part of the heresy. It is not respectful to the gods to have women in the clergy."

Hirizjahkinis smiled. "You are sure your goddess agrees?"

The priest ignored her question. "In fact," he said, "we understand that other women have been serving as clergy at Erchkaii. That will cease immediately; they will be stripped of their offices." He consulted his scroll again. "Where is the one called Yaioni?"

"She has already resigned from her office," Lemoes said. After a moment's hesitation, he added, "There is also Uliverat, but we have not seen her, either, for some days. She was not among the dead—"

"Do not concern yourself with that one. She has been accounted for," the priest said quickly, and Nora knew the name of at least one of the witnesses who had testified at her trial in Nenaveii.

The discussion moved to the subject of Oasme. The priests from Nenaveii had already heard reports of his role in the massacre, although—Nora was interested to hear—he apparently had not yet had his own trial. The Ghakis would take him back with them, his fate to be decided later.

If he were smart, Nora thought, he too would just blame everything on the renegade High Priestess.

Lemoes was also to go to the temple in Nenaveii, the priest announced. He was young and impressionable, he had been exposed to unfortunate influences, and it was important to ensure that he was schooled in orthodox doctrine and practice. Erchkaii itself would be reseeded with properly trained clergy from Nenaveii so that heresy would not have a chance to grow again.

It's just a power grab, Nora thought, they're taking over Erchkaii. Given that she had effectively resigned as Erchkaii's High Priestess twice already, she was surprised to find herself growing indignant. But the Nenaveii priest's crack about women clergy had been grating. She thought about all the pilgrims who had come from Nenaveii because they could not be cured at the temple there.

"I am sorry," Lemoes said, "but I must remain here."

The older priest frowned impatiently. "It is not your choice."

"That is true," Lemoes agreed. "It is the will of the goddess."

A web of purplish veins darkened the priest's cheeks. "That is exactly the kind of dangerous blasphemy that has poisoned this place," he said. "You have taken a vow of obedience, have you not? It's not your place to consider the will of the goddess; you follow the direction of your superiors. You will fast until we reach Nenaveii, and there you will learn how the gods are properly honored."

Oh, why not, Nora thought. It was twilight; oil lamps were burning throughout the room. She did a quick spell, and the flames turned inky. The room became a jungle of flickering, blue-black shadows.

The visitors from Nenaveii cried out, and then the older priest pulled himself together. "You are a magician of some repute, Lord Aruendiel," he said. "This is one of your magical deceptions. You should be ashamed to practice such trickery on holy men."

"I would be," Aruendiel said. "But I had nothing to do with this."

"You are lying."

"Only a fool or a good swordsman would call me a liar," Aruendiel said steadily. "Which one are you?"

From the Ghaki nobleman there came an odd noise, quickly squelched. "Let's not get distracted by a trifling misunderstanding, Erefex," he said to the priest. "What is more important is what we have already accomplished today."

In the gloom, Nora could just make out that he was pulling at his mustache. "His Gracious Majesty will be pleased to know that the wench who caused all this trouble has been removed, and the temple of Erchkaii will continue its excellent works under the patronage of the Most Holy Royal Temple at Nenaveii. All very satisfactory to His Majesty," the nobleman said. "Where the boy goes is trivial. The will of the gods should always be respected—as we always do," he added with sudden vigor. "Praise Sisoaneer!"

Nora, taking her cue, turned the lamp flames back to a more conventional yellow.

In the restored light, the priest Erefax looked somewhat paler than before. The nobleman grinned under his mustache. "Ah! Marvelous. I would have liked to have seen that snake. How big was it, would you say?" he asked Hirizjahkinis.

"Big enough," she said. "Are you going to tell His Majesty about it?"

"Eh." The nobleman's big face creased with a look of wry acumen. "He is a busy man. It depends on what he needs to hear about. A giant snake that eats criminals—well, I suppose he will want to know about that."

After the Nenaveiians had filed out, Hirizjahkinis and Aruendiel lingered in the refectory. So did Nora, taking a seat near them. She gripped the table in front of her as a precaution, just in case the invisibility spell tried to whisk her out of their presence. The other two looked around the room, and then at each other.

Hirizjahkinis laughed. "I taught her that spell for the flames!" she said with some pride. "It is very persuasive, in the right circumstances."

"She is fortunate that that Nenaveiian priest is no kind of magician," Aruendiel said. "But it was a welcome sign nonetheless. Is she here, can you tell?"

Hirizjahkinis blew air out of her cheeks. "I am sure she is—but even the Kavareen cannot tell for sure. That invisibility spell is so messy, it muddles everything."

"It's not just a simple invisibility-silencing spell," Aruendiel said. "There is a confusion spell that's part of it, I'm sure, and some kind of misdirection spell."

"Oh, tell me about it," Nora said. "I've been going in circles, it feels like. Or everyone else is." She stood up, lifted the bench she had been sitting on, and dropped it with a bang. Both Hirizjahkinis and Aruendiel started, then looked around quickly for the source of the noise. "Well, at least you heard that," Nora said.

Eyes on the bench, Aruendiel nodded. "Interesting." He held out his arm. "Here, Nora. Pinch me. Hard."

Pleased to have attracted some attention, Nora groped at his sleeve. "I can't get a good grip," she said. The thin black wool felt both slippery and insubstantial under her fingers. "All right—there."

"Harder!"

"You asked for it." Grimacing, Nora squeezed her thumb and finger together, pinching what might have been a fold of Aruendiel's flesh, although it did not exactly feel that way. "That has to hurt."

"I feel nothing at all," Aruendiel said. He rubbed curiously at a wrinkle on his sleeve, and Nora felt a vague, blunted touch on her hand. "There is a numbing component to the spell, it seems," he said. "I think, Nora, if you were to bludgeon me with something large and heavy, I would be aware of that. Otherwise, your touch is imperceptible."

"I figured that out already," Nora said. "Although I'll remember the part about the bludgeoning."

"Be careful what you suggest to Nora, Aruendiel," Hirizjahkinis said. "She may be getting very irritated with being invisible."

"Oh, yes," Nora said as Aruendiel rolled up his sleeve. On his sinewy forearm, under the lace of coarse black hairs, were two reddening spots. She winced a little when she saw them. "Ouch. I'm sorry."

"Very interesting," Aruendiel said. "The flesh is harder to deceive." He rubbed the red spots thoughtfully.

"You did pinch hard, little one," Hirizjahkinis said. "But it is nothing that Aruendiel does not deserve."

"I've had worse injuries," Aruendiel said. "Listen, Nora. This is an old and very complicated spell—"

"Olenan said it was her father's."

"—and I think it is the same one she used to use, long ago, to conceal herself—and me, sometimes—when we traveled in unfriendly countries. She did not teach it to me, and I was too green to unravel it. I can only guess at where and when Olenan learned it.

"Because it is partly a misdirection spell, which is a kind of unluckiness curse, it can twist and thwart your will and the will of others. Mostly to lead you away from those who might detect your presence,

But it also means that an improperly chosen counterhex could make the spell stronger."

"Great," Nora said. "Does that mean we can't even try to take it off?"

"Nora, when Tuthl Nes put a misdirection spell on me, I thought that I would never get rid of it," Hirizjahkinis said. "I was completely lost in Anjorabal for a month. Fortunately, the weather was lovely." She grinned, her dark eyes glinting. "A spell like that, you have to trick. You do not march away thinking, 'At all costs I must get back to the port immediately.' You have a nice breakfast, and then you stroll among the dunes, and look at the ocean, and you think, 'I wonder if the port is this way? No, I do not think so.' Then you admire the jessem flowers, and walk a little further, and suddenly you are at the port."

"I would like a vacation like that," Nora said. "Does that mean I should just think about something else for a while?"

"I sometimes wonder, Hiriz, whether you ever shed that misdirection spell completely," Aruendiel said. "But I must take more time to study this invisibility spell. The library here is not extensive, and it is poorly organized, but there are a few volumes that may be of use."

"The library mostly has healing spells," Nora said. Of course, being invisible, especially when you didn't want to be, might be considered a disease of sorts.

"I will find the right counterhex soon or devise one," Aruendiel said. "Have courage, Nora."

"And it is not a terrible thing for you to be invisible right now, anyway," Hirizjahkinis said. "At least until those greedy, silly priests have left. The fat one looked so disappointed that he could not bring you to justice for all the crimes you have committed."

"The fools," Aruendiel said. "They will not touch Nora, visible or invisible. I will make sure of that." Abruptly he gave a snicker of dour amusement. "You saw—the cowards would not even venture here without two and a half dozen of the Ghaki king's men to protect them from the heretics of Erchkaii."

"If I were you, little one," Hirizjahkinis said, "I would go see if those holy men can feel your invisible pinch any better than Aruendiel can."

They were trying to cheer her up, Nora thought. It almost worked.

Chapter 36

The next day Nora decided to see for herself what the library held in the way of books on invisibility and its cure.

When she entered, there were several scrolls and a thick bound volume open on one of the desks. Aruendiel had been here already, probably last night, but he was absent now. The unluckiness part of the spell kicking in, she thought. She leaned over the desk to see what he had been reading.

One scroll was a treatise on the anatomy of the eye, a second dealt with magical cures for blindness, and the third was in a language she didn't know, but it had alarming illustrations of human figures with misshapen animal limbs. The open book was about ways to induce madness. Aruendiel had been making notes on a wax tablet in his tight, jagged script, apparently working out a counterhex to one of the insanity spells.

Nora picked up the stylus. *Do you think I'm mad?* she wrote. *I am starting to wonder, myself. I am here, but I am not here. You are so close, but I can't reach you. I wonder if you will even be able to read my note.*

She spent some time examining the library shelves. On the far side of the little octagonal library, where she and Oasme had rarely ventured, she found a shelf full of scrolls recording what seemed to be case histories. Some of the notes were in Ors—badly or archaically spelled, but mostly comprehensible. She made her way through one scroll and actually found a case that involved invisibility: a pilgrim who wanted to be made to vanish because of hideous deformities. She left the scroll on Aruendiel's desk with another note.

Nora wandered outside and took the river path. By habit she followed it up the Stairs of Healing and along the bottom of the ravine running her hands over the carved walls. Prayers and praise to a goddess who was more of a mystery to Nora than ever. The damp, ferny shade here was appreciably cooler than the sunnier, more exposed hospital complex. Summer was not far away, she thought. How long had she been here? The yellow and red wildflowers that now lit the banks of the stream looked tough and grassy, ready for long hot days.

Hearing voices, Nora turned to see Lemoes and Yaioni walking behind her on the path, their heads together. She slowed and drifted near them.

"—decided not to rebuild the temple in the old place," Lemoes was saying. "There will be a shrine closer to the hospital. The architect comes from Nenaveii tomorrow or the next day."

Yaioni sniffed. "The old temple was too wet and musty. Uliverat said that it made her joints ache."

"And it was a long way from the hospital for the sick pilgrims to come."

"They don't care about the sick pilgrims! It is just money."

"Want to know the real reason?" Lemoes grinned shyly. "They are afraid of the giant snake. I saw their faces when they heard it swallowed the High Priestess. Afterward, Erefex said that it was dangerous to disturb the old gods, and he sent a letter to the High Priest in Nenaveii this morning."

"But the snake didn't eat the High Priestess!" Yaioni's eyebrows arched with indignation that anyone might expect her to believe such an obvious falsehood. "The magicians told us that a spell made her invisible. Although they might have lied," she added reflectively.

"Well—" Lemoes looked slightly abashed. "I think they would rather let the Nenaveiians believe the High Priestess is dead."

"Do you think she is dead? Or invisible?"

"I don't think she is dead," Lemoes said. He was silent for a moment. "Some of the pilgrims on the ward say that they have seen strange things. Not really seen them, exactly, but they feel that someone is nearby, and then their pain is gone."

Yaioni gripped his wrist. "Do you know what some of the *ganoi* are saying?"

"What?"

"That she was the goddess, the real one. While the other one was pretending."

Lemoes frowned blankly. "Wait, the High Priestess, the one called Nora, was really the god—"

"Yes, that is what I am telling you. The *ganoi* say that the real goddess came to earth to get rid of the liar goddess, and she did, and then she disappeared."

"You're kidding," Nora said.

"No, that is not true," Lemoes said. "I know it's not true."

"Oh, yes, you know because you are such good friends with the goddess," Yaioni said dismissively. "She comes to visit in the middle of the night."

"No," Lemoes said slowly. "Not anymore."

Yaioni raised her eyebrows. "She is angry with you? Or—perhaps she has found someone else."

Lemoes shook his head. "It's not her will to come to me. Not now." His tone was guarded.

"Oh." Yaioni gave him a long look. "Well, I was only telling you what the *ganoi* say. They are very ignorant." She pointed ahead. "You see the altar? All those flowers and the food? More than we ever had in the temple before! Did you put it there? Or is it all from the *ganoi*?"

If anything, the altar in the middle of the river was more lavishly decorated with offerings than it had been the day before.

Lemoes shook his head. "I only brought a few wickflowers. Well, they are doing honor to the goddess—the real goddess," he added with a slight emphasis. "This is still her holy place. Holier than it used to be, even."

"I will be glad to leave it." Yaioni gave an exaggerated shiver. "I am tired of these people who might be goddesses, or not. If Nora is the goddess, I would be vexed to worship her."

He laughed, then asked, "When are you leaving?"

"As soon as Lady Munthos is well enough to travel." That was one of the pilgrims recovering in the hospital, Nora recalled. "I will be her nurse all the way to Thallaas and perhaps farther," Yaioni went on. "Then I would like to go to see my son. He is six now, I think. He was only a baby when I left. I want to be his mother again. Before he turns into a man.

"I suppose my husband will try to kill me, but—" She shrugged. "I know a little more about the arts of power than I used to, and I am sure he is still an idiot. And you? There is no reason for you to stay here. It is a wretched hole."

It was Lemoes's turn to shrug. "I pledged that I would stay here all my life. When the High Priest spared me at Falis Woana." He glanced at Yaioni. "That was before you came here."

She curled her lip. "Ah, you were one of those prisoners, too? Sent by the king? That's what Uliverat always said, but I did not believe her—she thought everyone was a criminal. Did you do something very bad?"

"Yes, I did," Lemoes said gravely.

"But you must have been very little!"

"I was old enough to keep watch, even if I wasn't old enough to strike the blows. My brothers did that."

Yaioni waited, but he said nothing more. "The priests won't care about your promises to the goddess," she said finally. "They will still want you to go to Nenaveii."

"It won't happen." Lemoes's eyes were fixed on the white streak of the waterfall ahead. "She won't let it happen."

Yaioni made a noise in her throat that could have been either sympathetic or exasperated. After a moment, they turned and retreated down the path. Nora didn't follow them. Instead, she waded through the shallow rushing water to the improvised altar.

It was banked with the red and yellow wildflowers and some branches of white blossoms. Under the flowers was a layer of greasy black ashes and burned bones. There were bowls of milk and a cloudy amber liquid—beer, Nora established with a sniff—and an earthenware dish of wild strawberries.

Nora tasted one of the strawberries. It was not quite ripe.

She let herself contemplate the possibility that the invisibility spell would never wear off or be removed. That she would remain a voiceless phantom doomed to eavesdrop on the real life going on all round her.

I would make a better fake goddess than Olenan, Nora thought. I wouldn't kill my followers. I wouldn't even ask very much of them. They could believe whatever they wanted. I would help them as much as I could, with magic or in other ways, and look after them, and in return

I'd survive on their offerings and the satisfaction it gave me to know that I was doing good.

She pictured herself explaining to her younger sister that she was now a goddess, or at least working as one. Ramona wouldn't buy it for an instant.

And Erchkaii didn't need another fake goddess, anyway.

Nora splashed back to the stream bank and gathered her own armful of the red and yellow blooms. She left them on the altar and did a spell to send ghost flames licking over the offerings, the fire caressing and brightening the flowers without blackening them. Gold and crimson petals flickered and danced in the still air.

"Please, Sisoaneer."

At the library, Aruendiel's place was still vacant, but Hirizjahkinis was at another desk, braids dangling over a scroll. Out of habit, Nora greeted her. Hirizjahkinis did not look up. There was no sound but a faint, occasional rustle of paper. Nora picked up a book and slammed it to the floor as hard as she could.

Hirizjahkinis gave a jump, then grinned. She got to her feet stretching her arms. "Are you here, little one, or did that book fall by chance?"

"It's me," Nora said. Hirizjahkinis's gaze stopped at a point about three feet to her left.

"Let us say that it is you! I am glad for the interruption. I am doing no good here. I am not much help in taking your spell off. I am sorry for that! It is a double rebuke for me to come into this library. All these books of magic—completely useless to me now!" She shook her head with a clicking of beads.

"Maybe just give it a rest for a while, and see what happens?" Nora asked, thinking of spilled wine and an unbroken wineglass. Magic could be more persistent and surprising than you dared to hope. She put the question gently, as though Hirizjahkinis could hear her.

"There is always the Kavareen! He might be able to take away your spell, if I let him—roam free. Aruendiel is dead set against the idea

Perhaps he is right." She sighed, and the corners of her wide mouth tightened in a way that looked unnatural for her.

"I agree with him," Nora said. "I would rather have you be you than the Kavareen, even for a minute."

"Aruendiel thinks I should go back to Semrland with him, to be his student again. And he wants to try to rescue me from the Kavareen, I know."

"Is that even poss—?"

"I told him no, I do not need rescuing. He has a better student than me now, one who is more gifted. And I have a reputation to guard in Semr! The king and his lords have been good clients. I do not wish them to hear that I cannot muddle through the simplest spell, because if I am a magician again someday, they will not want to hire me.

"So I will go back to my country instead. But I mean to say," Hirizjahkinis added, "I will not leave until this absurd invisibility spell of yours is gone. It is very unlucky to say goodbye to someone if you cannot see her face, did you know that?" She gave a decisive nod and swept out of the library with a slap-slap of her slippers on the stone floor.

A half conversation like this one was better than nothing, but afterward Nora felt more desolate than ever.

Hirizjahkinis was just here, she wrote on the wax tablet on Aruendiel's desk. *I am glad that you have made peace with her. I'm still not sure I understand exactly what she is now, but she is still Hirizjahkinis.*

She looked over the shelves again and pulled out a couple of case studies. Sometime later, the sound of a heavier footstep jolted her out of her reading, and she looked up to see Aruendiel. The library seemed smaller with him filling the doorway and then settling his long legs under the desk.

"I'm here," Nora said.

Aruendiel reached for a book, opened it. Nora watched his gray gaze run up and down the lines of text, as quick as a wolf tracking prey. After a minute he turned a page. He picked up the stylus and began to write on the wax tablet. Then he saw that Nora had written there and drew in his breath. He touched the wax with his fingertips.

"Nora, are you here?" he asked, like Hirizjahkinis, and looked around the library so intently that Nora felt that somehow she had to make her presence known. She lifted the book she had dropped before—although it was really too fragile for this treatment, the front cover was already loose, she noticed guiltily—but before she could drop it, Aruendiel was speaking again.

"Nora, you are not mad," he said seriously, his eyes still moving over the room. "The spell that afflicts you makes everyone around you a little mad, unable to see what should be obvious. You are not alone; remember, you are not alone. I am looking for you." His brow creased further. "I hope—I pray to all the gods that, aside from this wretched spell, you are well. Do you have enough to eat? That snakebite—did it make you ill?"

Aruendiel paused, and she could tell from the way his eyes narrowed that he was concentrating on a spell. The tint of the air shifted subtly. Sunlight sliding through the tall windows changed to a pale violet, then turned ruddy when it touched the floor. A sudden movement near the locked shelves startled her. A human figure, an old man in a gray robe. Aruendiel also saw it, and his crooked shoulders hunched with disappointment.

It was the shade of a long-dead priest, Nora guessed. Silently she and Aruendiel watched the ghost shuffle across the room and disappear through the wall. The light in the room changed again as the visualization spell faded.

"Nora!" Aruendiel rose from the desk abruptly. From the way he roared the syllables of her name, she thought for an instant that he could see her. "Nora, where are you?"

She let the book fall. It struck the floor with a thud, and the loose cover flew off. She winced. He seemed to notice nothing, however. That was odd; Hirizjahkinis had actually jumped at the sound. Nora stared at the book—another treatise on eyesight, she noticed now—while Aruendiel stepped right over it, heading toward the other side of the library. *The spell makes everyone around you a little mad, unable to see what should be obvious to them.* After a minute, Nora puzzled it out. Hirizjahkinis had heard the book fall only because she wasn't expec ing the noise. Aruendiel missed it precisely because he was looking for some sign from Nora.

Quickly she went over to the desk, picked up the stylus, and wrote on the wax tablet again. *I'm fine. I'm right here. I wish I could talk to you. But it is easier to signal to you when you are not expecting me. Otherwise the spell will distract you.*

She moved away as Aruendiel came around the shelves, carrying a couple of scrolls and a codex. This time the book lying in the middle of the floor caught his attention. He stooped and picked it up, frowning, and moved back to the desk. To her disappointment, he did not look at the tablet at once, but paged through the book pensively.

After a few minutes, he picked up the tablet. The black eyebrows snapped upward; a look of relief flickered across his face.

"This particular verb, 'signal,' has a specific naval connotation that is not quite right in this sentence, and at some point we must review the potentive subjunctive." He cleared his throat. "But I have never liked anything you have written so much as this, when I can see your words freshly written on the wax and know that you are here and well."

Nora grinned invisibly at him. "So long as men can breathe or eyes can see, so long lives this, and this gives life to thee?" she said. "Words seem to be the most substantial part of me these days."

Aruendiel's gaze moved around the room once again, reflexively searching its angled walls, and then he unrolled one of the scrolls that he had brought to the desk. "I propose to try something. It is a little crude, but let us see. A similitude spell, with some modifications."

From inside his tunic he pulled a pocketknife. Slipping the blade out of its leather sheath, he pricked the tip of his finger. A drop of blood splotched the floor. Immediately a shape arose, a shadow that gained form and color. It grew taller, blurred details coming into finer and finer focus as Aruendiel watched with critical attention.

Nora, with an inkling of what he was up to, still felt her scalp prickle as she recognized what he had conjured.

"And that would be me," she said, stepping closer. He hadn't gotten the height quite right; she was an inch or so taller in real life. The faintly translucent image, she was interested to see, wore her red wool dress, which she hadn't worn for quite some time. Where was it? Still back in Aruendiel's castle, she guessed. And yes, those were her features, her squarish chin and brown brows, the white scars on her cheek—no flattery there, but the overall effect somehow pleasing. Aruendiel's Nora smiled to herself with quiet luminosity. The real Nora wondered what she was thinking.

"You have me with long hair again," she said to Aruendiel, to cover up a rush of self-consciousness that for an instant felt more powerful than any invisibility spell.

He seemed to be inspecting the replica of herself even more carefully than she was. "It's not exactly right. I am no artist. I cannot see what is lacking. Well, it is not you, Nora," he added with a faint, irritated sigh, "only your copy. Put it on as you would a garment."

"A garment?" Nora considered what to do. From behind the simulacrum, she stepped forward, boldly shouldering her way into the other Nora's body, and thrust her arms into her twin's arms as though they were sleeves. The shadow-self felt cool, insubstantial, yet oddly tight around her own body.

Aruendiel's eyes focused directly on her. He sees me! Nora thought

"Can you hear me, Aruendiel?" Almost as soon as she spoke, Nora knew that it was no good. His expression did not change; he did not answer. She raised her arm. The arm of her copy did not move.

After a moment, Nora saw from his face that he knew it, too. She slid out of the other Nora with a subdued sense of disappointment and release. Aruendiel regarded the image for another long moment.

"No. It is very pleasant—it is restorative—to see your face again but it will not do, I want to see the real thing." He raised his hand, and the other Nora shimmered and dissolved. Only a fleck of dried blood remained on the floor.

"That's probably best," Nora said. "Although that was a nice version of me. Even the hair."

"Nora, I regret—" He stopped, and was silent.

"Yes? I'm still here," Nora said finally.

Aruendiel passed his hand over his face. After another long moment he said: "That is, this enchantment of yours was meant to punish me—so Olenan said."

"To be fair, I don't think she minded having me suffer along with you."

"What I mean to say is that Olenan is not entirely to blame. She wanted to punish me by separating you from me. But I had divided us already."

Nora leaned forward to see exactly what was in his face. "Oh. You mean, when you slept with Olenan?"

"I was too quick to take offense when you spoke perfect truth to me," Aruendiel said. "You quite rightly called me old—ugly—and so forth."

"That! I am so sorry—I am *still* so sorry—"

"Faitoren magic, I thought. It compelled you to speak the truth that was in your heart, instead of comfortable lies." He gave a crooked half smile. "But I have thought more about something else you said to me, when we were talking about Hirizjahkinis.

"You said that true affection sees through change—through even the blackest enchantment—to what is unchanged. I have not been that clear-sighted with you. I let myself be blinded by, well, old habits of mind. That is folly for a magician. Worse for a man."

His mouth twisted. "Olenan chose a cruel and clever spell when she hid you from my sight. I know this now: if I had first seen you clearly, we would have been spared much wretchedness and ill-fortune, you and I both. I am well punished for my dullness."

Nora made a move to grab the tablet from his hands, then thought of something better. So far, the invisibility spell had done nothing to impede her magic capabilities. She cupped her hands and summoned a flickering ball of light from a freshly kindled fire in the refectory kitchen. It squirmed excitedly in her hands.

Aruendiel half turned, his gray eyes reflecting fragments of the glow. Good, he could see the light she held—even if he could not see her. Then she asked the flames to do as she told them.

A plume of sparks rose into the air and traced letters there, twisting like glowing wires: *You have seen me more clearly than anyone since the day we met.*

The letters faded. She wrote again: *You found my real self when the Faitoren had made me forget it. You saw that I was thirsty for magic. You found me in the darkest places underground.*

Her words went dark again. The light in her hand dimmed; the fire was tiring. Once more she wrote: *I'm invisible, and you are still here, looking for me.*

He smiled at that, as lightly as a leaf falling. His broken face was sad and quizzical and curiously alert. "Nora, if I hadn't seen your grace and wit and sweetness before this, I'd be a blinder fool than the eagle who hunted the sun. And I know what it is to be thirsty for magic. Yes, I saw that in you." In a slightly different tone, he added, "As I suppose Olenan saw it in me. I owe her that much."

Olenan. Nora felt her spirits cloud slightly at the mention of her name. It would be some while, she saw, before she could rid herself of the nettlesome fear that Olenan, with all her power, with all those years lived in the dim and glorious past, had in some sense known Aruendiel better than Nora ever would.

Nora hesitated, then summoned more firelight. In a way, it was easier to write this than to say it aloud: *Did she still see you truly, this time? She said you would want to die.*

"Ah." Aruendiel tilted his head. "Well, I would not want to live the way Olenan did. She lost the habit of ordinary life long ago. Even before she decided to be a goddess. For myself, every time I've wished to die I've been thwarted. And curiously"—he raised an eyebrow—"I find that I am content to have failed."

"That is unlike you, Aruendiel," Nora said. "But—that's good."

"Olenan was wrong about a good number of things," he said. "And I would never have come near her again, except that she had already ensnared you. And still afflicts you. But I won't let her win this last contest. All curses can be lifted, and we shall lift this one, I promise you. I will have you back in my sight and touch and hearing, and I will not lose you again."

Nora gave a half smile that she suspected looked somewhat troubled, if anyone had been able to see it. *How to lift the spell?* she wrote. *You said it might grow stronger if you tried to break it.*

"It might. But I want you to have a look at this." Aruendiel opened the book that he had brought over from the shelves. "This spell here."

She peered down at the big, dog-eared pages, brown with age, as he leafed through them. Experimentally, she leaned against him, but could sense his body only as a kind of mass next to hers. She sighed, then read down the page where he had stopped.

"That's to protect a woman in childbirth," Nora objected. "And I'm not pregnant."

"It's a very old spell," Aruendiel said. "It's like your invisibility spell in that it's made up of a lot of different spells linked together. The old magicians liked to do that, to concentrate their power. But it means that if one link breaks, the whole spell fails. You see, how this part, for the baby's breathing, connects back to the strengthening spell? And the spell against hemorrhage and the spell for milk are inverses of each other? Clever, not entirely practical."

Nora squinted at the faded script. "Complicated. I see, it's all connected. If this part goes, the next one goes. And so forth. So what is the weak link in my spell?"

Aruendiel turned the page. His long finger traveled down the lines of brushstrokes. "If you wanted to break this obstetrical spell, you could start with undoing the anodyne portion, which is fairly simple. But any part would do, if you have the right counterhex."

"Well, that's the problem, isn't it?" Nora said.

"That is the difficulty, of course." Aruendiel read a little further, then suddenly closed the book. "For an enchantment like this—" He looked searchingly from side to side, his gaze still trying to find Nora. "You may be the one who is most likely to break it. You now know this spell better than anyone else living. There are weaknesses in it—"

"Like what?"

"—that only you will discover."

Great, Nora thought, rubbing her aching eyes as she bent over yet another spellbook. I still don't know how to cast an invisibility spell—or a confusion spell, or a misdirection curse—let alone work out the counterhexes to them.

A slim scroll titled *How to Make Clear What Has Been Obscured* raised her hopes, but it turned out to be an essay on magic to determine whether a person is lying and what the actual truth might be. She tried a couple of the spells, on the theory that her invisibility was a kind of lie. They seemed to have no effect.

It was dark now. Aruendiel was gone, summoned to the hospital to see to a pilgrim with seizures. So far he had not returned. She was growing hungry. No doubt as soon as she left, he would be back—that would be the unluckiness spell kicking in.

Eventually Nora stood, stretched her cramped muscles, and went outside. It was past dinnertime, but in the deserted kitchen she made a supper of some leftover porridge and goat's milk. Afterward, she walked slowly through the temple complex. No one bothered to light the torches these days, but now she knew her way even in the dark. A light breeze was blowing, and she could hear the gurgle of the river nearby.

Overhead the sky was flooded with stars, more numerous and brilliant than Nora ever remembered seeing in her world. Were they the same stars? Even at home, her knowledge of the constellations was uncertain; the notion that a certain group of stars was supposed to look like a winged horse, she had found, was more distracting than helpful. She'd heard Aruendiel mention the Spinning Wheel, the Goose, and the Dragon. Probably every world had a constellation called the Dragon.

Then she spied what she recognized immediately as the Big Dipper. The sight of its angled handle and bowl gave her an unexpected comfort. She wondered what they called the constellation here and raised her hand in a private greeting.

She turned back at the Stairs of Healing, having no wish to visit the ruined temple in the dark. There might be other ghosts prowling around here besides me, Nora thought half seriously. She followed the riverbank downstream, listening to the wind whispering to the trees, watching starlight lace the water with silver shadows. The river's dim mirror would not show her own form, of course. She was almost getting used to it now.

But there was a reflection on the surface of the water, almost at her feet. A woman's face, dark hair—Nora gave a start of excitement. Was she visible again?

As soon as she leaned forward, though, she saw that she was mistaken, because the reflection did not move. It belonged to another woman, standing on the bank next to Nora. Except that there was no one there.

"You thought I was you, didn't you?" the reflection said. "And you are disappointed."

"No, no," Nora said, reflexively polite. The face in the water was too dim for her to make out its features clearly, but the voice was somehow familiar. Not Olenan's, thankfully. "We've met before, haven't we?" Nora asked slowly.

"Do you remember?"

"Yes. In that cave, the goddess's cave. You told me to leave."

"I did."

"You saved my life!"

"Quite likely, although I only pointed out the obvious course of action."

Nora frowned. "Was there another time, too?"

"Oh, that never happened," the reflection said.

"No?" For some reason, Nora found herself wanting to laugh. It was hard to tell, but she thought the woman smiled. "That's what you said before, I remember. Why are you here?" A hopeful thought occurred to her. "Are you going to break my invisibility spell?"

The woman shook her head. "I never learned enough real magic to do something like that. I will tell you this, though: all spells can be broken, but the answer is not always found in books.

"Sometimes you have to feel your way out of an enchantment. Olenan told me that. Aruendiel knows it, too, but often he prefers to forget."

Her Ors had a slightly antique flavor. Nora wished that she could see the woman's face better. "You knew Olenan—and Aruendiel? How?"

"Olenan? She helped me, long ago. Aruendiel—" The reflection shrugged. "It's difficult to explain."

"You're a ghost, aren't you? Are you—" Trying to piece together fragments of the stories she'd heard, Nora made a guess. "Aruendiel's wife?"

"After my time," the woman said severely.

"Hmm." Was there to be no end of Aruendiel's old girlfriends? "Are you Warigan?" Nora asked suddenly.

"Very good. Perhaps you are as clever as Aruendiel thinks you are. He has learned to appreciate clever women, I will give him that. But cleverness isn't enough for a woman. Do you know that? It won't help you live to a good old age."

What had Olenan said, at the end, when she had flung Warigan's name at Aruendiel? Nora tried to remember. An accusation—she'd called Aruendiel ruthless. "Aruendiel did something to you, didn't he?" she asked with some apprehension. "What was it?"

"He never raised a hand against me, if that's what you're thinking," Warigan said. "No, I died to save his life."

Nora was aghast. "Why? What happened?"

"He wouldn't want me to tell you. And I can't talk about it, even after all this time." She smiled grimly. "I was pleased to die. I didn't want to live. But sometimes I regret it, now."

So many hints, so much obscurity. Nora wondered if Warigan was deliberately trying to distract her. "I'm very sorry. That sounds painful. Is that why you're here, with me?"

"Oh, I don't have the chance to converse with many people these days. It must be your idiotic invisibility spell that lets you hear me. Or you're excessively fatigued. How are you going to break the spell, by the way?"

"I don't know." She could hear an appalling bleakness in her own voice, but there was no reason to put a good spin on things when, after all, she was talking to someone who was also invisible. "I'm wondering if I'm going to be this way forever. A ghost, like you."

"You're not a ghost." The woman almost snarled at her. "Don't be absurd. You have a body, a living body."

"Right," Nora said quickly, seeing that she had been tactless. "Sorry."

"I'm not offended!" Warigan said, although Nora did not believe her. "What I mean is, it's always more difficult to enchant a living body than a ghost. Obviously it can be done, but the flesh is harder to deceive."

"That's what Aruendiel said. When I pinched him."

"It's an old axiom about transformations—why they're so unstable. Usually." She grimaced.

Nora was silent for a moment, then she asked: "Where is he?" She was fairly confident that Warigan knew this, although she could not say why. Sure enough, Warigan said: "Sleeping."

"Good. Take me to him," Nora said.

"Why?" For the first time, Warigan seemed surprised.

"Because you're right, I'm tired, and I'd like to sleep, and I don't want to be alone anymore. And if I set out to find him by myself, I'll get lost or distracted, or he'll wake up and go wandering away, thanks to this damned curse of mine."

"You're sure?"

"Yes!"

"Very well." Nora felt strong, rather bony fingers wrap around her wrist. They tugged her away from the riverbank. "Come this way."

Nora followed, stepping cautiously in the darkness. The woman led her up the sloping bank toward the hospital complex. The burble of the river grew quieter.

"Why do you ask if I'm sure?"

"Because I think Aruendiel meant what he said today, that he does not want to lose you again."

"How did you know he said that?"

"I heard him say it." The ground was level now, easier to walk on. They skirted the hospital building, where threads of light gleamed through the shutters. "He'll want to marry you, you know. He'll insist on it. Will you enjoy being a great lady? Now that I've seen you, I wonder. Well, it's better than starving."

"You're jumping ahead," Nora said dryly. "I don't want to lose Aruendiel, either, but no one has said anything about marriage. He was talking about the spell, anyway. And he would never marry a commoner."

"Perhaps. I think that after a ridiculous amount of shilly-shallying, he has finally decided what he wants. Men often have trouble figuring out. What do you want?"

"I want to be visible again, I want to be with Aruendiel, I want to be great magician, but first of all, I want some sleep."

Warigan laughed, not unkindly. "You have some dangerous ambitions. Well, sleep is a blessing, usually. Rest well."

Abruptly the grip on her wrist loosened and was gone. "Warigan?" Nora called softly. "Warigan?" She heard only the distant chuckle of the river. "Rest well yourself, whoever you are," she whispered.

Nora turned in a slow circle to get her bearings. The hospital was behind her. To her left, a darkened, low-slung building. The visitors' dormitory. The entry door creaked in mild protest as she went inside. She could smell hints of the vinegar that was used to wash the floors.

His was the second room on the right. There was a locking spell on the door, but it was one that he had taught her. Interesting.

She pushed open the door slowly and caught the sound of Aruendiel's breathing, soft and regular. The room was almost but not completely dark. Gradually she could make out his shape on a bed across the room, the rumpled blanket not quite ample enough to cover his long limbs completely.

Nora slipped off her gown and sandals and padded across the floor. Aruendiel lay with his back toward her, a coil of his dark hair just visible against his pillow. She lifted the blanket and inserted herself under it, folding herself against Aruendiel. He grunted in his sleep as she put her arm around him, but he stirred only slightly. She doubted that even if he were awake, he could feel anything; for herself, it was as though she were embracing him through layers and layers of wrappings, like a statue swaddled for shipping.

If you break one part of the spell, she thought, you break it all. She nestled closer to the almost imperceptible warmth of Aruendiel's body and her nostrils found the pleasing sharp scent of his skin.

Her mind drifted as she let herself relax into the slow rustle of his breathing. Lazily she pictured her mother cocooning her grandmother's cut-glass pitcher in plastic. Her mother was planning to mail it to Nora, but Nora wasn't sure she had given her the correct address.

It was growing warmer under the blanket. Nora poured Aruendiel lemonade from the glass pitcher. Her mother must have sent it to the right address after all, she realized. That was a relief. But how was it delivered?

Nora woke dozily to find that Aruendiel had turned over, and that one of his arms was draped over her waist in a pleasantly possessive way. Aruendiel muttered something sleep-jumbled. "It's only me," Nora said, closing her eyes.

When she woke again, they were entangled further, Aruendiel having taken more territory as she slept. He pressed solidly up against her from behind, one hand cupping a breast. Men had an instinct for that, always, awake or asleep, invisibility spell or no invisibility spell, she thought.

"Are you awake?" she whispered. No answer. Nora rubbed his arm, feeling the silky friction of his arm hairs under her fingers. She wriggled gently in his arms, making enough space to uncurl her right elbow, which was full of pins and needles, and then she said, "Aha," because in jostling against him she had just discovered that one part of Aruendiel, at least, was paying her close attention.

"Apparently," Nora said, "the flesh *is* harder to deceive."

Aruendiel groaned something that might have been assent, and his arm tightened around her. His fingertips slid down her body, making an unhurried survey of its angles and concealed crevices. *Licence my roving hands, and let them go, before, behind, between, above, below,* Nora thought, turning toward him. And his hands roamed everywhere on her body, reaching all the way down to pet and pinch her toes, as though he were intent on mapping every inch of her.

His kisses were swift and hungry, not always precisely aimed. Nora saw, as the air in the room grew gray, then brightened, that Aruendiel's eyes were shut. She knew why. He was afraid of what he might not see if he opened them.

She kissed his skin and savored its salty tang. "It's not a dream," she said. But it was not until he thrust his way inside her, fierce, gentle, and insistent, that she knew for certain that the spell was dissolved.

For a moment she thought about Aruendiel the magician, and it seemed to her that she held a sky full of stars in her arms, while an answering brightness was dawning in her own body.

Aruendiel shuddered and subsided to lie next to her. Nora let her finger trace one of the hard white scars on his torso, and then felt suddenly bashful. He still had not opened his eyes.

"Aruendiel?"

He turned his head. His eyes held the silvery calm of the dawn sky, and they looked at her as though they would never stop. "Nora," he said.

Acknowledgments

This book was a long time in the making, and it would never have come out into the world if not for much encouragement, support, hard work, and sage advice from many good friends and lovers of books. I can't begin to express my thanks to Margaret Sutherland Brown and Emma Sweeney for their belief in this book and their brilliant counsel all along the way. I am incredibly grateful to Catherine Wallach, David Gassaway, Jeff Tabnick, and everyone on the Recorded Books team for the fantastic work they've done to bring this novel to readers as an audiobook original, and I am still swooning with delight over Alyssa Bresnahan's absolutely perfect narration. Thank you to the amazing designers who have shaped this print edition, Patrick Knowles and Iram Allam, and to copyeditors Tricia Callahan, Judy Lopatin, and Kelli Rae Patton, who saved me from myself countless times. If there are any errors of usage in the text, they are solely my responsibility.

As this novel went through its many drafts, it benefited enormously from the comments of many brave and discerning early readers. Catherine, Denise, Emily, Trever, Gail, Heather, Kathy, Lesley, Pam, Jim, Robin, Sally, Tonie, and Xenia, thank you for the thoughtful advice that made the book immeasurably better, gave me inspiration, and kept me sane. I am very fortunate to have you as my friends. Thanks to Beth and Laura for generously sharing their medical knowledge so that I could better describe the healing spells that Nora casts; any errors or incongruities are mine alone. I can't begin to express my gratitude to Dave, who offered wisdom and good cheer when I needed those things, and who has been more than humanly understanding about all the hours that I've spent in other worlds.

Finally, I owe a great debt to all the readers of *The Thinking Woman's Guide to Real Magic*, especially those who asked with kind impatience about its sequel. I'm grateful that you have let Nora and Aruendiel live in your imaginations as they live in mine.

Printed in Great Britain
by Amazon

26050816R00249